The Crocodile Princess

for Jean and Paul

1

Yuri Shunin was drinking a Tiger beer with Ariadna and Dmitri, his colleagues in the Soviet embassy, and asking Ariadna about her private audience with Prince Sihanouk, head of state in Cambodia:

'It was arranged between the two governments,' Ariadna said, 'that I should play the cello for the Prince in his palace.'

'Arranged at the highest level, then?'

Ariadna ignored Dmitri's teasing. 'Yes, yes, at a high level, Dmitri Alexandrovich. The Prince especially enjoyed the Bach sonata I played.'

They were drinking in the *ZigZag* and Yuri was noting the growing contingent of younger staff from the British embassy, including his secret friend, Keith Entwistle, and glancing occasionally at Hok Suhana, the reactionary conspirator, seated alone in a far corner, reading. Yuri was about to experience a moment of *déjà vu*, as Ariadna was talking about her Bach cello sonata, and there was a power failure that extinguished all the lights in the bar. The sudden darkness briefly silenced everyone, so that the chiming of the bells of cyclopousses, near and far, was eerily loud.

Yuri had decided recently that he experienced *déjà vu* more often than most people, and that it felt to him as though *déjà vu* provided a brief glimpse of a previous existence of the kind that Buddhists believed in. A previous existence, or a glimpse into a life that an alternative Yuri, a variant Yuri, was living concurrently.

The darkness persisted, but, as the *ZigZag's* private generator was coughing into life, Dmitri said, 'Well certainly your playing is of a very high standard, but the Prince has a certain reputation.' As the lights were flickering back on, Dmitri folded his arms across his chest, and raised his eyebrows pointedly at Ariadna.

Ariadna squirmed with irritation. 'He flattered me, of course. And in fact he asked me if I would like to have a part in a film he is going to direct.'

With her dynamic figure, highly-defined cheekbones, and cold blue eyes, Ariadna was certainly beautiful enough to star in a film. She was the daughter of a famous physicist and a slightly less famous musician. She had said hardly anything all evening, but she had clearly found their conversation lacking, and Yuri knew that her exquisite vacancy was only apparent, that her father had taught her about sub-atomic particles, which were only one of her intimidating hobbies. Soon after she arrived in Phnom Penh he had watched her, in this very bar, tear apart an empty packet of *Sobranies* and doodle on it, but he had found, when she left, that what she had doodled was an equation fraught with Greek letters and other incomprehensible signs.

Yuri was contemplating the idea of Sihanouk as a film director when the moment of uncanny familiarity, of *déjà vu*, occurred, as Peter Cook, the tall young man from the British embassy, surprised Yuri by strolling across to the table where Hok Suhana was sitting and placing a sheet of paper in front of him. On his way, Cook glanced unashamedly at Ariadna, who was sitting next to Yuri – that was unsurprising. But Hok Suhana, who hardly looked up and left the paper sitting there on the tabletop, was arousing increasing interest in the Soviet embassy in Phnom Penh, where Yuri worked as a personal assistant to the ambassador. How could this English fop have a link with such a serious character, with such a dangerous subversive?

The rainy season had just started, a couple of weeks early, and the swollen Mekong was beginning its annual feat of reversing its flow and drowning the lake, the Tonle Sap, expanding it to four times its dry season size, so it overwhelmed the nearby forest. Yuri had been thinking of the fish that were at that moment being lifted suddenly higher. He had imagined being such a fish, giant salmon carp, say, or tropical sand goby, finding itself rising and rising into the forest canopy, a fish out of its depth swimming among branches and leaves, where birds had perched. There was even a fish called a climbing perch.

Then he had been startled out of his reverie by this strange conjunction of people, which disoriented him with *déjà vu* and slowed the moment. Dmitri had just moved the conversation on and was talking, as he did so often, about the U.S. nuclear missiles stationed in Turkey – they could reach Moscow, he was saying, but not Leningrad – Ariadna, cultural attaché, staring towards the long mirror behind the bar, and the Englishman, (quite new – maybe he'd been in Phnom Penh for six months?) ambling across and leaving the sheet of paper which Hok Suhana acknowledged only with a brief, irritable nod of the head.

Yuri felt an urgent need to snatch that message, but there were so many people around that evening, and he wasn't sure he wanted even Dmitri and Ariadna, to know – Dmitri might try to stop him, might argue it wasn't worth it, and he didn't have a strong argument on his side, it was only a powerful instinct that this message meant something important. More worrying were the four other people at Cook's table, Keith Entwistle, Bill Noon, Reginald Armstrong, and a secretary. Yuri liked Keith, and they had become friends, (horribly fraught as that was, between a Russian and a British diplomat) because Keith leant him jazz records – Charlie Parker, Dizzy Gillespie, bebop masters scorned by Yuri's bosses as evil flowers of capitalism, whose music was difficult to acquire back home. Yuri's friendship with Keith meant that he was knowledgeable about the staff in the British embassy, and meant that he knew that Keith liked to refer to the pretty secretary, the thin blonde with the very light-skinned complexion, as his girlfriend.

Keith was seated close to that girl, and another startling thing happened, just after the incident with Hok Suhana, when Yuri thought he noticed her glance furtively in his direction, and then look confused and look quickly away. Armstrong, the disabled communications man, was sitting with Noon, but they weren't talking to each other, and looked as though they were only half involved with the group. It was the presence of Noon, also, that had slowed the moment, because, like Hok Suhana, he'd been discussed at the Russian embassy – he was the British military attaché, but had aroused attention because he frequently drove out of Phnom Penh at night. He'd been spotted driving in the direction of the province of Battambang, in the north-west, where there were several villages known to harbour rebels. Yuri and Keith had smiled acknowledgement at each other earlier in the evening before settling into their separate groups.

Ariadna suddenly decided to leave, and strode away with an abruptness that seemed charged, but surely only because it was her, just as the perfume that lingered after her couldn't really be unique to her, as it seemed, the perfume still sitting in the chair between Yuri and Dmitri. The two men avoided each other's look and stared ahead at the chairs and tables and door of her recent spoor, rueful about her unavailability, but Yuri told himself that he had more important matters than Ariadna on his mind. Then he and Dmitri watched Cook enter her spoor and unashamedly follow it, and they shook their heads at each other in moralising horror.

Even Hok Suhana had noticed Ariadna leave, and glanced up from his book. Moscow was aware of a number of factions in Cambodia, and Suhana's was amongst the least formidable, a reactionary cadre with links to the military, and more royalist than the royal family. Yuri's own sympathies were with the leftist groups that opposed Cambodia's self-indulgent princeling, the playboy Sihanouk

– anything would be an improvement on him. But Suhana should certainly be watched: the peripheral vision of the plump Cambodian must have caught Ariadna's gait, its high proportion of sideways to forward movement, its high wiggle quotient, and he glanced after her, but quickly returned to his book, and didn't notice Cook following her.

The bar was filling, and the chat between Yuri and Dmitri was sporadic, partly because Yuri was anxiously eyeing Hok Suhana, but he was amazed when the political conspirator left the sheet of paper sitting on the tabletop when he eventually went to the lavatory. Without consulting Dmitri, Yuri dodged swiftly through the tables and around the standing groups, one of which had gathered near Hok Suhana's table. Yuri used that little crowd as cover to snatch the sheet of paper and carry it back to his table, folding it roughly and one-handedly as he went. Dmitri looked at him quizzically, but he explained what it was, and they examined it together: it was entitled *The Crocodile Princess* and contained three references to Dagenham.

Alone, later, Yuri stared at the wall of his flat and reflected gloomily that his problems had originated when he had become partly Australian. His first diplomatic posting, when he was 24, had been to the embassy in Canberra, and he had allowed himself, then, to be more influenced by Western thinking than he should have done, and had fraternised with Australians more than he should have done. That had started on a very hot day when, driven by baffled desires, he had charged into the city centre late on a Saturday night and entered a bar where he had fallen into conversation with a man who invited him to a house party. There he had heard Dizzy Gillespie for the first time, and had been astonished and excited. But he had also got tangled up in an argument with a tall, gaunt man who had screamed at him about Stalin's atrocities, a man who equated Russia with mass murders and nothing else – for foreigners, if such horrors have occurred, your country will be summed up completely by them, and everything else will be erased, the horrors will be like a room that's crammed with a ferocious shouting so that no other sounds can be heard. Yuri had been forced to lift the gaunt man up and hold him tightly against a wall until he calmed down, but he found himself infected, nonetheless, and felt, later, that the gaunt man had been right – that the weight of such atrocities should dominate how a country was regarded. And once you dwelt on that, everything else felt futile and pointless.

He glanced wearily at the page he had stolen from Peter Cook: it was either a coded message, or it was trivial nonsense.

2

'No no you're not going to catch me,' shouted Joe Keane, the American ambassador in Cambodia. He stared in the face of Norodom Sihanouk looming on a billboard above him, Sihanouk dressed all in white and with a shaved head, saintly Buddhist, his serenity a rebuke to Keane's desperate, breathless driving forward of his cyclopousse, his bicycle rickshaw, his pedalling ever more frantic because the finishing line was a huge jacaranda tree only forty yards past the billboard, and Peter Cook was gaining on him, now only fifteen yards behind, and calling to him, taunting him with his growing nearness, about how he would imminently overtake, about the superiority of Cook's own cyclo, about how Joe's contraption was wonky, about how Joe himself – worst of all, this, as Joe was gasping more and more for breath – was an old man, was past it... and Joe was dizzy now, standing up on his pedals, then sitting down again, and the cyclo was so unwieldy, and four times heavier than a normal bicycle, and he could feel his head sicken, where dazzling-white enormous Sihanouk in the silver of the nearly-full moon was swimming in his eyes above him – or no, too bright for that, because in fact lit from below by a carefully placed lamp, so now, as he approached, Joe could see lizards running all over the god/king... lizards (and he thought this ludicrously, even painfully, given what he needed to concentrate upon) attracted by the insects on Sihanouk that were, in turn, attracted by the lamplight... and then he thought about that thought and knew he was observing his thought self-consciously still because of the opium he had smoked earlier, at Madame Chhum's, the opium whose pungent taste even now lingered between his teeth and inside his tongue, somehow both sweet and bitter, the opium that made thoughts wrap themselves around each other, twist inside each other and open

11

passageways that led past tens of doorways which might open at any moment and lead down other passageways... and it was being too deeply inside that thought that led him not to notice he was veering to the right, not to notice so that now he had to wrestle the cyclo leftwards, still half-hoping to go forwards as well, still somehow to win because the tree was only twenty yards ahead, but it was no good, the front wheel was pointing left but the weight of everything behind it, the hooded seat and the wheels and Keane himself, was dragging it still to the right, so that his back right wheel was slipping more and more into a shallow ditch, and he made a final effort, standing on his pedals feeling that his breath was squeezed hard as though his lungs might burst, but no, it was no use, and he slipped further into the ditch and the whole ungainly contraption toppled onto its right side, and he saw Cook go flying past him to the jacaranda where he stopped and jumped out of his cyclo and danced about with his arms in the air.

Joe was trapped under the cyclo, his right leg jammed under the pedals, and he could feel the pain starting there, in his right knee and all around it. He tried to push the thing off himself but he was too weak and it seemed to push him back deeper into the ditch, which was very wet, so he submitted to that and settled back with a groan. He watched a frog hopping around his feet, and gazed at an empty packet of Capstan cigarettes in the midst of cicada corpses and next to the shed tail of a lizard. The pain made him think he was the fall guy once again – once again he'd been had. He noticed that the pedaleur's trousers were dangling out from under the passenger's seat, where the Cambodian had stowed them, folded neatly. He watched Cook dance and whoop and he could see the two pedaleurs trotting up the road towards him, one of them gesticulating wildly, but he closed his eyes and the moment expanded vastly, containing a query, fundamentally, about how he had sunk literally so low, and he blamed Cook for that, but no he ought to blame himself for being so easily led. He had always been easily led, when he was supposed to be a natural leader. But he was going nowhere now when before he'd been destined for a great future. He'd made bad tactical errors, so that he should've risen high with the rise of the Kennedys because he'd supported them before their rise, but he'd been too outspoken, impractical, too idealistic. And he had told a stupid joke about Bobby Kennedy. That was how he'd ended up in Cambodia where he could simply be ignored, which was far worse than being reprimanded, which meant attention was paid to you, far worse when no-one even thought about you. He was nearly forty now and no-one was thinking about him, and now he'd goofed again, he'd screwed things up. All of this, in that expanded moment, was the background to what he thought, but in the foreground still, repeatedly, was the image that had seized him at the same time as the opium, which was snow catching on the hair and eyelashes of Mary O'Neill as he kissed her. Not his first kiss, which he couldn't remember, but this one, perhaps his hundredth kiss, lovely freckled Mary O'Neill, smiling in the snow as he dared to move in close to her, with snow also finding his own eyes, which now, as he lay back in this icky Cambodian ditch, which no doubt harboured tropical spiders and cockroaches, and huge leeches, welled and threatened to spill, because that foreground image held the same colour as the background, which was loss and regret. Because he remembered how upset Mary had been when he ended it with her, which was a bad mistake he'd committed because his friend Jack had told him Mary was too skinny. At Madame Chhum's this had suddenly seemed like the worst mistake of his life, from which all the others had followed, he'd been thinking this as the girl, Sisopha, had passed him the pipe, which she'd prepared, this girl who was so attractive and was far skinnier than Mary O'Neill – and, there, too, at Madame Chhum's, he had laid back as he was doing now, thinking of snow on freckles, snow on soft brown hair, and the simultaneous warmth and melting cold of that kiss from twenty-four years ago.

Cook reached him before the pedaleurs, and managed to haul the cyclo off him, and put it back fully on the road, and Joe said, from his prone position, 'I could've lost a leg,' and saw Cook wince, and remembered that the Englishman claimed to have – Joe thought it an affectation – a phobia about one-legged men. Cook recovered swiftly from that, and stood beside the cyclo with his hands behind his back and a careless, distracted air, humming a tune, as if defying the pedaleurs to say anything was wrong, ignoring the fact that Joe was still lying across the ditch, and that the back right wheel was conspicuously buckled. Its owner shouted at Cook in Khmer, and then, in Khmer, at Joe who was struggling to rise, and Cook helped him, but his knee wouldn't take his weight. The pedaleur calmed enough to shout in French, and Cook replied in French, patronising him, with Joe hanging on his arm, but Joe felt horribly remorseful, knowing that the man depended so much on his vehicle, his family depended on it, he stared sadly at the faded cotton of the man's shirt and shorts, and even more sadly at his palm-leaf hat – it was possible that he even slept in the cyclo. He remembered that the man's trousers had fallen out of the cyclo when Cook hauled it upright, and he limped over to the ditch and found them, and folded them carefully, and limped over to the man and handed them to him.

As he performed that action, he felt as though he were looking down from a steep height at himself performing it, so that it seemed ceremonial, like a symbolic action which might be performed in an embassy – here I, the American ambassador, hand to you the emblematic trousers, and with this action I bestow upon you, with all the power invested in me by my great nation, full and irrevocable trouserhood. He glanced sideways at Cook, feeling that this was an idea that the young Englishman had infected him with, but for a moment the pedaleur too responded ceremonially, receiving the trousers as though they carried stately significance, placated by the solemnity of the moment. That was brief, however, and he shook himself out of his inappropriate awe, and resumed his tirade, again in French. Joe understood that the man would be in a tizzy that his Chinese boss – all the cyclos were owned by Chinese businessmen, who never drove them – would be furious about the buckling of the wheel, that the expense caused by the damage would be equal to months of the pedaleur's wages. It had been difficult to persuade the two men to part with their vehicles in the first place, they had refused until Joe offered them a thousand *riel* each, about thirty bucks, and even then they were anxious, rightly as it turned out. Joe nodded at the shouting pedaleur and raised his hand slowly and moved it from side to side placatingly, and when that didn't work, raised both hands, and moved them slowly, in a massaging motion, looking the man in the eye. He could see Cook smirking at this and realised that the gesture might easily be taken as a mime, an instructional mime, of how to propitiate a pair of spectacularly intimidating breasts.

Joe worried that, aside from that, these signs might, for all he knew, be offensive to a Cambodian – it was so easy to get your protocol wrong, like one of his predecessors who'd gone to the Cambodian Royal Court immaculately dressed, silk hat etc, but took his two big dogs with him, not knowing that Asians don't like dogs. What unsettled Joe, as he looked at the cyclo boy, was the conviction that struck him often when he thought about Cambodians, the conviction which he felt guilty about but couldn't suppress, that they were a degenerate race. When he thought about the astonishing temple complex at Angkor Wat, he was in awe at what giants the Cambodians had been in that period so many centuries ago, for Angkor Wat not only had an unearthly beauty, but was built on a massive scale that expressed the extent to which Cambodia dominated and conquered its neighbours. But look at them in the twentieth century. They had shrivelled to nothing.

Joe needed to focus now because he didn't want this small incident to start a domino effect that might publicise what he'd been doing that evening. Focusing, he pressed his palms together and bowed, as he'd been taught to do when backing out of a room away from a local dignitary, and this again silenced the pedaleur for a moment, though it clearly baffled him rather than soothing him. Money, he realised, was the *lingua franca* – the almighty dollar, and then he had a terrible fear that his wallet might have been lost, at some point during all the distractions of the evening, as he searched his jacket and trousers before he found it in the jacket's inside pocket.

Sighing with relief he looked up from his wallet before he opened it and noticed a burly and tall Western figure approaching from the direction of the jacaranda which had been the finishing post and hurry through the pool of greater illumination surrounding the Sihanouk billboard – the figure's pace was striking because it conveyed agitation and also because it was generated by a conspicuous athleticism, despite a slight limp. As the man got closer, Keane was sure he'd seen him before, but he needed to concentrate: in his wallet he found only 800 *riel* and felt that wasn't enough to ensure the pedaleur's co-operation. He turned to Cook but Cook had turned towards the new man and was acknowledging him. Then Cook directed the man's attention to Joe and said, 'Have you met Joe? Joe Keane – the American ambassador?' The two men directed a puzzled frown at each other.

'Once, I think,' the Englishman said.

'Yes,' Keane agreed, 'at...'

'Joe, this is Bill Noon, military attaché – Major Noon.'

'Ah yes – must've been one of those cocktail parties.' Joe glanced around, puzzled. 'Nice night for a stroll?'

Noon's mouth opened as though to speak, and then he didn't. He tried again: 'Yes, couldn't sleep – the heat, you know.' The three of them stood awkwardly, while the pedaleur looked up from one to the other of the much taller men, and Joe tried to imagine how they looked from the Cambodian's point of view: *long noses*, that was the term Cambodians used for Westerners. Joe moved in closer to Noon and Cook and whispered, 'Bill, this guy's got a problem, and I'd like to help him out. I was about to ask Peter as well, if he's got any spare cash.' He showed them the notes in his hand. 'I've got 800, but I'd like to add more.'

'800 is already a lot, you know, to a chap like him,' Noon said.

'Yes but still and all... his cyclo is badly damaged, and I feel some responsibility...' Keane glanced at Cook. 'I'll pay you back, pal, naturally.'

Cook and Noon looked in their wallets and came up with another 735 between them. Keane thanked them, then turned to the pedaleur and, looking deep into his eyes, said, 'Je suis désolé, très très désolé, et je préfère que vous...' He shrugged and put his forefinger vertically over his mouth, and then despaired – because the shushing gesture might mean something utterly unpredictable to a Cambodian... 'Comprenez?' he said, showing him the pile of notes, then putting them, one by one, highest *riels* first, into his hand. The pedaleur watched this carefully, then was seized with a distraction that made him look away, in the direction of the dome of the Grand Market, before he nodded with tired resignation, looked up at Keane and put his forefinger vertically over his lips, and wandered over to his cyclo.

'Well, better be going,' Noon said.

'Yes. Great to have met you again,' Joe replied, shaking his hand.

As they watched Noon stride vigorously away, Joe said, 'Very odd to be out strolling at this time of night. Suspicious, if you ask me.' Cook only raised his eyebrows, and Joe had second thoughts: after all, what serious mischief could you do – political mischief that is – in the small hours that you couldn't do better in daylight? Evil is banal and happens when the sun is shedding its benevolent rays. They decided it would be better now to walk from there to their separate residences, though Cook was embarked on a complex jive where at first he kept saying 'Ill Met by Moonlight', but then moved on to how good Bill Noon would be in the jungle and from there to a book he was reading on jungle survival that had been written by another Brit army type called Captain Hilary Pecksniff-Protheroe. Joe's leg was hurting badly and Cook was annoying him, and annoyed him even more when he said, 'Did you know that a single tree in the Cambodian jungle has more ants than the whole of the British Isles?'

Joe set off walking, desperate for the point where their paths would diverge. 'You mean *species* of ants?'

'You might say that, Joe, but you are mistaken. Because formicographers have identified this tree and it's one single heaving pullulating conglomeration of ants from its formicating roots to its formicating canopy, and these ants are marching up and down its trunk all day and night bumping into one another carrying bits of leaves...'

As they passed the billboard, Joe noticed a large white owl swoop from some nearby trees towards it and snatch a lizard from Sihanouk's white robes; he saw the lizard's tail dangle from the owl's beak as it flew back to the trees.

3

The British Ambassador in Phnom Penh, Christopher Hartnell, had a number of reasons for remembering a day two months earlier, in late March. It had started with a row with his wife Edith, which was based on a misunderstanding about how much he was expressing affection for Cambodians when he said that they were uninterested in facts. He was barely awake when the domestic battle had started, and still staring in a daze at the mosquito net, feeling stunned with tiredness. Edith didn't understand how much he aspired to that Khmer condition, how much he increasingly felt that this attitude was more likely than scientific rationalism to provide access to the most essential truths. And Edith didn't understand, and he was reluctant to explain to her, how deeply weary he was, how exhaustion pressed down upon him daily, and that therefore it was genuinely true that he admired Cambodians for being clever and lazy. Edith anyway was in a petulant bad mood because a terrible dream had woken her, she had called out in her sleep and writhed in the bed and that had jolted Christopher, also, from his sleep. She had dreamt that the head of a statue of Prince Sihanouk had been severed and dumped in a pigsty under some manure – she had seen his face covered in pig excrement.

Christopher didn't understand why that was so terrible and he tried to lighten the mood by illustrating Cambodian ingenuity, by describing an irrigation method he had seen, with a hundred wonky waterwheels splashing cupfuls of water into a Heath-Robinson network of bamboo tubes that led to Lilliputian gardens, terribly inefficient – but still working well enough to aid the growth of all the vegetables they needed. But Edith had refused to listen and had shouted at him that he needed to understand Buddhism: she kept insisting Buddhism, Buddhism, and Christopher wondered why, at such moments, her voice sounded a bit American and croaky.

Edith was a great admirer of Prince Sihanouk as a Buddhist politician, and she was always informing Christopher about how his religion had taught Sihanouk a 'middle way' between the two sides in the Cold War, and helped him to fight against tremendous odds, opposing the haughty and devious French, and his country was tiny and had always faced much larger enemies who wanted to invade – the Thais, the Vietnamese, the Chinese, the Japanese. No end of invasions.

Christopher shuddered to remember the time, a year or so ago, when he had lectured Sihanouk – the Foreign Office had insisted that he must. Christopher had told him that his continuing efforts to oppose communist influences from China and Vietnam were very much appreciated, but he needed to be aware of the danger of communist insurgency in Cambodia itself (and he told Sihanouk that Britain had clear intelligence that this was happening). He needed to blunt the communist case by redistributing a little wealth, and by opposing the widespread corruption. Christopher remembered flinching and looking away as he made himself say that Sihanouk needed to tackle the corruption in his own court.

The Prince had listened to him with a blank expression, and then had looked Christopher straight in the eye and asked him what he thought of *nouvelle vague* cinema, said that he personally found it fascinating, Godard and Truffaut were technically brilliant, but that, still, it was a little *avant garde* for his own taste. And Christopher could only smile wryly in reply and nod a *touché*.

It was on this same day in late March that Peter Cook's famous first encounter with Prince Sihanouk had occurred. Relations had been icy between the Cambodian regime and the Embassy, but there was then a slight thaw, no doubt occasioned by Sihanouk's skittishness, – and anyway, as it turned out, very brief. But the Prince had warmed long enough to attend a cocktail party and had circulated amiably, so that Christopher was cautiously – you never knew with Sihanouk – cheerful about the way the evening was going. But then he noticed that, by some unfortunate shuffling of the party's *dramatis personae*, Sihanouk was now face to face with Cook, who, even in his brief time in the Embassy, had earned a reputation as indiscreet. Edith had told him that Keith Entwistle was upset because the secretary he'd been painstakingly wooing for over a year, Sandie Hamilton, had taken up with Cook within a week of his arrival: Christopher noticed, with some personal interest, the emphasis that Edith had placed in her aside explaining this when she had said that Cook was *very* handsome (Christopher was no good at judging these things). But Edith had said that Keith was feeling ghastly, he was really quite wretched.

Now here was Cook in what looked like a rapid colloquy with Sihanouk, which involved, on the part of the Embassy's new Third Secretary, much arm waving and face wringing. As Christopher was watching this mime, Wilfred Jamie, the Head of Chancery, joined him, and whispered 'Head him off, for God's sake, head him off'. Christopher shook his head and shushed Jamie with a finger across his lips, then crooking the finger in Jamie's face – a couple of the Prince's acolytes were nearby, and mustn't know they were anxious. Keith Entwistle joined them and nodded towards the odd pairing and nodded more deeply, a rolling nod, to suggest he might intervene. Christopher again shook his head and the three faced each other casting sidelong glances at the dangerous scene. There had been a rapid interchange, initially, and the pair were attracting glances from everywhere in the room – Sihanouk of course did that naturally, but the man he was engaged with also looked unusual, his hair a bit unruly, his suit somehow a statement of anti-formality. The interchange was followed by a longer passage in which Cook was performing, stretching his eyebrows and mouth. Christopher and Jamie and Entwistle watched this openly, struck with such anxious horror that they could no longer conceal it, as they saw the look of dumb amazement on Sihanouk's face. How long did that moment continue as Sihanouk's amazement grew?

Cook ended his performance. He looked at Sihanouk whose lips were parted – bewildered, surely, and uncomprehending. And the chatter had ceased across the room because everyone had turned to watch. Then Sihanouk was seized with a spasm, as though someone had prodded him sharply. And he threw back his head and emitted a very loud, high-pitched giggle, and the whole room joined in, because the sound itself was so peculiar and marvellous.

With that collective laughter in his ears, relieved, sipping his whisky, Christopher warmed to Sihanouk who was still smiling broadly, flushed with pleasure, and nodding to Cook who was suavely signalling his intention to move away and join some of the other junior staff. It was true that the Prince had human failings, an amorous disposition, and skittish – very volatile in his responses to the British. But he had been under awful pressure, and the Americans had treated him with contempt, so it was not surprising he harboured resentments. Christopher and Wilfred and Keith were still gazing at the perfect oval face of the neat Prince in his beautifully tailored suit, his sober tie, the top pocket where the whiteness of the handkerchief echoed that of his shirt. His dark brown complexion showed that he was a true Khmer – that his lineage (unlike that of some others in the ruling elite) – had not mingled with the Chinese.

But the three of them then, simultaneously, turned their gaze towards Peter Cook, who had achieved something daring and extraordinary with the Prince. Christopher realised that he needed to manage Peter, not least because he aroused such strong responses in the rest of his staff:

'And why…' Wilfred Jamie said, 'why has that callow peacock come to this backwater to flaunt himself?'

Wilfred's being so affronted struck Christopher as a form of self-advertising, as indignation that a junior member of staff should attract so much attention. He was more concerned about Keith's reactions and puzzled by the smile that Keith was aiming at Cook, who you would have thought he must surely hate. Keith was just the sort of man that Christopher thought deserved to be successful, a man whose father was a north-country electrician, and who was annoying sometimes in his attempts to conceal his origin when you could so readily discern it from his gestures and vocabulary. But the Ambassador was determined to advance Keith's cause because he was a man who was very intelligent and had gone to a grammar school and worked diligently – the diplomatic service must comprehend that sort of Englishness.

Christopher was pleased that Edith was looking after Keith, was mothering him, but he thought that Peter might be a dangerous friend for him: when he had tried to impress on Peter how hard Keith had worked, how he had always wanted to be a diplomat and had therefore diligently studied his Classics, Peter had dismissively said, 'yes he had to have the Latin for the diplomatin'.' Keith had worked at Sandie as diligently as he had at his Greek, and then Cook had come along and taken her in just the way the local lord might have exercised his privilege over a pretty wench who had been nurtured on his manor.

'Dirk Bogarde – now *there* was glamour,' Wilfred Jamie was proclaiming. 'Did I tell you, Chris, that I knew him in Jakarta in '45?'

Christopher was pretty sure that he had, but he only smiled. Sihanouk's giggle had spread an excited cheerfulness across the room.

'Pip, we knew him as then. Glamour yes, but he was also very efficient, a real genius with aerial photography. He edited the Divisional newspaper, and read the news on Radio Batavia. Wonderful speaking voice. I used to talk to his secretary, a lovely Eurasian girl. Pip got things done, but he was great fun as well, had a small panther called Ursula.'

Christopher lit a cigarette and pondered what Cook had done. The answer to Wilfred's question about why Cook had come to Cambodia was that he had undergone some sort of crisis. So the whispered word had been from London, and they wouldn't be less vague than that, some life-changing event that had knocked him badly sideways for over a year. The implication, clear if not extensively stated, was that they were relying on Christopher – who had grown close to Peter's father when they were both posted to Nigeria – to look after his friend's son, be tolerant and nurse him along. Evidently there were risks with such a man, and the service generally avoided risk as its premise, but often taking a risk would bring greater rewards. Keith was risk-free but he wouldn't make Sihanouk laugh without six months' notice to write the joke. Hearts and minds. Cook surely had great potential for winning hearts and minds, and Christopher needed to think hard about how to deploy him to the greatest, and safest, effect.

Christopher noticed that Keith was gazing at Sandie who was flushed with excitement as she chatted with Cook. Assuming an expression as innocent as he could manage, Christopher asked Keith how he was getting on with Cook. Keith composed himself and shrugged slightly and nodded, 'Oh, he's great, really great.' His north-country accent was heavier than usual. 'Very witty. He showed me a script he's writing, which is awfully clever. Actually.'

'A script?'

'For a film, I think. It'll be too long for the telly.'

'He's writing a film script?'

'Yes – out of hours, of course'

'I see.'

Keith was blushing. As Christopher noted the blush, Keith blushed a deeper red and it spread further into his forehead and neck. 'It's based on the Faust legend. Peter studied languages you know at Cambridge, must've read Goethe I suppose – it's just awfully clever how he adapts the Faust idea for now, in Britain. There's this anti-hero type who lives in Dagenham, and he...'

Christopher was starting to find Keith too annoying to watch as he squirmed and blushed, feigning this idolatry.

The Ambassador had actually shut his eyes, his discomfort was so acute, because he was starting to think the idolatry was real. But Keith was continuing, 'The Faust idea – it's accurate for Peter because he's like someone who's been given a wish, but it turns into a nightmare... He was bullied at school, and he needed to fight off the bullies, so he wished to be uproariously funny, but then he couldn't stop – he couldn't ever say *anything* that was serious...'

Keith trailed off because Sandie had come over and was very polite to Christopher but was looking, really, at Keith, who managed a smile. 'Keith,' she said, 'we need you to come over to the piano because we want to sing some songs.'

'Oh, I'm sorry Sandie, I really can't...'

'Please, Keith....' Her look was reproachful.

'I'm not feeling that well, actually, I wouldn't even have come this evening...' he glanced at Christopher, 'if it hadn't been such an important occasion. I'm coming down with some sort of lurgy...'

'Oh you know that's made up, and you're fine *really*... it won't do to be the prima donna...'

'That isn't it, at all. I'm...'

'Dreaded lurgy – just nonsense, like that word. Lurgy.' She pronounced the word contemptuously and turned her look to Christopher, who nodded agreement.

Keith's posture had stiffened with resistance, but Christopher's equal dismissiveness about *lurgy* defeated him, and he slackened with consent and followed Sandie to the upright piano where Cook and a couple of others of the younger Embassy staff had gathered. Keith at the piano threw himself into a frantic series of notes and Cook shouted 'You ain't nothing but a hound dog' and started to gyrate in a fashion that even Christopher recognised as an attempt to parody Elvis Presley. The others, when Cook started another of these, protested loudly, and persuaded Keith to play something else – and then they were all harmonising songs that were vaguely familiar to Christopher and whose obsessive refrains admonished little Susie to wake up and proclaimed that a prodigious quantity of 'shaking' was in progress. Christopher noticed that Sihanouk was standing, almost shyly, to one side, watching the performance, tapping his feet and nodding his head in evident enjoyment, and realised that the Prince would love to join in, and pointed that out to Wilfred and said, 'Can we invite him to take part, do you think?'

'Surely not.' Wilf was vigorously shaking his head.

'But he really looks as though he wants to. He's a musician after all. He's written songs.'

'No, no. He can easily take offence.'

'What we need is a saxophone.'

Christopher was fretting at the improbability of this when Reginald Armstrong, the communications man, stepped awkwardly in front of him, saying, 'Excuse me Ambassador, I can get one.'

'You can, Reg? That would be marvellous.'

Reg bustled stiffly away and Christopher was unnerved, as he often was, by the idea of a man called Armstrong having only one leg, but he was grateful to him now. Christopher assumed that for some reason Reg had a saxophone in his tiny room of lights and dials where he sent and received Morse code. And he was quickly back with the gleaming instrument in his hand, and Christopher carried it reverently over to Sihanouk and said, 'We'd be very honoured if you'd play this for us, as we know you can.' Sihanouk smiled doubtfully but allowed Christopher to lead him over to the piano where Christopher asked Keith if he would discuss with Sihanouk what they might play. Keith did and very soon was playing the first notes of *Petite Soeur Angélique* and Sihanouk was joining in with tentative interjections on the saxophone. It was nervous and self-conscious at first, but both men evidently loved the music and soon forgot the strangeness of their duet in their absorption in the possibilities of the tune, first one and then the other cleverly finding surprising avenues it could be led along. They followed that with *Le Temps des Cerises*, this time confident from the start, the working-class Lancastrian and the princely descendant of the venerable Khmer royal family, in unexpected harmony, enjoying each other's inventiveness.

Christopher was delighted but he thought it would be preferable if there could be others joining in and singing, and remembered he had heard Sandie occasionally, *sotto voce*, singing *La Mer*, the hugely popular song by Charles Trenet. Sihanouk was giggling at a slightly mocking rush of tinkling notes that Keith was improvising, when Christopher asked Sandie if she'd sing. She feigned reluctance, but quickly assented, and the players were soon arranging themselves, and Christopher walked over to his wife who was talking to the journalist Hector Perch. Christopher said, 'This will bring back memories', because the song had been everywhere when they had visited Paris early in their marriage. Hector Perch slipped away and left Christopher and Edith standing side-by-side listening. Sandie's voice was surprisingly assured and powerful, and Christopher had forgotten what a marvellous, evocative song it was, *La Mer*, and he turned to Edith feeling stirred with a nostalgia that made him celebrate what an exciting and vivid life he had led, and touched her shoulder and was shocked to see a tear fall from her chin and then two others running down her cheeks. 'Edith,' he said, 'oh dear.' He tried to look her in the face but she turned away, refusing to look at him as he said, 'Edith, darling, it's marvellous isn't it?' And then she was moving away and he watched her heading out of the room, and followed her, but once out of the room she was almost running towards the exit of the Embassy, and he knew he couldn't follow her there.

Christopher felt dismayed that this meant that some sort of new marital trouble was afoot, and he hated those periods – the worst had been in Nigeria when she lost the baby, and that had been simply terrible and lasted almost a year. He had been sensing recently that Edith wasn't at her happiest. He felt annoyed then because it had otherwise been a brilliantly successful evening and he wanted simply to celebrate that and not fret about personal trivia. It was his annoyance that led him to drink and smoke too much for the rest of the evening, and to linger in the Embassy when most people had left, feeling, as he had often felt, that his marriage was harder work than his work.

In the early hours of the morning he and Peter Cook were amongst only six people remaining and Christopher was leaning against a wall when Cook sauntered by, then Cook leant against the opposite wall and they smoked together silently for some minutes. Christopher finally said, 'We all need to be very careful these days, Peter. All of us in the diplomatic service and such. Britain has lost its empire and we can't find a role. We're on a sticky wicket now as a nation.'

Peter smoked, and blinked, and then, still slouching against the wall, nodded at Christopher. 'A sticky wicket, yes. Russia and America – the bowling's positively bodyline. Our leggie's lost his googly. Our offie's lost his flight. We've lost our umpire and we can't recall the rules.'

They gazed at each other lengthily, blinking and slightly open-mouthed, Christopher settling his back against the wall. They pulled on their cigarettes. Christopher smiled. 'The sun has set behind the Imperial Hotel, and bad light has stopped play.'

4

Keith Entwistle emerged from a long meeting with the Ambassador and the Head of Chancery where he had felt, as usual, out of place. The sky blinked and then shuddered, disclosed brief veins of fire, and roared as though it was ripping itself apart. Keith watched it through the window of his office, thinking that he was the Second Secretary in the Embassy, but he was from Vulgaria. He heard *Rose, Rose, I love you*, the tune that was trapped between his ears because he had heard it so often squeaking from loudspeakers all over Phnom Penh. He constantly needed to translate, for H.E. and the others, from his native Vulgarian, but his vocabulary was often not correct tonally, and they would adopt slightly sceptical postures in response. Wilfred, the Head of Chancery, had often told him off for snatching at the knee of his trouser leg when he sat down, and for holding his elbow too rigidly, and at too self-conscious an angle, when he drank his coffee. A week ago, the Ambassador had sent him home for wearing a brown tie. Watching the sky wincing from its own internal fire, Keith thought that the Ambassador clearly liked Peter (the Third Secretary) but regarded Keith as a project to be philanthropically pursued.

It was early June, deep into the rainy season, and near the end of the working day, and Keith watched a heavy downpour fall into the garden of the Embassy, watched it splash up vigorously on the gravel path, and he hoped it would stop before he planned to leave, which was soon. Despite his problems of assimilation, he felt strangely happy, watching the powerful rain from his desk, and hearing *Rose, Rose, I love you*, which he had encountered in several Chinese dialects, and whose familiarity was soothing, and whose ebullience he enjoyed because it struck him as defiantly cheerful as though determined to be in love.

He felt charged with an energy that was so powerful it was unnerving, because he didn't know how to direct it. He smiled, remembering a conversation with his Russian friend Yuri Shunin, because bald young Yuri had said that the Russians suspected that pop songs contained coded messages. Keith remembered Yuri saying this in that strange accent of his, with its bizarre hybrid of Russian and Australian: Yuri had struggled to think of examples of these coded messages, but then had suggested *Wake Up Little Susie*. Yuri had looked offended when Keith had laughed, so Keith had tried to placate him with flattery, suggesting that the Russians were themselves so literary and sophisticated that they couldn't believe a simple truth, which was that *Wake Up Little Susie* really was every bit as inane as it appeared to be. But Yuri had said he was only choosing that song as an example, but that *Little Susie* might easily represent a small country like Cambodia, which was being exhorted to stir itself and recognise the truth as the West understood it. When Keith had asked who this code was directed towards, what people exactly were supposed to receive and interpret the allegory, Yuri had merely given him a patronising look which had implied that Keith was hopelessly naive.

Noticing the rain subsiding, Keith jumped from his chair, grabbed his bag and headed for the exit, but then, on his way out of the Embassy, encountered Sandie Hamilton just outside the doorway, performing some sort of hairpin adjustment, but when she turned to him he was sure she'd been aware that he was behind her, and that her surprise was feigned. 'Oh Keith,' she said, 'two or three of us are going to the *Zigzag* – do you want to come?'

Keith looked back into the hallway at the portrait of the queen, a reproduction of the Annigoni picture. He remembered that Sandie, when a group of Embassy girls were asked at a party who would be their ideal man, had answered 'Prince Philip'. Just about the opposite of Keith – aristocratic, ruggedly athletic, insouciant. Keith replied, still looking away, as though to her majesty, 'Can't tonight. Terribly hungry, for one thing.'

'I was going to pick up something on the way.'

The cicadas were unusually loud and shrill and sounded like panic, like the shrieking of his nervous system, to Keith, who had resolved to avoid Sandie. 'Peter's coming is he?' Keith straight away regretted 'coming' rather than 'going'. Already, he'd made it impossible not to go.

Sandie grimaced. 'Not that I know of.' She gave him that look which meant he was being childishly awkward if he didn't do what she asked.

Keith was feeling much more relaxed, an hour later, after a baguette and a bottle of beer, sitting in the *Zigzag* at the table he and Sandie had always favoured in the days before Peter came to Phnom Penh: he noted that no-one else had shown up, though that might, of course, have happened by accident. He enjoyed the sense of familiarity as Sandie recounted, lengthily, the story of the latest farce that was occupying her section of the Embassy, the business section. The mode was tried and trusted, elaborate farce, and the response (amused exasperation) so expected it was reassuring, and he could set his face in the required shape and sip his beer and glance around contentedly at the Cambodian bar that pretended it was in Marseilles. He didn't need to formulate the sort of sentences that Sandie would approve of, only to nod and smile ruefully, so he was alarmed when he saw Hector Perch enter the bar because he'd introduce a random factor Keith didn't want. Still listening to Sandie's story, Keith watched Perch order a drink and then glance around until he noticed Keith, who managed to return his smile. And then he was sauntering over, gaunt, grey, looking a bit like Spencer Tracy, but in a neckerchief today that added some flamboyance to his usual look of the worldly reporter, the formidable foreign correspondent. Keith had been very surprised when Perch had decided to extend his stay in Phnom Penh, and had even moved out of *Hôtel le Royal* and into a flat of his own: why would such an important journalist decide to linger in a backwater? Did he have inside information that he wasn't divulging? It struck Keith as ominous.

'May I join you?' Perch asked, with his hand on the wooden chair he was about to occupy, and Keith said of course and introduced him to Sandie as Perch placed his glass of whisky on their table.

Perch leant back in his chair and sipped and smiled and let out a moan of exaggerated frustration as he said, 'What a day! How am I supposed to report from a place that hasn't heard of the telephone?' Prompted by Keith for more detail, he described how he had typed out his story as a telegram but then the censor hadn't liked it.

Keith was intrigued. 'Why was that?'

Perch shrugged. 'Maybe my bribe wasn't enough.' He hurried on: 'Anyway, I tried all afternoon to get a phone line, and finally got one but was cut off after a couple of minutes. So I had to go to the airport to find someone willing to take the story with them – which I did in the end, a business type I'd seen here before.'

Keith had noticed how guarded Perch had grown in response to his curiosity, so he was being mischievous when he asked, 'So what was the story?'

Perch dipped his head and smiled wryly, signalling he knew what Keith was up to. 'Oh, the usual – what other story is there? Sihanouk and his latest alliances.'

'You saw him the other day at our party?' Sandie asked.

Perch turned towards her. 'I did, yes. As a political leader he makes a great saxophonist.'

'But he does play well.'

'I couldn't say. Keith's the expert there.'

'He's really not bad, actually, considering,' Keith said.

'Considering all the hardships he's faced, scraping the money together to buy the instrument, finding time to practice after all the hours of back-breaking work...'

'I mean considering that blues and jazz are not the natural idiom of Khmer royalty.'

'Yes that's true. Keith will've played you his jazz records, Sandie? He and I have spent many pleasant evenings together.' Perch smiled at Keith, who knew that Perch was now firing a warning shot, that he might introduce the randomness Keith hadn't wanted, the danger he might mention that they'd smoked opium together and, even worse, spent an evening at Madame Chhum's. If Hector said that dreaded name, how could Keith possibly insist on the distinction that needed to be made in his case – that, yes, he had smoked the opium, but had rejected the girls?

'They're not really to my taste,' Sandie said, fastidiously.

'Very pleasant evening though, and such fascinating developments. Sihanouk enjoying himself like that, and the odd moment with that chap Peter Cook – who I've been told some very unlikely things about.'

'What are they?' Keith asked.

'That he was once an up-and-coming comedian.'

'He was.'

'Well not if he was the one who appeared in the Edinburgh fringe doing satire with three other Oxbridge types.'

'Well he was,' Keith insisted. 'What makes you say he wasn't?'

'Because I saw that show, got a tip-off from a friend that it looked like something big.'

'Oh you did? Was it... good?'

'Amazing. Not just funny. You could see these young men were very clever, certainly – but also that they were determined that things must change, that they had it in for the whole status quo. The Peter Cook in that show did a parody of Macmillan that was absolutely ferocious, made him look like an old buffoon.'

'Well I've heard Peter do that impression,' Keith said, 'and yes it's very funny.'

'But not just that, you see – meant to change things. And this chap, *your* chap – he's nothing like that.'

'Well he'd look different on stage, for one thing, wouldn't he? And it was a few years ago...'

Sandie had been trying to say something, and the two men had spoken too aggressively for her to speak, but in the pause at that point she said, 'And he went through a terrible time after he left that show. I'm sure that must have changed him quite deeply.'

Impatiently exhaling cigarette smoke, Perch said, 'It wouldn't make him lose all his talent would it? I mean that Elvis Presley parody he performed the other day – it was awful. Your man can't sing, his movements were... jerky – all wrong, nothing like Presley.'

'I thought it was very funny...' Sandie started.

'The Edinburgh chap, though, – he'd have done that *far* better. The man I saw that night was thoroughly confident, everything he did was perfectly timed, and word perfect.'

Sandie wanted to say something and leant forward and opened her mouth but then looked at Keith and stopped.

Perch smoked agitatedly and pondered then said, 'Unless he's been got at.'

'Or unless,' Sandie said, 'the Peter we have here, in Phnom Penh, is a lost twin of the other Peter. A twin who was separated from Peter at birth.'

Hector gave a shout of laughter, and Keith, watching Sandie, with her look, then, of defiant puzzlement, felt a pang of love for her, because she seemed, so much of the time, to think with predictable conventionality, but occasionally, as in this very odd moment, said something disorientingly off-beat. But then Keith started to worry that this twin idea was a product of Sandie's secret closeness to

Peter: feeling uncomfortable, he offered to buy a round, even though most of their drinks were still unfinished. Sandie said no, but Perch asked for another whisky. While he was standing at the bar, Keith noticed Perch lean across to Sandie to say something confidentially: Sandie leaned towards him and listened, and nodded, readily accepting his point.

When Keith returned, Perch said, 'Maybe he's been brainwashed.'

'Oh, this is barmy.' Keith was on edge now – this line of conversation was irritating him.

'No, seriously,' Perch insisted. 'I can see, thinking about it, that the man I saw that evening would alarm the powers-that-be, and they might want to silence him...'

'This is typical of you, Hector – as I've told you before, you're paranoiac.'

'No but really I've written about this quite recently. There are ways, now, that they can change someone completely. Kidnap them and isolate them, deprive them of sleep, keep them hungry so they're physically weak, then play tricks on their mind.' Perch turned to Sandie and continued, patronisingly, 'Once the victim is vulnerable, they can be manipulated in all sorts of ways. Deprive them of daylight and switch the lights on and off to shorten the day to a couple of hours or stretch it to a couple of days. And then make them repeat things, even nonsensical things, after their torturer – repeat them or they get an electric shock, or a good old kick in the shins. Once the victim is in a thoroughly suggestible state they can be moulded however they want them to be.'

'You notice, Sandie,' Keith said, working hard not to condescend, as Perch had been doing, 'how Hector keeps saying "they" and "them" without specifying who these people are who might want to torture a rising star of light entertainment?'

But Sandie was frowning pensively. 'It's true, you know Keith – maybe he's told you himself? – that he feels like an entirely different person from the one who went as an undergraduate to Cambridge? He told me he sometimes feels like he's pitched up here out of the blue, as though he can't remember how he got here. And he certainly seems the square peg, don't you think? He sometimes seems so lost...'

'Well,' Perch said, smiling, 'it's one of the features of brainwashing – "thought reform" is the preferred term now – that they make you forget everything about the process they've put you through.'

Keith lost his temper. 'We all feel lost don't we? It's the human condition... I feel lost much of the time, but somehow, when I am, it's not perceived as anything like as loveable.'

Keith regretted his anger as Perch smiled more broadly, and said, 'Keith's an *existentialist*, did you know that, Sandie? Bit of a beatnik on the quiet.'

But Perch left soon afterwards and then the evening went well enough for Sandie to agree to go back to Keith's flat. When they got there, though, Keith was mortified when he remembered he had painted his sitting-room completely in black, partly because it seemed to confirm Perch's beatnik jibe, but especially because Sandie groaned with horror when she saw it, and declared it to be the colour of mourning, which seemed to destroy Keith's chances – ironic because Keith had done that painting on rebellious impulse at the point when Sandie had chosen Peter ahead of him. Even now Sandie couldn't stop talking about Peter, talking about *his* sitting-room, how light and airy it was, and how, eccentrically, he kept a set of dominoes on a card table and kept rearranging the pieces, so sometimes, when you went, they were set out inches apart and in lines, and sometimes he'd placed two together with another on top – several like that, like a tiny

Stonehenge. Keith knew what the punch line was there, but didn't want to tell Sandie, didn't want to talk about Peter at all, but it was partly because of that, and partly because Keith felt so inexperienced when he thought about Hector Perch – so intimidating because he had lived so variously, travelled so widely, exposed himself to so much danger – that, after Sandie had refused his offer of whisky, and he had made coffee, and she had seated herself in the single armchair, he said, 'A strange thing happened to me in my third year at Oxford.'

Sandie said she needed more milk and went and got it for herself.

When she came back he pressed on: 'Yes, in the Michaelmas term. It may have been because I'd been in the Labour Party, and I'd spoken quite a bit at the Union on political questions. But I was... approached then.'

'Approached?'

'Yes. I was in a Wimpy Bar. A man came and sat at my table. Very shifty, he was...'

Sandie grimaced. 'I don't want to hear about...'

'No. No. Not that. He told me that the people he worked for had been interested in me for some time. They knew about my background, and my political views, and were certain I must have powerful reasons for hating the English establishment, how it had oppressed my family for generations. They also knew that – despite that – I had, since I was young, wanted to enter the diplomatic service, and that his people thought I might be especially helpful to them for that reason. I was very naive then, not yet twenty-one, and young for my age, so I didn't really catch on to what he meant...

'Oh Keith, this is terribly dangerous...'

'Well of course I soon started to catch on, to see what he was getting at. But I thought I'd play him along. Partly I was just curious, I wanted to find out what they were like –

these people he worked for. But then I backed out pretty swiftly.'

'Did you report it?'

Keith hesitated. 'Well I told my tutor, but he didn't seem to make much of it.'

Sandie looked indignant. 'He didn't?'

'No, he behaved as though it was quite common.'

After this, Sandie seemed to find Keith freshly interesting, and she told him that, while he'd been at the bar, Hector Perch had told her that he thought Keith highly intelligent and destined for great things. Keith thought it must have been this combination of circumstances that encouraged Sandie to allow herself to rest in close proximity to Keith on his sofa, and then to tolerate the extending of a clinch in which the shape of a surprising range of her body parts were evident, so that his hopes were raised with an almost unbearable intensity, to an extent which shifted from hope to feverish alarm as he started to fret about his ability to cope with the demands of the final stage. His left hand had advanced an astonishing, and then terrifying, distance up her leg, so that it was grasping at the suspender there, before she finally said, 'Better not, darling,' and he could settle back on the sofa, sighing with relief, and hearing again *Rose, Rose, I love you*, with a picture in his mind, from the James Bond novel he was reading, of a woman painted all in gold.

5

Instead of taking a seated luncheon, Christopher Hartnell was strolling, feeling reluctant to return to the Embassy, and tempted, even, to retreat to his Residence, to claim that he was unwell, which wasn't entirely untrue. There was a series of interviews scheduled for the afternoon which all made him feel slightly queasy, especially the one with Bill Noon's wife, Hilda, who was clearly upset about something. It wasn't his job to deal with that sort of thing, and he'd wanted to refer her to Edith, but she had insisted it was him she wanted to see. He was strolling because he liked to stare at the street life of Phnom Penh – all the bicycles, the cyclos, the occasional Citroen or Peugeot, and the new Volkswagen Beetle, and the workshops where punctures were repaired, or watches mended, or where plastic covers were welded onto documents. He hurried away from one of the workshops where the smell of raw latex was especially strong and turned his stomach, dodged around some broken paving – and saw, in the road, an elephant carrying a huge howdah bristling with wood. Even now a sight like that amazed him, reminding him that he made his living in a place where elephants went strolling by, and he paused and watched it intently. Then he strolled on and saw a large billboard with a portrait of Prince Sihanouk in football kit, a billboard that wished the Prince, in Khmer and French, a long life, and called him "the sport-loving father". He saw a cart that was selling clothing, and he bought a *kramar*, one of those chequered towels that Cambodians wore round their necks like a scarf, or like a turban on their heads, – he thought he'd send it to his nephew who lived in London. Odd to think of himself *shopping* – something he'd never do in Britain. Then he thought that eating might settle his stomach, which was only slightly querulous, and he approached a cart where dried beef was being grilled over charcoal, and tenderised, and bought some served on a lotus leaf with pickled papaya.

Chewing and swallowing, he felt the whole of his upper body welcome the food, his chest and even his shoulders saying *yes yes yes* to the mingled impact of meat and piquant fruit – smoky tang, contrasting textures, now crisp, now solid but yielding – absorbing it with a clear conviction of its rightness and goodness, like a profound relief, as he entered Psar Thmei, the Grand Market, under its high dome, and its arches of reinforced concrete, and stumbled into the reverie which had recently been seizing him, in which he was standing in fields by the side of the Thames not far from Cirencester. It was a landscape he knew well – he had spent many summer months there when he was growing up because one of his aunts lived there, but he had never previously dwelt on it as he'd been doing in the past few months – the call of snipe, a cloud rift dazzling the slow reedy current of the brown water. He shook it off, recalling a much more recent and odd image he'd caught on the edge of his vision just before he'd entered the market, and which he'd not then wanted to shift his focus towards – Cook standing and chatting with someone unexpected. He turned back and exited the market and looked across the road – and yes it was Cook, across the road from the market, talking to a Chinese gentleman who Christopher was sure he'd seen before but wearing a Mao suit, not the casual clothes he was wearing now. The obvious seriousness of their conversation intrigued him – he watched the thoughtful nodding and the frowns of concentration of their exchanges, and then Cook glanced furtively across the road and saw him and was taken aback, but recovered himself enough to wave a greeting and call 'Hello'. The Chinese man slipped away and Cook crossed the road and, indicating the remains of the food in Christopher's hand, said, 'Snatching luncheon as you go?'

'Just strolling. Taking a breather in the market.' Christopher scrutinised Cook, whose movements were jerky, and whose face was a little flushed, which struck him as very unusual, because the man was generally so self-possessed.

'Ah, yes, well...I'll leave you to it. To your musings...' And, before Christopher could reply, Peter had turned and was crossing the road.

Christopher didn't know what to make of this, and didn't want to make the effort to make anything of it, but resolved to try to remember, at some other point, where he'd seen the Chinese gentleman, which was almost certainly at some sort of formal occasion organised by one of the embassies or by Sihanouk's government. It was the weariness that oppressed him when he thought of such diplomatic gatherings, that led him back to the Thames: it was a fantasy of retirement, which he reprimanded himself about because it was mere self-indulgence in a man of only 56, but nonetheless he was increasingly diverted towards the idea of a small village near the Thames, of a cottage with an abundance of pink and yellow roses growing in front of it. He had made the mistake of mentioning this to Edith once, a few months ago, and she was furious about it, and withered him with her scorn – she hated any talk of ageing, of bodily aches and pains, any mention of declining memory or drive.

He had wandered back into the market, with its functional form influenced by the Munich school, its bare concrete contrasting with the tropical colour of the fruit and flowers, mango and durian so strongly scented they were unnerving, they smelt to him like an indiscretion, like an inappropriately overt sexual reference. Hundreds of big, blatant durian hanging from awnings, with yellow and red ribbons tied around them. He gazed at these but he couldn't escape his Cotswold's village with its small church dating from before the Normans, the light subdued yet warmed by stained glass: those pews in his head while in his sight rambutans were spiky with quills – rambutans, pineapples, oranges and bananas, and bowls of lotus buds whose petals he loved, so crisp and sweet, in salads. He would miss such things about the tropics but, daily now, he saw himself strolling to the small village shop and strolling back holding *The Times* and pondering the headline, feeling the detachment from it of a man retired from politics, strolling back to his cottage where he would sit in his garden and read it slowly and fully, saving the cricket reports for last.

Back at the Embassy, Christopher dropped the *kramar* onto his desk, then, in the kitchen, drank some tap-water, thirsty for it even though it was brownish and warm, thinking that smoking too much made him dry, but there had also been that beef and papaya. He returned to his office and changed out of his shirt, which was soaked with sweat, and he had a clean one for that purpose on a hanger on a hook on his wall. Then he pushed the wooden chair out from behind his desk into the open – because he didn't want to seem too formal when he spoke to Mrs. Noon – and removed some papers from an armchair so she'd be able to sit there. Just as he noticed some tropical mildew on the faded chintz of its cushioned seat, he remembered where he'd seen that man Cook was talking to – it was at an evening of the Royal Ballet where they'd gone to see Bopha Devi, an evening at the Dance Pavilion in the Royal Palace. Bopha Devi – Sihanouk's daughter, and an eerily beautiful dancer, the vivid focal point of the dance company: he saw her strangely long and fragile neck and heard an echo of the plangent stringed instruments. That fellow had been there with a group of others from the Chinese embassy, all in their Mao suits. He dismissed the thought and swatted at the mildew, raising some dust from the cushion. There was a knock at his door and he called 'Come in', but, instead of Mrs. Noon, it was red-faced Reginald Armstrong who entered saying he'd asked Hilda Noon to wait because he needed urgently to show Christopher what he'd found in the Embassy garden. And as he said that he was displaying a set of papers in his hands and raising his eyebrows exasperatedly. Christopher felt a wave of exhaustion spread through him as he took the papers from Armstrong and noticed their level of importance and consequent secrecy and said, 'Ah yes, Reginald, that's really not good at all. It's really most unfortunate.'

Armstrong walked over to the window and, pointing at the lawn there, said, 'Yes, Ambassador, I'm afraid I found them there.'

Christopher felt extremely irritated at the man's tone, but only shook his head contritely and said, 'Yes, most unfortunate.'

'Clearly the ceiling fan blew them out of the window.'

They both looked from the ceiling fan above Christopher's desk to the open window, and then back again. 'Must have. Yes, I suppose.'

'I know it's *terribly* hot, Ambassador, but even so anyone on the staff – the gardener, or the cook, might've picked them up. I didn't, of course, read them but they...'

Armstrong really was insufferably officious. 'Yes quite. The heat is very distracting. The Americans, of course, have air conditioning.'

'Maybe you could move your desk away from the fan?'

This was too much. Christopher was on the verge of losing his temper but restrained himself, feeling anxious that Armstrong might have a secret role, an idea that had been planted in him a couple of months earlier. The Ambassador had attended, then, for the first time, a reunion at Magdalen, his college in Oxford, and he had found the whole evening very unpleasant. First of all, he was shocked at how his contemporaries had aged, and felt resentment towards them for looking so superannuated, so bald and grey and wrinkled. But then, much worse, he had been taunted, towards the end of the gaudy, by Alec Crawford, an old antagonist (Christopher could hardly even remember the *casus belli*, something about a girl). Crawford was now in the Foreign Office, and told Christopher that he was regarded there as a joke, and only allowed to stay in post because Phnom Penh was considered such a backwater. Later still, very drunk, Crawford had laughed at Christopher and declared that the disabled communications officer in his Embassy had covertly been given powers – it was preposterous, and Christopher refused even to think about it, even to contemplate the idea that a Cockney amputee… But he was sure that Crawford was just maliciously pulling his leg.

'Yes, Armstrong, *thank you*. Look here, I'll deal with it. Thank you. I must see Mrs Noon now. Could you please send her in?'

Armstrong sighed and left and Noon's wife entered. They exchanged awkward platitudes about the humidity then Christopher nodded towards the armchair and she seated herself in it, filling much of the space it offered. Christopher avoided looking at the cleavage of his colleague's wife, who had chosen a blue dress which displayed a surprising extent of it, striking in such an ample woman, and he regretted, then, choosing seating which stationed him a couple of feet above her, so that he had to fix his range of vision on her face, with extreme rigidity. 'Well, Hilda, you and Bill, I would've said, have taken to life in Cambodia very readily.'

Mrs. Noon shook her head, and he knew he'd overdone the tone of robust cheerfulness. 'No?'

She shook her head again. 'No, Ambassador, we...' She stopped.

'It's not an easy place, of course. Challenging. Very. But you army types are generally most adaptable, and Bill has a very distinguished record – Suez and so on, most distinguished there, despite the obvious...' Christopher could see the woman shifting impatiently, which made him self-conscious that flattery, for a diplomat, was the most predictable of tactics, 'Of course, I don't need to tell you...'

'Bill is a fine man. None better.'

'At least here you are together. When he was on army duty he was posted away from you, but now you can be together under the same roof.'

'Bill is a fine man. But being under a roof isn't his strongest suit.'

'No. A bivouac, eh? Out under the stars...' Christopher chuckled too loudly and was stopped abruptly by the woman's severe look, which annoyed him by making him feel slightly foolish.

'To be frank, Ambassador, Bill has been behaving very oddly. Lives in a world of his own. Hardly talks to me. Insists on sleeping in a different room to me, says he finds he can't sleep when we're in the same room. I sometimes slip into his bedroom in the small hours and find he's not there, that he's left the house altogether. And when I ask him about it he says the heat keeps him awake – so he goes for long walks in the city to tire himself out so he can sleep. And sometimes I know he takes the car – God knows where he's driving to.'

Christopher glanced down at his hands and thought that there must still be some spores of mildew invisibly smeared on his fingers. He rubbed them on the back of his trouser leg. 'It may well be, of course, that the adjustment to a more civilian way of life is difficult for a man like Bill who, after all, has been a soldier from a very early age. Conditioned to live amongst a large group of men.'

'Have you noticed how well Bill gets on with your wife?'

Christopher was so unnerved that he allowed his eyes to stray momentarily below the woman's face – and then swiftly corrected them. He pondered this: Edith had hardly ever mentioned Bill, though what she'd said had been positive enough. In terms of attractiveness, in so far as any man can judge such things, Bill would rank far higher than himself, the man was so powerfully and athletically built – but then would Bill actually want Edith? It seemed unlikely.

'My wife gets on well with all the Embassy staff. She works very hard to oil the wheels.' He hoped he had managed to inject sufficient chill into his response, in the face of the woman's aggression.

'You've not noticed them tête-à-tête in our little gatherings?'

'Can't say I have.' Embassies had always been rife with sexual intrigue, especially in remote places like Phnom Penh, where adultery was one of the very few diversions on offer, but he and Edith had been largely immune from all that – for himself, he thought that the complications involved could never be worth the gratifications, though he sometimes half admired those who'd been willing to accept the risks, and he sometimes regretted the lack of excitement in his own experience. He felt a sudden spasm of anger, felt it actually at the top of his stomach, just under his ribs, and, when he spoke, it made him slightly breathless: 'Edith and I, Mrs Noon, have been married for a long time.' He glared at her and saw her cheeks wince as though she'd been slapped, and then she looked away, and then they spent a long moment as they both stared at the floor.

'I'm very sorry, Ambassador, this wasn't... I didn't mean...' she was almost inaudible now.

'Mrs. Noon...'

'Please call me Hilda.'

'Hilda, I...'

She made a choking sound in her throat. 'I just feel terribly alone, here.'

He saw a couple of tears spill down her face. 'It's terribly difficult for Embassy staff in places like Phnom Penh, when they're so far away from their families, and their usual systems of support.' He pulled a handkerchief out of his trousers and reached it across to her. 'I'm very sorry, Hilda, that isn't terribly clean, actually,' he said, when he saw her wipe her cheeks with it.

'It's fine. You're very kind.'

'I'm sure that Bill is just going through a difficult time. A period of adjustment.'

Hilda smiled weakly and shook her head. 'No, it's something much... deeper than that.'

'You know that the Embassy wives get together quite frequently – they're tremendously supportive of each other, and they organise all sorts of social events... whist drives and... such...' Christopher trailed off because Hilda was looking at him quite intently now, and he was surprised because her tear-smudged face aroused him with the sense of his authority. Suddenly he was the Ambassador in his Embassy and this young woman was appealing to him because of the power he could wield. He settled back in his chair and enjoyed this feeling of arousal, which was not something he had felt for a while. Not something he had even wanted to feel and, now he thought about it, Edith hadn't approached him in that way for a few months. That had been a relief – but might it not suggest that Mrs. Noon was right and she now had other outlets? It was true, when he thought about it, that she had seemed a little distracted recently, a little more cheerful.

As he thought this, they'd been looking into each other's eyes for an uncomfortably long time, and Hilda now said, 'You know, Ambassador, it would really cheer me up if you could do for me – I don't want to seem impertinent – if you could do your Sihanouk for me.'

'My Sihanouk?' As Christopher said this he realised what she meant and remembered that, recently, at the end of an especially drunken Embassy gathering, when only his staff remained, – but, still, it had been embarrassingly indiscreet – he had performed his Sihanouk impersonation.

'It's so funny, Ambassador. That nervous little giggle you do where it's brief at first and then it's almost nothing but the giggle, and the same French phrase again and again. And how you start out shrill and get shriller and shriller. And... funniest of the lot where you get so shrill you can't be heard – so you're just *miming* the words – as though it's beyond the range of human hearing.'

Christopher felt a growing alarm. 'Well, you know, Hilda, it was really rather improper of me...'

Hilda ignored him. 'You know that our house is not very far at all from your Residence?'

'That's true isn't it? I remember now – Edith and I came round to see you once didn't we?'

'Yes you did. And I've sometimes thought, when I've been there on my own – as I often am – how nice it would be if – when you're on your way somewhere – you could drop by perhaps...'

Christopher felt impelled then to jump to his feet, saying 'Well I'll bear that in mind, Mrs. Noon.' Grabbing the *kramar* from the top of his desk, he said, 'This is splendid, don't you think? – I bought this earlier in the market...' and he opened it to display its chequered pattern.

And later, when she'd gone, he imagined going to her house, contemplating how that visit would go – how, at some point, he must move across the floor towards this large young woman. And he actually shook his head at how grotesque it was, that idea.

6

Wilfred Jamie, the Head of Chancery at the British Embassy, was waiting for Alain Jouve to join him for luncheon in a French restaurant called *La Lanterne*, which adjoined a hotel owned by the same French proprietor. The man's Cambodian wife had seated Wilfred by a window that looked out onto the small asymmetrical square with its post office, which was painted white, a police station, and some mango and prakop trees. It was all very provincial, like everything else in Phnom Penh: he was often irritated by the city centre, which was so small you were always running into people you knew. This was a place of frequent power cuts and brown tap water, and he disliked feeling belittled by the low status of the tiny Embassy, rated by the Foreign Office at Grade 4, below even Vientiane, and of course the British had never been powerful in Indo-China. Considering those limitations, *La Lanterne* was exceptional: he and Alain often had luncheon there because the chef was very skilful – Alain had known that because, being an insider, he knew that Sihanouk often borrowed him.

Just after he sat down, Wilfred noticed that *eminence grise* of a journalist – what was his name? – seated at a corner table deep inside the restaurant. As he did so, the man returned his look and smiled and nodded, quite vigorously. Perch. That was his name. Wilfred was surprised by the vigorous nodding, which seemed to signify Perch's whole-hearted approval, and Wilfred was baffled about why the man should feel that, much less signify it so conspicuously. Nonetheless, he smiled and nodded back before confusedly turning away to gaze at a group of three Frenchmen who were drinking aperitifs at an outside table next to the neat shrubs that separated those tables from the street. He recognised their look, so pale, always slightly agitated, these bankers and businessmen, flotsam and jetsam scattered in the wake of Cambodia's independence from France. Watching them, Wilfred felt the sensation he had felt since early adolescence of being at an oblique angle to the world, of being an interloper who watched others and could never be one of them. In later adolescence he had articulated that thought further, so that he regarded himself as resembling an agent who was always slipping backwards and forwards across frontiers, was constantly under cover amongst foreigners, observing the detail of their lives but never participating, one whose identity was never fixed, and whose briefcase contained seven or eight passports with faked photographs. Ruefully, as a young adult, he had wondered, though, whether this wasn't just a melodramatic way of coping with the knowledge of his father's disapproval of him, his father's feelings of deep distaste for his son's daydreaming passivity.

Just before he left the Embassy Wilfred had encountered Edith Hartnell, who was wearing a new dress and had had her hair done, and looked suddenly younger, and laughed a lot telling him a story about a casino at Kep on the Gulf of Thailand, which had been attacked by a gang of thugs who smashed all the furniture and windows and mirrors. He had found it hard to understand why this was so funny, but she explained that it involved a *high personality* in Phnom Penh, and possibly even a *high bourgeois feminine personality*. He knew that the last phrase must refer to Monique, Sihanouk's consort, who was *bourgeois* by contrast with his other wife, but he found it impossible to follow the intrigue she described – something about the casino being smashed by its own proprietor who was tired of paying the toll imposed by a corrupt *royal highness*. He was delighted to see Edith look so happy, because she was such a marvellous person, and he had been saddened by how defeated she had appeared in the past few months, when she had repeatedly complained to him about being dogged by horrific dreams. That had been alarming because he had worried she was becoming unstable, so her exhilaration this morning was very cheering, but it was uncharacteristic of her to take such an interest in politics, and to be so knowledgeable about it, and to repeat those phrases of Cambodian English with such ironic pleasure, and there was an edge to her laughter which was disquieting.

Alain was late. He was often late, but his work was unpredictable. Mostly he worked in the French language part of the radio service, which, out of loyalty, Wilfred sometimes tried to listen to, but he found its style far too hectic, rapid speech and music in a cacophonous montage. But Alain also did some work with Sihanouk's speech writers and it was that which gave him inside knowledge. He was so fascinating! Wilfred thought about the fine bones of Alain's face, his delicate cheekbones, but then, Alain was like that everywhere – everywhere he had such delicate, protruding bones, in his wrists, in his chest, his collarbones, the curving lines of his ribs, in his knees. Jamie smiled – yes his knees, it was true! Alain had knobbly knees, and the idea was so incongruous, in one so elegant. He wondered if he dared to say that to Alain, to tease him about it, or would it irritate him?

When Alain finally arrived, Wilfred was shocked to see that his face was badly bruised, especially around his eyes.

'Poor boy,' he said, 'what happened to your face?'

'It's nothing,' Alain said irritably and sat down and grabbed a menu.

'Madame Quesnel says the onion soup is very good today.' Wilfred stared at Alain as he read the menu. He started to reach his hand across to his bruises, but thought better of it. 'Did you fall?'

'Yes. Drank too much and fell on my stairs.'

'Poor boy, you really should take more care of yourself.'

Alain looked out over the menu and raised his contemptuous eyebrows.

Wilfred was so unnerved by Alain's surprising tetchiness that when he thought about his knobbly knees he actually shook his head in horror, though Alain didn't see it because he was staring rigidly at the menu. And he found himself introducing his surprise, which he'd expected to have saved for near the end of luncheon, very early: 'You've never been to Tokyo have you?'

'No.'

'I thought we could go there...'

'Can't. No money.'

'Well I'd be happy to pay.'

'Very kind of you, but I couldn't possibly.'

'It would be my pleasure. Honestly. Alain, look: I'd love to take you there. It's a fascinating, exciting place – exotic, of course, but not like the rest of the Far East at all. Not provincial, really not provincial, but very cosmopolitan, very metropolitan, much more attuned to what's happening in the West. And I'd love to show you around.'

Alain looked up and made a *moue*. 'Provincial. God yes.' He stared with open distaste at the Frenchmen who had gathered with their mini-drinks at the bar, and their women who were using napkins to wipe sweat from their faces. 'Can you convey me to Paris or London? New York, maybe?'

When, as always, they ordered the onion soup and *coq au vin* and burgundy, Wilfred fretted, as he spoke the words to the plump Cambodian proprietress in her perpetual black sarong, about the sense of mechanical repetition, afraid of the staleness that was descending. 'Yes, admittedly, New York would be glorious... Perhaps...'

'No, don't be silly Wilfred. It is merely that I am being suffocated in this steaming place.'

There seemed no way forward from there, and each topic of conversation that occurred to Wilfred seemed equally futile. As they were eating their soup the red-haired proprietor wandered over, smoking a thin cigar, hoping, in

53

French, that the soup was good and, referring to Alain as a *plumitif*, tried to engage him in banter about the Cambodian obscenities which he knew (from previous hints by Alain) must have been removed from the French version of Sihanouk's latest diatribe against the Americans. Alain smiled wearily as the restaurateur repeated the word *chiens* – which had apparently featured very frequently – and barely maintained his politeness. When he left them, Alain sighed and said, 'I'm very sorry, Wilfred. I am really at the end of my rope.'

'No, it's alright. It's difficult here for a young person.'

Alain gazed at a toddler who was rolling around the floor near the bar, rapt in a desperate tantrum, and shook his head as its mother responded with nearly equal lack of control, so that the two vied with each other in extreme shrillness. 'I was eating in the *Nouveau Tricotin* the other night and that new fellow was there from your Embassy. The very thin fellow, with the long sharp nose?'

'Yes. Cook. His name is Peter Cook.'

'Well, I looked at him and I realised how out of touch I've become. How provincial I now am.'

'You're a hundred times better than him.'

'That's not my point.'

'Honestly, Alain. He's just a narcissist.'

'Well maybe he deserves to be.'

'I caught him looking in a mirror once, and he had the look of someone who has caught sight of something in a newspaper which is new and amazing.'

'But his clothes... they were so striking. Very dark shirts, Italian, I think. And a jacket...'

'Yes I've seen that. It's a box jacket. Heavy for here – he couldn't wear that for very long in this climate.'

'Exquisite tailoring. It made me feel so shabby.'

'He's trying to dress like a Regency buck. But he'll soon revert to sharkskin.'

'But he looked so modern. So I felt like living here has made me twenty years out of date.'

'You could get hold of those if you wanted.'

'I tried to speak to him. Just to ask him about his jacket. But he was very standing off.'

'Yes he flaunts himself.'

'And he was with that awful American, the ambassador.'

'Was he? Was he really? That's amazing. In a group?'

'Those two, and that girl... That Russian *salop*?'

Wilfred shook his head. 'No.' He was alarmed about the thought of a younger set growing that he was unaware of, because clearly Alain and others were there too. He realised that he hadn't been going out much recently, had been going to bed early, and the world was shifting towards youth.

'Yes. Those three.'

Wilfred felt a little dizzy, as though the ground were shifting under his feet. How much could he rely on? Edith's friendship, Christopher's support – the Ambassador was a friend who could be counted upon to continue supporting him. And Edith loved Phnom Penh and would never want to leave. But what else would stably remain the same? Alarmed, he said, 'Really? Eating together?'

'So ugly, that man. That red hair and pale skin. Those *freckles*.'

Wilfred didn't hear what Alain was saying, plaintively, for the next minute, because he was pondering this connection. When he started to listen again, Alain was saying '...and this ugly man was pawing him all evening, his hairy hands were all over that jacket.'

7

It was Sunday morning, and Keith Entwistle had decided to take a cyclopousse over to Peter's place because they needed to discuss arrangements for the party they were organising to celebrate Edith's fiftieth birthday. They had sent a request to London for an Elvis Presley costume for Peter but, when Keith had opened the diplomatic bag, he discovered they had sent some sort of military uniform. He found a cyclo near his flat and the pedaleur was a young man he recognised from several previous rides, and, as they started laboriously away into the road, the Cambodian asked him in French if he wanted a woman. Keith watched a couple of Buddhist monks, in their orange robes and with the umbrellas that shield their bare scalps from the sun, standing inside the gateway of a house waiting to be brought some food, and noted the patience on their faces, and thought of Nirvana, eternal peace and self-realisation linked to the ending of all desire. Was Peter really a Buddhist? Surely not, but it was impossible to tell because his ironies were impossible to penetrate – and they had agreed once that the ending of all desire might have its benefits (but then Peter might have ulterior reasons for saying that, considering Sandie). He thought about how Peter could start from a small idea like the initials H.E., His Excellency, referring to their Ambassador, and how he could improvise like Coltrane on a phrase like that, referring to how the Ambassador excelled, referring to him as *he he he*. Keith couldn't even remember now how the riff went, and even that convinced him of his own inferiority in that mode of thought, and he recalled Peter recently praising Dudley Moore, reminiscing about what a rapport Peter had enjoyed with him, and what a great pianist he was, and how funny he was, and that had made Keith feel lost and alone.

Keith thanked the pedaleur but said that he had urgent business to attend to at the moment, but the pedaleur said that he would return later in the day and take him to visit some girls, and all of them would be congenial and lovely, and there would be a choice – there would be some Cambodian ladies, but also some Vietnamese, some Chinese and some French. The broad boulevard was a soporific blur as Keith contemplated this impossible idea, so exotic to him, as he listened to the hissy breath of the cyclo's tyres and the squeaking of its pedals, and *Rose, Rose I Love You,* that Chinese tune, echoing repeatedly between his ears.

But then he was suddenly shocked by the thought that such a visit might actually be wise – because sex was an activity he needed to learn and this, when no emotion was involved, might in fact be the wisest place to learn it. He was unnerved by the idea that the wisest course could possibly be so thoroughly the opposite of conventional wisdom. But a woman would certainly expect a man to be confident and competent and he couldn't be either in a field of action he had never entered. He had heard a rumour, originating from the female members of Embassy staff, that Peter was very good at sex, and this aggravated his own position. Shouldn't he go to Boeng Snor, the red-light district, and learn what he needed to know? He imagined that part of the city, near the banks of the Mekong, where the road was lifted on a dyke above the level of the land, and he imagined entering one of the brothels which were on stilts and therefore level with the road, or one of the houses lower down that were on dry land in the dry season but floated on the water in the rainy months.

Keith was made aware of the long silence between them when the pedaleur said that he also knew boys who could be of service to him. When they arrived outside Peter's apartment, the pedaleur looked Keith solicitously in the eye and said that he, too, could be of service, and Keith registered the man's gold-capped teeth, and his dark skin, the skin of a rural Cambodian, and his powerful arms and shoulders. With that sudden intensity which Keith had noticed before in Cambodians, the pedaleur said that he and Keith could go to a place he knew where, for half-an-hour, they could be *heureux*, and then he would pedal Keith tranquilly along the river, so that he could be quiet and peaceful. And this would cost only one American dollar. Keith remembered it was Sunday morning, and thought how different this was from the church-going Sundays of his Lancastrian upbringing.

As he mounted the stone steps to Peter's flat, Keith shook his head from side to side to clear it of the clinging contamination of his interaction with the pedaleur, and wished he could acquire the invincible self-possession of men like the Ambassador which would allow him simply to dismiss such an interaction and move on to the next, or, even better, the unswerving determination of a man like Bill Noon, the military attaché, a driven purpose which carried him powerfully in a straight direction, unswayed by unwanted feelings. He knocked on Peter's door, and there was no reply, and he looked at his watch and saw he was twelve minutes late – he hated to be unpunctual but was surprised that Peter had left in that time. He blamed the pedaleur, for being too distracted to pedal at the usual pace, and he turned away towards the stairs but thought he heard a sound from inside the flat, which made him turn back again. He was raising his hand to knock again when Peter flung open the door saying, 'Keith, hello, hello,' revealing Edith sitting on his sofa. He flourished a hand gesture in her direction saying, 'Keith I think you know Edith Hartnell? Her excellency? Our S.H.E.?'

Keith was stunned. And S.H.E.? How could Peter have the nerve? But maybe he'd explained the H.E. joke to her? But even if he had – S.H.E.? Edith was smiling at him, but she looked uncomfortable and guilty – but, surely, if there was anything of that sort involved, they wouldn't have opened the door? Several desperate words which hated women, which he had heard used mechanically, obsessively, during his national service, and which he had found himself using then, during that time, crowded into his head and shouted.

'I'm very sorry...' he started.

'No, Keith, really. Don't be silly. Peter evidently forgot to tell me you were on your way,' Edith said, and stared at Peter moodily. 'There are just one or two things I need to say to Peter. Which I had started to say. So if you'll excuse us...'

Keith saw their eyes flit towards the door of the bedroom (the only other room) and skid away from it towards the French windows. 'Yes, if you'll excuse us, take a seat for a minute,' Peter said, and he guided Edith towards the French windows onto his balcony and closed the windows behind him. As he seated himself in an armchair, national service words were still blaring inside Keith's ears, as he pitied himself, left alone, excluded, as they chatted on the balcony. What a nerve Peter had with women! Keith remembered, soon after Peter had arrived, how, with an exaggerated leer, he had watched Sandie walking away from him, after she had delivered a document, and called out 'Your seams are crooked', and how she had half-turned but shook her head and scurried away.

How many things would Peter take away from him? Because Edith had done so much to support Keith and it wasn't too much, surely, to have that left alone? Baffled, he tried to imagine Edith naked, and he could only imagine her body with enormous difficulty, and, even when he did, he couldn't muster a sexual response. But that wasn't the point — he almost said that out loud. That wasn't the fucking point. He tried to calm himself. He saw, on Peter's table, that his typewriter had a piece of paper sticking out of it, and he wandered over to it and saw it was a script, with names and dialogue, and that numerous pages of a script were lying in a neat pile under the table. And he declared to himself that Peter was living inauthentically. Hector might mock him as an existentialist, but that was a genuine thing for Keith – the urgent need to live truly, to make true choices, life choices, not to behave with bad faith, but to choose bravely to live your true life. And Peter was living untruly. He had made a cowardly choice in becoming a diplomat, and opted out of his true path.

He was startled then by a knock at the door behind him and, when he opened it, found Reginald Armstrong there. He invited him in and explained where Peter was and gestured towards the sofa where Edith had been sitting. Then neither of them knew what to say and Keith felt his usual response to 'Reggie', as Peter called him, – a terrible discomfort that Reginald was a nightmare version of himself, unkempt, prone to sweat too much and bathe too rarely, lonely, sad, socially inept, but desperate to do the right thing and be accepted. Keith felt guilty about how, as a result, he shunned the 'communications wizard', which he knew was because he feared the contamination of this awful affinity between them. Reg's job increased his isolation anyway – he worked in a tiny room with earphones on his head, surrounded by black boxes, by oscillating dials and coruscating lights, a room that wailed with static as he sent and received Morse code. Keith felt guiltier about shunning Reg because Peter was strenuously friendly to the unfortunate man, which Keith suspected was something to do with his one-leggedness – he imagined, now, Reg awkwardly mounting the stone steps before he knocked on the door, and speculated about whatever prosthesis it was that he had inside one of his trouser legs.

Reg fidgeted and said, 'I can't stay long.'

'No, please, Reginald. Please wait. I'm sure Peter will be very pleased to see you.'

'It's not a social visit.'

'No?'

'No, I've got an important message for him.'

Keith squirmed with embarrassment at this spectacle of a man seeking attention in this way, of one so aware of his personal lack of intrinsic interest that he had to drum up something he was claiming was useful. 'I'm sure he'll want to hear it.'

Reg looked offended. 'Not necessarily.'

'Peter speaks very highly of you.'

'That's beside the point. I've tried to speak to him about this before.'

Keith glanced towards the typewriter. 'Well, Peter, you know, lives in a world of his own much of the time. Imaginative type.'

'That's as maybe, but some things he can't afford to ignore.'

'Well if you tell me I'll let him know about it and tell him it's important.' Keith noted with some discomfort the condescending note he was sounding.

'It's true, you're his best friend...'

'Hardly...'

'He trusts you, that's clear. You seem very close, so maybe you can persuade him where I've failed. It's to do with an association he seems to have struck up with a local schoolteacher...'

'Well Peter visits schools you know. He does "hearts and minds", so schools are a big part of that.'

'Yes yes, the point is that this Cambodian teacher...' Reg paused and looked as though absent-mindedly towards the French windows, 'this is to do, you understand, with a message I happened to intercept?'

'You must do that all the time.'

'No no, but sometimes. The point is that Peter's name has been linked to this teacher, but he is much more than a teacher.'

This was a nod and a wink. Keith nodded but didn't wink. 'Much more than a teacher. That's your message?'

Reg nodded with a self-congratulating melodrama.

'Rest assured, Reg, I'll tell Peter and impress its importance upon him.'

Keith was very relieved to see Reginald go and, thinking there might be a joke he could make of "more than a schoolteacher", which Peter might enjoy, turned his attention back to the manuscript that was lying under the table. He skimmed it briefly until he noticed movement on the balcony, suggesting they were coming back into the room, and returned it to its place, thinking something should be done about this waste of talent, that some way must be found to make people aware again of this audacious comedy.

8

Yuri Shunin woke up that Sunday morning longing for the sleepy gloom of midwinter afternoons in Leningrad when he was a child looked after by his grandmother who was very devout. He grieved over the loss of that warm gloom lit by the blazing coal fire and the icon lamp, and the marvellous stories his grandmother told him about Christ and the saints, about their miracles. His education had taught him to dismiss those fairy tales, and he did, he did, but he still regretted their loss and sometimes wished he could return to that state of mind, and sometimes pondered how, in different times, he might have become a priest, because the religious feeling he learned from his grandmother had sunk into him very deep. He turned in bed onto his back and saw himself in priestly robes conducting a service, then thought that this sense of alternatives had arisen because of an insult fired at him the previous night by a small Frenchman who had approached him telling him that his name was Alain, insisting that he learn his name, and asking him about Nureyev. Yuri had told him that he knew nothing about ballet and didn't care about Nureyev, but this Alain kept touching his shirt and speaking right into his eyes and saying he knew that Yuri was lying, that Nureyev was fascinating, he had created a huge sensation in Paris, and he could tell that a man like Yuri would know *all* about him, and about the background to his defection. This Frenchman kept making a strange shape with his mouth, a crooked *O* shape like a pained sturgeon, and Yuri had pushed him away, but the scoundrel had actually learned a Russian word to insult him with, and which had so infuriated Yuri that he had punched him. He shuddered with embarrassment now, and felt thoroughly for the first time the sickness of his hangover, as he remembered punching that face, and felt the shame of having punched someone so much smaller and slighter than himself.

He hauled himself stiffly upright, and felt an abrupt bout of dizziness, but bravely maintained his upright position until the dizziness subsided. He stepped stealthily out of bed, trying to evade his dizziness by ducking under it before rising to his full height, thinking now about Ariadna who he wanted to speak to about the message that Cook had tried to pass to Hok Suhana. It ought to be easy to speak to her, given how few her duties seemed to be. He wondered why she seemed to have so much free time, but then dwelt for longer on his growing admiration for her, on the irony she used in response to the male wonder she constantly inspired. He felt a growing understanding of that response, of the cleverness behind that irony, its knowingness and dismissiveness – 'Ah yes', her response, was saying, 'it is true my breasts are remarkable, thank you for noticing, but the observation is hardly new.' He entered the role of Ariadna, which was anyway a role that Ariadna herself was constantly playing, and was struck with awe at the adeptness with which she played it.

All day that Sunday, though, Yuri felt he was not at home in his own Yuriness, that he was unsuited to his own role: Ariadna was a magnificent Ariadna, but he was an unconvincing Yuri. This Sunday's Yuri didn't fit with the usual Yuri, as though, if he looked in the mirror, his outline would flicker, and his right side would step sideways out of his outline, like someone observed with double vision. There was a continuity problem – the camera had moved away and, when it returned, he was wearing a different uniform. From his adolescent years he had felt those breaks in continuity, felt that if you travelled somewhere, for example, you would be a different person in that new place.

The next day in the embassy he performed his routine duties quickly enough to allow himself half an hour to seek out Ariadna to discuss Cook. He went to her tiny office and found the door ajar but Ariadna nowhere around, but he was so intrigued by her that he slipped into the room, which was chaotically untidy and charged with her distinctive perfume. On her desk he noticed an open folder and couldn't resist looking into it and saw it was ten or so pages about the American ambassador Joe Keane. He paused and listened, then looked outside the room to make sure Ariadna wasn't approaching before he skimmed its pages: it was a *zapiska*, and provided, in painstaking detail, biographical information about Keane's Irish American background, his boyhood in Chicago, his early links with the Kennedys, his education at Yale, and even personal information about his early girlfriends, his current marriage and two children, his tastes in clothes and music and sports. Yuri skimmed all this very quickly while listening hard. Then he heard the distinctive clicking of Ariadna's stilettos approaching in the corridor as he glimpsed, at the end of the dossier, a section which speculated on Keane's weaknesses, just at the moment he had to put the folder back on her desk at what he hoped was the right page and angle. Yuri stood looking away from the dossier as Ariadna entered. She started back in surprise, raising her hand to her mouth, and took a moment to recover before she snapped, 'Yuri Ivanovich, you've no right...'

'Oh I'm very sorry, Ariadna, I've only just come in here, into your office, because I thought you must be in. Your door was ajar...'

'That is not relevant. You mustn't...' She glanced at the dossier. 'You must respect this room. It is my private space.'

'Certainly, Ariadna, you are right. And I apologise.' Yuri saw that Ariadna was not being placated. 'Really, Ariadna, please forgive me.' She was very intimidating.

'Oh very well. What was it, anyway, that you wanted?'

'If you have time, I would like to discuss the Englishman Peter Cook.'

Ariadna shrugged. 'Alright. Take a seat.' She nodded towards a wooden chair and Yuri seated himself there. Ariadna sat down in another wooden chair, the only other furniture, except her desk, in the room. 'I have read the copy of the coded message which you gave me.'

'Coded message?'

'What else could it be? Here is a man at the British embassy who has passed a message to a known Cambodian subversive.'

'Certainly, that was odd. I think we need, though, to consider the nature of the man who wrote that "message".' Yuri was anxious not to indicate how much of his information about Cook had come from Keith Entwistle, and thereby reveal the closeness of his friendship with a British diplomat.

'What about him?' Today Ariadna was wearing a simple black dress and her brown hair had been cut a little shorter. Yuri thought that she looked so beautiful that he couldn't return her gaze, but he worked hard to look her in the eye when he said, 'As I'm sure you know, he was a comedian.' He had wanted to gauge Ariadna's reaction because he was sure that she had interacted with Cook more than she was willing to admit. Once again, though, he had to look away, as though Ariadna were a painfully bright light.

'How is that relevant?'

'I think he might be *pulling our legs*.' Yuri said this phrase in English, and there was an unsettling moment when he pictured hands grasping a foot and violently tugging – he imagined that Ariadna was imagining the same thing.

'Pulling our legs?'

In Russian Yuri said: 'Yes. Teasing us? Do you not think, from your knowledge of him, that this might be possible?' Yuri was now inquiring more bravely about Ariadna's dealings with Cook, who was evidently fascinating to people of both sexes – he was handsome and charming, with very flourishing hair, and Keith was impressed by him, to an extent that Yuri, to his surprise, felt jealous about.

'To what end?'

'Maybe just for fun.' Yuri smoothed back the little vestige of hair he retained at the top of his brow, and touched, gingerly, the itchy sunburnt scalp behind it.

'Fun?' The concept was alien to Ariadna.

'Or possibly a diversionary tactic. Like a conjuror, who makes his audience look in the wrong place. Perhaps he is diverting our attention from something more significant.'

Ariadna frowned. 'I think you're wrong. We may need to send the message by Cook to Moscow, to ask their advice. It is evidently a typical piece of Cold War obscurantism in the form of an allegory.'

'I agree that's possible. When I discussed it with Dmitri he talked about the Russian children's stories where the crocodile swallows people and dogs but is benevolent and opens his mouth and lets them out again. But I'm sure he was distorting the meaning of the crocodile with Russian associations. But I'd like him to be part of this discussion.'

Yuri went to fetch Dmitri.

As the two men entered her office, Ariadna handed Dmitri the sheet of paper on which 'The Crocodile Princess' was typed and said, 'the crocodile clearly represents Cambodia.'

'Or Indochina generally?' Yuri said.

They paused while Dmitri studied the story. Then Dmitri said, 'This sentence here, where the parents of the princess are called "Croc Monsieur and Croc Madame"…'

'Calembour,' Ariadna said.

'Yes, that's a pun. Two meanings,' Yuri agreed, but then he smiled ironically, 'but does it have a third or even a fourth?'

Ignoring this, Ariadna said, 'The crocodile might represent Indochina generally, but the Crocodile Princess is an important figure in Cambodian cultural history.'

'Ah, I didn't know that,' Yuri admitted.

Ariadna sighed dismissively. 'You should... Well, for one thing, you should travel more here. There's a jungle village on the Mekong called Sambaur – you must have heard of it?'

'The name is familiar.'

'There is a stupa there – a funerary tower, conical? – dedicated to the Princess Nucheat Khatr Vorpheak. In 1834 she was bathing in the Tonle Sap near Oudong which in that period was the royal capital. She disappeared. Three months later her body was discovered, miraculously without decay, inside a crocodile.'

'This is a true story?'

Ariadna smiled. 'What do you think?' She actually waited for an answer.

Yuri frantically pondered. 'Some of it?'

'The crocodile must have swallowed the girl in one piece, and then swum for around one hundred and ninety miles without digesting her, from Oudong to Sambaur where it was killed and then opened up.' Ariadna fixed Yuri with a questioning smile.

'Still, *some* truth behind it?'

'Certainly. Because they took the body and cremated it, and then erected the stupa. And the little girl was a princess and very beautiful, and, because she was young, regarded as without sin, and the miraculous circumstances surrounding her death indicated that she was especially favoured by the "Tevodas", the gods who reign in Cambodia and protect the kingdom. And a medium at the royal court soon claimed that the princess had contacted her, and a long line of *astrologues* claimed the same, so that the Crocodile Princess is said to have exercised a benign influence in Cambodian affairs right through the nineteenth century and even to be influential now – so Cambodians think she helped them get rid of the French in 1953.'

'It's a beautiful story isn't it?' said Yuri, who surprised himself by feeling moved, 'though in the Cook version the Crocodile Princess is quite a different figure...'

'Yes. She's an actual crocodile...'

'Yes, but terribly at odds with her background. Born to a human family, a working-class family in Dagenham, and under-sized and with a clubfoot. And these simple people are baffled by her being a crocodile.'

'That's quite difficult to interpret. Also her prodigious musical talent, her ability to play piano concertos, and jazz, and to play the violin so it sounds like a baby crying. But I would say that this is a tribute to Cambodia in the figure of the Crocodile Princess, a tribute to Cambodia's great potential despite its tiny size and awkward circumstances. In Cook's narrative it is Britain saying to a Cambodian subversive that Britain recognises Cambodia's hidden importance.'

'Yes some of that seems to fit. But you've spoken to Cook, so you must have a sense of what he's up to.'

'No, no.'

'You *have* spoken to him.'

'No. He has spoken to me. I have said nothing in reply.'

'He is clearly interested in you, so you could easily discover...'

'I won't be used in that way.'

'I'm only saying if you spoke to him...'

'He is a lost and callow young man, and he speaks a version of English that is incomprehensible to me.'

'But that's exactly what we're trying to comprehend.'

'I can't stand to listen to a person who talks about the Cold War and says that Mr and Mrs Kruschev are huddled around a meagre coal fire, and speaks of heat-seeking snowballs...'

Ariadna said the phrase *heat-seeking snowballs* in contemptuous English, and Yuri decided it was time to leave the discussion for the time being.

9

Ever since her arrival in Cambodia, Edith Hartnell had been drawn to the Buddhist idea of self-negation, but she often felt it as too easy, a temptation towards passive, submissive drift, especially because it was associated for her with an image of the Mekong river which sometimes arose in her so powerfully that it threatened to overwhelm her sense of self. Repeatedly she thought of how the river could change itself, of how it fell ten yards in the dry season, so that it looked subdued and depressed where stony reefs and islands pushed up out of it, but roared back again when the rains flooded into it and swirled with currents that spiralled and were heavy with silt and carried bottles and broken trees and the corpses of pigs and water buffaloes. Edith lost herself watching these changes then recalling them as she drifted off at night into sleep: for some months she had been plagued by nightmares and she had chosen to contemplate the Mekong, at first, as a calming image. So she had deliberately imagined, step by step, its course, from its origins as a trickle out of a Tibetan glacier in the Himalayas, identifying with its gradual, relentless growth as it was joined by mountain streams and melting snow, identifying with its changes as the land around it, in south-western China between Burma and Thailand, altered, so it plunged down steep gorges. A river, like a person, is transformed by its surroundings, so she then identified with its new, warmer self in the borders of Laos where it flowed through the hills and jungle vegetation, falling further into Cambodia through a series of rapids, and slowing as it entered southern Vietnam and then wandered past Saigon into the South China Sea.

Often, though, Edith felt she wanted instead to solidify herself, and fortify the distinctiveness of her boundaries. At those times she liked to call upon the image of Katharine

Hepburn, who Edith had loved since she was fourteen, and whose career she had followed step by step, responding to each of Hepburn's successes and setbacks as though they were her own. Edith adored Hepburn's smiling self-confidence, her effortless robustness, so different from the vulnerability of actresses like Marilyn Monroe. Hepburn in her films moved in the company of men, declaring her equality and independence with an easy implicitness which indicated high intelligence, and which quietly defied men to think otherwise. Edith had often, in tricky moments, called upon the image of Hepburn to carry her through, and recently her film memory had replayed to her, over and over, a moment where Hepburn, in a beautifully tailored jacket, has paused at the bottom of stairs, with a long cigarette dangling out of the corner of her mouth, and gazing downwards at her hands extracting a match from a matchbox, as Spencer Tracy is approaching along a corridor, out of sight to her. Hepburn looks up as Tracy turns the corner and into the stairs. They almost collide, but then stand facing each other, very close, but half-smiling into each other's eyes, Hepburn, because of the stairs, for that moment looking down at Tracy from above.

Edith loved Cambodia, where she had passed many hours of magical vividness that still haunted her, such as the evening with the Royal Cambodian Ballet performing, in a clearing in front of Angkor Wat, while lamps illuminated their slender limbs and necks, and their long arms and fingers, and flickeringly hinted at the vast shadowy complex of temples and the dark depths of the jungle surrounding it. She loved, in particular, Phnom Penh, because it was a French city bewildered to find itself in the tropics. Its pastel-coloured buildings, and its venerable villas with their walled and orderly gardens, and its gratuitously spacious boulevards, were nostalgic for the Midi. And yet it was also a Buddhist city of pagodas and stupas, and yes it was surrounded by grand, broad rivers, the Mekong, the

Bassac, and the Tonle Sap, which could magically transform itself by reversing its flow. And these watery presences were inescapable because they infiltrated the air and light of the city and imposed a profound riverine calm in which small sounds, especially the bells of cyclopousses, reverberated.

Edith was meditatively following the rhythm of her breathing, and listening hard to the cyclo bells, attempting to determine which she could hear, which was furthest away, and trying to focus on her knowledge of the city's calm, because she could still taste cinders in her mouth from the dream that had woken her that morning, cinders that had drifted in the sky from a scorched horizon. Christopher had surprised her by being sympathetic when she had again woken shocked, gasping for breath, he had stroked her head and calmed her, and apologised for not being sympathetic enough in the past, and not making more effort, also, to understand her menopausal symptoms. That had reminded her of how attentive he had once been, sensitive even, and more so when he started to reminisce about their early days, and she had recalled how marvellously comprehending he often was when he was young. He had amazed her sometimes, then, with the worldly breadth and depth of his knowledge and insight. But his sympathy that morning only unsettled her by feeling like yet another disorientation, and it only made her feel guilty and unnerved about her current adultery, and made her question it, if only briefly, in a manner that was unwelcome. She was walking now towards the park, still feeling guilty, when she wondered – given how he moved from the one subject to the other – if Christopher regarded her nightmares as another menopausal symptom, and was simply dismissing them on that pretext?

She was pondering that, when she encountered Peter Cook. They had hardly even said hello, when he said: 'I've invented a new school of Buddhism. Previously, there has mostly been the Great Vehicle…'

'Mahayana: the universal way to salvation,' Edith Hartnell said dubiously. Edith was on her way to her fortune-teller at Wat Phnom.

Peter was now strolling alongside her. 'The great universal vehicle to salvation. And there has also been the Smaller Vehicle…'

'Hinayana, which is focused on suffering, and stresses the need for renunciation and perseverance.' Edith was uncomfortable because she was accustomed to being mocked about her interest in Buddhism, which was often linked to the mockery of her having "gone native". 'There is also…'

'In both of these traditions the key point is that the Buddha is sitting down…'

'He is in the lotus position, a cross-legged *asana*…'

'Sitting there in his lotus, sitting there very still…'

'As an aid to meditation…'

'In his lotus, totally still, meditating. And he's been doing that for centuries. Meditating, in his lotus, in the 6th century BC, and then the 5th century BC, all through the Greeks and Romans and the Christians, in his lotus sitting very still meditating, through the Dark Ages, still sitting there through the Battle of Hastings and on and on and on, sitting very still, in his lotus.'

'I need to go in this direction now,' Edith said, pointing, because they were nearing the end of Norodom Boulevard, and she needed to enter the park. It had occurred to her just that morning that it was logical to have a comedian in the diplomatic service because all diplomats, in her experience, liked to think of themselves as great wits and performers. To have a comedian diplomat was an obvious extension of that tendency: her husband liked nothing better than to compose an after-dinner speech that would cause uncontrollable hilarity in the assembled guests. Everywhere she had travelled with Christopher she had encountered diplomats who were comedians manqué, and would recount the latest episode involving quaint foreigners and alarmingly fallible Embassy staff, as though the relentless decline of Britain were only a queasy joke. Peter had taken the same turn as her and was now saying:

'Through the Renaissance, and the Industrial Revolution, still in his lotus, on and on, totally still. But my school of Buddhism is not the Great Vehicle, or the Smaller Vehicle. It is the Faster Vehicle, and it's reflected in a vision I had one day, an epiphany, as Christians would say, and, in the Faster Vehicle, the Buddha… stands up!'

'He stands up?'

'Yes, he unfolds his sacred knees and stretches out his holy legs, and he plants his godly heels on the earth and straightens out his body length-ways and… stands up!'

'I see.'

'And then…he moves about! He ambles, strolls, wanders, strides hither and thither…'

Edith smiled tolerantly, and, as they walked together in silence past the bandstand, and the kiosk that sold soup and ragout, she thought that the older diplomats ought to be tolerant towards Peter and Keith and the others because Phnom Penh was a marvellous place for the middle-aged, but it was very testing for young people who had to content themselves with the gay chatter at cocktail parties, or evenings spent dancing to the radiogram, or venturing to one of the smarter cabarets where a dancing-girl from Hong Kong or Saigon would partner you for a shilling a minute, tremendously expensive. But she said, 'So you are close friends now with Sihanouk?'

'No. I wouldn't say that at all,' Peter said.

'But you visit him in the Palace?'

'Not at all the same thing, Ambassadress.'

They watched a man go by who was carrying two fish, whose gills had been threaded on a bamboo string, and then a woman carrying a large oval tray of mangoes.

'An unusual privilege.'

'In fact I went there yesterday. But Sihanouk had replaced himself with an actor. I was ushered into the Presence, except it wasn't – it was this man who resembled Sihanouk only slightly.'

'I'm surprised. That's so rude. It seems unlike him.'

'It was funny actually. The actor looked wrong, but he played the part perfectly. Everyone imitates Sihanouk's laugh, the famous, high-pitched laugh…'

'Yes, Christopher does that…'

'Christopher does it well, yes. This actor, though, he was astonishingly good.'

They stopped briefly to watch a man on a bicycle, wearing a white fedora, standing up on his pedals as he hauled two massive rolls of straw matting behind him on a two-wheeled pallet.

'What unnerved me, in the end, was that this actor seemed better at being Sihanouk than the Prince himself. Sometimes, when Sihanouk laughs, it seems forced, it seems like he's performing, it feels as though "Prince Sihanouk" is a role for him. But this actor made it seem perfectly natural. He was watching me knowingly throughout. I got out of comedy just in time.'

They moved on and were soon approaching the stupa where the *astrologues*, with their incense sticks and their little slates and charts, sat cooling themselves with fans. Edith was greeted by name by the fortune-teller she had visited before, and given a pin. She paid her three cents, closed her eyes and prayed, and stuck the pin into the pack of palm leaf cards. The fortune-teller took the one that Edith had picked, stared at it and pondered, then said (in the Khmer that Edith later translated for Peter): 'Monkeys can outwit tigers. The hare can outwit the crocodile.' Turning to Peter she said: 'And you, young man, like the wily adventurer Tmenh Chey, will survive humiliation and hardship by using your wits.'

10

Those lines by W. H. Auden, "he often had/ Reproached the night for a companion/ Dreamed of already", haunted Wilfred Jamie as he directed the arrangements for Edith's fiftieth birthday party. He had been reproaching the night very often recently because Alain had been avoiding him so he felt abandoned even though nothing explicit had been said. And perhaps Alain would return and it was only a brief phase they were going through. The poem is called 'The Secret Agent' and is one of those where Auden talks about spies, and that's about the 1930s, an age of anxiety, Soviet Russia, Nazi Germany, – but it's also a code for talking about how the homosexual is always under cover, always pretending to be someone he isn't. So at the start the poem talks about public things, a dam, a railway, and bridges, but then moves into these lines about loneliness – in the same way Wilfred was bustling about the Embassy, arranging furniture, talking to the cook, but he was occupied most seriously with his fear that Alain was lost to him. Though he was also wondering about what it must be like to be a real spy like the Cambridge Five, recruited, when they were students, by the Soviet Union, and especially Guy Burgess who a friend of his had known quite well in the Embassy in Washington DC. Wilfred, out of loyalty to his friend, and his difficult situation there, hadn't wanted to tell anyone that Kim Philby might also be a mole, given his closeness to Burgess. It was as though that Auden poem had been prophetic about spies who were doubly under cover.

Wilfred was performing tasks that Edith normally performed but clearly couldn't for her own party, which was supposed to be a surprise. He had volunteered to organise it because he considered Edith to be one of his best friends – she was the only person in Phnom Penh he could talk to about Alain, and they had often spoken confidingly to each other, though Edith had only hinted at her dissatisfactions with Christopher, with his lassitude and his habit of ignoring her, especially reprehensible because of how much he relied on her to run the Embassy. She was indispensible there in helping its members to like each other, and in building and maintaining relationships with others in the diplomatic community – he was amazed by her ability to remember names – and with Cambodians, where she excelled because of the depth of her knowledge of Cambodian culture and language. He could always recognise the moments where Edith was especially impatient with Christopher because, instead of saying so, she would propose that they go to the cinema. Edith loved Katharine Hepburn, and was overjoyed when there was a film starring the feisty actress, but otherwise they didn't care much what the film was. So they had seen many American, British and French films all subtitled with ideograms, and even, occasionally, Hindustani epics set in Baghdad that featured star-crossed lovers, and genies, and horses that could speak and fly. They would sit together and admire these marvels while mosquitoes alarmed their ears and bit their necks and hands and ankles.

Wilfred was anxious about the cook, who was Chinese and cooked his own cuisine quite well but was unreliable outside it. One Christmas he had imported turkey and Christmas puddings, and had cooked the turkey acceptably but had put the Christmas puddings in the oven at the same time and they had emerged, inevitably, as impenetrable cannon balls. Christopher had been inconsolable because he'd been looking forward, so intensely, to this little bit of culinary England at Christmas – even now Wilfred remembered, acutely, the depth of sadness on the Ambassador's face as he refused to give up on his pudding, as he applied more and more pressure with his futile spoon. So Wilfred had told the cook not to spring any surprises and to stick to what he knew best, and he'd ordered a birthday cake from a versatile bakery that he thought was more or less reliable.

Wilfred saw Keith Entwistle come in and asked him to help him to move the long table over against a wall. Little delicacies, dim sum, and crispy duck with pancakes, and the like, could be set out on the table when they were ready. Wilfred asked Keith if there was anything more he needed for the music he was going to play later and Keith said no, but he was concerned about Peter's part in it because they'd sent off, over a month ago, for an Elvis Presley outfit and had been sent a Charles de Gaulle uniform instead. 'That Elvis Presley impersonation is just awful anyway,' Wilfred said, 'the boy has absolutely no sense of rhythm.' Keith smiled and hurried away, saying there was paperwork he wanted to get done before the party started. He had recently told Wilfred that a pedaleur had made a sexual approach to him, and Wilfred had warned him to avoid that cyclopousse in future because many pedaleurs worked for the secret police.

He started to lay out napkins and forks on the table, wondering why the gap of ten years between him and Alain seemed so much more than it was, especially when people always said how much younger he looked than 45. Wilfred was slim and agile and had a full head of hair, which was touched only slightly with grey, and it was ten years almost exactly between him and Alain – Wilfred born in 1917 and Alain in 1927. Was it self-dramatising to say that the ten years seemed more because Wilfred had lived through a far more draining part of the twentieth century? His generation had grown up under the shadow of the First World War, had been adolescents in the depression, had fought in the Second World War, and had experienced as young adults, in the background to their lives, the great horrors of the death camps and Hiroshima. It was true that Wilfred sometimes felt a terrible weariness as though these events had really dug themselves deep inside him, and they marked him as entirely different from those born later – or maybe it was just that he lacked the refreshing frivolity of someone like Alain who seemed mostly indifferent to world events.

When the guests started to arrive Wilfred felt he could relax and he drank a gin and tonic as he greeted people. He was relieved by how well everything was going at the start and glad they'd chosen to restrict the invitations to Embassy staff together with close friends, some British businessmen, and journalists like Hector Perch, some staff from the American and Australian embassies – all very Anglo-Saxon, with little chance of cultural misunderstanding. Edith's movements had been manipulated to ensure she entered at the right moment, and the surprise had been maintained and her pleasure was clearly genuine when she saw the gathering of people closest to her in Phnom Penh. Wilfred was delighted to see Edith smile as she made her entrance, he felt proud of her, watching his tall, blonde, slim friend, with her asymmetrical, expressive face, long nose and thick lips.

Keith on piano had combined with one of the secretaries who played the violin to provide a suitably unobtrusive light classical background. Everyone was mingling happily except Bill Noon, the military attaché, and Wilfred watched him standing on his own and drinking heavily and wondered if he should try to speak to him, but he found Noon intimidating because of his formidable, craggy looks, and his habit of frowning and silence. He wondered what it must be like to be as built for action as the major was, to be so focused on doing rather than thinking, or where all your thinking is directed towards an active purpose, undeflected by doubts.

Wilfred was alarmed when he saw the secretary replaced by Peter Cook wearing the de Gaulle uniform, and astonished when, despite that costume, Keith launched into an Elvis Presley tune and Cook pouted, and gyrated his hips inside the absurdly long and buttoned-up trench coat, and shouted "You ain't nothing but a hound dog" with a haughty demeanour and a French accent. The younger Embassy staff thought this was hilarious, and so too, tentatively, did some others of the guests, but Wilfred thought it preposterous. Many of the older people present watched with open-mouthed disbelief, and Bill Noon looked thunderous. Cook was some sort of chimera, a hybrid of Elvis Presley and de Gaulle, or de Gaulle in the process of transforming into Elvis Presley, and Wilfred was angry that something as grotesque as this was dominating Edith's party. Even so, there was something arresting about it, something obviously superior to Cook's simple Elvis Presley mimicry, because now his lack of rhythm, and his inability to carry a tune, seemed part of the de Gaulle element, part of the general's woeful inability to do rockabilly vocals. The version of 'Heartbreak Hotel' started out with the usual words about finding a place to dwell on Lonely Street, but then Cook was singing that he, de Gaulle, had fought a war in Indochina and got himself a shiner and was feeling sadly minor, and in the next verse he was bemoaning how he'd had to leave Algeria and was becoming more and more inferior. And all the time he was intoning this, the two stars on his flat hat were glinting in the electric light, and Cook was gyrating and replacing Elvis Presley's throaty American *uh-uh-uh* with a French *hein hein hein*.

The reception of Cook's performance was getting warmer and Wilfred was starting to think he might need to reassess Cook, and reassess his attitude to the social changes Cook evidently represented, when he found Bill Noon suddenly looming over him and frowning viciously.

'Stop staring at me,' he whispered ferociously.

It took Wilfred a long minute to recover before he could say, 'Don't talk nonsense. I wasn't staring.' Had he been staring? Not at all. Not much. Not at all.

'Every time I look up there you are staring at me.' The stench of whisky and cigarettes was hot on Noon's breath.

'You're really, Major Noon, not that interesting to me.'

'Well keep your perverted eyes to yourself.' Noon's whisper was a compressed shout.

'Look here, major: in the diplomatic service, unlike the army, you need to learn a more open-minded attitude.'

'You and your French pervert friends. You should be careful. You could get into trouble.'

'Oh...' Wilfred tried to walk away but Noon caught him by the shirt and tugged him back. Wilfred gasped and glanced around to see if anyone had seen. No-one had.

'Let go of me you bigot.'

'In the diplomatic service, Wilfred, there are great dangers in living the way you live.'

'Not here, major, not here. They don't have those prejudices here. It's you who should be careful. Driving around at night the way you do.'

Noon looked taken aback. 'That's no-one's business.'

Wilfred glanced away and saw Edith talking earnestly with the secretary, Sandie Hamilton. 'You should be careful because there's a lot of evidence you're linking up with the rebels in Battambang. That's not my business, you're right, since we're talking about each other's business. But when you're doing that you need to be more discreet about it. Half of Phnom Penh knows what you're up to. And it's very brave of you, given how unpredictable those characters are. But it's clearly work you're not accustomed to – you're used to doing the manly thing, out in the open. Whereas for this work you need to be discreet. You know, Major Noon, it's supposed to be *secret*.' He spoke the last word as though he was teaching it to a child.

Noon gave Wilfred a pinching sort of two-fingered push in the chest before he marched away, and it took several drinks and about fifty deep breaths before Wilfred was composed enough to call the attention of the whole room to the ceremonial handing-over of Edith's present, which the staff had clubbed together to buy. He managed that, and then Christopher gave a brief speech about how indispensible Edith was in the Embassy and how she also had, he was forced to concede, a certain level of importance in his own life, before he handed over the antique which Wilfred had been delighted to find, a very finely carved statue of Buddha which he had known that Edith would love. It was very unfortunate that it happened to be at that moment that a huge brown rat appeared and wandered across the room just in front of the piano. There were cries of horror, and some of the women actually stood on chairs as though they were in cartoons or a sitcom, before Cook and Entwistle chased the rat away, with Cook making scooping motions at it with his two-star hat.

11

'It's odd,' Kenneth Allsop said, 'how just saying the word *Dagenham* gets a laugh.'

Dudley Moore, sensing a slight, was quick to agree.

'Don't get me wrong, Dudley, – it *was* funny, the way you timed it. I just meant...'

'No you're absolutely right. Quite a few English place names are funny like that. Hard to know why.'

It was the Thursday evening of the week in April when Yuri Shunin had stolen Peter Cook's *Crocodile Princess*, and Dudley and Kenneth had appeared together at the Oxford Union and were drinking now in the bar of the Randolph Hotel, where they were both staying that night.

'And they loved the organ joke.'

Dudley smiled. An Oxford-related story – how, as an undergraduate, he got an organ scholarship. And then he wanted to do a little graduate work, so he got an extended organ scholarship. His organ had been extended a lot recently, growing alongside his growing fame.

'But they laughed, those students, at the mangle story.'

Dudley was becoming uncomfortable, now, with Kenneth's tone. He had seen Kenneth a couple of times on television, seen him as a formidably combative interviewer of politicians, and he had felt intimidated at the prospect of sharing a platform with him at the Oxford Union, fearing that he might easily humiliate Dudley by exposing him as trivial-minded. So he had been relieved when they met and Kenneth had been in a genial mood, adapting himself to the nature of the Oxford Union event by being relaxed and even attempting frivolity. Now, though, Dudley felt that Kenneth was overdoing it, and his tone was that of a man who thought he needed to tread carefully with the person he was speaking to, because that person was sensitive and vulnerable. It annoyed him to feel he was being patronised, and all the more because he *did* feel himself to be sensitive and vulnerable. 'Well, it *is* funny isn't it?'

'Yes, but not *just* funny.' It was Kenneth now who was shifting uneasily in his seat – he was being forced to explain himself flat-footedly, and more than he wanted to, as though he was cornered. 'If you're talking about your mother, and you're saying that she prepared your evening meal at the kitchen table, and that table had a mangle under it, so that as a small child you saw the top half of your mother but a mangle instead of her lower half, so you thought the mangle *was* her lower half, and then you're saying that you thought you'd come out of that mangle instead of a womb, so that your birth was...'

'Mangled?'

Kenneth's laugh was very nervous. 'That's funny, but there's a lot more going on in it.' He drank from his glass and took a breath.

Dudley smiled at him mischievously because he was deliberately unsettling him now.

Kenneth nodded acknowledgement of what Dudley was up to. 'It made me laugh, but I thought it was... poignant, as well.' Kenneth excused himself then, saying he needed the lavatory, but it was clear that he was more in need of some respite from this line of conversation. Dudley noticed, as Kenneth walked away, that a young woman in glasses was gazing at him, but when she saw him return the gaze, she looked very quickly away. Dudley took comfort in the idea that his reputation had grown enough for someone as famous as Kenneth not simply to opt to walk away altogether from a conversation he was finding so unnerving. Their table was near a window and Dudley glanced across at the Ashmolean museum, thinking he'd never gone there as an undergraduate. He heard, then, distinctly, the fugal section from the funeral march of Beethoven's 'Eroica' symphony. And he knew it was the road outside the Randolph that was playing it to him, because, as an undergraduate, he had walked down that road so often when he had recently listened to the version of it conducted by Otto Klemperer, which he had bought then.

Dudley reprimanded himself for this mental departure. A psychiatrist had told him that he ought to focus on the here and now, that the answer to his fretful restlessness was to focus on the present moment and to be inside it. But he found his mind always sliding away into other places and other times, and driving himself towards the future. He tried hard to sit still and just be present in the Spring, in the Randolph at 10.45, but he kept hearing that Beethoven fugue, and dwelling on the evening that had passed. He had never met Kenneth Allsop before, but all evening he had been trying to remember why the name was so familiar to him, and personally familiar, not just the way that people on television are familiar. Still gazing at the Ashmolean, Dudley remembered that Peter Cook had mentioned the name to him. It had been the only time that Peter had ever said anything emotional to him, and it was just before he did his vanishing act. He had mentioned meeting Kenneth Allsop and... what was it? It had some connection with Tarzan, Dudley was sure of that.

After Kenneth had resumed his seat, there was an awkward silence between them, and Dudley was aware that Kenneth was thinking very hard, and then he saw him smile with relief and realisation before he said: 'Did I tell you I saw you in *Beyond the Fringe* in Edinburgh? One of those very early performances.'

Kenneth had evidently found the conversational departure that he needed, but Dudley was sceptical about whether he was telling the truth – many people claimed to have been there who simply couldn't have been. 'Did you really? They were very exciting, those early ones.'

'They were. Well, certainly, the one I saw. Who was that man?'

'Peter Cook.'

'Yes. He was extraordinary... You *all* were, but there was something about him...'

'He was full of ideas, Peter, – for comedy. Ideas just flowed out of him.'

'You must miss him.'

Dudley shrugged. 'He could be very difficult as well. Very.'

'Worth it though surely?'

'Maybe, I was often not sure. But clearly that was a way of things that wasn't meant to happen.'

'What changed?'

'I don't know.' Dudley shrugged and smiled, 'Something to do with Tarzan, apparently. He started to say something to me, which I guessed later was what had done for him, but he never finished... his sentence, even.'

Dudley noticed Kenneth nod as though with realisation, and glance sideways as though pondering his realisation, suggesting that he understood something about Peter and Tarzan which Dudley himself didn't understand.

'Where is he now?' Kenneth said.

'I heard he became a diplomat.'

'No!'

'Well his father had been a diplomat. And his public school had produced a lot of diplomats. Specialised in it.'

'But that Welshman who replaced him, Waldo Vaughan? How does he strike you?'

'Jonathan Miller's idea. Very political. Very clever, some of it.'

'Not to your taste?'

'No.'

'I must say, Dudley, that I'm intrigued by Waldo Vaughan. I mean I think there's something genuinely satirical about him. Not that you and Cook and the others weren't genuine...'

'We weren't satirists really.'

'No. And I'm not saying you should have been, because you were very funny. But Waldo Vaughan is much more challenging.'

'I was afraid we were going to be arrested sometimes, he was so irreverent, so angry. And I'm sure that made us less popular than we would've been.'

'You think?'

'Hard to know, but Peter was easier on people. There's something not British about Waldo, and you know he's said to have links with Russia? And with communists in Britain? I've heard him on the telephone speaking some kind of Eastern European language. Bulgarian, something like that.'

'Really? Any chance Cook could make a comeback? Where is he?'

'I don't know.' Dudley was starting to feel gloomy, and they lapsed again into silence, and Dudley remembered a moment at the Union earlier when an earnest young man had asked Kenneth about the injury he had suffered in the war, which had led to his having a leg amputated, and which must mean that he had to deal with constant pain. There had been an extended moment of collective embarrassment until Kenneth rescued things by briefly acknowledging the truth of what the boy had said, and then moved on swiftly to talk about his current project, which was about nature conservation.

'Did you know,' Kenneth whispered, then, 'there was a girl staring at you all evening?' He stood up then and walked over to the young woman in glasses and spoke to her. Shyly she followed Kenneth to where Dudley was sitting and reached into a briefcase and brought out a long-playing record. 'Would you mind signing this?' she said to Dudley.

Behind her back Kenneth waved a silent goodbye. 'Not at all,' Dudley said, 'would you like a drink?'

12

In late August, when Yuri Shunin had let slip a remark about Cuba, Keith Entwistle had not wanted to press him on the subject, because he could see that his friend was embarrassed about his momentary indiscretion, and Keith was constantly anxious not to appear to be using their friendship in any way. But rumours intensified during September, and the topic of missiles, stationed only ninety miles from the USA, grew in heat and intensity amongst the knowledgeable diplomatic community in Phnom Penh. The tension rose almost unbearably as more details about the crisis became evident in October, and the whole world watched Kennedy and Khrushchev squaring up to one another. Keith fretted as everyone in Phnom Penh fretted, as mutual suspicions sat on the city like another humidity.

Keith and Yuri continued to meet to listen to jazz, but avoided the obsessive topic, so it haunted their talk like a guilt that was supposed to be secret but was well known to both, as solos on piano or saxophone wound themselves around Keith's living-room, unaware of the apocalyptic moment. Keith was anxious that no distance should open up between him and Yuri because he thought that the Russian understood him better than anyone else. Certainly Yuri understood him far better than either Peter or Sandie, who reminded him of the people he had met at Oxford. He had found there that most of the other undergraduates had already led interesting lives: their parents had taken them on holidays on the continent of Europe, and had introduced them to talented and successful men, and they had been introduced, also, to youthful social circles where they had mingled with others, like themselves, who could share their stories of travel and the plenitude enjoyed by the offspring of the well-to-do and powerful. With these opportunities, and the confidence that radiated daily upon them from the success of the households that nurtured them, these young men had acquired girlfriends, and that experience had added to their stock of knowledge.

By contrast, before he went up to Oxford, Keith had never travelled anywhere further than Morecombe and Bridlington, and the council estate where he grew up was characterised above all by how little happened there, and he moved in no social circles at all, and never came close to acquiring a girlfriend, but spent all his spare hours studying. The major problem that he found as an undergraduate, therefore, was that he had nothing to say when the conversation was about anything other than ideas and facts learned from books. Keith repeatedly found himself in a conversation where a fellow undergraduate was describing an incident that had happened in Paris or Rome, and he was expected to supply something similar in reply, but he could think of nothing except stories that would crash the occasion into sad bathos, that would feature, for example, eating fish and chips on a drizzly pier. So he slipped gradually into the habit of inventing stories about himself, and of fretting about whether or not he would remember the details accurately if his friends ever referred to one of these narratives on a later occasion.

Keith had found it impossible to sleep after the party for Edith because he had made an arrangement with Sandie to meet her for a drink in the *ZigZag* and she hadn't turned up, and he had guessed that she had disappeared somewhere with Peter. He had tormented himself all night thinking about this, and it had got tangled up with these memories of Oxford, of feeling thoroughly at a loss, but also with an image from the James Bond novel he was reading, about a hoarding advertising a film starring Marilyn Monroe. The image was so strange that he had to work hard to understand it: the hoarding was twenty-feet high, and the moon was behind it, so that the film star's face was in shadow, but the key point was that the hoarding concealed, inside itself, a shack inhabited by a Russian agent. Bond hides across the road from the hoarding and is given a gun with a "sniperscope", and he runs the sights of the weapon across the vast stretch of Monroe's hair, and the "cliff of forehead" and the "two feet of nose" to the "cavernous nostrils". This picture of a shack inside Monroe's enormous head haunted him, perhaps partly because the actress had died a couple of months earlier. He imagined, as he often did, what it would be like to be Bond, so attractive to women and so fearless. He wondered about his own physical bravery, which had never been tested: if he were called upon, in a tight spot, would he respond courageously? Even to ask the question was self-deception, because he was, so obviously, a coward just as much as he was a liar.

He felt angry, but he knew that his anger was inseparable from the powerful affection he felt for both Sandie and Peter, and the two emotions clashed with each other and fought, so that he partly wanted to distance himself from the pair of them, but couldn't face how drab everything would then become. This emotional battle mingled as well with the Elvis Presley tunes he had played during the evening, and his admiration for Peter's talent for improvisation, his facility in finding de Gaulle words to sing to those tunes, – had Peter made them up on the spot, or had he worked some of it out in advance? And the sound of his own playing of "Heartbreak Hotel" had echoed in his pillow and he had spent hours, half-asleep, working on a stanza of his own for de Gaulle to sing:

Once down Colonial Street
We found a place to dwell
But now we're beating a retreat
Back to the Heartland Hotel

He liked the way the word "Colonial" echoed the word "Lonely" in the original song, but it was stilted, somehow, in a way that Peter's lines weren't. He puzzled over Peter's facility, about how easily, for example, Peter could mimic Yuri's bizarre accent, its mixture of Russian and Australian, slipping into a monologue and referring to Keith as 'Keith Ernieovich, *mate*.'

He decided that he needed to speak to both of them about what they were doing – not "confront" them, but try to make them understand. He had to wait for several hours until it was late enough on a Saturday to pay a visit, and then he set out on the way to Peter's flat where he was sure they'd gone. He saw the pedaleur who had offered him sexual services and avoided him after what Wilfred Jamie had told him about pedaleurs who worked for the secret police. He soon found another and they set out with Keith having second thoughts, feeling embarrassed with himself for taking this outlandish step, where emotion was so much on the surface, and a scene might easily be created. Peter and Sandie were both from middle-class families, and his working-class ignorance of their codes would be on the surface, so that they would both regard him as beyond the pale. He would arrive and see them and they would recently have had sexual intercourse and he would stand there in front of them like a red-raw thumb. He thought of turning back, but the dilemma, and his lack of sleep, and the lulling effect of the cyclo's slow gliding progress past the familiar street scenes, made him glaze over in a fuzzy passivity as he was borne along, hearing *Rose, Rose I Love You* echoing between his ears. So he was very surprised, and stirred, when he felt a hand on his and saw it belonged to a woman who was passing in another cyclo, and she smiled at him and said '*Bonjour*, where are you heading today?' and for a couple of minutes they were hand in hand, with their cyclos running in parallel, as Keith struggled to think of an answer. He was suddenly convinced that the best course would be to follow this cheerful young woman – who was Vietnamese, he thought, rather than Cambodian – to follow her cyclo and spend the rest of the morning with her and not say anything at all about Peter and Sandie. Maybe, if he did that, anyway, he'd lose all interest in that conversation. But then it was too late, and probably his face had seemed very grim, because the woman's smile had faded, and her cyclo slipped ahead.

So he was left to his original mission, still unhappy with himself for having set out on it, but seemingly unable to stop. He knocked on Peter's door and waited, but there was no answer. It was possible that his uncertain state had made him knock too quietly, so he knocked again, harder. The door was opened then – but by Peter's Cambodian maid, who Keith had seen before. Keith felt very relieved, and irrationally cheered by the maid's welcoming smile of recognition – to arouse a warm response made Keith feel less spurned than he had felt, because he had felt, he realised, spurned by the world in general, and not just by two individuals. The maid said that Peter wasn't there that morning and looked only slightly surprised when Keith asked if he might come in anyway, or even when, ten minutes later, when she had done her cleaning, he asked if he could stay, saying he was sure that Peter was on his way.

When the maid had left, Keith settled himself into the armchair where Peter normally sat, and understood that he had asked to be able to stay there in order to imagine what it was like to be Peter. Seated in his chair he looked towards the small table where the dominoes had been arranged in a new pattern and smiled at that silly joke, and he took out a cigarette and smoked it as he knew Peter often did while sitting there. He gazed towards a large, framed photograph, on the wall, of Angkor Wat, and noticed, just below it, a strange glint of metal catch the light. He walked over to it and took a closer look and saw it was the perforated tip of a small wire that stuck out slightly from the bottom of the frame. It reminded him of something he had read in a novel, and he decided that, next time he was in Peter's flat, he would pretend to notice it for the first time and draw Peter's attention to it.

He looked towards the French windows and the balcony where Peter had spoken with Edith, and he thought he had been stupid to think anything could be going on between them, then he wandered, still smoking, across to Peter's bedroom and gazed in. He rejected the idea of entering there, sensing that it was too intimate, and reflecting on what a shame it was that Peter had lost his way, that he really shouldn't be in Phnom Penh, shouldn't be in the diplomatic service, and that he must be encouraged to return to his previous life, because he had a great, original talent and that mustn't be wasted. He wondered what he could do to help Peter to return to his genuine, authentic life, and he returned to the armchair, feeling peaceful and pondering how powerfully he felt about Sandie and Peter, and that what he should do was to renounce Sandie altogether so he could simply be a close friend of the two of them as a couple.

He glanced at the small table with the dominoes, then at a larger one where Peter's typewriter was sitting. He wandered over to it and saw it must be a new script because it contained dialogue where the speaker was named as 'Prince Sihanouk'. He glanced under the table, this larger one with the typewriter, and saw quite a thick manuscript with the title page on top, and he saw that the title was *Bedazzled*. His cigarette dropped some ash onto the pages as he picked it up and flicked through it, and then he made a decision to take it with him.

13

'Busty protuberances?' Peter Cook said when Joe Keane was searching for words to describe what the Russian woman Ariadna possessed, while being slim everywhere else – Peter had just supplied him with her name. Because the American ambassador was meditating gravely on the understanding with himself that he had reached, surprisingly recently, that he preferred thin women. Yet here was another surprise, because now he found himself strongly drawn to this Ariadna, who was certainly not flat-chested. This topic would normally have engaged Peter's rapt attention, but this evening he had been talking all the time about a book he was reading called *Jungle Survival*, by Captain Hilary Pecksniff-Protheroe (Peter kept repeating the name in a rhythm that meant you could *hear* the hyphen), who was a Brit army guy who had escaped the Japanese and lived for two months in the Malayan rain forest, and had made a specialism of the subject enough to write a manual. And having suggested the phrase about protuberances, Peter had returned immediately to the question of how you avoided the most venomous snakes, and the most persistent ticks, and then needed to apply an edibility test to anything you ate – you had to avoid plants, for example, with milky saps, except for dandelion, coconut and goat's beard.

Joe and Peter were eating in the big Chinese restaurant with the French name, the *Nouveau Tricotin*, when the three young Russians had entered and Joe had noticed Ariadna – he'd seen her before in the same restaurant – as soon as she walked through the door. He was sure that she had glanced in his direction but then had pretended not to, he was sure he wasn't just hoping that into existence. Peter had told him her name and that she and her friends worked at the Russian embassy, and given him some details about her background that led him to suspect that Peter, too, was interested in her, and Peter had readily agreed that if the Russians had many women who looked like Ariadna then they could be deployed as formidable weapons in the Cold War. Ariadna, he said, was an accomplished cellist and had done research into quantum mechanics. The Russians were soon found seats not far away, and when Joe and Peter had finished eating, and the Russians hadn't started, Peter had introduced Joe to this youthful trio, apologising to the men for not knowing their names. Joe had immediately tried to engage Ariadna in conversation about something he remembered from the cello repertoire, but she had not responded, so he wasn't sure if she spoke much English, and she had refused even to look him in the eye.

Joe and Peter, as they left the restaurant, had invited the Russians to drink with them in a nearby bar when they'd eaten, and then they'd gone there and drunk some Tiger beers, Joe thinking during the first about the oddness of the American ambassador issuing such an invitation to Russians. Especially given the reports he was hearing about a crisis on the horizon arising because the Russians were secretly basing nuclear missiles in Cuba, within striking distance of major American cities, which was astonishing provocation. He knew that even being out and about, as much as he had been, in Phnom Penh, was odd for an American diplomat, because their embassy staff kept themselves to themselves more than the staff of other embassies. And that had happened because of Joe's restlessness, and because of Peter's influence which still surprised and unnerved him when he thought about it coolly. They were unlikely friends – Joe's father was a fervent Irish republican and had inculcated his hatred of the British insistently into his children, so Joe's friendship with an Englishman of the governing class would certainly shock the old man. It was true that Peter's anti-establishment attitudes had been a major reason why Joe found him congenial, his parody of the British prime minister stirred Joe with an inkling of the powerful contempt that motivated it. Nonetheless, he was constantly aware of his own ignorance of the complicated English attitudes that were entangled with that contempt, and he preferred Chris Hartnell's mimickry of Sihanouk – the way Hartnell caught the silly shrillness of Snookie's voice was uncanny and very funny.

The Russians hadn't shown up, which made Joe gloomy. Though he'd made a resolution earlier not to go to Madame Chhum's that evening, he then felt very tempted when Peter said they should – because he needed some distraction from the longing he was starting to feel for that Russian broad, a longing which had begun when he first saw her over a fortnight ago. But it was a very bad idea on about eight different levels. He started, as a discipline, to count them: political career, wife, children, personal respect...They left the bar and started to head in the direction of Madame Chhum's, or rather to look for cyclos to take them there, though Joe was still arguing with Peter about it, and with himself, saying he should take a rain-check, but telling himself he could go and not smoke opium. For opium was the real problem because it had altered his brain, and he was thinking then about the curvature of the top of his brain inside his skull, because opium made him think that he could feel his brain, that it could quiver as the opium molecules entered its raw surface, he could feel the surface of his brain as though a finger were touching it and it was slightly flayed or scalded. He was still limping badly from the cyclo smash. The doctor had said the knee was badly bruised and he'd damaged a ligament, and it would take months before he was fully recovered, so he was limping along beside Peter, in the hot night, sweating inside his lightweight tropical suit, and arguing with himself about opium because he excitedly imagined one of the girls preparing a pipe, her fingers in the bowl squeezing the paste and working it into a pink pill and then threading that onto a needle, to release its potency, and lighting it. He imagined wearing a sarong and sucking at that moment on the pipe, as the girl held the needle across its bowl, and inhaling that peculiar smoke which would open the corridor again where there were many rooms that could be entered and which led into a labyrinth of other corridors. One of those corridors would take him to the route that led from the girl Sisopha to his teenage love, Mary O'Neill, and on through snow and the ditch where his cyclo overturned, and ending in lizards and a swooping owl. Sisopha, who had showed him that his erect cock was long enough to accommodate both her tiny hands, one on top of the other: you'd need twelve inches to accommodate the hands of an American woman in that way. Hundreds of times since that night he had been locked in that corridor – Sisopha, Mary, snow, ditch, lizards, owl, this sequence that opium had invented and imprisoned him inside. Those were the pictures, but there was also an emotion that attended them – the feeling, terribly oppressive, that he had made numerous wrong turnings, that he had goofed, that he was a fall guy – and this sequence kept repeating itself, like relentless variations of *déjà vu*.

So why should he want the opium? – And still and all he did. But thinking all of this had slowed him down even further, and Peter was hundreds of yards down the wide carriageway, he must've gone ahead to secure cyclos, but Joe's knee had stiffened and was hurting him at every step, and he leant against a large tree which was on the margin of Phnom Penh's little park. He watched a couple of prostitutes walk by carrying baskets of oranges and bananas and saw a man approach one of them and buy a banana and then disappear with her into the bushes. Then he saw another in a close-fitting long dress who wasn't carrying fruit and was unusually tall and slender for a

Cambodian woman, and she held herself in a dignified, almost stately fashion. Joe thought she was tremendously stylish and elegant, perhaps because of her subtle make-up, and the dress was actually the traditional long wrapped skirt, the sampot, in black silk, and her top was white and embroidered. When she looked at him there was sympathy and warmth on her face as though, in fact, she had noticed him before and seen him limping and in pain. Joe found it moving that a stranger was responding to his plight and felt almost tearful when she approached and brushed her fingers gently against his face. He smiled at her and she kissed him on his neck under his ear and ran her hand behind his back and caressed him there and tightened her grip, very slightly, on his back, then ran her hand lower over the seat of his trousers. Joe shook his head and said 'No no' but she looked him straight in the eye and smiled again and nodded and took his hand gently and set off towards the park. When Joe tried to follow he found his knee had frozen and he cried out in pain, but she turned to him and led him, waiting patiently for him to move more easily. Finally they reached the point where the darkness of the park deepened and the woman pressed him back gently against the trunk of a large tree and kissed him reassuringly on his cheek and ran her hands over him everywhere gently, encouraging him to relax his body, which was still stiff with pain.

Joe settled back and allowed the woman's hands to massage him into relaxation and he felt his body untighten with relief, his body understanding that it was this that he needed above all – these knowing hands moving everywhere so that his arms and legs and his stomach and chest could soften, when all the time normally, day to day, at work, and, even with his family, they were hard and unyielding because they were aware, always, of dangers lurking. And it was at the point where he had thoroughly slackened, and his eyes were closed, that he felt the sudden heavy blow into his groin. He opened his eyes and realised that she had kneed him there and the pain was shocking in both its ferocity and its unexpectedness and he felt helpless as she started to remove his wallet from where he always kept it, deep inside his trouser pocket. He recovered quickly enough, though, to grab her right arm as she thrust her hand into the pocket, and to fend away her left as she tried to hit him with it, so they were fighting now. Joe was surprised by the prostitute's strength as they wrestled hand to hand and then he grabbed her hair and was horrified when it came away in his hand, and the hair under it was short and he understood that this was not a woman. He was able to dismiss the shock of this enough to maintain his grip but then the transvestite managed to slip his right hand out of Joe's left and produce a short thin knife which he drove into the top of Joe's thigh.

The pain was so terrible that Joe couldn't stop the man in the dress from stabbing him again in a similar place and he collapsed to the ground crying out and holding his thigh, which was bleeding heavily. Even the ground hurt him because it was hard with tree roots thrusting from the soil, and the transvestite was punching him repeatedly around the head so that he felt helplessly groggy. Then he felt himself being dragged deeper into the park, the man had grabbed the top of his jacket and was using it to drag him over the rough ground further and further from the road. Joe shouted 'Help! Help!' and thought hopelessly about how far away Peter was now and he recognised, in the moonlight, the lily pond and the crocodile fountain where he had occasionally gone for pleasant strolls with his small son and daughter. He kept shouting 'Help! Help!' but he didn't believe that anyone could hear him and he wondered if he was going to survive this because the man might use the knife to finish him off. He knew he was completely helpless and that his life was no longer in his hands.

So he was surprised when suddenly he wasn't being dragged any more and he turned around and saw that the transvestite had been knocked to the ground. A large Western male with a very straight back was gazing coolly at the prone figure in the dress and telling him he was disgusting and he'd better leave if he knew what was best for him. The transvestite rose slowly to his feet, not looking at this new person, then found his knife and ran at him. Joe recognised the man that Peter had introduced after the cyclo smash, whose name was Noon – he couldn't remember his first name, but he was Major Noon. And this Noon guy just treated the knife with contempt, he stepped calmly to one side and punched the transvestite hard in the side of his face, which sent him sprawling. And the transvestite gave up then, scrambled to his feet and ran away, and Noon gave him a kick in the tail. Noon turned to Joe and asked him if he was OK and Joe said he thought so but he was bleeding, and the truth was that so many different parts of him were hurting it was difficult to say – the blows to the head still made him groggy and being dragged over the ground had torn the skin of his buttocks and he was only beginning to feel the full extent of his injuries as he calmed after the fear that gripped him before. More composed now, Joe thanked Noon and started to explain how the problem had started but Noon dismissed that part of it – just shrugged and looked him in the eye with the implication, man to man, that the start of it was just the sort of thing that happened that needn't be discussed. Joe felt great warmth for this guy, who had plenty of moxie, but not only that, understood things, and was looking now at the wounds to his thigh and saying, 'That's not too bad, actually, that creature's knife must've been pretty blunt. It's bleeding, of course, and we'd better be aware of that. But it's too high up on the thigh for a tourniquet.' Joe asked him then why he hadn't thought of detaining the guy so he could be arrested, given how much he could control him, but Noon said it was best to avoid involving the Cambodian authorities whenever you could, especially given (and here he looked Joe straight in the eye) the positions both of them held. That made Joe feel foolish, it was so obvious. 'Can you walk, do you think?' Noon asked, and helped him to his feet and put his arm around Joe's waist to hold him up as he attempted his first steps. But Joe cried out as he felt the screaming protest that came from his right leg when he tried to move – it was the same leg that had been injured before. 'Yes, well, it's better, anyway, if you keep that leg held up to slow the bleeding,' Noon said, and, at the same time, he swept Joe off his feet and started to carry him. Joe was astonished by how easily Noon did that, because he weighed a hundred and seventy pounds and Noon had done it as though he was a small child. 'Try to raise the leg, if you can,' Noon said, 'because gravity will slow the bleeding – that's as good as a tourniquet,' but he was anyway tilting Joe so that his head was below the level of his legs.

Noon carried him like that to the boulevard and Joe noticed the earthy odour of Noon's sweat and how he wore his wristwatch facing inwards, towards himself. Noon carried Joe along the almost deserted Monivong Boulevard for five hundred yards searching for a cyclo, and then there was a power failure and all the streetlights were extinguished and Joe gazed upwards at the patterns of the millions of stars that were now, in the urban darkness, suddenly so bright and numerous that the sky was deeply encrusted. And he thought, during that strange jaywalking journey, that he had kissed one man that evening and now he was in the arms of another.

14

In the Cotswolds village where he will retire, Christopher Hartnell is the warden of the small Norman church and brings his diplomatic skills to bear on the parish council. He is friends with the young vicar, who has only recently graduated, and who tells him about the latest thinking in theology. Christopher tells the vicar about what he knows, from his diplomatic wanderings, of Islam and Buddhism, and they compare these religions with Christianity. Christopher has made friends with a former Liberal MP, and a retired merchant seaman, and the three of them regularly meet for luncheon in the village pub. In summer they often watch test cricket together on the television, and, in winter, the rugger internationals. Christopher has taken up gardening and has built a large greenhouse with a special section, a little hothouse, where he grows tropical fruit – mangoes, rambutans with their spiky quills, and durian with their addictive flavour but unsettling smell of rot. These fruits cause a sensation at the village fetes, where the durian, in particular, arouses amazement and revulsion. Christopher's cottage has a view of the river and he spends long afternoons watching the light shift across the water and listening to the call of snipe. You have to have lived in the tropics to appreciate the English shifts in weather, the subtle gradations in the light, the numerous, barely distinguishable, shades of green. On spring afternoons, as the days are beginning to lengthen, he sits by his greenhouse in a big overcoat as the light fades, drinking a gin and tonic and listening to a blackbird perform its elaborate song.

Christopher was in his office eating a sandwich and reading *The Natural History of Selbourne*, and it occurred to him that Edith was somewhere in the background in his retirement reverie, but was only a shadowy figure. He was due to see Peter Cook later, and he shook off the marginal image of Edith and resumed the idea that had occurred to him earlier that morning, which was that, in becoming a diplomat, Peter had been translated. Peter was a brilliant linguist and had mastered Mandarin admirably, and his Khmer was improving apace, and Christopher reflected that, when you thoroughly learned languages with such alien syntax, they changed the shape of the brain, they shifted around your internal furniture, so that you became a different person.

Suddenly anxious, he wandered over to his window, seeing it was open, and looked out and saw his fear confirmed. Gasping with exasperation, he hurried outside, hoping Reginald Armstrong hadn't noticed, and picked up the papers that had once again been blown out onto the lawn by his ceiling fan. One of them labelled itself *Urgent* and contained absurd allegations about Bill Noon, which tried Christopher's patience – it was one of the tedious side effects of the current international situation that fingers of this sort were constantly being pointed. It was true that Bill's army background would fit the profile of a spy, but for Christopher (with his long experience of intelligence types in embassies) the key test was the ability to type: all spies could type because they needed to be able, off their own bats, to operate their communications equipment. By contrast, few diplomats could type, and Christopher knew for a fact that Bill had no clerical skills whatsoever.

Until recently, he reflected ruefully, he would have been confident that the Foreign Office would have told him if they were planting a spy in the Embassy, but now he actually felt he couldn't be sure. The taunting by Alec Crawford, at the Magdalen gaudy, had rattled him more than he wanted to acknowledge – that idea that Reginald Armstrong had been raised, in the Embassy, to the status of an alternative power to himself, however absurd the notion actually was. But more and more the sense that you were ignored, discounted even, if you had spent your life working in far-flung embassies, was taking its toll on him. Just a month ago, Christopher had sent the Foreign Office a report, very well-written by Keith, about Sihanouk's current outlook and the state of things in Cambodia, including the threat, or otherwise, posed by communist insurgents – and it had barely been acknowledged. Wilfred, in his cups, had suggested that the Foreign Office was a dinosaur that had received, some years ago, a heavy blow to the head, but the pain was only now gradually reaching places like the Embassy in Phnom Penh, which were the dinosaur's toes.

The paper about Bill had come from the Australian embassy and followed a phone call, which had made similar allegations, but the written version provided dates and times when Noon had apparently behaved suspiciously, where the problem wasn't that he was a spy but that he was being too conspicuous about it. He supposed that he would have to raise the subject with Bill. But he remembered that Hilda Noon had told him an odd thing about Bill at Edith's party. She had approached Christopher late on, and kept touching his arm in a way that unsettled him, and fixing him with an intense look, and she told him that, earlier in the week, Bill had walked into the kitchen where she was cooking and had stopped abruptly when he saw a pan of brown lentils that was boiling on the cooker. She said he had let out a groan of horror, just at the sight of this pan, and, without saying anything, had turned around and marched quickly away. Her implication was that Bill was becoming impossible – that he'd reacted to lentils boiling as though he'd seen a ghost.

So he wasn't looking forward to a conversation with Bill. Meanwhile, he had an equally repugnant task to perform relating to his Head of Chancery and he drew up the armchair to face the desk and removed some papers from it, but decided to keep his wooden chair behind his desk –

because he needed, regrettably, to retain a formal atmosphere considering what he had to say. When Wilfred arrived Christopher indicated the armchair, and, after thanking him for the great job he'd done in organising Edith's party, and listening patiently to Wilfred saying it was the least he could do, and after he had done his best to ignore the insinuation that Edith's husband wasn't doing enough to show his appreciation, he said, 'This is an unpleasant task for me, Wilfred, because, unfortunately, a couple of complaints have been made against you.'

'A couple?'

'A couple yes.'

'Am I allowed to know who made them?'

'I think it would work for us altogether better if I don't reveal that.'

'And what exactly were these complaints about?'

Christopher was amazed that Wilfred was asking this question, 'I think we know...'

'Was Bill Noon one of the people who complained?'

'An altercation between you was overheard at the party. Which is not to say that I'm agreeing that he was one of the people who complained.'

'You know that he's a spy.'

'That's absurd – and anyway it's not relevant.'

'Everyone except you knows he's a spy, Christopher. And it is relevant...'

'Look, Wilfred, please calm down. It doesn't help that you consort, I mean that you've been seen in the company of, Jean Barré.' This had always dismayed Christopher, who considered himself tolerant of homosexuality, but Barré, the editor of the semi-official newspaper, *Réalités Cambodgiennes*, was simply monstrous, clownishly anti-American, and with a *louche* past connected to Nazi collaborators in France. And also an obese, jowly, and bald man observed regularly pawing his fresh-faced Cambodian catamite in scandalously public places. It had horrified him that Wilfred moved in the same company as Barré, though he had perhaps been wrong to bring this up at this moment.

'Oh Christopher, that's really not fair. Barré is really not a friend of mine. He's a French journalist who knows other Frenchmen I know who move in those circles.'

'Nonetheless, Wilfred, it would be decidedly preferable if you removed yourself altogether from those circles. But this isn't the point – which is, as I say, that complaints have been made...'

'But how can I defend myself against them if you won't specify who made them?'

'I don't want you to defend yourself against them. I just want you to take them as a warning sign. Phnom Penh, as you know, is a tolerant place, which is one of things we all enjoy about it, but that doesn't mean we don't need to be careful.'

'I *am* careful.'

'You used to be, but I think you've recently become significantly less discreet.'

'Again, Chris...'

Christopher gave him a disapproving look.

'Again, Ambassador, I can't respond to these criticisms unless you provide me with examples.'

'And again, Wilfred, I don't want you to respond. I'm asking you just to believe me.'

'That's not fair.'

'Fairness is beside the point. Whether the complaints are fair or not is also beside the point, which is that they've been made. The fact that they've been made is what concerns me as the person in charge of this Embassy.'

'So you're warning me?'

'Yes.'

'Well fine then. I'll think about what you've said and try to be more discreet.'

'I'm pleased to hear it. But I've also made a decision – which is nothing to be alarmed about. I've decided that these complaints are a sign that you're not at your best at the moment. Would you agree that there's some truth in that?'

'Not really. I'm perfectly alright.'

Christopher was feeling the strain of maintaining the formality. He stood up and moved his chair from behind the desk and nearer to his Head of Chancery. 'You know that's untrue – don't you Wilfred?'

'If Edith has been telling you...'

'No no, not at all. But you've not, lately, been at all cheerful.'

'Things have been a little difficult for me, it's true, but...'

'That's pretty obvious Wilfred. So I've decided you need a rest. I want you to leave Cambodia for a couple of weeks. Go back to Scotland and see your mother if you like. But just leave and go somewhere else for a little while.'

'I'm grateful for your concern, Ambassador, but it's really not a good time at the moment for me not to be around. It's a tricky time in my private life and...'

'I've made up my mind, Wilfred, that I want you to take a break.'

Christopher felt that Wilfred had made this interview much more difficult than it need have been, and he was relieved to see Wilfred replaced in the armchair by Peter Cook, and to be in a meeting in which he needed only to convey a trivial piece of information, which was that a local schoolteacher called Hok Suhana had mislaid a piece of paper that Peter had given him and would like another copy. 'Oh yes,' Peter said, 'I remember. It was a story I told his pupils which he said they'd enjoyed, and he wanted a copy of it.'

Needing to relax, Christopher asked what the story was.

'It was called The Crocodile Princess.'

'I know that one.'

'I really only took the name, Ambassador. In my story the Crocodile Princess lives with a working-class family in a provincial part of southern England, but she's a foundling and gradually they realise she's part of the royal family and they eventually arrange things so she's accepted in Buckingham Palace. But she never forgets her roots and the working-class family are allowed to visit whenever they like.'

Christopher realised that he was still tense from the interview with Wilfred now that he felt himself relax hearing this piece of pointless whimsy. He settled back in his chair and wiggled his neck a little recognising the stiffness there he often felt when he was tense. It was a great boon to have Peter around because he was such a source of harmless distraction, which was particularly helpful given the fraught political situation, which seemed to be building to a horrifying climax with the business in Cuba. The story was typical of Peter, and he thought he must be marvellous with children, because, although he was very sophisticated and knowledgeable, there was something fundamentally childlike about him, an essential innocence. He felt very protective towards him, fatherly, and started to worry that Peter's innocence might lead him to make blunders which would be all too conspicuous in Phnom Penh, where the diplomatic community was a tiny village which watched its inhabitants with minute, and distorted attention. So he felt it necessary to warn Peter about dangers that arose from the Cold War, about an atmosphere that was charged, all the time, with suspicion, and then Peter informed him that not many people knew the actual origins of the Cold War.

'They don't?' Christopher asked.

'No because the Cold War started when Mr and Mrs Khrushchev were shivering in their parlour watching their television, with blankets over their knees, when they saw Jack and Jackie Kennedy in their bathing costumes in Florida. And Jackie was wearing a skimpy bikini, and Jack was in his trunks and he was lovely and tanned and youthful...'

'It's true he's very young-looking, I met him once...'

'Yes, he's all handsome and young and that, and he and Jackie were carrying their deck chairs over the front in Miami, just by the promenade, and setting them up on the sand, and Mrs. Khrushchev said, "Why should those Yankees have all that nice sunshine, Nikkie, when we have to sit in all this tundra, we have to sit in all this permafrost, and wear fur all over us, like this fur hat," – and she took off her fur hat and waved it at Mr.Khrushchev – "you're a very powerful man, Nikkie, why can't you fix it so the sunshine gets shared out more equally – a bit more tundra for them, a bit more sunshine for us, more of an equal distribution on the rays-of-warmth front." And Mr. Khrushchev shivered and said, "Good point, chuck, I'll see what I can do." So he started a war to try to make the Americans colder, and he got his scientists to work on it – including clever Germans who had escaped to Russia during the earlier war – and they invented frosty rays which they started firing at America, and heat-seeking snowballs...'

'Heat-seeking?'

'It's very new technology. Heat-seeking snowballs, and before long the whole world was shivering along with the Russians...'

15

Peter Cook was daydreaming that he had remained in *Beyond the Fringe*, and the show had been an outstanding success and had transferred to London where the reviews had proclaimed that it was groundbreaking satire and represented a new spirit, not just in comedy, but in British culture. He daydreamed that it had been so successful that it had transferred to New York where even its Englishness had aided its triumphant progress, and it was regarded as such a phenomenon that even President Kennedy felt the need to see it. He had asked these young comedians to travel to the White House to do a private performance, but they had refused – they were anti-establishment, after all – and so he had travelled to New York to the club where they were appearing just to see them. Even in the midst of a major crisis, as tension continued to rise over Russian missiles in Cuba, the possible beginning of the Third World War, which would be fought with nuclear weapons, Kennedy was in the audience, – with his security men on all sides with walkie-talkies in their hands – as the Oxbridge four went through their routines. Peter daydreamed that he could see Kennedy in that audience, with a rueful, self-conscious smile, watching Peter's merciless impersonation of the president's friend Harold Macmillan.

It would be a simplification to say that the crisis that had transformed Peter Cook's life was about the boundaries of comedy, and, even more so, to say that it was about the comic nature, or otherwise, of one-legged men. It would be more accurate to say that a strange coinciding of moments relating to one-legged men unearthed a melancholy that might otherwise have remained latent in Peter for much longer.

Peter had written a sketch called 'One Leg Too Few' in which a one-legged man auditions for the part of Tarzan, and he had sent it to Kenneth Williams who had employed Peter as a writer even when Peter was still an undergraduate. Williams, who was fastidiously versed in Freud and Bergson on comedy, had been appalled by the sketch, and Peter, when he had gone to meet the established comedian and actor, who had always intimidated him, had been quite badly unnerved by Williams's indignation about its poor taste. Peter was taken aback because he regarded the sketch as one of the funniest he had written, he thought it was hilarious: but his confidence was unsettled by Kenneth's angry insistence on the fraught care that was demanded whenever comedy approached subjects where suffering was involved.

He put the anxiety behind him for a time, telling himself that Kenneth was just being melodramatic, but then it arose again in combination with another when he reprimanded himself over a remark he had made to Dudley Moore, who had been telling him about his working-class upbringing in Dagenham. Dudley had told him that his mother used to stand preparing their supper at their kitchen table, which had a mangle underneath it, and he had grown up thinking that the lower half of his mother was a mangle, and that he had emerged out of that mangle instead of a womb. And Peter, unable to resist, had said, 'Mangled?'

Dudley had been hurt by that remark because he was extremely sensitive about his own physical deficiencies – he was very short and had a clubfoot. That is nothing like as big a disability as missing a leg, but the two things got tangled up for Peter, especially when it was proposed that Dudley should play the one-legged auditioner in that sketch. Peter regretted hurting Dudley, who was arousing in him an increasing admiration and warmth, together with an obvious rapport when they worked together that struck him as very promising.

The incidents with Kenneth and Dudley began, very gradually, to put doubts in his mind – was the sketch only funny as long as you weren't thinking about a *real* man who had suffered an amputation? It would probably not have struck him in that way if his general mood hadn't anyway begun, inexplicably, to darken: but was it only funny if you weren't thinking inside the part (and not, no, no, definitely not, the severed body part!) of the one-legged man, of how he might experience lacking his other leg? He was already feeling himself to be prone to a depression related to this anxiety about a potential cruelty at the heart of his comic impulse when he encountered a one-legged man in a pub at lunch-time during the run of *Beyond the Fringe* in Edinburgh. He had been thinking that 'One Leg Too Few' needed to be played differently if it was going to work properly. He was occupied, in fact, with thinking this through, when a man at a neighbouring table struck up a conversation, which led, before long, to his description of what it was like to have your leg removed. Peter didn't believe in fate, or any concepts of that sort, was not at all superstitious, but he was shaken by this coincidence, and remembered the horrified edge to Kenneth Williams's voice as he condemned Peter's terrible misjudgement.

It was the final coincidence that toppled Peter over the edge. After the performance, that same day, of *Beyond the Fringe*, he encountered the television presenter Kenneth Allsop in the bar. Peter had always admired Allsop's interviews with politicians because he was able to unnerve them so thoroughly with his knowledge and authority, and he asked the journalist if he had enjoyed the show. Allsop said that he had, but that 'One Leg Too Few' had made him feel uncomfortable. When Peter asked him why, Allsop explained, matter-of-factly, that he had lost a leg serving in the RAF during the war.

The next day Peter started to feel as though he was being pursued by one-legged men. He walked through a city-centre street in Edinburgh where, along its length at different points, there were three war veterans displaying their stumps in order to gain sympathy and cash. He sank into a black mood of a sort he had never felt before, but which was, despite that, eerily familiar, as though it had been lying in wait for him all his life. It resembled boredom, but boredom grown so extreme that it had changed from being a passive state into an aggressive one, it was a boredom turned violent. He went into a pub meaning only to drink a half, or a pint at most, but he found himself unable to stop drinking, and as he drank his mood darkened further, and he imagined writing horribly misjudged sketches about the holocaust or the Bomb, and not being able to decide the point where comedy shouldn't enter. He left the pub but went to an off-license and bought a bottle of Scotch and went back to his digs and drank himself into a stupor that made him unable to appear that evening for the next performance.

He felt unable, after that, to go back and face the other three, partly because he didn't know how to explain what had happened to him – didn't know himself, and it was really not funny. He had thought that, out of the other three, he might try explaining it to Jonathan Miller who was after all not only a fellow performer but a doctor, so doubly qualified – perhaps there might be a medical way of describing it? But then you would be talking about psychoanalysis, and Peter loathed all things of that sort. Somehow his mouth had been open at the wrong moment and a black mist had slipped inside him and spread upwards into his brain and then downwards into his chest and limbs and its grip grew tighter the more he struggled against it, and he couldn't move. So for several months he hid himself away and felt cripplingly sorry for himself, and he recurrently remembered dead tadpoles in his bed, a childhood memory from wartime, when he had left a jar of tadpoles by his bedside and had knocked it over in his sleep, and woke to find ten dead tadpoles on his pillow.

For those several months he drank and drank and it was finally his parents who rescued him, and his father was very understanding, which for Peter was a remarkable thing because his father had been so distant when he was a child – literally distant for much of his childhood because he worked abroad in the diplomatic service. Peter felt sure he couldn't go back to performing, and it might well have been because his father was so understanding that he gravitated gradually towards his father's career, and the one his school had most prepared him for. So, with a little help from his father, he found himself one day, when the black mist had started to thin, and wearing the suit he had bought, on his father's advice, from a tailor in Sackville Street, walking into the Training Section in Carlton House Terrace. After a brief nod at the Head of Personnel, he was sent down a back corridor to a plywood cubicle where a departmental clerk asked him which 'hard language' he wished to learn – for example, Japanese, Russian, Persian, Amharic and Chinese. He selected Chinese, signed the Official Secrets Act, notified the Foreign Office of his next of kin, agreed to small deductions from his salary towards the in-house medical scheme, and was sent to the School of Oriental and African Studies. Peter had always had a facility for languages and had studied German and French at Cambridge, and it was during this period in London, living in a small flat and learning Chinese, that he started to feel his stability return.

Learning Chinese didn't, of course, guarantee that you would be sent to China, and Peter wasn't sure what process had led to his being sent to Cambodia and whether or not it was a coincidence that the Ambassador in Phnom Penh turned out to be a former colleague of his father in Nigeria. After the terrible sense of being undermined that he had experienced, though, he was left with a continual knowledge that he could, at any minute, be undermined again, so the feeling of being looked after was very welcome to him, and Christopher Hartnell, and especially His Excellency's wife, Edith, were welcoming, and had helped him to settle comfortably in Phnom Penh, which was reassuringly small and utterly safe. These characteristics had seemed perfect when Peter first arrived and it was a couple of months before he had started to seek out more dangerous diversions and had found them in the form of Joe Keane and Madame Chhum. His new, surprising, association with Prince Sihanouk offered even more possibilities. Shaking himself out of his daydream about President Kennedy, Peter pondered the reality of this link with an entirely different ruler as he headed towards the Royal Palace to meet him. He was riding the scooter he had recently imported from Singapore and thinking that his attitude to that other ruler, Harold Macmillan, had always been misunderstood, that he hadn't meant his impersonation to be at all cruel, that it was actually an affectionate tribute to the sort of men his father had always worked alongside.

Perhaps, when he had approached Sihanouk at the Embassy party, he had been thinking along these lines about rulers. He had slipped easily into conversation with him and had been surprised by how amiable and quick-witted he was, and the Prince had managed to surprise Peter into momentary silence by whispering a ribald reference about Sandie, which amused Peter because Sandie preserved such a sexually innocent surface. It had been a relief to Peter to have the secretary referred to so lightly because he was already wearying of the gravity with which the tangle with Keith and Sandie and himself was being treated, and his relief had encouraged him to embark on a monologue of his own, which at first had seemed to baffle Sihanouk but then had made him laugh. They had stayed in touch ever since, and, because he had complained about the humidity keeping him awake, the Prince had sent him a box fan, with rotating blades, which had proved to be very effective, and Peter had felt he needed to give the Prince something in return, and so had started to write a musical about Cambodia, and had given the Prince a starring role. This idea had occurred to Peter because of Sihanouk's musical ability, so that Peter had thought that the Prince would be taken with the notion of adding music to Peter's words, if those words were appealing enough, but also because the Prince – when he had heard about Peter's show-business background – had revealed his growing interest in cinema, and his desire to direct films set in Cambodia. Even so, Peter was starting to feel uncomfortable with the corner where he now found himself as a diplomat who had been befriended by the local ruler, where his own role was prescribed so thoroughly. It was one thing to write affectionate satire, from a distance, of the British prime minister, especially when the affection was so thoroughly encoded in what appeared to be savage comedy – it was another thing entirely to find himself following the relentless logic of a friendship where his own sense of himself was being almost as endangered as it had been by his period of drunken depression, where his personal style was being undermined, and he was being led dangerously close to sycophancy.

Peter steered his scooter along the front face of the Royal Palace which ran parallel to the river, past the esplanade, and then parked it at the start of the gardens so that he could walk along the pathway which led from the royal houseboat to the palace gates where he found the guard asleep and had to wake him to inspect his invitation and allow him to enter. Peter found it hard to take the palace seriously because the buildings seemed an elegant fantasy with their tall, golden spires, their steep roofs tiled in green and blue, and their pagoda-like eaves which stretched themselves upwards so flamboyantly, and all of this wavering in the shimmer of heat. That impression was increased once he was inside the palace and was greeted by the Prince who showed him around and revealed an interior which was surprisingly simple and homely, and Peter even felt a little sorry for the Prince (especially given his touchiness about references to his country's smallness and backwardness) as he showed such pride in the holy throne room, and then, inside a glass case in the palace museum, a black bowler hat which had belonged to one of Sihanouk's ancestors. The hat looked scuffed and worn, and its brim was tarnished slightly green, but, stitched on one side, it sported a circle of diamonds which the Prince said weighed fifty carats. Sihanouk was descended directly, he wanted to insist, from the ancient line of kings who had built the magnificent temples at Angkor.

During these initial exchanges, in a painstaking effort at politeness, Peter worked hard to speak in Royal Khmer, which he had learned for this encounter in an effort to oppose his own tendency to irreverence. Sihanouk was amused by this at first and replied in the same language, but soon tired of its ponderous circumlocutions and – as he led Peter to a small office with a desk and seated himself behind it and indicated a wooden chair for Peter to sit in – pointedly switched to French to ask about Peter's interest in weather-betting. Peter was dumbfounded that Sihanouk knew about this because he had only shared his interest in it with Keith and Sandie and he had to work hard not to be too distracted by anxiety about how the Prince had found this out, about how much the Prince had made inquiries about him. He hadn't thought much about it before, but realised, then, that the Prince had displayed knowledge of his early career, which he had not, in fact, revealed himself. Sihanouk was looking at him deliberately, in order to make it clear that he possessed this power over him, that he had knowledge about Peter whose extent Peter might not be able to guess, but his raising of this particular subject was especially undermining because weather-betting was strictly forbidden by the Prince's own government. Blithely ignoring this point, Sihanouk asked Peter if he was aware that weather-betting had started amongst the Chinese community thirty years ago, amongst some workers in a sausage-factory who noticed the suddenness with which rain starts and stops in Phnom Penh, and had started betting on the time it would start to rain and how long the rain would last. Their bosses had found out about it and had soon abandoned their sausages and set themselves up, full-time, as weather bookmakers. Sihanouk's tone throughout this had been gentle amusement, as if he had simply been enjoying the sense of what loveable rogues they were, those Chinese, but now he looked Peter directly in the eye and said, 'However, you need to be careful.'

'Yes, your highness, I know. I was recently warned for standing on my balcony and looking at the sky. I was accused of *studying form.*'

Peter said that last phrase in English, and was treated to one of Sihanouk's famous high-pitched laughs. But then, taking possession of himself, the Prince shrugged dismissively and said, 'Oh that is merely officious.'

'I wouldn't want to have to claim diplomatic immunity...'

'No no. I mean you are at a disadvantage with these Chinese gentlemen because the betting, being illegal, cannot be recorded, and therefore it relies on word of mouth. And sometimes it rains in one part of Phnom Penh but not another? And then, of course, the rain is supposedly verified by a cigarette-paper which is placed at the bottom of a pipe?' Sihanouk waited for Peter to verify this.

Peter could see no way out of admitting this knowledge, and said, resignedly, 'That's true, yes, your highness. There's an official drainpipe, and the cigarette paper is placed in the grid at the bottom.'

Sihanouk smiled. 'But you're aware that when the rain is only slight, the moisture won't reach the cigarette paper,

118

because the drainpipe causes it to evaporate because the sun had heated it previously so much? And sometimes the bookmaker packs the drainpipe with old bread to absorb the moisture? And then, conversely, if it suits him for rain to have fallen, the bookmaker melts a block of ice on his roof to moisten the cigarette paper, and you're powerless to oppose him, because sometimes in Phnom Penh rain does indeed fall out of a clear blue sky.'

Sihanouk looked triumphant now as Peter squirmed, so that Peter was desperate to shift the subject to his musical, and asked the Prince if he had found time to read the plot outline and sample pages he had sent him, and the Prince said that he had, and was very interested in the idea, but also felt some anxieties about it. Peter felt uncomfortable with the thought that he was approaching Sihanouk in a similar way to that in which, in the past, he had approached Kenneth Williams, worried he was explaining the obvious, but worried nonetheless that his point might be missed. That had been awkward enough when it was an established comedian he was wooing, but the discomfort was much greater now he was speaking to a God King, however much the reality of the slightly rotund prince denied his titles. With that discrepancy in mind, the need to be fully aware of the gulf between Kenneth Williams and a descendant of the kings who built the temples at Angkor, Peter drew the Prince's attention to a speech where he was introduced with a full list of his attributes: 'Great king with heavenly feet, better than all others, descendant of angels and of the god Vishnu, excellent heart, supreme earthly power, as full of qualities as the sun, born to protect men, supporter of the weak, he who knows and understands better than all others...' But Sihanouk waved all this away, saying, 'Yes yes that's very kind. As I understand it though, you're focusing the musical on Bon Om Tuk?'

'Along with Angkor Wat, your highness – and I thought the temples there might form a backdrop to some of the scenes – Bon Om Tuk is the most famous feature of Cambodia outside the country, so I thought the key scene in the musical could be the one where you cut the string that stretches out across the water. Because, anyway, that *is* remarkable, that the river at that time of year changes the direction of its flow. Actually turns itself around.'

'Yes, yes,' Sihanouk said impatiently.

Aware of that impatience, Peter still dared to say: 'Does your highness really believe – if you don't mind me asking – that it's actually necessary for you to cut the string to ensure that the flow reversal happens?'

Sihanouk shrugged. 'Better to be safe than sorry.'

The Prince was turning the pages that Peter had sent him, and Peter contemplated the idea that Edith Hartnell had propounded to him, without fully endorsing, that Sihanouk was a genius, who had won his country independence from France with a series of deft manoeuvres – made more effective because the French had seriously underestimated him, had regarded him as a trivial playboy, – and now he was playing off the West and the communists against each other, welcoming overtures from both but refusing to be subsumed by either. But there was also the other view that Sihanouk had inherited mental illness from his inbred family, and was seriously unstable, and had won his victories by luck, the view that mad unpredictability had worked by chance in his favour by disconcerting his adversaries. Maybe, in fact, he was a Mad Genius, just as Peter was a Sad Clown, and this was a meeting of two clichés?

Sihanouk looked up and said, 'This passage here is the one that most concerns me.' He passed the page across to Peter. 'Here, I am worked from above by strings. I am a puppet...'

'The point there, your highness, is that this is how you are sometimes depicted. Sometimes as the puppet of America, sometimes as the puppet of China. The crucial point there is when you burst free from the strings to cut the string across the river and then you sing 'When the river changes its mind', the song I'm still working on...'

'I'm not sure I could sing...'

'Or you could mime it. Or someone else could sing it on stage, while you played along on the saxophone. But it needs your presence on the stage. Well, not *you* always, but someone playing the part of you. And you see the verses I've written so far:

> Though Russia with the U.S. clashes
> All the past will be left behind,
> Though thunder roars and lightning flashes
> When the river changes its mind.
>
> Though Russia with the U.S. clashes
> Cambodia still is unaligned,
> Though thunder roars and lightning flashes
> When the river changes its mind...

'Yes, Peter – but what makes you so sure that Cambodia will stay unaligned? Is your musical dictating my foreign policy?'

'No no.'

'Aligned. Unaligned. Everything will be different, anyway, in a month's time once this Cuban disaster has worked itself out. If the world survives at all. Do you want to write a song, Peter, that predicts who will be aligned with who when the superpowers have stopped threatening to blow us all up?'

Confronted by this question, Peter felt bewildered and abruptly took stock of what was happening, of Sihanouk as a sophisticated Asian ruler and himself as a callow Englishman a long way from the Devon of his childhood and the Cambridge of his early brilliant youth, and was horrified that his musical had been a terrible presumption.

So he was only bewildered further, now, when Sihanouk asked him if he knew a young woman who worked at the Russian embassy, who was a cellist. Peter admitted that he'd spoken to her once or twice. 'Yes, Ariadna, she is called, this young lady,' Sihanouk said, 'and the Russians sent her here, to play her cello, and she plays it very sweetly. Bach, and so on. And of course she resembles an apsara...You know the apsaras?'

'Handmaidens of the gods. Semi-divine – sculptures of them at Angkor.'

'Quite, yes – she is shaped like them, and speaks very good Khmer. But it is very annoying that these foreigners think that Cambodia is small and backward and therefore that its ruler must be naive and stupid.'

16

In Edith Hartnell's nightmare, Prince Sihanouk had been imprisoned in the Royal Palace, which was surrounded by soldiers wearing dirty rags, and he was wandering through the grounds, and through the museum, past the four crowns, the one worn when riding an elephant, the one when riding a horse, the one for sitting in a carriage, and the one for walking, and he wandered past the stupas in the shape of flames that surround the silver pagoda, and he was blowing on his saxophone but it only made the sound of tiny chicks as he approached the walls and the palace gates that were supposed to protect him, but the ragged soldiers wouldn't let him leave, they forced him to turn back.

She woke and took a minute to understand that it was early evening, she could see, through the open doors onto the balcony that it was dusk, and she had fallen asleep in Hector Perch's bed, and she heard him catch his breath between two brief quick snores one after the other. She examined his face closely, noting the bigness of his features, the large prominent nose and ears, then the thin mostly grey hair, and she remembered what Keith had said about Hector, about how hard he was to argue with because he had such definite opinions about everything. She remembered Keith's intimidated tone and thought that the problem wasn't just that men had all the power but that they felt most strongly about each other, that they responded most urgently to the fascinatingly different kinds of power that each of them owned and expressed. She was drenched in sweat – the tropics were the worst place to experience the menopause because you could be sweating in two entirely different ways simultaneously, and she was fervently looking forward to the cooler, drier season that was now only a couple of weeks away.

She turned onto her back then slipped out from under the single sheet that had been half-covering the pair of them, moving stealthily in order not to wake Hector because she wanted to maintain the silence until she had time to compose herself. She stepped away from the mosquito net, and noted again the maps in different scales that covered one side of Hector's floor, with asterisks over in the west of Cambodia. Then she glanced at the clutter on his table, realising it was research material: she flicked through the magazine which Prince Sihanouk edited and which showed him successively helping a farmer to dig an irrigation channel, making a speech to the National Assembly, strolling in uniform past a line of soldiers, directing a film, and bestowing gifts on monks. The other material there was also centred on the Prince – a rolled-up poster, a notebook, a set of postcards, all displaying him in his many roles.

Edith tiptoed into the bathroom where she made a sideways stride into the bath and rinsed herself. She felt a little dizzy, and it was a physical sensation, but it reflected, also, her disorientation at finding herself again in this wrong place, this guilty corner where she shouldn't have strayed. Through the open window she heard a sudden, ferocious downpour, heard it drumming violently on the road outside the building, as she ruefully contemplated her nakedness, and the slight sag of her stomach, which was still creased from the bedsheets. She yawned and felt a familiar rancour about the damage which had been inflicted upon her by Britain and the vestiges of empire, inflicted even upon her body, felt again that rancour about what the nation had drained out of her as she had supported Christopher in diplomatic jobs in strenuous locations around the world. Worst of all had been the baby she had lost in Nigeria when she was thirty-eight, the baby it had taken her a long time to conceive. She had prematurely gone into labour, and had suffered a terrible journey on potholed roads to a hospital with primitive facilities where her treatment had been thoroughly inadequate for the complications of her condition. When she had first arrived in Cambodia she had been asked by a Cambodian woman, at a small gathering for drinks at the Embassy, if she had children, and she had said no, and the woman had said 'Oh, I'm terribly sorry.' Cambodians are focused upon family, so the assumption was natural for that woman, though it was a remark that a Western person would never have made: what made it so startling for Edith was that, in her case, it was all too accurate. And it was an attitude that she had felt was too little shared and understood by Christopher, who did sympathise with her loss, but had never properly weighed how terrible that loss felt to her, and Edith was sure that the drift they had suffered over the past decade had begun in the aftermath of that lost baby in Nigeria, when the shortcomings in his response had made him seem like a stranger to her.

Edith, nonetheless, couldn't recognise herself in the role of the unfaithful wife. As a younger woman she had thought it inexcusable for anyone to deceive their spouse, had thought that there could be no circumstances when you could be excused for involving yourself in secret with someone else – that everything should be done honestly and out in the open. If you were powerfully attracted to someone else then you must end it first with your spouse. Her marriage with Christopher, though, was much bigger than the two of them because it involved the whole Embassy, and her resentments had made her rebel against the idea that her patriotic duty, and her responsibility to Wilfred and Keith and Bill and Hilda (and their young daughter) and Peter and the rest should entirely trammel her emotional life. She had needed an assurance that she existed beyond her official role, especially when the intimate side of that role, with her husband, hardly existed any more, because he ignored her increasingly as he sank deeper into the persona of a fat old man, who complained constantly about being tired, and about one kind of physical ailment or another – his bunion, his tinnitus, his stiff neck. During the first month or so of her affair it had been a matter of a couple of occasions when she had strayed, she hadn't regarded it as anything at all established and fixed, and it had only been in the past fortnight that it had felt defined enough to justify the word 'affair', which still frightened her. It had therefore been as recent as the last week that she had begun to feel hypocritical in the stance she had adopted towards Sandie and Peter, and embarrassed about a couple of her attempted interventions, especially the one where she had visited Peter in his flat and then been discovered there by Keith. She had even begun to wonder if Sandie and Keith and Peter didn't resemble younger versions of herself and Christopher and Hector. Because Christopher and Keith represented plump inactivity, and Hector and Peter represented flamboyant energy. She understood Sandie's attraction to Peter, and how she might feel an urgency about herself, given the conspicuous fragility of her prettiness, with her extreme fairness of hair and skin that meant she had to pencil in her eyebrows.

Hector was only a couple of years younger than Christopher, but he was charged with a drive that made him radically different to her husband. He remained restlessly curious. Earlier that day, he had been telling her about a trip he had made, that week, to the far west of the country, to a settlement called Pailin in Battambang province. It involved a very difficult journey, but he had felt determined to go there because he felt that, if he was going to understand Cambodia, he needed to understand places that were very different from Phnom Penh, and Pailin was far away near the border with Thailand, and was a gem-mining settlement controlled by the Burmese. So he had taken a train to Battambang, the provincial capital, and that had been straightforward, but then he had to travel the rest of the way in a terribly slow old bus on a road that started out uneven and broken but then, when it climbed steeply, almost vanished altogether, and resembled something indistinctly cleared of vegetation, so that the last fifty miles took over four hours. Hector's account had been amused, and he had clearly been fascinated by Pailin, which consisted of one main street, without tarmac, with wooden houses on each side, that had verandahs and two storeys, and which was surrounded by hills of tropical forests, and whose mines were in fact only open-cast ditches.

Edith had enjoyed Hector's account because of the vivid enjoyment which he had so clearly felt in undergoing these discomforts, and his unconcern about the dangers involved in visiting such a lawless area. His vivacity contrasted with her husband's jadedness. As she strode sideways out of the bath and started to dry herself she contemplated the idea of physical bravery, which Hector certainly must have because this journey he had made was only mildly dangerous compared with the war zones he had inhabited in the past, and the countries he had visited precisely because they were about to erupt into civil disorder. She thought then about Bill Noon, who, like Hector, made light of the dangers he had lived through, but who had obviously been shaped by them. She had repeatedly encouraged the military attaché to talk about his experiences but he would only convey limited information, and always insisted that those experiences couldn't be properly described to people who hadn't been through them. His insistence was gentle, so Edith had been upset, a couple of days before, when Bill had shouted at her. She had been reading to Bill's young daughter, Andrea, reading a very short story by Peter Cook that Andrea loved to hear repeated, and which was called 'The Crocodile Princess', and she had noticed a small smudge of chocolate on Andrea's cheek. Edith had wet a handkerchief by licking it and then had dabbed it against Andrea's cheek to clear the smudge, and Bill had happened to come in at that moment and, for some reason, lost his temper. She was aware that she was fussing, and aware that she had that tendency, and Christopher had told her off for showing too much interest in children, when it wasn't her business, but Bill seemed a little out of control, and had frightened her. He had apologised almost immediately, but she still felt upset now, remembering it.

She heard Hector stirring and she slipped on his dressing gown and moved into the kitchen and put the kettle on. Bill shouting at her was more upsetting because she felt an affinity with him: he had a wound in his leg, which sometimes made him limp slightly, and she had also been wounded serving her country. She wanted to be able to put it like that because she was sure it was true, but she didn't feel able to say that to anyone except Chris, and he had raised his eyebrows when she'd said it, meaning she was dramatising herself. She couldn't say it to Bill, self-evidently, because it was emotional talk, and disallowed on those grounds, especially with a near-stranger. But she wanted to say it, the affinity part, not least because Bill was tremendously attractive, with his big body, and his face which was battered but also somehow sensitive. He was unnervingly attractive, in fact, because she found it hard to hide the fact she thought so, and she knew that Bill's wife was aware that she felt that way, and that Hilda disliked her, understandably, for that reason, though Edith was obviously no threat.

She passed Hector a mug of tea because he was sitting up now with a sleep-stunned look on his face and he thanked her and smiled and asked her if she had also slept. She said that she had and asked him to tell her more about what he'd been saying about the crisis in Cuba, about feeling frustrated that he wasn't closer to the action, when it was so major. Edith disliked the look on Hector's face in response to her prompting, the look of a man who wanted to be allowed to wake up before he was quizzed, and who also felt a little guilty. Hector shifted a little in the bed, and said 'Oh, you know, it's not that I want to be away from here, because, as you know, I'm very fond of it here – and of you, of course – it's just that it's so far away from this world-changing event. And it's so awkward here, trying to get the inside information I'd normally have ready access to.'

Hector said this very slowly, as though it took a great effort to find inoffensive words, and Edith felt, watching him sigh and struggle, a strong impulse to leave, so she backed away into the bathroom, where Hector kept the one mirror he owned, a shaving-mirror, and started to make up her face, but bridled when another rush of sweat to her cheeks thickened her powder and made it uneven. 'Don't go, Edith,' Hector called, 'I just need to wake up properly.'

'No, no, it's fine, really. I need to get back now. They'll be wondering where I am.' Edith walked away from the bathroom towards the balcony.

'Stay just a little longer.'

'No I really can't.'

Hector's flat was near the Old Market and Edith could see now, through the balcony, the railings of the market, and, beyond them, the petrol lamps of the Khmer traders being lit.

'I wanted to ask you, though...' Hector was standing in the doorway now, watching her try to smooth her powder, and his tone was gentle and chastened, 'if you know anyone who might be able to interpret Chinese for me?'

'Peter Cook speaks some Mandarin.' Edith was amused by the sight of Hector's nakedness, his grey body hair and shrunken penis, as he asked a business question, and amusement made her warm to him.

'Would he be willing to interpret for me, do you think? I need to speak to someone at the Chinese embassy.'

'I should've thought so. As it happens Christopher tells me that Peter knows someone quite high up in that embassy.'

Edith had turned to face Hector as she said this and saw his look of surprise.

17

'We ought to go and celebrate now all that nonsense is over,' Keith Entwistle said.

'It is certainly relieving,' Yuri Shunin replied.

'We could go to the *Zigzag* and celebrate there?'

'Certainly, we could, certainly.'

Yuri and Keith continued seated, however. The Russian pushed himself deeper into Keith's sofa, and Keith, in his armchair, closed his eyes and nodded a little to the solo piano of Erroll Garner. Yuri was still on edge and mostly, he thought, because of the missile crisis, and he was still trying to get used to the idea that the danger had passed. 'Would you mind, however, if we remained in your flat?' He had chosen to visit Keith as the best way to smooth his unease because the atmosphere in Keith's flat was always so utterly relaxed. Sometimes, when he saw a statue of Buddha in the lotus position, he supplied it with Keith's bespectacled, slightly chubby smiling face, because Keith seemed so serene to Yuri that he carried serenity around with him, and his flat had deep layers of it which had fallen from Keith's person and accumulated. Keith sometimes spoke about his existentialism, but surely no other existentialist could saunter as cheerfully towards the void as Keith. Yuri closed his eyes and listened to Garner accompanied by the trilling of the refrigerator, and the whirring of the fan, and then a brief downpour hitting the nearby pavements. He opened his eyes and saw ants flying into the electric lamp.

'We could stay here of course, but the ending of that nonsense is worth marking with a drink?' Keith said.

Reluctantly, therefore, Yuri accompanied Keith into the centre of Phnom Penh, where they expressed, as usual, their shared scepticism about the Chinese who had for some years been in control of that part of the city, dominating it with their own taste for signs in neon, and for cinemas and radio shops whose loudspeakers echoed from their doorways, and where, in 1949, they had opened a casino with a deadly attraction for too many Cambodians. Straight away Yuri was oppressed by the noise, and complained to Keith about the Chinese love of electrical amplification. A tannoy above them thundered lines, marked at intervals by over-emphatic cymbals, delivered by a fervent actor, and then a troupe of drummers, in silk which danced in the rhythm of their drumming, drowned out Yuri's words. Keith only smiled his enjoyment of the scene – he was humming that awful Chinese love song about a rose and Yuri felt, as he usually did when they ventured out together, as though he and his secret English friend were committing adultery, and that he needed to be wary of being spotted by other staff from his embassy. They couldn't agree on a place to drink, because Yuri, impossibly, wanted somewhere quiet. So they were standing watching a pale-skinned girl, probably Vietnamese, singing a song of exquisite, languorous suffering out of the open casement of a first-floor Cantonese restaurant, when Yuri spotted Keith's girlfriend strolling along with Peter Cook. They were heading towards the spot where the singer was performing, and were only thirty yards from it, and then Sandie noticed Yuri and Keith and stared directly at Yuri, looking stunned. He felt, at that moment, that she gazed deeply into his eyes, and she shocked him with how attractive she looked, which struck him as somehow well beyond the simple components of her appearance.

Panicking, Yuri seized Keith by the arm and spun him away from the approaching couple, saying, 'Sorry Keith, I can't stand this, mate. I can't stand it any more. Have you no alcohol in your flat?'

'I have some scotch.'

'Scotch is great.'

Back at his flat, Keith poured two large helpings of the whisky into teacups, explaining that his glasses had mysteriously disappeared. 'Best to be here, anyway, Keith, because I need to hand over to you a document.' He fixed Keith with a significant stare. 'A document which I bought from a local man, and which he claimed had originated in your Ambassador's office.'

Keith frowned. 'And how did this person come by it?'

'I was sceptical of course, so I interrogated him closely about it. He said that the document was just at the exterior of your Ambassador's window. He said that documents could quite often be discovered there. His story seemed plausible to me.'

'Plausible. How?'

'Given what I know about His Excellency.'

'I see. Can I see it then?'

'Later, Keith. Rest assured. I am doing this as your friend, so you needn't be alarmed...Ah, *She's Funny that Way.*' Yuri sipped his scotch and tapped his foot in time to this Erroll Garner tune that he and Keith both loved. And Keith, being Keith, didn't want to press the subject, and they both settled back and listened without speaking for fifteen minutes or so, and Yuri contemplated his increasing disaffection from the policies of his own government. The United States, and the West, in general, were far worse, with their lies and hypocrisy, and all that fuss about missiles in Cuba when they had missiles in Britain and Turkey which could easily reach the Soviet Union. In school, when they had studied *War and Peace*, he had wanted to skip the parts where Tolstoy had extended his polemic against war, against Napoleon and generals like him, but now he felt he understood that pacifism, felt that he increasingly shared it. And he had got weary of the way that Ariadna and Dmitri and the others had ranted about the missile crisis, weary of the endless confrontations between power blocs. And weary of how Ariadna and Dmitri speculated constantly about what Bill Noon and Peter Cook were up to – one a soldier, the other an insidious diplomat who was forever building bridges with key political figures. His own embassy had a link with a group of insurgents based near a mining town on the border with Thailand and they said they had not had any contact with either Bill Noon or Peter Cook, and didn't know of any group that had, but these groups were scattered and disconnected, they weren't under any central command, so it was impossible to be sure.

'How is your friend Peter Cook?' he asked.

'A bit sad recently. A bit lost, I think.'

'Why is that?'

'Oh Peter isn't suited, really, to diplomacy.'

'No?' Yuri thought that Keith was unwilling to speak.

'He had an awkward meeting with Sihanouk. He found himself co-opted in a way that made him uncomfortable.'

'Sihanouk?'

'Yes Sihanouk took a shine to him. Gave him a present. Spoke to him a couple of times on the phone. Invited him to the palace.'

'No. That's odd isn't it?'

'Not really. Sihanouk has his whims of course.'

'But still...'

'And the Prince wants to keep up with the times, and he's interested in show business. And Peter has that background.'

'Is that why they sent Cook in the first instance?' Yuri had blurted this before he had chance to censor it.

Keith looked at Yuri a bit quizzically, but then his sleepiness doused that slight flame, so that Yuri wasn't even sure if Keith had even grasped the implications of what Yuri had said. And then Keith opened his eyes and said, 'Talking about Peter, come and have a look at this. I'll show you what Peter should be doing, instead of doing something he's unsuited to.' He was calling Yuri over to a table where two piles of paper were sitting, and both had the single word *Bedazzled* on their top page. 'This is a script that Peter wrote and I liked it so much that I asked a girl I know, who works at the American embassy, to make a copy of it for me.'

'And how did she copy it?'

'They have a machine there, made by a company called Xerox, that makes copies of printed pages by photographing them.'

'So clever.' Yuri flicked through the pages, first in one pile then the other.

'It's the latest thing, this machine called Xerox 914, and it uses a process called Electro-photography.'

'How ingenious those Americans are!' Yuri tried to suppress the note of irony in his voice by moving quickly on to: 'And the characters are Stanley Moon and George Spiggott?'

'It's a modern re-telling of the Faust story — Stanley Moon is the Faust figure, and George Spiggott is the devil.'

'That sounds most ingenious...' Yuri was struck with embarrassment by his repetition of the word, which made him sound patronising. He smiled awkwardly at Keith, but good old Keith only nodded knowingly back and smiled cheerfully, and said, 'you know Yuri, maybe you and me should go some time to Madame Chhum's?'

'You've been there?'

'Once, yes. A journalist called Hector Perch got me drunk and took me there.'

'Ah, it was against your will, then?'

Keith chuckled. 'To be honest, Yuri, I think I might not have had the courage to go there if I hadn't been coerced.' He was turning over the long-playing record and lifting the needle onto the groove.

Keith's music, and his whisky, and this frank, self-mocking, confession, made Yuri warm to Keith even further, and he thought about Madame Chhum's. He had never smoked opium, and was sure he didn't want to, and then he thought about the women in that establishment. It wasn't only the missile crisis which had put him on edge, it was also the thing about himself he was always pushing to one side, which flickered continually in the corner of his eye, and which he was always turning away from, because it frightened him, and now he felt it looming larger there, felt that it was going to force itself into the forefront. Maybe Madame Chhum's was the diversion he needed to forestall it? 'What happened, Keith, when you went there?'

'Very little, actually. I felt constrained by Perch's presence.'

'Why was that?'

'He's quite intimidating. He's older, in his fifties, and quite famous. You've heard of him?'

'Possibly.'

'He makes fun of me. Not maliciously, you know, but it means I never really relax when he's around.'

'Whereas, with me, the enemy, you feel entirely at ease?'

'It's true, Yuri, you *are* the enemy.' Keith poured some more scotch into Yuri's teacup. 'I've been instructed to lead you astray in order to extract government secrets from you.'

Yuri was so shocked he laughed abruptly and loudly. Did Keith feel so comfortable with Yuri because he sensed his disaffection? And what was the extent of Keith's own scepticism? Yuri was sure that Keith was not a slavish supporter of his own country, whatever his official line had to be, and Keith had occasionally let slip to Yuri hints of his scepticism. On the other hand, the idea that an Englishman and a Russian could go comfortably together to an establishment like Madame Chhum's required a much bigger leap of imagination.

They relapsed into the silent camaraderie of scotch and jazz and Yuri could feel his unease dissolving. Then Keith said, 'So, Yuri, perhaps you can show me the document you mentioned?'

'I'm afraid you will have to pay me to see it.'

'How much?'

'I think I'm prepared to let you own it outright for twice what I paid.'

'And you're sure that it originated in my Ambassador's office?'

'Absolutely.'

'Alright. What did you pay for it?'

'Fifty riels.'

'I see, yes. About ten shillings.' Keith stood up and walked across to his jacket and took his wallet from a pocket and extracted a note. He passed it to Yuri saying, 'There's a hundred riels.'

'Thankyou.' Yuri reached into his briefcase and handed Keith some soiled pages. Keith leafed through them and looked up at Yuri, nodding wearily.

It was a seed catalogue.

18

'So I'd like you, Dudley, to tell me that story again. The one you told me in our last session. Because it seemed to me that there was something about it that struck a chord with you – if you'll excuse the pun.' The analyst, Donald Taylor, chuckled.

Dudley frowned. 'If you say so. Mozart and Haydn used to set each other feats to perform on the piano.'

'It was about a competition between them?'

'Yes. They were both virtuosos on the piano, as well as being great composers.'

'So their friendship reflected a sense of mutual admiration?'

'Yes.' Dudley paused. He wasn't sure he liked the direction this was taking.

'Go on.'

'So one day Mozart had written a piece which he challenged Haydn to play. And Hadyn was attempting it, but he found that, at one point it required him to have his hands at the extreme right and left of the keyboard, and then, at the same time, to play a note in the middle. So he pointed that out to Mozart and claimed it was impossible. So Mozart played it – and, at the point where that note needed to be played in the middle, he ducked his head at the keyboard and played it with his nose.'

Somehow, repeating a story he loved with the sense that his analyst was going to impose an interpretation on it made him feel miserable. Even though he was paying lots of money to hear those interpretations. Striking a chord! All that day he'd been hearing a dissonance from Bartok's fourth string quartet, from a disc a friend had leant him, a nightmare sound from the second scherzo, and scherzo after all means joke, and this was really not funny. All plucked. Why would anyone want to use their talent to invent a noise so unsettling that it sounded like the worst news you could possibly hear? And he could hear that dissonance again, now.

'We've talked a lot about your sexuality...'

'You're bored with my sexuality?'

The analyst with his abundant grey hair and his neatly trimmed white beard looked at Dudley reproachfully. 'Of course not. And anyway, Dudley, you're not here to entertain me.'

'Perhaps I'm bored with my sexuality?'

'That's possible. Would you like to talk about it?'

'You just said we've talked too much about it.'

Taylor sighed. 'You know that wasn't what I said.'

'Did you see the article in that newspaper yesterday?' *The Daily Mail* had run a piece on how Dudley was seeing two women at the same time: fortunately they seemed not to know about the third. The photos were embarrassing. So far he'd heard from only one of the women, who wasn't amused.

'I'm not interested in tittle-tattle. What we're dealing with is how *you* feel about it.'

'Pretty exposed at the moment.'

Taylor stared at the carpet, which looked as though it came from Turkey or Bokkhara, the sort of place Dudley still found impossibly posh. He doubted if his analyst understood that psychoanalysis for Dudley might be influenced by its taking place in softly gleaming leather armchairs in a high-ceilinged residence in Hampstead, but Taylor was officially retired, so it would take place in his house, or nowhere, and he was supposed to be one of the best.

'The impact of fame is an issue we might broach eventually. One or two of my analysands have been quite famous, so I'm not a stranger to the issue. In your case, evidently, it is entangled with your sexuality, which may well have been a driving force in creating it. And no, I'm not bored with that discussion, and, if we find ourselves returning to it, then that is for a genuine, underlying reason. We've discussed the relationship between your sexuality and your childhood, but of course that doesn't exhaust the subject, and its impact on your life now is also, obviously, germane.'

Dudley heard again the sound of those plucked Bartokian strings and thought that films were genuinely saying something about the real world when they used background music as motifs, genuine at least for people like himself whose minds kept replaying musical fragments. 'A couple of my friends have told me they've had dreams where they find themselves naked in a restaurant or a cinema. Being famous can feel like that.'

'It's something you fear, but also something you desire. All those eyes turning towards you?'

'Yes yes. We've talked a lot about my lack of self-esteem...' Dudley hesitated.

'Please, Dudley, stop worrying about repetition. If something is repeated it's because it's meaningful.'

'But I bore myself with it...'

'Boredom is beside the point. There are much worse things than boredom, much worse people than boring people. Don't frown, please, I'm not saying you're a boring person. And it's true, in your profession, boredom must be avoided at all costs. But *not* in my profession. If your low self-esteem is the question that we need most to address, then we'll keep addressing it. If it's your low self-esteem that drives your compulsions, and leads to your being haunted by a sense that something is missing, then we will need to keep returning to that.'

'But you were interested in the Mozart and Haydn story.'

'Only because it appeared to fascinate you. When you told that story you acquired a kind of brio...that's a musical term also is it not?' He chuckled. 'Brio, yes. Often, when you're describing yourself you seem lethargic – and, believe me, I'm not complaining – but when you told that story you were animated as you are when you perform on television. So I wanted to explore the reason why it appealed to you so much.'

'But it's a great story, isn't it?'

'Certainly, yes. But no more so than other things you've said when you've appeared lethargic, for example when you've described sexual encounters, which, for many men might inspire the most brio. That is to say that you're driven towards those sexual encounters but often remain unfulfilled by them. What I would like you to do, before our meeting next week, is to think about the times when you have felt at your happiest. Which might, for example, only be quite brief, might only be for a couple of hours at a time.'

19

It is autumn in the Cotswolds village where Christopher Hartnell will retire. The light is chilly and angled low, especially in the long, misty twilight, when the sun peers redly through the elegant elms and limes, and the massive oaks and beeches, whose yellowing leaves are still thick on their branches, but just beginning to drift down across the village green, and the cricket pitch, and the churchyard with its ancient, lichen-encrusted stones. The river begins to swell and also carries yellow leaves on its tannin-tinted, gently rippling, surface. The urgent clamour of geese overhead is heard at regular intervals, and that migratory plangency would once, in Christopher's youth, have unsettled him with the instinct for journeying, but now only endorses the luxurious pleasure of sitting still. Throughout the village there is the heavy odour of woodsmoke, of leaf mulch, and of sodden tilth, and there are blackberries on the brambles, and pears and apples heavy on their branches, and Christopher is gathering harvest offerings in the church for the festival that will soon take place – as they approach the equinox and the period of the harvest moon, offerings of vegetables and fruit from gardens and farms – when the congregation will sing hymns about God-given plenitude. But there is bad news because Christopher's friend, the old sea-dog Bob Murphy, has recently died of a heart attack, and Christopher is pondering what he will say at the funeral, when he will deliver the eulogy.

The yellows and browns of that autumnal Cotswold village mingled with Christopher's irritation as he remembered a conversation that morning with Keith Entwistle, who was deferential, undeniably, but had been determined to finish and amplify his point beyond the time when Christopher had clearly indicated that he had understood it. Keith meant well, certainly, and was only echoing the exhortations that Christopher himself had made to be careful, but there was an element of insubordination in his tone. He had to admit that, however much he exhorted his staff to be careful, Christopher himself had never taken to the Cold War, he hated a diplomatic culture being structured around the paranoiac petty-mindedness fostered by that superpower antagonism, because he had become a diplomat in the first place because he subscribed to much nobler ideals. So, in practice, the need to pay attention to whether or not mostly trivial documents were blown out of his window was very annoying, especially because (due to Reg Armstrong's busy-body interventions) he kept reminding himself that he needed to pay that attention. He was approaching the small square, which contained the post office, strolling, as he often did, at lunchtime. His Keith irritation, and the Cotswold yellows and browns, mingled with the whiteness of the facade of the post office in his actual vision, when he suffered an odd hallucination. He was still perhaps a hundred yards from the post office, on his own side of the street, when he saw a man and a woman leave the French restaurant, *La Lanterne*, which was opposite the post office. Both were western and middle-aged, and Christopher was misty-eyed with his meditativeness, but he had the sudden impression, through the heat haze, that the woman was Edith. That impression made him shake himself awake, but then he realised that he must've been mistaken, because, just before the woman climbed into a cyclopousse, the man kissed her on the cheek before hurrying away out of the square.

Christopher had asked to see Peter Cook, who duly called on him in his office soon after he arrived back at the Embassy, where Christopher asked him if he'd heard any Cambodian jokes. Peter shook his head, and Christopher said, 'Well, for example, there's the one about the mosquito which finds itself battered by a storm and looks for shelter and finds it in the...er...private parts of a female elephant.' He paused to check Peter's reaction and saw him nod solemnly. 'When the storm has blown over, the mosquito is approached by one of his friends who asks him: "Were you aware of where you were just now?" and the first mosquito says no, so the other mosquito tells him. So the first mosquito flexes his biceps and says "Well, it's a great shame I was unaware of that because, had I known, I would certainly have done something about it." '

Christopher laughed, but stopped abruptly when he could see that Peter was only smiling politely. 'My point, anyway, Peter, is that this is what Cambodian humour is like, and that's relevant because I'd like you to be our buffoon.'

'Buffoon?'

'Yes. I've decided we should enter a boat in the race during Bon Om Tuk, because it will be good for our relationship with the local community. As I'm sure you know, Bon Om Tuk is the biggest event in their calendar, and understandably, given how astonishing it is for their major river to change the direction of its flow. Keith has agreed to be our drummer, because the boats have a drummer who beats time and the oars are wielded in time to the drum, and Bill Noon has been training our team.'

'Yes, Sandie has been telling me about that.'

'Good. It's been some years since we entered a boat, but I'm convinced that this is a good time to start again, especially now that Sihanouk has taken up the role of cutting the cord across the river to mark the end of the race and symbolically free the waters to flow down to the sea. I'm sure he would see it as a well-judged tribute to him. But the role of the buffoon is also crucial here, bloody crucial, so we'll need you to strike the right note.'

'I see.'

Christopher opened the drawer in his desk and produced a piece of paper. 'So you need to be aware of the

sort of thing the buffoon says, which is, for example...'
Christopher cleared his throat, put on his reading glasses,
and read: '"Your women are fine, Mr Frenchman, their
skin is white and good; but their noses are long, and the
noses of our women – they are short".'

He stopped and looked at Peter from under his glasses,
and noted that Peter was looking uneasy. 'Their noses –
they are short?'

'Yes, that's right. Here's another: "The Khmer girls make
love all the night, the Vietnamese all the day, the *mademoiselle*
from France, they say, only makes love in the evening".'

'They say? Would that be the *mademoiselles* who say that?'

'Here's another: "It has rained a great deal this year, the
river has broken its banks. There will be much rice and joy.
All the women are pregnant, either by their husbands or by
their lovers. It doesn't really matter. Aya!"'

'Aya?'

'Aya! Yes. And here's the last example I have: "Oh you
women, lift up your sarongs, so that I can tell who amongst
you pleases me the most. Aya!" Now Peter, do you think
you can emulate this?'

Peter said, 'Aya! Ambassador,' nodded and strode hastily
to the door.

In the silence that followed Peter's departure,
Christopher listened to his tinnitus. Normally it sounded
like hundreds of cicadas, but now it sounded like water
hurrying over stones at the edges of a broad river, and
Christopher waxed unexpectedly sentimental about the idea
of a river changing the direction of its flow, thinking of the
word *watershed*, and of the endless, regenerative possibilities
of change.

145

20

In the bedroom at his ambassadorial residence, Joe Keane stroked the bandage under his trouser leg as he read a letter to his wife from her mother. He had found the letter on the bedside table, and he listened hard in case his wife climbed the stairs and caught him. She was downstairs reading to their three-year-old daughter while their Vietnamese cook was preparing their dinner. He looked up, thinking hard about what Marianne's mother was saying, and saw a lizard raising its head above the sill outside the window he was standing next to, and he thought of a swooping owl, and then backwards through the opium chain of association he was locked inside: owl, lizard, insect, light, Sihanouk. Increasingly, in this chain, Prince Snookie wore a smile of sinister knowingness, and, this time, when the associative loop reached him, the Prince smiled as though with insider knowledge of what Joe's wife and her mother were saying about him to each other. It was clear that Marianne had defended him against charges that her parents were making and that her mother was commending her for her loyalty but insisting that Joe was a great disappointment to them. Joe grimaced: they had never liked him, never liked his Irish background – their own was German and Scandinavian – never liked his being a Democrat and a politician, because their allegiances were to the Republicans, and to business. Her father was a senior executive in the Chrysler Corporation. They had been appeased when his career prospects had started to look promising, but clearly felt cheated now those prospects had seemed so disastrously to wane. The letter reminded Marianne how much she was unsuited to living in a cultural backwater, how much she enjoyed opera and theatre, and sophisticated, well-connected company. Joe stared at the lizard, which had lifted itself deftly onto the sill, and listened hard – there were street noises but only muffled sounds from below, no footsteps on the stairs, and told himself he was right to read the letter, because the charges were unfair and he needed to compensate for the unfairness with knowledge he wasn't known to have. He felt a rising fury, partly because he agreed that Phnom Penh was a hopeless place to be condemned to, and because he deserved better, and because he'd just discovered that the job he thought he might get in the Treasury department had been given to one of his oldest friends.

During dinner, Marianne tried to start a number of conversations about her day, about what their six-year-old son Michael had said about his school, and about her visit to the Grand Market, but Joe had been able to say little in reply, he tried to muster the effort, but failed because he was brooding about being overlooked for a job he was so thoroughly suited to, given his background in economics. The opium loop of association, so vivid, loomed oppressively to him because it declared with shocking explicitness an area of his experience which he could never share with Marianne, and all the more because increasingly he was finding that a pair of green-blue eyes, above a pair of high sharp cheekbones, were gazing through that loop, the face of Ariadna, which he struggled hard not to name. That sharpened his anxiety because he acknowledged, however reluctantly, how much he needed Marianne's support at that moment. Being forced to acknowledge that, though, also made him resent her, made him rebel against the lack of freedom the need entailed. It was worse because, aside from the support of his wife, he felt almost no support from elsewhere, and that was proven by the way he'd been overlooked, so it felt as though his existence was hardly recognised, so thoroughly had he been ignored. The friend he thought he had in Washington, who had the ear of Douglas Dillon, the Secretary of The Treasury, had promised that he would press Joe's case, and stress his credentials, but that had come to nothing, and there had been a long silence before Joe had heard he wasn't getting the job, so that, humiliatingly, he'd spent a couple of weeks thinking that he still stood a chance when the decision had already been made against him. He brooded now over the image of himself in a state of misguided expectancy, of innocent hope, and cursed himself as an ingenuous idiot. That image of himself made him want to hurt someone badly, to find a culprit and kick them hard and repeatedly.

'There'll be other jobs,' Marianne said gently when they had left the table and were seated on the couch drinking wine, and Joe knew that her gentleness was in sympathy for the journey he had just made, torturously slow because of the heavily bandaged knife wound in his leg.

Joe nodded, 'I know. I know.' He reminded himself about the story he had told about the wound, a story whose details had been over-elaborated because of his severe anxieties about the grotesqueness of the truth. Now he had to remember all those details.

'Anyway, I'm learning to love this place. It's fascinating in so many ways. Today in the Grand Market...'

'You're better than I deserve. I know that Phnom Penh is far from ideal for someone with your interests in the Arts and all. You're being terribly patient.' He gazed at Marianne's tasteful possessions, which she had shipped here: the Kazak carpet, the set of Wedgewood pottery, that glass thing from Murano, those big vases from – where? He'd forgotten. There were also items she had bought more locally, the Chinoiserie she had started to study, so he had begun to wonder if she was going native like Christopher Hartnell's wife. He unnerved himself because he felt a strong desire to shun one of these pieces, to turn away from it as though it contained a terrible message: at its centre was a figure who was human but seemed to be turning into porcelain, and who was sitting under a shimmering pagoda between two monkeys in human clothes, and there were birds on hoops and terraces that seemed to appear out of nothing and lead nowhere, and a crocodile holding a parasol.

'Patience is what we need. This is just a step on the ladder. A man with your talents – they can't keep you down.'

The pain in Joe's leg had subsided to a throbbing ache. Their son had gone to bed but their daughter Christine was still up because she'd been waking recently in the night and they had the idea that delaying her bedtime would help her sleep through. She kept stepping across them on the couch. 'It's not just not getting the job that hurts. It's the personal part of it, that my friends won't help me, as though there's something wrong with me at a personal level, that I'm someone whose friends aren't warm towards. The advancements I've had have come from strangers who've recognised my talent, and my friends have refused to help. So that time...' He looked at Marianne and recognised the patient look on her face and felt strongly the knowledge of how often she had heard this lament. He recoiled from the echo of the self-pitying whine in his voice and felt a new surge of impotent rage at the people who'd condemned him to this position, condemned him to hear this awful sound issuing from his own mouth. 'Oh for God's sake let's change the subject.'

'You mustn't think of it as personal. They're not thinking that way. They have their own ambitions and concerns.'

Joe saw how Marianne's blonde hair shone in the lamplight, and how her pale skin had acquired a glowing and slightly red tan, and he noted the pleading look on her beautiful, intelligent face, and felt how much he loved and needed her, and remembered the couple of occasions when he had slapped her and torn her expensive clothes. The first time was because she hadn't understood the predicament he'd been patiently explaining, a predicament like this one.

The second time was because she understood it only too well and was being a patient angel, and that had infuriated him even more. Had there been more than two such occasions? He didn't want to remember: a tendency towards self-loathing was relentlessly growing in him and he queasily knew he must oppose it. As he told himself this, Christine was stepping across him and he didn't pay enough attention so she got her right foot caught under his bad leg and he recoiled too suddenly and pitched her onto the floor where she banged her head. There was a horrifying moment of silence before she screamed with the shock of the fall and the pain and seemed to turn towards Joe accusing him as she screamed. Marianne darted towards her with amazing swiftness and swept her up and pulled her towards her chest and soothed her and started to carry her around the room to distract her and Joe shook his head ruefully and brooded further about personal betrayal.

He wished that Marianne wasn't around so he could smoke some opium. He had hidden some in the pocket of a pair of his trousers in his wardrobe, but even there he couldn't be sure that Marianne wouldn't interfere – nowhere was safe from her organising. He remembered the stupid joke he had told about Bobby Kennedy, and which had spread like a disease. The sad truth was that he had always unnerved himself, even when they were at Harvard together, with how strongly he felt about Bobby, how glamorous he thought Bobby was, how exciting his company, his darting intelligence and wit, his pizzazz. When Bobby was away he had pined for him, and it was anger at that pining, revolt against it, which had made him make that piss-ant remark about Bobby's *socks*.

He had virtually no friends in Phnom Penh, and he fretted that rumours about his misdemeanours in the city might be drifting back to Washington, and he certainly found Sihanouk impossible to deal with, so alien, so difficult to fathom, and so capricious. Systematically capricious. Yes, virtually no friends in Phnom Penh unless you counted Peter Cook who was more like an addiction than a friend, an addiction that reminded him of his addiction to Bobby. Cook had abandoned him that last time, and he would've been in serious trouble if the Brit army guy hadn't appeared. Bill Noon. He had made inquiries about him and discovered there were long-standing rumours that he was a spy. And then it occurred to him: Noon had shown up on a couple of occasions when Joe had been with Peter Cook. Wasn't there some sort of *pattern* there?

21

There had been nothing dramatic when the police arrested Hector Perch. They hadn't burst into his flat at 4 o'clock in the morning. They hadn't needed to handcuff him and throw him into the back of a van because he had been taking his luncheon alone in *La Lanterne* in the small square that also contains the post office and the police station. He had just written a marginal note in the article he was currently constructing, and was putting the top back on his fountain pen, and listening to the government radio which was playing in the restaurant, transmitting one of Prince Sihanouk's songs, "The Rose of Luang Prabang", when he glanced up. He was sitting near the window so he observed the two policemen leave the police station and stroll across the square and into the restaurant, but he was thinking hard about the ordering of his paragraphs so he hardly noticed them until it was suddenly clear that they were looking at him. 'Monsieur Perch?' the shorter one said, and Hector nodded. 'Is it good, your camembert?'

Hector looked down, ludicrously, at his cheese. 'Very good, in fact.'

'Well you must finish it then.'

'Yes. Thank you.' Hector was struck by a feeling of *déjà vu*.

'And your wine as well. That is also good?'

Hector shrugged. 'A little young, perhaps.'

'Ah yes.' The policeman spoke as though he had already known that. 'The white is better here I think.' He lifted a chair from a neighbouring table, and seated himself next to Hector, on his right, and his colleague did the same on Hector's left.

'Take your time, Mr. Perch. However, when you've finished your luncheon we would be grateful if you would

152

accompany us across the road so we can ask you a few questions.'

Hector reflected later that this was the last time that the police spoke to him in French: once he was in the police station they spoke only in Khmer. They handed him over to a superior officer who asked him questions in Khmer and raised his eyebrows when Hector replied in French. Hector asked if he was being charged with any offence, but he was aware that even his French wouldn't stretch to anything subtle or complex. The new, higher-ranking, man frowned as though he found Hector's French deeply offensive, and spoke to the policeman who had remained silent in the restaurant, who then led Hector down a corridor, opened a heavy door and shoved him inside, where Hector stood for several minutes feeling too astounded to be alarmed.

Hector had only been arrested once before, and that had been in Havana where charges were concocted against him by the corrupt right-wing regime which he had offended by writing the truth: but he had often felt that arrest, or worse, was looming, and had, quite frequently in widespread countries, pre-empted the strike against him by leaving. He looked around his cell and saw a single window which was opaque with frosted glass of the kind with wire inside it, and a rough mattress on the floor, and thought that there had been no warning that a move against him was about to happen. He knew, though, that it was likely that the authorities had been aware that he had met with the insurgents when he had travelled towards the Thai border, to Pailin, and he had quoted the views of those rebels in an article he had published in *The New Statesman* a fortnight earlier. It was highly likely it had taken that intervening period for the article to reach the attention of the Cambodian authorities, and the views he had quoted were scathing about corruption and luxurious privilege in the midst of general poverty, and he had made no attempt to hide the fact that those views closely resembled his own.

He winced now, remembering that he had also referred to Sihanouk's 'sickly smile' and said it reminded him of Liberace.

He sat down on the mattress and leant his back against the wall, reflecting that it was ironic that it should be in Cambodia that a threatening act should be made against him when nothing had happened in far more dangerous and violent places. He felt contempt for Sihanouk and his self-indulgent cronies but he was sure that they were not serious characters, that they were harmlessly Ruritanian, even if Cambodia's geographical position was currently endowing it with an inflated importance. So he decided that he should treat his arrest as an opportunity to catch up on some sleep: he urinated into a pot that had evidently been left for that purpose in the corner of his cell, stretched out on the mattress and went to sleep.

When he awoke it had grown dark and he was struck by how utterly silent it was. He dozed for a while, but it seemed a long time before any light struggled through the opaque window, and he thought about Edith, and argued with himself against any idea that he had started the liaison with a sense that it might provide him with inside information – not at all, he had been attracted to her from very early on and, since that time, he had grown increasingly fond of her. What inside information was available, anyway, of any worthwhile kind, from the British Embassy in Phnom Penh? It was a little Ruritania of its own, with Edith's husband bumbling around ineffectually. It struck him that Edith was the first menopausal woman he had been involved with, partly because many of his encounters had occurred on a paying basis in establishments whose similarities and differences in their varied locations around the world were a source of intense fascination to him.

It was a very long time before anyone in the police station acknowledged his existence, it had grown dark and light again twice before they did, and he had drunk all the water in the jug they had left quite early on, not regarding it as a precious resource. So he was very thirsty and hungry by the time he was taken to another interview with the higher-ranked policeman. Once again the man spoke only in Khmer and merely shrugged when Hector repeated the words *soif* and *faim*. Was this a kind of Cambodian joke? To conduct an interview in a language of which the interviewee had only the very slightest knowledge? However, Hector's attempts to extract single words of Khmer that sounded familiar to him from the policeman's questions reminded him of a single word of Khmer which he did know, and which he had quoted in his article: *b'ngreek*. He was sure that the policeman had been saying this word quite regularly, like a refrain. Sihanouk's father had used the word obsessively, so that his populace had started to repeat it in comically mundane situations. It meant *enlarge*, and the old king had endlessly repeated that Cambodian industry, and her army, and her diplomatic corps, and her population, must be enlarged. At meetings he had famously shouted *B'ngreek- b'ngrun- b'ngreek- b'ngrung* and it became a popular joke. In his article, Hector had poked fun at Sihanouk as a petty dictator who wanted to enlarge himself – but maybe now the joke was on Hector.

As the days passed, Hector wondered what Edith must be thinking about his disappearance and whether she would be making inquiries about him. It would be difficult for her because of the secrecy she would still need to maintain. He remembered that the joke in his article had occurred to him because of an incident between Edith and himself when she had boldly reached inside his underpants and started to squeeze and they had both, simultaneously, said *b'ngreek*, like a moment of telepathy. That referred, partly, to Hector's own unusual largeness there, which Edith had remarked upon from the start. Partly because he mostly celebrated that largeness, and enjoyed the feeling of potency that it gave him, he had been insensitively slow to realise that it made Edith apprehensive because of her menopausal dryness. He reprimanded himself about that because he should have understood more quickly given the problems he had encountered in establishments in Japan, and in Vietnam, where the women, being so tiny, found him difficult to accommodate – that had led him, out of embarrassment, into unfamiliar abstinence in those places.

It had seemed suddenly important that they had simultaneously thought the same esoteric word, especially because, later, they had again found themselves thinking exactly the same thing, in similar words, when they had been discussing the Embassy personnel. Edith used, about Keith Entwistle, exactly the same words that Hector had been thinking: that, because of Keith's working-class origins, he was unusually down to earth and clear-eyed, entirely undistracted by fantasy, entirely focused on the job at hand.

But he remembered now, with some alarm, something else that Edith had once said to him about Cambodians. They had been walking by the river and, because it was the dry season then, the water had sunk all the way down the concrete embankment, and they had watched the numerous sampans, and the ferries and the large cargo boats on the river, and Edith had explained to him the Cambodian concept of *kum* and how it baffled her because it was so at odds with Buddhism. She explained that it was a shockingly excessive form of vendetta – not an eye for an eye, but both eyes and the nose, not a tooth for a tooth, but your whole upper set. Hector missed Edith badly, then, remembering how very fond of her he had felt observing her bafflement, and feeling protective towards her ingenuousness, her strong determination to understand a pointless violence at odds with the official belief in benevolence and tolerance – which was also so evidently her own fervently and naively held belief.

With a fervency, then, of his own, and with an absurdity that must arise from his reduced state, he wished that Edith could be with him at that moment to interpret for him. It was hearing her speak Khmer that had first startled him into a more powerful feeling for the Ambassadress, had moved him away from the complacency in which he had thought that he was engaging in a brief fling. Part of that complacency was his dismissiveness about the liberalism he had attributed to her, which he regarded as typical of the milder opinions which had sustained the Empire. But watching, on their walks together, her interactions with Cambodians in their own language, watching her engage with them and make them nod with agreement, or smile broadly, or even burst into laughter, unsettled him, and shocked him into a disoriented admiration that deepened his response to her in a most inconvenient fashion. For it not only meant that he needed to change his plans for the future, it also called upon him to rethink his dismissiveness and regard what Edith did in Phnom Penh as a form of praxis, albeit deeply alien to him, which was not about soft-pedalling conflict, but about engaging with Cambodians and really attempting to understand. He began to think it was a form of self-transcendence, and it undermined him even further to find himself overturned politically by such an attitude.

22

Sandie Hamilton had been taken aback when H.E. had asked her if she would be willing to row for the Embassy in the boat race in the festival of Bon Om Tuk. But the Ambassador had been very understanding when she had gone to him to complain about Wilfred Jamie, and that had been a great relief to her because she had known that he was great friends with the queer Head of Chancery and had thought he would simply dismiss her complaints. Instead he had listened sympathetically and ordered Jamie to go away for a while. Sandie enjoyed the sense that she had won a victory over that horrible man who had treated her with such contempt. (Head of Pansery – she had tried that joke out on Peter, but he had only smiled absent-mindedly.) So when, soon afterwards, the Ambassador had asked her if she would be willing to do this rowing, she had felt disposed to listen to him even when he seemed to be asking her to do something rather undignified. He had explained that it was a hearts and minds exercise, that the Bon Om Tuk was very important to Cambodians, because it celebrated a key naval victory by Jayavarman VII, and the Embassy entering a boat in it would constitute a respectful gesture which he was sure that Prince Sihanouk would heartily welcome. And he had asked her if she would also be willing to approach two other secretaries (she could choose which ones would be most suitable, and they could be chosen from either the diplomatic or the business sections). Being given this responsibility made her feel gratifyingly recognised and gave her the sense that it might portend good things for the future.

So she had made her choices. She had chosen Cynthia and Joan, because they were the ones she found the easiest company, and the three of them had presented themselves, with some sense of novelty and excitement, at the river at the time appointed by Major Bill Noon, who was in charge of it all. Sandie felt intimidated by the major, who always looked so serious, as though even leading his little daughter by the hand was as grave as driving a tank. He was certainly impressive, and the rumours that he was a spy added to his mystique because there was anyway something terribly deep about him, as though his mind was always elsewhere. He did lose his temper quite often but you respected him even then because there was something formidable and explosive about it, quite unlike that petty, screaming temper of Wilfred Jamie. She had been surprised when one of her chosen secretaries had said that the major was very attractive because he was much too menacing-looking for her own taste, she thought him ugly, in fact, with those deep creases in his face. Even so, she found it bewildering that he showed no signs at all of thinking her attractive, that there was no sign of anything remotely like a man's response on his part, so that he treated her as though she were a small boy – she found that very unnerving.

That strangeness had been compounded because the whole exercise involved her and the other secretaries forgetting that they were women: in fact they were officially not female because H.E. was anxious that Cambodians might not like women being involved. Women weren't explicitly banned, it was just that there was an assumption that they didn't compete, so she and the other girls were dressed up in overalls and caps to disguise them. And it became increasingly clear that they were just there to make up the numbers. Major Noon taught them the basics of how to row and keep the oars going in time, but it was clear when they were actually out on the river that the three girls weren't expected to contribute much to the actual propulsion of the boat. But then that was almost as true of everyone other than the major – even the other three men were hardly more than passengers compared to the military attaché who was the 'engine'. This was the word one of the men applied to Bill, meaning he sat in the middle of the boat and powered it along mostly on his own while the rest of them tried not to get in his way, though they often *did* get in his way because of the difference between how quickly and how far he could fire his oars backwards, and the slowness, and the short distance, of the rest of them, especially the three girls. At the start the boat was constantly coming to a halt because the oars got tangled up with each other, and the major had to adjust himself to the gulf in oar-firing distances, which required patience that he conspicuously didn't possess.

The whole thing became an awful ordeal. She had twice got long splinters, from the oars, lodged deep in her palms, and had got stiffness for days in her arms and legs, but had only been dismissed by Bill when she had told him about them – she shouldn't be stiff in those places, he had told her, because that showed her technique was poor, and that she hadn't followed his instructions properly. They had to practice in the early morning, just as it was getting light, in order to avoid the worst heat and humidity, but, even so, by the time they were finishing, it was already terribly sticky, and Sandie hated the thought of herself in the overalls and cap, and with her hair and face thoroughly soaked with sweat. It turned out that Cynthia and Joan were close friends and they tended to whisper together and exclude her, and, at the second practice, when they were getting changed, she overheard Cynthia telling Joan about the dominoes that Peter had arranged on the table in his flat and she explained the joke to Joan, who laughed. Though the laugh sounded a bit forced, as if she felt she ought to think it funny, but didn't really, or didn't really get it. Sandie couldn't quite hear the explanation and it occurred to her that Peter had never explained the joke to her. As she zipped up her overalls she felt all the strength leave her body. She forced herself to walk towards the boat, but, as she was sitting down, she felt terribly weak and dizzy, and had to call out to Bill saying she wasn't well. She had been worried he would lose his temper, but he was surprisingly sympathetic, and helped her out of the boat. She had the freakish idea, then – and thought she might mention it to Keith, who enjoyed it so much when she said such things – that it seemed very out of place, almost impossible, that Major Noon and Peter Cook could co-exist, because they were so alien to each other, the Major so entirely removed from anything comic, and Peter so immersed in it.

At the third practice they had been joined by Keith who sat at one end of the boat drumming and they were supposed to row in time to his beat. So it was no surprise that, on the day of the festival, he was there in that role, but it was a great shock to her to find that Peter was also there and had a role in the boat. Sandie thought that Peter had been avoiding her for a couple of weeks and she had been desperately wondering how to revive the fire between them, going over and over that first night when she had set out to attract him, and had worn her brown linen dress whose unbelted plainness she knew was especially becoming for her figure. She had worn a very brief petticoat under it and she remembered how Peter, at a point in the evening when she had thought that things were still not fully decided, had simply taken off his clothes and slipped into her bed. She had never known a boy before who had done anything as bold as that. She had been flabbergasted, and still gasped remembering how she had pulled the dress over her head then, and removed other undergarments, and stood facing him wearing only that petticoat.

And now here was Peter, on the day of the festival, wearing his de Gaulle uniform, and being horrible to her, standing with a very stiff back and tilting his head upwards and away and refusing to speak anything but French except for the phrase *method acting*, talking about Marlon Brando and James Dean, and saying very slowly that the *langue anglaise* was *merde*. She had been trying to say that she needed urgently to speak to him, that they needed to talk seriously, but he persisted with French, when he knew she didn't understand it very well, and it was awkward anyway because Keith was there and she had to whisper, and Peter had been bending down cupping his hand to his ear like a hard-of-hearing old person, and frowning, and grunting in a French way. And then Keith came over, laughing hysterically like a hopeless nitwit, and Peter spoke in French to him so that he could interpret, and Keith informed her that the general was very preoccupied at the moment with pressing matters of state, especially connected to Algeria, and groups of secretive insurgents who were plotting to assassinate him. So now Peter and Keith were clubbing together against her, and she felt, standing between them in her overalls and cap, like a thirteen-year-old boy who was being mocked by adults. This sharing between them of an in-joke was especially juvenile, and they just seemed terribly pleased with themselves, as Keith addressed Peter as general or president, or Mr. General President, and Peter would get furiously indignant when Keith said that the general was a *bouffon*, and Keith kept repeating *bouffon bouffon*, and laughing hysterically, as though the word itself was somehow a marvellous witticism.

She wanted to dismiss them and get on with the rowing, but when they were underweigh it suddenly struck her that the Embassy boat was entirely different to the others in the race. Their boat was English, and a different shape altogether to the Cambodian dragon boats, where the rowers sat or even stood in rows of two and used long paddles instead of oars. Maybe it was being unnerved by Keith and Peter, but she found this sudden realisation, of a radical difference so obvious and yet not previously recognised by her (when, after all, she had seen the dragon boats numerous times) made her dizzy with disorientation.

But then, when she truly entered the rhythm of the rowing, she was amazed by how well it was going and found herself thoroughly enjoying her part in a marvellous, exotic spectacle, with about fifteen boats competing on the broad, magnificent tropical river, with the sound of xylophones drifting across the water, and fireworks exploding high overhead. She looked forward to the part after the boats had competed, which she had enjoyed in previous years, and which would embody the importance of the whole event, when the Prince, wearing a golden helmet and carrying a crimson scabbard, would cut the symbolic cord. The colours shimmered in the sun – some of the rowers wore black trousers and red shirts, some wore sampots tucked under yellow shirts, some had black shorts and purple shirts, and others white shirts and red berets. Two of the boats were manned by the Mohammedan people, the Chams, who rowed standing up.

She was astonished by how well the Embassy boat was doing, because somehow they had found a rhythm that propelled it with exhilarating swiftness and they were in fifth or sixth place, hurtling across the water with a fluency they had never previously managed, as Keith drummed and drummed at great speed. She had her back to Peter, who was standing at the back of the boat, and she managed to ignore what he was saying at first, she heard only a sort of rhythm with a long refrain which involved something about Russian women, but eventually she couldn't avoid turning her head briefly to look at him and watched him saying 'Aya!' and stamping his foot in time to the oars. Once she had seen him, though, she seemed to hear him better and noticed how this 'Aya' was said at regular intervals and the refrain was about how Russian women were only interested in attraction as it related to forces of gravity and mass. She then started to understand that the refrain was a culmination of a set of remarks about the sexual habits of women of different races, and she found this outrageously unamusing – that French women preferred this time of day, and Khmer women another, and English women might possibly be persuaded if you happened to catch them off-guard in a chance couple of minutes during a time it was impossible to guess, and Russian women etc etc. What was especially infuriating was that, now he wasn't speaking to her, Peter wasn't speaking French any more, he was speaking in English with an exaggerated French accent, and she knew the part about Russian women must be connected to that arrogant girl at the Russian embassy. She started suddenly to feel exhausted, to feel weak, so that she forgot the rhythm and got her oars caught up in Cynthia's and that created a domino effect with the other oars, and the whole thing was worse because they happened to be close to another boat at that point. She wasn't sure what happened after that before she found herself in the water, desperate to avoid being struck by oars, swimming under water with her eyes shut until she felt she was away from the boats enough to surface, when she found that Keith was next to her, asking if she was alright. She knew then that he must have followed her, to make sure she was safe, and she felt awkward and embarrassed about that, and a bit annoyed because she knew she was safe anyway – she was a strong swimmer. They were swimming to the side of the river when she was surprised to see Keith's friend Yuri there waiting for them, and when they were out of the water he greeted them saying how anxious he'd been – saying this not just to Keith but to her, frowning with concern and looking at her with his intense brown eyes.

23

'You know, in truth, everything about Rudolph Nureyev.'

The taunting voice from behind Yuri Shunin at the bar was Alain Jouve's, but Yuri turned with a swiftness that was intended to intimidate the Frenchman, and was delighted with its success, as he noted how the small man stepped back with a disconcerted grimace. He surprised Jouve further by replying, 'What if I do? What then?'

'I know you do. And you do not think him a bourgeois, or a decadent.'

Yuri shrugged and paid the barman, and gathered up the drinks, and pushed past Jouve, catching him deliberately on the shoulder with the point of his elbow. Once back at his table, though, with Ariadna and Dmitri stalely repeating their usual chat, he thought that this brush with Jouve had been the most enjoyable part so far of the evening at the *ZigZag*, and it was already late. When he had arrived at the table, as well, he had been unnerved by the impression that they had been talking animatedly and had abruptly stopped when they saw him returning, and that had deepened his growing fear that they were excluding him, and were sharing doubts about him. They were becoming stale for him because their opinions struck him as wholly predictable, but he knew that their conformism was no worse that it had been before – it was only that he was becoming increasingly impatient with it, and he was anxious that they might be aware of his impatience. His confusion was so loud inside his own head that he was growing convinced that they must be able to hear it, and that they must even be able to guess at the odd desires that accompanied his confusion, to catch the shadows from him of the vivid images which disturbed, excited and then sickened him, as though they leaked out of his ears. He drank his Tiger beer much too quickly as he listened to

Ariadna expressing her scorn for the role of the U.S. in the recent missile crisis, and watched her poodle, Dmitri, fawning and nodding his eager agreement.

Yuri glanced around, and stood up, and, when the other two looked at him, he pointed at his empty glass and headed towards the bar. It was a Friday night and the *ZigZag* was so crowded that he was only a couple of yards from their table before he was surrounded by people, and he welcomed the sense that Ariadna and Dmitri could no longer see him easily. Jouve was suddenly there – he was so tiny that it was easy for him to disappear in a crowd, but Yuri knew that he must have headed for a point where they would coincide. Jouve took a self-conscious step towards Yuri and said, 'Last time you very badly damaged my face.' He reached out his hand and touched Yuri's arm.

Yuri shrugged. 'You deserved it.' He stared doubtfully at the hand that Jouve had placed on his arm and said, as though with resignation, 'Nureyev was born on a Trans-Siberian train near Irkutsk in Siberia. His mother had been travelling to Vladivostok where his father was stationed. His father was a Red Army political commissar. He grew up in a village in the republic of Bashkortostan.'

'A very poor background.'

'By 1958 he was very famous, but he was mistrusted because he was a rebel, and refused to conform. So the authorities refused to allow him to leave the Soviet Union.'

'Imagine how frightening that would be. How isolated you would feel when your colleagues and your bosses were always pointing their hands at you. Whispers about you all the time. So you could never be yourself.'

'But then the Kirov's leading dancer had to drop out of a tour to the West because of an injury and they were forced to let him go.'

'And in Paris he was adored. In *Firebird* he wore a turban with a spray of feathers, and an ultramarine costume with a white sash, and his thighs bulged inside his tights, and he

166

held himself like a cat, and he announced himself by running across the back of the stage.'

'And in June last year, at the airport in Paris, he defected with the help of the French police.'

'And then he could translate himself into something other.'

Yuri watched Jouve pronounce that last word as though its stress were on its last syllable – oth*eur*, to rhyme with voyeur.

'Something oth*eur* – an entirely new and extremely fulfilled version of himself.'

They were being jostled on each side, the bar was so full, and the smell of sweat and smoke was so dense it was a taste in Yuri's mouth. He tensed because he and this thin Frenchman in his tropical-weight Parisian suit in dark blue, with a white silk handkerchief just visible in its breast pocket, were now, for a long moment, only gazing at each other. Then Jouve reached across that divide and loosely grasped a corner of Yuri's shirt near his elbow and tugged it, nodding his head towards the door. Admiring Jouve's courage, given how he had been punched by Yuri before, Yuri followed him, partly because Jouve appeared to be speaking in code when he spoke about Nureyev attaining his otherness, as though he had made inquiries about Yuri. But then what inquiries could he have made that would have revealed such a carefully hidden hankering on Yuri's part? He had been anxious that Ariadna and Dmitri had guessed this about him, but they wouldn't have told Jouve. Was it possible that they had whispered it to someone else, who had passed it on? He knew that there had been some sort of interaction between Ariadna and Peter Cook.

Yuri couldn't recognise himself as he followed Jouve out of the bar, as though his arms and legs were being operated by someone else, and now, where his will had been, which he located behind his forehead, there was only a hurt and shocked numbness. A sudden waft carried the stench of the monsoon drains into his face, a fetor like a warning of something underhand, secreted in a mildewed corner and rotting.

But there, across the road, and high in the sky above the buildings, was a thin moon lying prostrate, and Yuri remembered that he had seen moons like that before in Cambodia, but he didn't think he had ever seen one in Russia, that was so thin and lay so horizontal, – maybe it was an angle created by looking from the tropics? Its oddness struck him as having an unguessable connection with what was happening to him. How could his government send Russians to such strange places and expect them to remain unchanged?

They were standing now next to a half-lit wall and Jouve said, 'What are you looking at?' He was stroking Yuri's face with a single finger.

Yuri nodded at the sky and said, 'There. The moon.'

Jouve turned and looked and said, 'Ah yes it's beautiful. So romantic.'

Yuri gave Jouve a warning look: he felt he was being coerced. Jouve tugged his shirt again and led him along the wall to where the light didn't reach, then he stretched upwards and kissed Yuri softly on the lips. The stubbly scratchiness of the skin around Jouve's mouth shocked Yuri and made him suddenly and alarmingly conscious of what he was doing, and there was also the slight funk of Jouve's male sweat, half-covered by cologne. He felt aroused but angry and he pushed Jouve away heavily, and Jouve stumbled backwards. How could Jouve have known that Yuri felt this desire, when, after all, the desire wasn't thoroughly clear to Yuri himself, was only an alien mood that sometimes settled on him? If it was evident to Jouve, was it also evident to others who knew him? Yuri watched Jouve recover from his stumble and move towards Yuri again and reach his hand onto Yuri's head and say, 'You should get rid of this absurd 'illock of 'air.'

Yuri grasped Jouve's thin shoulder and stared at him and squeezed hard – he wanted Jouve to know how strong he was, and how dangerous. 'Illock of air?'

'Yes, this grotesque...tuft.' Jouve was pushing two fingers through the strands of hair that remained at the front of Yuri's head.

They stared at each other and Yuri watched Jouve smile his taunting smile and Yuri now enjoyed this because it was so novel to him and he enjoyed, also, Jouve's comic posture and his satirical smile. Jouve was twisting himself exaggeratedly to his right, tucking his right shoulder under and looking up, with his eyebrows raised from behind his other shoulder, and it was very silly. Yuri laughed. 'Illock of air!' Now that phrase seemed like one of the funniest things that Yuri had ever heard. He had made inquiries about Jouve and found he worked for Francophone radio, and he had listened to it and been amazed by it, by how noisy it was, by how it darted from one subject to another, and from music to speech. He found it very exciting and somehow youthful, and it had made him feel more intrigued about this Frenchman who had singled him out and taunted him. Even Jouve's association with the editor of the newspaper *Réalités Cambodgiennes*, Jean Barré, intrigued Yuri, because the Soviet straitjacket Yuri had inhabited all his life made him yearn for the unorthodox and the unpredictable, and the mysterious loucheness of that gross Frenchman, with his incomprehensible link to Sihanouk, was fascinatingly exotic. He felt a powerful temptation, driven by a lifetime of frustration, to annihilate his former self by burying it in dangerous and ambiguous addictions.

Yuri knew it was unwise simply to drift away from the *ZigZag* without saying anything to Ariadna and Dmitri, especially when they were already growing dubious about him, but he wanted to cast off his usual caution thoroughly and recklessly, he was desperate not to care, and Jouve was leading him away, as though the crucial point had already been decided, and chattering about his work, and his circle of outlandish friends, and Yuri was fascinated by Jouve's cynicism and his jadedness about bare-faced corruption in high places, and his dismissive tolerance about sexual extravagance and experiment in low places, and his tone and his experience were so far removed from Yuri's habitual life that he found he needed to continue to listen, and that he needed to enter Jouve's world and understand it, and be, to some extent, a part of it. Especially because Jouve's knowledge gave him a different insight into questions which had already been troubling Yuri – about the activities of the British military attaché Bill Noon and his connections to others, in particular the American ambassador, who was also friends, Jouve said, with Peter Cook, who was himself somehow involved in secret machinations with Major Noon. Cook had also somehow inveigled himself into the favours of Sihanouk and had become a regular visitor to his court. Jouve enjoyed himself hugely describing a grotesque rumour involving Joe Keane and a transvestite, that Keane had paid a Cambodian boy to dress up as a woman, but the boy had taken offence and had beaten Keane up.

So Yuri felt it to be almost a privilege when he was sharing a cyclo with Alain, and the cooler night air was rushing into his face and he was laughing because even quite trivial things that Alain said were very amusing when they were pronounced in his preposterous accent, and the humdrum streets of Phnom Penh seemed more vivid and exciting. Alain's flat turned out to be surprisingly spacious, and it was very tastefully furnished, with matching rattan sofa and armchairs, plushly upholstered. Alain seated Yuri in one of them and bustled into his kitchen and emerged with a bottle of Chablis in an ice bucket, which he placed on one of the two large drums, which stood like side tables between the armchairs. Alain was still chattering, and offered Yuri a cigarette and lit it, and Yuri listened in a daze and gazed at the curved sword, which hung on the wall between two long knives, and Alain told him the sword was from Laos, and the knives were Shan knives. Alain poured the wine into long glasses and said, 'You must've been concealing your emotions for a long time.'

'No, I...'

'No, really, it is very clear. And there are many men like yourself, who are denying who they are essentially.'

Yuri reached across to the other drum, to drop his ash into the Bakelite ashtray there, and noticed now, and realised he must've not wanted to look too closely before, that it was mounted on a teak stand which had been inserted into the skull of what appeared to be a tiger with its bony mouth full of perfect teeth. Yuri felt a violent urge to stand up and leave but Alain was expounding his theories about widespread repression and he felt that the weight of Alain's speech was forcing him back into his soft chair, and he felt profound relief at the idea of being passive and allowing himself to be led where this man wanted him to go, of entirely handing over his powers of will and self-determination.

24

Dudley Moore was trying to buy heroin for Lenny Bruce. He had been driving around in a dense fog for nearly two hours, squinting through his windscreen at the dissolving walls of sulphur that swallowed the light from his headlights and reflected it back as a diffuse, grimy, yellowish glow. His neck was stiff from hunching his head forward to peer above his steering wheel, and strain above it from his short height, as his car crawled along to addresses he'd been given by a couple of jazz musicians he knew, including one in Stepney and one in Hackney. But he had found no-one in, or had been been treated to blank and amazed faces and turned swiftly away. At one point he turned off the Third Programme because a Bartok string quartet had been playing, with those chords that sounded like sudden sharp dismay, like a terrible diagnosis, and it reminded him that he might never compose the symphony he had always wanted to write – he might never compose it because his mind wasn't capacious enough, his mind couldn't extend itself into the vast territory that a symphony needed to discover, but also because the modern world was all wrong for the sort of big, generous statement he would want his symphony to make. These chords by Bartok bullied him into understanding that his sort of major affirmation was no longer possible.

Then he went south of the river, to Catford, to where he'd been told Harry Farrell lived, and he liked Harry, who was a saxophonist who Dudley had played with a couple of times, and he was a relaxed and funny man, and an accomplished musician, one you could tell thought about it hard and was working at making something of his own. Dudley pressed the buzzer, the button he thought must be right, but it was answered by a young man who looked like a teddy boy, who said that Harry lived on the third floor, and to go up. Dudley had noticed the slight flicker in the teddy boy's face, the one that indicates recognition, or at least *that* puzzlement – *haven't I seen you somewhere?* And *that* starting to say something and stopping, that meant he wasn't quite sure and didn't want to name the wrong star, *that* turning away surprised by shyness, showing Dudley the 'duck's arse' at the back of his hair as he climbed the stairs. But the puzzlement had been combined with a smile, and Dudley liked that, because it felt welcoming, it seemed to say that this member of the public felt well disposed to him and his reputation. It meant all the more that a type so foreign to Dudley, a teddy boy, had treated him to this shy smile.

Dudley found the door in the dim stairway and knocked. There was no response for several minutes then a gruff voice called 'What?'

'Harry? It's Dudley.'

'Dudley who? Fuck off.'

'Dudley Moore.'

'Fuck off. I'm asleep.'

'Sorry, Harry. Can I have a word?' Dudley was trying to call through the door, but, at the same time, to keep his voice low because, after all, he was in search of something illegal.

'Can't hear you, because I'm asleep.' It was nearly four o' clock in the afternoon but Harry could've been playing until four in the morning.

'Sorry, Harry.'

The door half-opened. Harry was drawing a dressing gown around his ample body but Dudley caught sight of a hairy chest and paunch above a pair of skewed Y-fronts. Harry stared at Dudley balefully, 'I'm sleep-walking.'

Harry hadn't opened the door fully to say this, and he didn't open it any further as he turned and walked back towards his bed, but Dudley followed him, abashed, into the room that smelled of ancient nicotine and bed sheets long unwashed and half-dried towels. 'Saw you on the telly the other night,' Harry said.

Harry's tone wasn't encouraging. 'Oh?' Dudley said anxiously.

'Playing, yes. Some sort of variety show.'

'Oh yes, it was...'

'Uncanny resemblance to Errol Garner in style.'

'Well I love Errol Garner.'

'We've always known *that* haven't we.' Very deliberately he drew the curtains back from his casement window and stood in front of it and nodded as though he'd just been given terrible news. 'Again. Fog. Again.'

'Fog again, yes,' Dudley said, and felt like punching himself in the face. Should he just leave now? Instead he seated himself gingerly on an armchair, pushing a shirt and a jumper to one side, to make enough room. The light was dim and the room was freezing cold but sweaty.

'You can't see it now for the fog but there's a tree about ten feet in front of this window.'

'That'll be nice in the Spring.'

'Not really, you see, because this is a soot tree.'

'Soot tree?'

'Yes. Instead of leaves it has soot. It has adapted to its surroundings, it's – like a form of camouflage. Green would draw too much attention, so it just secretes soot. More and more soot accumulates on its branches. It's a survival strategy.'

Harry sat down on the edge of his bed and closed his eyes for a couple of minutes and let his mouth sag open and Dudley thought he might just slip away while the saxophonist wasn't looking. Instead he said, 'It's a tribute. Playing like that for me is a tribute to Errol Garner.'

Harry opened his eyes and stared at Dudley with his sagging face, his heavy features, his scruffy beard, 'Tribute?'

'Yes. Bringing him to a larger audience.'

'So you acknowledge that that audience on the telly hasn't heard Errol Garner?'

'Well yes.'

'How can they get it then?'

'Get it?'

'Get it that it's a tribute?'

'Well they need to hear it first and then...'

'No, Dudley, because they think you invented that. They think it was you who invented that style of playing. So if, then, some members of that audience hear Errol Garner...'

'But what can I do? That's how I love to play, because I love Errol Garner and...'

'It's stealing, Dudley.' Harry was sounding less angry now, more understanding. 'You've taken that and then you play it with that cheeky smile on your face, and everybody loves you. I mean I can see how it happened, and I know how badly you need to be famous.'

Dudley found the tired, understanding manner more upsetting than the angry one, especially because he recognised the truth of the last statement and recognised that people like Harry, who he respected, must be saying that about him. 'Is that so wrong, Harry?'

'No, no, Dudley. There's a lot of chance involved though in the fame business don't you think?'

'Maybe, partly, but...'

'Of course there are people like Einstein and Picasso and Miles Davis. They're famous for a definite reason. They're just exceptional people, aren't they?'

Dudley, faced with Harry's questioning stare, was forced to nod. 'They're exceptional yes.'

'But other people – there's a lot of chance involved. Being in the right place at the right time, knowing the right people. Having a face that fits.' Harry gazed intently and lovingly at Dudley. 'You do, Dudley, you do. I mean you have a *lovely* face.'

'There's a lot of hard work, Harry.'

175

'Yes I'm sure. But there's a lot of people working hard in mines and factories. And they don't appear very often in *The Daily Express*. Have you ever imagined, Dudley, a world that was even just *slightly* different, where chance had worked differently for all the famous people, and all those names were different?' Harry was reaching into a pack of cigarettes and putting one in his mouth. He offered one to Dudley, who shook his head; then, looking around for matches, Harry took the cigarette out of his mouth. 'Strange-sounding names – you wake up one day in this skewed world and where before there was Rock Hudson and Doris Day you've got Cliff Gibson and Laverne Knight. And these aliens look quite similar, these body-snatchers, the man is also tall and dark, and the woman is blonde and toothsome, but you do a double-take and you can see they're quite different? Your bearings would be completely lost.'

Dudley squirmed slightly in his seat and noticed, under his left buttock, something hard and compact, which he extricated. It was a box of matches, which he handed to Harry, as he said, 'A world like that would be completely different from ours.'

'No it wouldn't, you see.' Harry was lighting his cigarette. 'Because Cliff and Laverne aren't Einstein or Picasso. They're not even Richard Burton. They're just carbon copies of Rock and Doris, and thousands of others could be copies like that. They don't do anything that makes even a slight difference. Like, say, – just as a random example – Errol Garner.'

Dudley felt himself shrink inside the armchair, felt himself shrivel until he was tiny, thinking about the symphony he would never be able to compose. He was a long way now from being able to raise the subject of heroin, and it took a huge physical effort for him to haul himself out of the armchair, mutter that he had to be going, deliberately inaudible, and leave. Outside it was even colder than before, and the fog was thicker and more yellow now because it was reflecting the streetlights that were coming on, and the traffic was heavier, and he stared at all the vehicles before he climbed into his car, needing to rest before he started to drive, and then he heard the newsboys calling above the traffic noise, like warning voices in the fog. He opened his car door and seated himself behind the wheel but couldn't face driving so he switched on the Third Programme and recognised Beethoven's fourth symphony and found it, even from this small source of sound, astonishing, and sat listening to it all the way through. He drove north then, across the river, and parked somewhere in the City, and then fell asleep – like Harry he had been playing until the early hours of the morning, but unlike Harry he'd been playing in a fashionable club where Lenny Bruce had also been appearing. When he woke he felt too groggy to drive so he climbed stiffly out of his car and headed down the street looking for a pub, and found a big Edwardian place. He ordered a whisky and sat at a table near a couple in their forties who were holding hands, and noticed, also there, a Chelsea pensioner, two ancient women, a pair of very young lovers, also holding hands, and another teddy boy.

He gazed out of the window at the street where the fog was less obvious now in the dark but was still there inside the darkness, drifting visibly sometimes in the streetlights, and he thought about Harry's tree of soot and how that soot was falling all the time on Londoners and falling on all the buildings and the Thames, and the river carried tides of soot and coal dust and industrial chemicals and household filth and rolled it along relentlessly to wash ashore in the wharves at Battersea and at – no no no, he had to stop this direction and think elsewhere, because he was famous and lived a great life. Last night, in the basement of the *Red Stoat*, the club that Waldo Vaughan had opened in Soho, he had played and played for hours, and a growing crowd of fashionable young people, with a very high proportion of single and beautiful women, had gathered around him. And they had all adored him, and Lenny Bruce had joined them, this very hip American comedian, and had seen all these people adore him, and Dudley insisted to himself that his life was full and vibrant, and he wouldn't be bullied by jealous people like Harry into thinking otherwise.

He wished that, in a moment like that in the *Red Stoat*, he could live fully in the here and now, because even then he somehow stepped outside it and looked forward, or elsewhere. He felt, now, he should dwell on the *Red Stoat* moment, now that the Thames and its tides of shit started to wash through him, and he tried to remember what his psychoanalyst had said and to grasp onto it. And he remembered him asking Dudley when he had felt happiest and Dudley had had to go through a long process of removing sex from consideration, because it loomed so large. And now, sitting in that City pub, he recalled an evening with Peter Cook after one of the performances at the Edinburgh fringe when they had been drinking in Dudley's digs, when they had made each other laugh and laugh and laugh, so that tears had streamed down Dudley's face, and he felt that then with a sharp pang of loss.

He couldn't bear to go on looking for heroin, and he couldn't bear to go and admit that to Lenny, who had seemed so desperate for the drug. So he went back to his flat thinking a sleep would help. And he found there that his agent had sent him another film script and he glanced at the title page, which said *Bedazzled* by Keith Entwistle.

25

The first time that Edith Hartnell knocked on Hector Perch's door and found him not there she was surprised but didn't think it especially unusual. It was unusual because it was so early in the morning, half past eight, and Hector wasn't an early riser, but she hadn't arranged to be there. She had wanted to surprise him, as she had done once before, early in their affair, when she had knocked on his door at a similar time and taken warm croissants. She had sent him back to bed and made coffee and then sat on the side of his bed, and she had often recalled how excited and happy she had felt at that moment, perched there next to Hector with the taste of fresh coffee and warm croissant in her mouth early in the morning near the start of the rainy season. Her strong feeling when she received no answer to her knock was only regret at not being able to repeat that marvellous occasion. But maybe the attempt at repetition had anyway been wrong, and she felt pathetic standing in front of his door with the warm paper bag of croissants hanging limply from her hand.

After that she had telephoned Hector's number several times, and she had started to worry that he was avoiding her, so when she knocked on his door the second time she was worried that they were heading for a confrontation, or that she might even find him with another woman. As she stood alone in front of his door, she could hear the sound of government radio from an adjoining apartment, a broadcast of one of Prince Sihanouk's speeches: Cambodia was an island of peace, he was saying, and Cambodians were superior to the Vietnamese and the Thais. A shaft of light fell across her from a window just beside the door, and she experienced a sudden vision of herself from above, as though she were in a film and the camera had been shifted to a lofty height. She looked down at herself from this steep perspective and saw a middle-aged woman in a light floral dress, a woman who had spent a long, deliberate time on her hair and make-up before she had set out, knowing that her over-preparation marked her anxiety that she was on the verge of a most unwelcome change. From that height, then, she was sure that this change was taking place on the briefly illuminated landing.

She was half a mile away before she was conscious of herself again, knowing she must have walked down the stairs and the intervening distance without seeing what was around her. She looked then and understood that she was walking down a boulevard and heading for Madam Penh's hill and understood why she had taken that direction. She realised, also, that she had been remembering the moment when she had been jilted when she was sixteen-years-old, and that this moment had recurred to her throughout her life. She thought again, as she always did, how strange this was, given how early in her life this experience had happened, that she should dwell on it so much later in life, as she did now, at the age of fifty. But she had dwelt on it because the moment had been so painful, unbearably painful. The boy had been nineteen, and when he had said he didn't want to see her again they were beside the river in Shrewsbury where she grew up, and he had tried to mimic deep sadness, but his acting was so poor that his lack of concern was utterly transparent. So she had felt hopelessly powerless and empty, even though they had only been seeing each other for about a month, and little of a seriously sexual kind had happened. That pain had engraved itself deeply, and she recalled it again in this different place, this Phnom Penh boulevard, and in this different time, when the distant girl in Shrewsbury was in most other ways a stranger to her.

She approached the stupa near Madam Penh's hill and deliberately chose an *astrologue* she hadn't previously used, a very old man with an emaciated, wizened face, and waited her turn to pay the five cents, and whispered a prayer with her eyes shut, then stuck a pin into the pack to select a palmleaf card. The *astrologue* looked surprised at the card and gazed at her quizzically before pronouncing a sentence in Khmer she found difficult to follow, but which, repeated slowly several times, she understood to mean something like 'A squirrel can run across the surface of a trap but the elephant's great size may cause him to fall into the pit.' Edith was annoyed by this portentous nonsense, especially after the long ordeal of translation, and hurried away.

As she slowed and started to walk aimlessly through the streets she missed Wilfred and regretted how she had neglected him after the start of her affair with Hector – she should have confided in him because he was so understanding and she knew that she could trust him completely. She had been very angry when Christopher had sent him away, pretending it was a holiday, and she missed Wilfred now because she would love to be able to discuss Hector's absence with him, and she felt acutely that there was no-one else that she could trust enough to raise the subject with so that it wasn't poisoned by her own helpless bereftness, and so that it could be contemplated rationally and its range of possible explanations properly understood.

She was drifting now but found that she was heading for the Embassy and understood that she half-consciously believed that the answer to what had happened to Hector was most likely to be answered there. Once inside she noticed that Keith was standing in the doorway of the communications expert Reg Armstrong and she remembered that Hector had occasionally spoken warmly about Keith and it occurred to her that Keith might know something. As she walked towards him she heard the tone of what he was saying rather than words, though she did hear 'it's really not', pronounced emphatically. What struck her most, though, was that Keith was trying to appease Reg, to assure him about something, and then she noticed that he looked like a child who had been reprimanded. Keith had always struck her as childlike, as more immature even than his twenty-four years, and she had always found it hard to take him seriously, which might also explain why she had forgotten that Hector had praised him. Even so it was odd that someone in Reg's lowly position should feel entitled to reprimand another member of the staff, and, now that she thought about it, she remembered that she had heard of his warning Peter Cook and, even more remarkably, Bill Noon. She greeted the two men and noticed that Reg was seated with his earphones in his hand and his head inclined to one side and a rueful look on his face as though he was contemplating a new taste in his mouth that he was sceptical about. 'By the way,' she said, 'I was approached the other day by a journalist who writes for *Réalités Cambodgiennes* who wanted to do a piece on the Embassy, but I thought we'd better get some advice about it from someone with journalistic experience. Do you know anyone like that?'

Keith shook his head, 'Can't say I do.'

'There's Hector Perch,' Reg said.

Edith looked at Reg and the flashing lights and dials and black boxes that surrounded him.

'Oh yes, of course,' Keith said.

'Hector Perch,' Edith said. 'Yes I think I've met him.'

One of the black boxes howled with static and she was conscious that Reg was watching her closely. She returned his gaze, 'Do you know how I could contact him?'

'Keith knows him much better than me.'

'I know the digs where he lives,' Keith said. 'But he goes to the *ZigZag* quite a lot and I normally meet him there.'

Edith almost asked when Keith had seen him last but thought better of it. 'Well I wouldn't want to intrude by visiting him at home...'

'Now you mention it he hasn't been around much recently, but he goes away quite suddenly at times –

182

Battambang, that sort of place. Takes a lot of risks actually. Has spoken to the rebels, even.' Keith glanced anxiously at Reg, who looked long-suffering.

Edith felt so queasy she found herself saying, 'Perhaps he has a companion I could...' and abruptly stopping.

A black box again uttered a broken wail, while the three of them looked away from each other. Edith wondered if the two men could guess anything from her tone of voice, but she thought that neither of them were the most insightful of people. What Keith said next proved her all too correct: 'Well no, he very much prefers to keep his options open, frequents some of those riverside places, amongst others.' Keith was smiling defiantly at Reg.

Hopeless, hopeless, Edith thought as she walked away – these young men are hopeless. She left the Embassy again because she didn't want to see Christopher, and she couldn't stop herself from walking, as though she might somehow come across Hector randomly somewhere unexpected in Phnom Penh, and she went to *La Lanterne* because she and Hector, foolishly, brazenly almost, had eaten together there on a couple of occasions. The door was open so she wandered in but they weren't really open yet, it was only 11.30, but the very plump French proprietor, who was smoking a thin cigar, recognised her and told her to take a seat and called to his Cambodian wife to look after her. She took a seat at a table near the window and remembered she had eaten at that table once with Wilfred – Hector and Wilfred, the people she had liked best in Phnom Penh, and both gone, and she felt a surge of anger and, at the same time, a sudden flush of intense heat. She wondered helplessly if she had simply forgotten something that Hector had told her, that she was simply getting something pathetically wrong, forgetfully wrong, and that this forgetfulness was another menopausal symptom, like the wave of sweat that now broke across her. The Cambodian wife, almost as large as her husband, bustled in, bound tight in a black sarong, and frowned impatiently and remained impatient even though Edith asked her in perfect Khmer if it was alright if she simply had a cup of coffee. She felt a strong desire to perform a Buddhist ritual she had seen where you release a bird and pray that your own soul will also be liberated, will be released from the misery of desire that drives your soul through one cycle after another of human meaninglessness, and she gazed across the square at the police station and felt that Hector was very far away.

At home that evening with Christopher she found it impossible not to compare him unfavourably with Hector. She couldn't blame him, on this occasion, for his lack of conversation which before she had contrasted with Hector's marvellous stories about his experiences around the world. All evening Christopher talked about his disquiet about the role he had given Peter Cook, how he had asked Peter to win over Sihanouk, how he had relied on Peter's charm to win the propaganda battle, and it had all seemed to be going very well. Peter had taken an enormous amount of persuading because it went so much against the grain of his satirical instincts, but Christopher had insisted that he must do it for the greater good, and even mentioned sacrifices that Peter's father had made for that greater good. And Peter had even written a musical to flatter Sihanouk, and he had shown it to Christopher, who had made some suggestions for revisions, and Sihanouk had seemed to respond warmly to it at first. But he was worried now that Peter was out of his depth because in fact they were all out of their depth, maybe even Sihanouk himself, given that this was a global problem, a global threat. But certainly in Cambodia the situation was darkening, and the regime was growing ever more repressive, was taking ever more violent measures against its own citizens, and against foreign residents who aroused its displeasure.

But Edith found that she was hardly listening to this uncharacteristic flood of talk. She was too distracted to listen properly but also Christopher's manner had become so stuffy she found it hard to concentrate and looked at him hostilely as a fat and irrelevant stranger slumped in his armchair with his copy of *The Natural History of Selbourne* sitting in his lap. She wondered if their marriage would have worked better if they had lived a conventional life in England, and she saw herself gazing from the window of a suburban house in the home counties, as Christopher arrived after a day's work. She saw herself go out to greet him as he emerged from his car and hugging him in the chilly air in early March when the daylight had extended itself far enough to be fading only at this point so that she could see celandines sitting up pertly on their lawn. But no – without the urgent and strenuous pressure of their shared exotic experiences encouraging a sense of solidarity between them they might have become estranged long ago.

When Edith woke in the small hours of the morning she wasn't sure if it was Christopher's thunderous snoring or her dreams that had woken her. Chris had implied that vivid dreaming was another menopausal symptom because her nightmares had started at the same time as the onset of that change. Feeling the bed shaken by her husband's snores she saw again the teenage boys who had loomed so large in all these dreams, the teenage boys whose uniforms were the black cotton pyjamas of Cambodian peasants but with scarves and peaked caps and with big cylindrical pockets on the front of their jackets. These boys marched into Phnom Penh whose boulevards were all deserted and they shouted through loudhailers ordering everyone to leave the city. Then they extracted the tyres from the abandoned vehicles and improvised sandals from the rubber, and they stripped the bark from the ancient roadside kokum trees and made fires with it on the asphalt to cook cats and dogs.

26

Bill Noon still missed army life, he sickened still for the company of other men in fields of combat, and seethed about the humiliation he had suffered when they forced him to leave. He could have coped easily, he was sure, with a proper wound, even with being disabled, but to be dismissed on such grounds – he had never learned to live with that. His acceptance of the role of military attaché, he thought now, was a capitulation, and he had succumbed to it because the humiliation he had suffered was so bewilderingly unanticipated: he could never have imagined being the species of invalid that they said that he was, where they were saying that he was not valid in the very heart of who he was as a man, that insult. That doctor adding insult to injury. Or lack of injury.

So from the start he had found the Embassy job a kind of slight, a job suitable perhaps for a man much older than himself as a sort of semi-retirement, but not for one still firmly at his physical peak. And of course his malady had followed him faithfully all the way to Indo-China, and only left him alone when he was thoroughly absorbed in action, as he was when he disarmed the pervert who was attacking the American ambassador, made him drop his shiv. He knew it was wrong to wish for more of that sort of action in civilian life where it could only be trivial. That was far from the ideals which had made him join the army, which were about dedicating yourself, sacrificing yourself, if necessary; contributing to the common good at the point when the contribution must finally involve military action, when you firmly believed that your country always had the common good as its most abiding principle. His actual experience had made him question even this most precious belief, and that questioning now played a growing role in the feeling of being undermined, which constantly dogged him and which he was constantly attempting to escape. He found it odd how much of this he shared with Edith Hartnell, who was also bitter and angry, and who also suffered from terrible nightmares. They had happened upon this connection between them near the end of a long social event at the Embassy, when Edith had casually said it was time for everyone to go home and sleep, and he had just as casually said that sleeping was a skill he seemed to have lost. Edith was such a bright woman that she seized upon this very swiftly and they were soon sharing their common ground. The difference was that Edith could remember her dreams in sharp detail, whereas he couldn't remember any of his own – only that whatever he had seen had made him cry out and throw out his arms, and made him sit on the edge of the bed staring out of the window, as though the danger was somehow coming from there.

The great temptation had been to stay indoors and drink, and drink he certainly had, though he had struggled hard to limit it. For months at first he had been unable to go outside because he felt that there was terrible, unnameable danger there, and that there were people there who were intensely hostile to him and who were clubbed together to attack him. He fought hard against that fear because it was one of his premises as a person, his *sine qua non*, that he was not fearful, so he had forced himself to go out and face whatever was there. That had been a terrible ordeal and remained a terrible ordeal for months and months and only gradually improved, and then sometimes got worse again, so that it felt as though no improvement had been made. But it had, very slowly, improved, and now it was crucial to him that he spend most of the time out of doors, even at night when he could only sleep if he had walked for miles and miles.

What he preferred was to drive, but that became very difficult during the rainy season when the roads were often flooded, or the bitumen crumbled and was pitted with potholes. Even the thought of the tides of frogs that hopped across the roads in the rainy season put him off, he didn't like the idea of driving over hundreds of frogs. So now he felt a great sense of relief that he would again be able to climb into his car after midnight and drive at great speed through the dark over deserted roads, because speed was like action in how thoroughly absorbing it was. When he was absorbed in action or hurtling along at great speed that thought, which was at the core of the fear, did not recur to him. As with going outdoors he had made himself face up to that thought when the instinct was to skid away from it, squeeze your eyes shut and squeeze it away, anything not to see that thought. Again, he had told himself that he was not fearful, Bill was not fearful, and he had deliberately watched that thought, which he wanted to run from: watched how the top of that lance corporal's head had been sliced off so that his brain was steaming into the cool air. And that thought was connected stupidly, painfully, to a word: *bivouac*. Like an unforgivable joke.

Did it help to watch the picture deliberately? Or was it best to skid away? Whatever he did, that picture recurred: the needle couldn't climb out of that buckle in the vinyl groove, it fell back and advanced again and played that same fragment of tune, and tried to climb out again, but fell back and repeated that broken music, and it couldn't move forward further into the music. The movement was halted and the picture would always recur.

But when the rainy season ended he felt an enormous sense of release at the prospect of fast driving under clear skies, under millions of bright stars. There was also, in a corner of that idea, the other one that sometimes nudged forward, the idea that he might, one night, force the accelerator down hard, force his car up to its maximum speed and aim it into a wall. He never imagined the moment of collision, only the huge speed before and then a simple drifting away like a vapour. But mostly the fast driving on empty nocturnal roads was meant to dispel that other notion, and on three consecutive nights he had driven out of Phnom Penh. He was a little dismayed, though, to find that the expeditions seemed less effective than before, that the terrible thought had adapted, or had gained extra momentum, so that it could keep up with his car even when it reached top speed.

Anxious, he left the driving for a couple of nights and took to walking once more, but then there was an incident at home that sent him onto the road again. In the evening, after their daughter had gone to bed, Hilda had started in again on her accusations that he was unfaithful, that he was having an affair with Edith Hartnell, and he had tried to answer patiently, but she had persisted – on and on and on. But it was when she changed tack and told him that everyone was saying that he was a spy, and persisted with that one despite his patient attempts to explain, that he finally lost his temper. He had never thought it remotely possible to explain to Hilda what really lay behind his behaviour, because she was a thoroughly conventional woman and would think he was mad. So he had tried to conceal his nocturnal expeditions as much as possible, and he had explained the ones he couldn't conceal as an expression of excess energy and a love of the Cambodian countryside at night. That evening in their lounge he had been patiently explaining how his expeditions helped to calm him so that he could sleep, but Hilda had been repeating the same sentences over and over and wouldn't stop and he had jumped up, so enraged that he didn't know what to do, except that he felt so violent that he needed to run away before he hurt his wife. Once before, in a rage like this, he had smashed a door to pieces with two blows from his fist. He jumped up and made a rush to leave the lounge, and he caught his foot on the table leg and went sprawling across the floor, but, as he started to sprawl, his arm

189

brushed a teddy bear that was sitting on a wooden chair and it ended up on top of his raging back.

As he started to drive past the swampy outskirts of Phnom Penh he squirmed at the picture of himself still raging but stretched across the floor, with a startled teddy bear riding his back, and shuddered at the indignity that might, in another context, have become slapstick humour. There were rice fields in the moonlight in a place where he had once seen twenty or thirty bright lotuses being knocked about by a downpour, as he pondered the way that horror can often overlap uncomfortably close with comedy. He parked his car remembering that Edith had once told him the difference between lotuses and water lilies, something to do with their leaves, but he couldn't recall what, and he walked very quickly into the rice fields and walked even quicker, almost running, along the footpaths between the rice-plots, wondering if he was, in fact, mad, and whether he should speak to Edith about it, because she was the only person it was possible to approach with a subject like that. He charged around and around the same plots of rice, along the same footpaths, staring at the moon, which was nearly full, indignant to find himself in such a grotesque battle, to find himself in an absurdly inglorious war of attrition with himself.

Back in his car he pondered how he was constantly warring with himself so that Cambodians in shops and so forth turned away from him in fear, the look on his face must, in those moments, be so ferocious, and here was this long-nose giant looking deadly when he was only trying to buy cigarettes. He pushed hard at his accelerator, worrying that he was, indeed, dangerous, and not fit to be around vulnerable people like his wife and especially his daughter, and thinking of the simplicity of that imagined collision with a wall. He smiled ruefully as he passed a sign that said ABSOLUTE PRUDENCE, then drove at great speed for miles and miles feeling that, yes, it was helping now, that he was calmer – when he noticed at the far reaches of his headlights a tree that had fallen across the road. He knew that he was travelling so fast that he must hit the brake hard immediately and then, as he started to slow, he saw that there were six or so men around the tree and realised they must be rebels who had improvised a road block. He was only twenty yards away from them by the time his car had slowed enough for him to try to turn it around and then he heard shots and his back window shattering. By the time he had executed all the gear changes and frantic steering required to turn around, two of the men were running parallel with his car, one on each side, and the one next to him had a rifle. The other, who was running next to the passenger seat, was shouting at the one with the gun, probably to fire at him, but Bill pushed open the door and caught the armed man hard in his chest. He heard shots again but knew they were coming from behind and he managed to accelerate at the same time as he pulled the door shut and he felt the car gather enough speed to carry him out of their range.

27

'Cambodia was a great relief, you see,' the Ambassador said, 'after some of the other places, which were very hairy – Nigeria, in particular. Edith was pretty cheesed off there. Terribly difficult country, with some barbaric practices. We knew Peter's father there, did you know?'

Sandie nodded.

'Alec Cook. He was the District Officer in the Calabar region. Scrupulously fair-minded. Tormented himself about some of what he had to deal with. Twin murder – that sort of thing.'

Sandie frowned, questioningly.

'This superstition – they regarded twins as a bad omen, so they...disposed of them. Horrible, but you had to be very careful not to be high-handed.'

Sandie found it hard to concentrate as the Ambassador discoursed further about Nigeria. She glanced at the bookshelves next to her chair, at big, heavy books in French about Angkor Wat, and political studies of different Asian countries, and then at the two muscular blades of the ceiling fan above the desk near the window, slowly revolving and lifting the illustrated page of a book of exotic birds which was lying open on top of the desk. Wishing the fan was set to a faster speed so that it dispersed more of the heavy heat, she turned back to the Ambassador who was telling her now about how he had once met Prince Philip, and she registered more fully than before an odd aspect of H.E.'s response to her. She remembered that she had been half-conscious on earlier occasions when they had spoken together that he tended to look a little self-consciously away from her, but she had dismissed the perception because of the Ambassador's being so old (older than her father surely?) and because he was – well, quite plump. But she felt now that she detected the definite sense that he found her attractive, and was talking about Prince Philip in order to impress her.

'I don't mean to say, of course, that there are no dangers in Cambodia.' The Ambassador had circled back to his earlier topic. 'Nowhere in the world is safe these days, outside western Europe.'

'I wasn't complaining, Ambassador.' Sandie had started their conversation by saying that she had been anxious recently, and she wanted to resume that theme. 'It's just that one has heard so much about traitors, about Burgess and Maclean and those people. And there could be treachery, don't you think, even in an innocent place like Cambodia?'

'Innocent. Well I wouldn't use that word. The Prince himself shouldn't be underestimated, he's very canny. And there are the rebels, of course, who have links with major players elsewhere.' The Ambassador offered Sandie a cigarette, which she refused. He lit one himself and inhaled.

Sandie said, 'Did you know that there was an attempt to recruit Keith when he was an undergraduate?'

The Ambassador exhaled his smoke and shook his head, looking taken aback. 'No. Attempt by whom?'

Sandie felt a brief surge of panic. 'Well by...Russians I should think.'

The Ambassador looked impatient, which was unsettling. 'Look here, Sandie. He told you this?'

'Yes. He was approached in a Wimpy bar. He was quite drunk when he told me.'

'I assume the implication was that he turned them down?' The Ambassador smiled now in a way that Sandie found annoying: a young woman could all too easily be treated dismissively.

'Yes, yes. But he habitually says very left-wing things. Things with a definite communist tendency.'

'That wouldn't make him a traitor.'

'No, no. But he has a very close friend in the Russian embassy.'

'Really?'

'Yes. A young man called Yuri.'

The Ambassador smoked and gazed at the ceiling, then looked profoundly weary. Sandie followed his gaze and watched how the cigarette smoke was parted by the ceiling fan, and agitated so that it shuddered.

'That's a bit worrying, certainly – I'll have a word with him. He does need to be careful because it's so easy to be compromised.'

'I don't want to get him into trouble, but...'

'No, of course not. You're absolutely right to let me know.'

'I worry about him, for his own sake.'

'Don't forget he's also very close to Peter, who has none of those tendencies.'

'But Peter can also be very disrespectful. He rarely has a good word for anyone with any power.'

'That's just a question of style. It doesn't reflect his politics.'

'There's something not quite right about him, a sort of anger, something very unstable. But it's Keith I'm worried about. He has other connections... There's a journalist he knows called Hector who is also very left wing. Hector Perch.'

'Perch? That's odd. I've heard that name somewhere recently. Very fishy.' The Ambassador laughed, but Sandie struggled to laugh in return, so there was a hiatus of adjustment with Sandie staring at the floor. 'Reg it was,' the Ambassador finally said. Reg. He mentioned a problem with someone called Perch. Something that wasn't *shipshape and Bristol fashion.*'

Sandie did genuinely giggle now, because the Ambassador was certainly a good mimic, and he had caught that voice of Reginald Armstrong's very well, the high-pitched Cockney. 'You know how Keith hero-worships people – always men, of course. As he does with Peter.

194

And I met this Hector once, a most unlikely hero if you ask me, so... But anyway Keith kept saying how brave he was, the dangers he'd faced on principle, in order to oppose tyrants and so on. But he also said that Perch had connections with the rebels.'

A spasm of irritation and distaste crossed the Ambassador's face. 'Alright, Sandie, I'll look into all of this.'

Back at her digs, Sandie noticed that Peter had left behind the book he had been showing her when he had stayed the night before, *Jungle Survival*, by Captain Hilary Pecksniff-Protheroe. Peter was so absent-minded, and always mislaying things – he had told her how he had lost his journal, even though he was sure it had been on the table beside his bed. Holding *Jungle Survival* she wandered over to her window and looked out: across the road was a billboard with a portrait of Prince Sihanouk dressed smartly in a lounge suit. She sat on her settee, hearing, through her open window, the chinking sound of near and far cyclo bells, and flicked through the book. She noticed how Peter had underlined sentences here and there, and sometimes only phrases, but how they were never to do with actually learning about how to survive in the jungle, but only focused on things that sounded funny: *You must at all times keep checking that leeches have not latched onto your person; the edibility test, I am afraid, is ineffective for fungi; your stride must be steady and sustained.*

Sandie listened to the cyclo bells and thought that Phnom Penh seemed so peaceful most of the time, but odd things were unnerving. Reg Armstrong for example, with his metal leg and his air, always, that he was keeping a secret, and his odd way of looking you in the eye when he said *Bristolfashion*. And more offbeat things like the rumour that vampires had infiltrated the Chinese population. Childish nonsense, of course, but she always thought of it when she went to the railway station because it was in the area surrounding it, for some reason, that Chinese vampires were said to be concentrated.

She lifted the jungle survival book to her nose and closed it around her cheeks, hoping that its pages had retained some of Peter's smell, because he smelled so marvellous, unlike Keith who wouldn't stop pestering her and stank of stale sweat and Imperial Leather and Brylcreem. She worried about Peter because he was so unpredictable and spoke over the top of her when she was speaking and said things she didn't understand, so only yesterday he had said he didn't recognise himself any more because he was living in the wrong genre and had been forced to write a musical and it was dreadful.

Sandie carried the book through to her bed and lay down under the mosquito net hugging it to her chest.

28

On the day he visited the Lycée Sisowath, Peter Cook found that Bopha Devi, daughter of Prince Sihanouk, was also visiting the school. The headmaster, a neat, compact, impressively-tailored forty-five-year-old, was clearly excited by this royal presence when he greeted Peter and ushered him through to the packed, intent hall. There the princess was wearing her green and golden costume and the striking headgear of Cambodian ballerinas, with its golden cap that framed the face on one side with a white tassel, and on the other with a red flower, and then mounted upwards from the top of the head to a sort of golden, slender, two-tiered steeple. Members of the school orchestra were playing drums of different sizes, cymbals, gongs, stringed and wind instruments, and a xylophone, as Bopha Devi instructed small girls, sporting humbler versions of her own costume, in the exquisitely delicate hand and head movements of Cambodian ballet, where the fingers and the neck drew conspicuous attention to their elaborate sinuousness. Peter noticed the unassuming patience of the princess as she held the necks and fingers of the girls and gently pointed them in the correct directions, and how gravely the girls followed her instructions, but remained heavier-looking – because so much flatter-footed, shorter-necked and more stubby-fingered – than their taller teacher. And he thought he understood why the Cambodian people were so fond of their royal family.

After half an hour of this, the princess turned to the orchestra and they stopped playing, then she nodded to one of the older boys, a boy who had been playing the cymbals, and he stepped forward and began to speak. The girls moved into the background, just in front of the musicians, who began to play again, and the boy started to sing, tremulously, plangently, in a vibrato of longing. The princess composed herself, removing from her face the smile she had bestowed on the girls, and, wearing now a look of wistfulness in her eyebrows and her eyes and her mouth, began to dance. The headmaster whispered to Peter, assuming his lack of Khmer, and Peter bent his head downwards closer to the headmaster's mouth, which was saying in French that the song was called 'Preah Chinnavong' and told the story of a prince who falls in love with a girl he has seen strolling in a garden. He promises to marry her and gives her a rare flower in order to prove his love, but she doesn't believe him. So he goes to look for more flowers, but she leaves the garden weeping. The prince is devastated and sets off to search for her, vowing once again to marry her. Peter watched the princess, fluently and lithely, drive her head and hands through a series of gestures that expressed the song's precisely modulated despair, and puzzled over how Sihanouk was a saxophonist who wanted to direct films, and his daughter was a prima ballerina, and how different this was from the public life of Britain's own royal family.

After the performance, the headmaster said that he would show Peter to the classroom where they would be expecting him, but he would have to excuse himself after that because he would be called upon to show the princess around. Peter explained that he would need somewhere to change, because he had to transform himself into a crocodile and no-one must see the metamorphosis in its stages of transition. The headmaster smiled his understanding and passed him onto his secretary with instructions to allow Peter to use his own study and then to show him to the classroom. Peter had borrowed the Ambassador's car in order to transport the costumes and on his way to the car park he thought about the story of the Crocodile Princess and how it appealed to small children like Bill Noon's daughter, but also to older ones like the pupils of this school. The major had asked Peter for a copy of the story because Andrea had requested it after Peter had told her the story once at a small informal gathering at the Embassy, and Peter had very quickly done so, partly because Bill had looked so haggard and lost when he had asked for it, looked as though his mind was thoroughly elsewhere. Andrea was only four or five, so the story must mean something else to the twelve-year-olds at the Lycée Sisowath: in their first response to it, Peter remembered that they had laughed in surprising places so he was sure they were finding a meaning in it that he hadn't intended. That had been a relief on that first occasion because he had been worried that the story was too young for them. As Peter lifted the costumes out of the car boot, he pondered the different understanding in a twelve-year-old Cambodian mind, and his knowledge that his own mind had been changed by Cambodia so that David Frost had commented that the sketches that Peter had sent him were different from Peter's earlier work. Frostie thought that wasn't a hopeless obstacle but that revisions would be needed of some parts of the material where the references were too esoteric.

Peter carried the costumes from the car back to the headmaster's study. It was quite a distance along lengthy corridors because it was a large school and the two pairs of footwear, the rubber thigh waders and the child's wellingtons, and the two cardboard masks, were awkward shapes and quite heavy. He stopped a couple of times to rearrange the items in his hands, with pupils skipping past him, staring, and he was sweating inside his suit, lightweight though it was, by the time he reached the headmaster's secretary who unlocked the door of the study. Once inside, he removed his jacket and his shirt and tie and pulled on the crocodile torso which had been constructed by Cynthia at the embassy and which was made of thick green material with wavy black ridges drawn all over it. Then he took off his trousers and pulled on the crocodile legs and tail, which had been constructed by Cynthia's friend Joan (Peter had noted that Sandie had refused to help, and obviously regarded costume construction as beneath her). He put his trousers on the headmaster's chair, but then thought that might offend Cambodian etiquette, so he hung them, with his jacket, on the hooks on the wall near a large cupboard. The crocodile bottoms reached to his waist and he was careful when he pulled them on because the material around the waist and crotch felt thin and flimsy and he worried about tearing it. He stepped into the waders, which ended parallel with his crotch: they belonged to Bill Noon, who had offered him others which reached to his waist, but they had left insufficient room for the tail section. The waders felt a little big and loose on him as he squelched down the corridor, with the smiling secretary beside him, to the classroom. Just outside it, he pulled on the crocodile mask, which Cynthia and Joan had collaborated on, and whose long cardboard jaw, with its two rows of big cardboard teeth painted white, sat at its top across his forehead, and at its bottom under his chin, so that (as he had noted in a mirror in his brief rehearsal) it looked as though his face was in the process of being devoured.

The children laughed uproariously when Peter waded into their classroom and a couple of them dashed from their desks and vied with each other to grab Peter's tail and carry it behind him as he weaved backwards and forwards in front of the blackboard. It was some time before they were quiet enough for Peter to explain that he had written a dramatised version of the Crocodile Princess story and that the headmaster had said that, if all went well, this class would be able to perform it in front of the whole school on their prize-giving day. He said this in English, as he was supposed to do, because it was officially an English lesson, but he said it also at times in French, which they knew better, and sometimes also in his unreliable Khmer, in order to be sure they understood. In a combination of the three languages, and with some mime, he further explained that he was playing the role of the true father of the Crocodile Princess, a man who had been sidelined by the British royal family because of a terrible misunderstanding, and who therefore had been forced to live in an obscure corner of Buckingham Palace where the only food was fish fingers and beans on toast. Peter again noted that they laughed in strange places and that they seemed to find the words Buckingham Palace inexplicably hilarious, and this confirmed his growing suspicion that, unlike Andrea Noon, these twelve-year-olds perceived his version of the story as a form of satire. Did 'Buckingham' sound like something funny in Khmer? If you tinkered with its first letter there were too obvious possibilities in English, but he could think of nothing in Khmer that resembled that sound. By contrast with the hilariousness of Buckingham, when he auditioned the girls in the class for the role of the Crocodile Princess, and said the main qualification was like that of Cinderella, in having the right size of foot, because the actress would need to wear the wellingtons, they simply stared. He realised that the Cinderella reference might not work in Cambodia, but feet were surely funny anywhere in the world? But now they were quiet, and they sat still behind their desks in their khaki shorts and their white short-sleeved shirts embroidered with their names and the letters LS, for Lycée Sisowath.

Surprised by the sudden stillness of the pupils, Peter was wandering absent-mindedly towards the teacher's desk when he stumbled slightly because of the ponderousness and looseness of his waders. He threw out one of his hands onto the top of the desk to steady himself but his momentum, increased by the heaviness of his mask, propelled his chest across the desk so that his stomach collided with its front edge. That winded him but he also felt a sharp point sticking into his stomach and, when he tried to pull himself away, that point tore open the flimsy material of the crocodile trousers. He extricated himself, noting that the point was a nail that had come loose at the front of the desk, but much more concerned about his costume. The pupils looked shocked as he turned to them, but their shock, as they saw the Englishman clutching his crocodile trousers, vanished, and they laughed even harder than they had at his entrance. Peter used this mood to audition his Crocodile Princess, calling for female volunteers and asking them to try on the wellingtons and the smaller crocodile mask. Then he auditioned the Dagenham couple who raise the foundling princess, checking how each of the girls looked in a pinny and a headscarf (supplied by Cynthia) and how each of the boys looked in a dark overcoat and a flat cap (a desperately exotic item in Phnom Penh, especially in diminutive form, but supplied, in the end, by Reg Armstrong). He established his cast and, by the end of the hour, they had made a very promising start on the three different scenes that were required.

Back in the headmaster's office, Peter removed his waders and, congratulating himself on a job well done, and secure in the belief that the headmaster would still be occupied with Bopha Devi, decided to sit and smoke in his chair. He thought, as he took cigarettes and matches from the jacket he had hung up on the wall, that diplomatting was a fascinating job and he might be able to combine it with some script writing – certainly the noises that Frostie was making were very encouraging. He moved the chair to give himself a view of the front of the school and seated himself, still wearing the mask, enjoying the idea of being the headmaster-as-Crocodile-King, smoking through his crocodile head. He looked down at his crocodile body with its human part, his Y-fronts, visible where, seated, he allowed the torn, green trousers to remain open. In a tobacco haze, he was gazing into the spacious courtyard that led to the Boulevard Norodom, admiring its coconut palms and mango trees, when he heard shouting and then what might even have been two shots not far away, which startled him to his feet and made him want to run to the refuge of his everyday trousers. He looked towards them, hanging on a hook on the wall, but hesitated as he heard a scream. He froze like that for a couple of fateful moments before he set off towards the trousers, but, before he reached them, the door was flung open and Bopha Devi was pushed inside, and the door was loudly locked from the outside. She was very angry but she looked, nonetheless, in astonishment at Peter and exclaimed 'Who are you?' in Khmer and then in French. Before Peter could answer, she said 'Why are you here? What are you doing?' Peter was half-way through his explanation and desperately holding up his crocodile trousers as he noticed that she was no longer wearing her costume, but was dressed in a simple green dress and was eerily beautiful, when she said that some madmen had tried to kidnap her and had shot her bodyguard. She had managed to run away with the help of the headmaster, but she thought that they were still after her. Grasping his mask, Peter frantically considered various possibilities of escape for both of them and dismissed them, and left his mask in place because it might indicate innocence. Nodding towards the large cupboard behind the desk he said, 'Maybe you could hide in here?' The princess looked doubtful, and he tried the cupboard door and found it was locked. He searched the drawers in the headmaster's desk and found the key just as someone pounded ferociously on the door and shouted 'Police, police, open the door!' He told the princess that they might be lying, opened the cupboard door for her and helped her to climb in and then locked the cupboard. The office door was flung open then and two policemen waving guns rushed in and grabbed his hands and forced them behind his back – the right hand that was holding up his trousers and the left that held the key to the cupboard door.

29

Dudley Moore was sitting in his dentist's waiting room, apprehensive about his appointment, when he glanced at the glossy magazine of a fellow patient who was a couple of seats away from him. With his tongue he reached under the upper-right molar that had become sensitive and then touched his cheek in that area, but looked quickly back at the magazine because it was turned to a full-page photograph of a face he recognised. Yes. It was his own face. Or was it? It was subtly not quite him. He leaned towards it so far that the fellow patient looked at Dudley and irritably angled the magazine away from him. Dudley was sure that the photo was him, which meant that the fellow patient was reading about Dudley Moore three seats away but didn't recognise him. Maybe toothache had transformed him completely, or maybe the famous version of Dudley was another person altogether, who lived in a different place. He remembered a story about Cary Grant being refused admission to a country club, and telling the receptionist who he was, and her saying that he didn't look like Cary Grant, and him saying 'No-one does.' The photo was of a person who never got toothache, and didn't have a club foot, but thousands of these mini-copies of him were travelling about on buses and trains and tubes, were sitting in waiting-rooms and hairdresser's and living-rooms, and, in a week's time, torn replicas of him would scurry along pavements and be carried by gusts of wind up to the height of tree-tops and roofs. His torn face would look down out of the sky.

The week before, he had visited his parents in the house where he had grown up in Dagenham, and he was sitting in the kitchen with its ancient mangle when his dad talked to him about an article he had read about Dudley. His dad said it described some of Dudley's experiences as an undergraduate at Oxford, such as meeting people at his college who had been to public school and were going to parties where they met debutantes who wanted to marry them. Dudley felt guilty because he had never talked to his parents about such experiences because he had felt that they would be so alien to them that they couldn't possibly understand them. Yet here was his dad uncomplainingly narrating highlights of Dudley's undergraduate life, narrating them as though he had no problem at all comprehending them in the terms in which they'd been put. What had unnerved Dudley, though, was that his dad had talked about them, not as though they were a record of his son's life, but as things that had happened to someone off the telly.

In the evening after his dental appointment Dudley went over to the flat in Battersea where Lenny Bruce was staying after he had been kicked out of his hotel because the management had found a couple of prostitutes in his room and syringes in his lavatory. The flat belonged to Waldo Vaughan but it was Lenny who had invited him over, and Dudley was apprehensive because Lenny was a big star but his lowlife habits were intimidating. Dudley and Lenny talked together about jazz, which was an enthusiasm they shared, and Dudley was intrigued that Lenny wanted to perform his comedy as Charlie Parker performed his music, that he went on stage and improvised and you could see that he was excited and was surprising himself, and even transcending himself, that he was reaching for a level that was unprecedented, and that might be attained as climactic moments were sometimes, if rarely, attained in be-bop. That was intriguing but exotic to Dudley, and he thought that most Englishmen (except, perhaps, Jonathan Miller) would shy away from such ambition and intensity and worry that it was pretentious, or self-indulgent, – but maybe that was why Lenny and Waldo could understand each other, because Waldo wasn't English, he was from somewhere very remote and rural in the middle of Anglesey. Most alien of all were the constant, repetitive swearing, and the astonishingly explicit, and sometimes aggressively bizarre, sexual references: Dudley was sure that he would never be able to participate in anything remotely like that himself.

There was also the risk that you would fail abjectly, and Dudley felt he'd seen Lenny do that, at least once, in his stint in England, and he knew that Lenny was as unpredictable off-stage as he was on it. When Dudley returned without the heroin the American had said he needed, Dudley thought that Lenny would be frantic with craving for the drug, but he only shrugged dismissively and asked if Dudley could shag some chocolate cake instead.

Cowed and disoriented, Dudley had set off immediately to find a shop where he could buy some.

Dudley wanted to spend the evening at home, not just because his mouth was sore after the tinkering his dentist had done, but because he had pre-recorded an interview for television which was going to be broadcast that evening and he wanted to watch it alone. And certainly not in the presence of Lenny and Waldo who were the most challenging people that Dudley knew. Waldo frightened Dudley because he was so anti-establishment that Dudley had been afraid, during the run of *Beyond the Fringe*, that the police would burst in and lock them all up. (Lenny frightened Dudley in a similar way, with his hatred of the police). Jonathan Miller had suggested that the Welshman should replace Peter Cook when Peter absconded – he had said that Waldo was a 'genuine satirist', implying that what Peter had been doing was a conservative imitation of the real thing. But Dudley had found Peter dangerous enough, and had thought his mimicry of the prime minister was shocking. Waldo Vaughan was much more ferocious – he also mimicked Macmillan, and just as accurately, but the words he put into his mouth were savagely political, and

Dudley was sure that the substitution of Peter by Waldo had made the show less popular than it would have been. *The Daily Express* was now conducting a campaign against Waldo, insisting he was a communist, and saying that his club in Soho had received financial backing from the electrician's union, which was widely regarded as having Soviet links. Dudley had his own suspicions because Waldo was the most angrily left-wing person he had ever met, and Dudley had overheard him a couple of times speaking a very strange language on the telephone, something like Albanian or Magyar.

Waldo wasn't around when Dudley arrived and Lenny told him that the Welshman had gone to sort out a problem that had arisen at his club in Soho, which was being threatened by local gangsters, and Waldo had gone there to negotiate with them. Lenny looked exhausted and cindery in the face, but Dudley was relieved to find him in a subdued mood, and tried hard to answer the questions about cricket Lenny was asking because he'd found a book about it in a local second-hand bookshop. Lenny showed him a diagram of the fielding positions and Dudley tried hard to explain terms like square leg and silly mid-off, understanding how strange they sounded when you hadn't heard them before. Lenny seemed genuinely disappointed when Dudley said that he wouldn't be able to see a game during this trip to England because it wasn't played during winter.

But Dudley was alarmed when he noticed a secretive smile igniting at the corners of Lenny's face as the interview was starting. He wanted to focus on his own performance so he didn't like this distraction, but he was also intimidated by Lenny's cynical and savvy attitudes to fame and publicity. He thought it was unfair, when he wanted to judge how he would seem to a mass audience, to be made most aware of an appraisal that was so foreign and atypical. He was concentrating very hard on how he was coming across when Lenny said, 'He's so cute this Dudley guy, so *cute*. Look at him how *cute* he is.'

Dudley unfixed his stare at the screen, at his monochrome self, and said, 'Lenny, please...'

'This interviewer, though, he's a real schmuck. How can Dudley Moore show how cute he is, how deeply cute, when this schmuck is asking such pain-in-the-ass questions?'

'Lenny, *please*...' Dudley was insistent, so Lenny controlled himself for the rest of the interview, but when it ended he said, 'Great packaging, there, Dudley.'

Dudley sighed with relief, and poured himself some whisky from Waldo's drinks cabinet. 'That's not how I want to think of it.'

'Whatever you want, it was very *effective*. I'll have a pernod.'

'I was trying to be sincere.' Dudley poured some pernod into a small glass.

'If *that's* what you were trying you really screwed up.'

'That was all true, what I said.' Dudley passed him the glass.

'Oh yeah. The childhood in DagenHAM.' Lenny pronounced the place name like a tourist from the Midwest. 'Piano lessons. Childhood prodigy.'

'I wasn't boasting.'

'No no it was all very modest. That was what was so cute. And no kvetch. Rags. Riches.'

'Not so rich.'

'No that was very funny, how you sidestepped that.'

'I'm not rich.'

'Not yet. That Dudley Moore on the *telly* just now, though – he's going to be a plutocrat. That much you could very readily discern.'

Dudley sipped his scotch. 'You've not been on television much yourself have you Lenny?'

'Ooooh, now that's very true.'

'I mean...'

'I know what you mean. Don't get me wrong, what you did there just now was *very* clever."

'And you're not clever?'

'I'm clever alright. But my jewboy upbringing won't translate like yours, for one thing.'

Dudley felt as though a big wave had jolted him, and another was on its way that would flatten him. He and Lenny faced each other with their drinks in their hands. 'It's just that I...'

'I know, Dudley, I know. This is not the face you show the cameras. The tsuris.'

'I can't...'

'You can't show the cameras anything but *cute*. And your public can't get enough of *cute*. Your women too. All those women, Dudley. *Cute*. That's why you're lonely.'

30

Monkeys and cockatoos were hooting at him, and staring and grinning at him, and chattering loudly in his ears, and he ran into a series of pagodas and was imprisoned inside them in high secret chambers, but worst of all was the crocodile that sometimes carried a parasol and had surfaced out of Marianne's Chinoiserie panel. Joe Keane was trapped inside this reverie which had been, in his first encounters with opium, delightful and exhilarating, the monkeys and cockatoos only funny and cheeky, and the pagodas vivid and spacious, but now they couldn't be escaped, they returned every hour or less, and the crocodile frightened him inexplicably. Sometimes, also, there was the tiny landscape in the Chinoiserie frame of a looking-glass that Marianne had bought and then demanded that they look inside together, with their faces side by side: there were stone steps rising between moss hanging among icicles where elongated figures ascended to a landing-place under a portico.

Joe Keane knew at the start he had retreated into these landscapes in order to escape from the mundane frustrations of life in Phnom Penh, but he pitied himself, also, because his stabbed leg had led him to further opium to relieve the pain, so his problem had been compounded by bad luck. The derision of the monkeys and cockatoos, the relentlessness of the crocodile, the paralysis that gripped the icy, mossy steps, were especially alarming because they carried a knowledge with them of how they were excluding the ambassadorial alertness he ought above all to cultivate in himself. Inside his high secret chamber he was aware of noises from below, of muffled shouting, and his anxiety was growing more acute that he was missing crucial signs, that Prince Snookie was increasingly anti-American, and his latest pronouncements and machinations required much closer regard. But Washington was also to blame because it was dismissive about Cambodia, and he had always felt ignored and patronised when he tried to draw the close attention of that self-regarding city to what it viewed as a tiny and irrelevant country.

The Prince was conspicuously absent from today's cocktail party at the American embassy. Joe was smoking a cigar by the kidney-shaped swimming-pool, gazing into the clear water sparkling inside its bright blue tiles. He had taken a break from his circulating, but his break was extending too far, and his lassitude contrasted with the exemplary behaviour of his wife, as usual putting him to shame. He watched her gliding amongst the three hundred guests, smiling, extending her fingers to apply the precise touch to the appropriate body parts, to elbows and wrists, chatting, gauging exactly the requisite smallness of her talk – she was the best diplomat in Phnom Penh. She was exquisite in the cocktail dress he had bought her and imported from Paris, perhaps his greatest success in recent months, a cocktail dress by her favourite designer, Cristóbal Balenciga, whose name he had carefully memorised. Silk, its white polka dots on navy blue, and displaying the marvellously delicate bones of her shoulders. How easy she made it all look, her gliding to and fro, and yet its actual difficulty was clear from how many of the other women let their stiletto heels sink too far into the lawns where they plugged and halted them in their ungainly stride. Joe had enjoyed the sight of a couple of them barefootedly retrieving their stuck shoes.

Perhaps it was Marianne's immaculateness that had made Joe impatient, that superior manner she had of doing everything perfectly, and of looking perfect, that gave him no room for manoeuvre. If for once she got a stiletto stuck in the lawn and tumbled over and grass-stained her Parisian dress, he could rush over and rescue her and feel she was endearing. Her being exemplary was stifling and predictable, including her patience with his shortcomings. That was why he found himself dwelling on Ariadna: such a high percentage of his thoughts were the wrong thoughts! A fortnight ago, when he had lingered alone at the *ZigZag*, reluctant to go home, Ariadna had actually approached him, and he had thought it tremendously bold. She hadn't been in the bar earlier and seemed just suddenly to appear. Seated herself at his table – a young Russian woman and the Ambassador of the United States late at night in a bar talking intimately! It would only be possible in a backwater like Phnom Penh. She asked him what it had been like growing up in America, what had it been like to be a child there, and what was his family like? Here was something utterly beyond the pale, well beyond Madame Chhum's, and he had found himself glancing nervously around, as they spoke. Ariadna was so naive and vulnerable, and he felt strongly protective, and couldn't that be possible? That they could just be friends and chat occasionally, and that would be enough, and it would be an outlet, the change he needed, and nothing more need happen? She said, in a whisper, she had sometimes fantasised about defecting: maybe, he insisted to himself, he could help her with that, and that would be enough. There might even be secrets that she knew that would be helpful. When she talked about herself, Joe noticed that she talked a lot about her father, the famous physicist, and hardly mentioned her mother. When Joe pointed this out, she bridled and said that her mother fought with her and treated her as a rival for her father's love, that her mother was always trying to undermine her. Joe had felt shocked by her sudden anger and had dwelt on that moment ever since because it revealed so much, and suggested that she really wanted him to understand her. So he was mystified, now, that Ariadna had completely ignored him a couple of days earlier in the *Nouveau Tricotin*: was it only because she didn't want the embassy colleagues who were with her to witness any connection between them? Maybe that was it, but surely she could have given him some covert sign of recognition, especially when he had deliberately taken the risk of leaving the table, where his colleagues and wife were eating, to walk by her as she headed for the bathroom?

Joe shifted his gaze to the long tables whose placement across the lawns had been supervised by Marianne, who had also, with their Vietnamese chef, organised the sandwiches and snacks that were displayed tastefully on the white linen that covered the tables. The guests were charging their plates and standing in small groups eating and chatting and he noticed Christopher Hartnell and Peter Cook in discussion at the far end of the tables. He watched Hartnell listening to Cook, who was evidently embarked on one of his monologues, and thought the Ambassador looked tired and fat in his tight-fitting white duck jacket and his white duck trousers. Joe felt sorry for Hartnell, the guy was an engaging character but he was so conspicuously lonely, he was so thoroughly without friends, and the look he was giving Cook was embarrassingly full of need. When Joe had first arrived in Phnom Penh he had been grateful to Hartnell for his advice, for divulging his insider knowledge, and he had thought that their relationship was like that between Jack Kennedy and Harold Macmillan, the younger dynamic man from the younger dynamic nation being advised by the elder statesman from the ageing nation. But Hartnell increasingly struck Joe as a burnt-out case, and he watched him laugh now and then gaze after Cook with a jowly face charged with longing, and shuddered to receive such an explicit insight into Hartnell's adoration of Cook, not faggoty of course, but almost as undignified. No wonder Cook could get away with so much when his boss was so in awe of him.

Joe watched Cook's progress along the tables, his brief encounters with each knot of people, and he noticed how he sparked a brief flurry of laughter in each group, leaving each ignition in his trail, and then he noticed that Marianne was progressing along the tables from the opposite side, so he could compare their effect, for Marianne left behind warm smiles, she left behind happiness rather than hilarity.

Unknown to each other, Cook and Marianne were converging, but they both carried positive charges so their convergence was only glancing, the brief touch of Marianne's fingers on Cook's elbow pushed them both away and onwards.

Like charges repel. As Joe thought this he felt a wave of realisation travel through him: if Marianne was the best diplomat in town then something similar was true of Cook. Ambassador's wives were always engaged in subtle, domestic diplomacy, and everyone in Phnom Penh knew that Edith Hartnell was far smarter than her plodding spouse. But Cook was also involved in the subtle and unexpected, in wiles that were feminine compared with the up-front tactics of mainstream diplomats, and it was typical of the British to invent a mode of cunning indirectness, like the wiles they had used when everywhere massively outnumbered to maintain their overblown empire. Here was a young man who was certainly witty, but whose charm also depended on apparent maladroitness, and it was this freshness and ingenuousness that had quietly conquered Sihanouk, had made a high-level contact in the Chinese embassy, and had seduced Joe himself. Joe had seen a connection before between Cook and the much more explicit figure of the burly spy Bill Noon, but he could now see connections spreading outwards from Cook in every direction like underground cables and pipes.

Could it be that Cook was a spy? Of an entirely new kind where the secrecy was achieved through sophisticated openness, of being hidden in plain sight? From this perspective other data could be re-assessed. That amazing incident in the school with Sihanouk's daughter, that doll Bopha Devi, where Cook had somehow ended up in a cupboard with a princess, and where you would've thought her father would be hopping mad. The whole city had been talking about that, but it was surely a diversion, it was meant to make you look in the wrong place, as a conjuror does as he performs his sleight of hand under the cover of out-in-the-open obviousness.

Christopher Hartnell strolled over and nodded at Joe's nearly-finished cigar and said, 'I have some here, Joe, that are far superior to that.' He produced a pair of cigars from his jacket pocket and Joe accepted the long one he was offered. 'They're from a small island, out of bounds to you. The approved method of manufacture there is for young ladies to roll them along their thighs.'

'To extend them to the requisite length?'

'Yes, quite.'

Joe gazed around and noted how the guests were arranging themselves hierarchically, each group sorted on the correct rung, like the American and British ambassadors. This exchange about cigars and thighs was an item in a summit meeting, and the next items were all initiated by Christopher and were focused on the superiority of facilities in the American, by contrast with the British, embassy. The swimming pool, the catering, and the yanks didn't have big cumbersome ceiling fans, but air conditioning even in the lavatories.

'But there's something I've been meaning to say to you, actually, Joe,' Christopher said, after grimacing and staring at the lawn.

'Fire away.'

'You remember when you first arrived I told you that American embassy staff had a tendency to keep themselves to themselves too much? Sequester themselves away in their own compounds?'

'I do. I thought about that very carefully. Not good at all for hearts and minds.'

'Yes, quite. I think, however, Joe, you may have gone a little too far the other way, overdone it somewhat, in the other...direction.' Christopher took two rapid sips on his cigar and looked over towards the swimming pool.

'You don't say. How so?'

'These are just rumours, you understand. And I know, of course, there is no truth in them. No truth at all. Phnom Penh is a small city, and the diplomatic community, as always, is a specialised village of its own.'

Joe felt queasy. 'What do the rumours say?'

'You're seen around quite a lot. Nothing wrong with that, far from it.'

'I like to unwind and take in the local colour.'

'Absolutely. But people can be very malicious. And our countries are fearfully unpopular in some circles.'

'This bush you're beating around...'

Christopher took two rapid sips on his cigar, and glanced left and right as though he was crossing a road, then leaned in close to Joe and whispered, 'It's being said – bizarrely untrue of course – that you're involved with a Cambodian...*boy*.'

Joe giggled nervously. 'No-one could believe that...I'm...'

'Obviously yes. But the truth isn't all that relevant here I'm afraid. What is being said, is that you're paying this boy to dress up as a woman...'

'Bill Noon. It's Noon who told you this isn't it? I can see your intentions are good, Christopher, and I will take this under advisement. Don't you think, however, that you should have your own house in order? I mean I can see that Bill Noon has obvious assets as a spy, but shouldn't he be more under cover? Isn't it the thing about spies that you shouldn't be able to look one up in the telephone book and call them?'

Joe noticed then a small, dishevelled figure approaching them across the lawn but was still startled when this man ignored him and touched Hartnell on the arm so that the

British Ambassador turned to face him. In a French accent the intruder breathlessly exclaimed, 'This is all your fault. It is all your doing!'

The Frenchness of the voice made Joe realise that this was the young, tiny person he had seen in the company of Jean Barré, in that group of frog fairies, anti-American fairies and Sihanouk insiders, fomentors of anti-American opinion at Sihanouk's court.

Hartnell had turned to the intruder. 'What are you talking about?'

The Frenchman was red in the face. 'It is all your fault!' he was shouting and struggling to breathe. 'Wilfred has been arrested!'

31

As he watched the water in the saucepan take on its expected urgency and quicken from the tiny bubbles of simmering into the frantic larger ones of boiling, Hector Perch felt a surprising contentment. He checked his watch: it was twelve minutes past nine and he would allow his two eggs to boil like this until exactly quarter past. It was the sense of being utterly in control of this moment that was so satisfying, knowing that the eggs would be perfect and also his toast which he would spread with Oxford marmalade. Oxford. He gazed around the kitchen and loved how small it was and yet how thoroughly it contained everything he needed, and felt gratitude again to his cousin who had understood so clearly what he had needed at this moment and supplied it to him in the form of a flat on the Woodstock Road. His cousin had understood what Hector had needed even before Hector had: he had needed, and still needed, to spend mundane days, to move slowly and watch eggs boil and calmly anticipate the spreading of marmalade. He checked his watch again and stepped towards the window and enjoyed the sight of English gardens dishevelled by winter, the trees almost bare, their remaining leaves hardly stirring, the sodden wooden fences, the low thick stratus leaking cold drizzle whitening here and there into sleet.

Repeatedly, since he had returned to Britain, Hector had experienced moments when he had felt himself double-take at what he saw because it was so entirely different from what had preceded it in Phnom Penh. He felt that now: as he gazed through this kitchen window in north Oxford it turned into a cinema screen that was displaying something from elsewhere, even though he could feel the scene enter the kitchen in the form of a thin draught through the side of the casement. He was disconcerted by the subdued light that sat on the damp surfaces of trees and fences and roofs and windows, and was hardly reflected at all, because his eyes could hardly believe that such a mode of light was possible. He wanted to reach through the window and finger the whole scene, to grasp it close, to reassure himself.

Hector had thought he was going to die in the police station in Phnom Penh, he had thought the Cambodian police were going flatly to ignore him to death. They only interrogated him twice after the first session, and each time the session was shorter and the police officer was less interested. They spoke to him only in Khmer and were dismissive when he replied in French and even more so when, out of desperation, he pleaded with them in English. Each time the Khmer word *b'ngreek* sounded more loudly in the questions of the interrogator, who, in the final session, yawned repeatedly. After that last encounter with the senior officer, the police covered, from outside, the window in his cell, so he could no longer tell day from night. They weren't trying to brainwash him, because even that might be too much effort for them, but Hector thought about the methods of brainwashing and understood that depriving the victim of the ability to gauge the passage of time was one of them. Even that on its own, combined with being utterly alone and regarded with hostile indifference, was enough to make him feel terribly afraid and vulnerable, and to start to question his sense of himself. On the second day they had given him some fish and noodle soup and it was delicious, but the food steadily decreased in quantity, as, also, did his supply of water. He was never treated violently but the knowledge that he might easily die slowly of neglect grew steadily stronger: die slowly in one of the major squares in the city, next to the post office and opposite his favourite restaurant where Edith might easily be dining, unaware that he was only two hundred yards away.

In his cell, he wondered constantly what Edith must be thinking. Would she simply assume that he had slipped away without telling her? She was always chaffing him, saying that he was an inconstant lover, that he would lose interest very quickly and abandon her – was this what she was thinking now? Or would she make inquiries and try to use diplomatic influence to track him down? At first he was sure that she would try to work out what had happened to him and would be able to make a good guess, but, as time passed, he lost hope: after all, he had been secretive, he hadn't told Edith about his meetings with the rebels, because he knew her politics were different from his own. How could they be otherwise when she had spent her life upholding the British cause? He grew increasingly weak and dizzy and was plagued by hallucinations: what did it mean that the crucial word *b'ngreek* had been a national joke in Cambodia? Could a joke really branch away into such sinister sidestreets? Enlarge, enlarge. Sihanouk's father had meant enlarge Cambodian industry, its transport systems, its population – but when Hector had repeated the word in that English context, in *The New Statesman*, its meaning had changed. And he saw thoroughly, in his prison cell, what he had kept before far in the background, below the threshold of his thinking. The joke harboured an unspoken racism that cartooned Sihanouk's smallness of stature, and, beyond that, cartooned the diminutiveness, generally, of Cambodians. So his gaolers had some right on their side, to some degree he deserved his punishment.

From the wireless in the lounge Hector heard the end of a sentence about David Frost and something about a funeral. He moved the dial on the wireless to the Third programme, and ate his breakfast beside the gas fire while listening to a sort of series that was featuring Delius all that week, a composer he had previously hated but who he was now making an effort to appreciate. Then he set off to walk into town, picking up a copy of *The Times* on the way.

He wandered into Balliol, his old college, and gazed at the staircase where his room had been in his first two years. Nothing had changed. He understood that this continuity was frightfully important to him, but he suspected it nonetheless, just as he suspected Delius: was he sinking, like a coward, into conservatism? It was easy to do that in England where even rebellion could be made to work conservatively, the way that David Frost and his cronies had turned satire into a style, all surface, that pretended to be subversive but was really just helping to maintain the status quo.

The night before he had watched television, starting with a comedy called *Bootsie and Snudge*, which annoyed him with its simplistic humour combined with its bland refusal to acknowledge the homosexual undercurrent in the relationship of the protagonists. By contrast with that and Frost's version of satire, he saw a clip, much later in the evening, on an arts programme, from a stage performance by Waldo Vaughan. Hector had been thinking about this clip all day: he had heard that this was the man who had replaced Peter Cook in *Beyond the Fringe*, and by coincidence the clip showed his impersonation of Harold Macmillan. The vocal mimicry was a little less accurate than Cook's, but the performance was more deeply researched – Vaughan impersonated Macmillan's limp, for example, and so acknowledged the prime minister's very distinguished war record. This was an old Tory but Vaughan's savagery was also accurate, so that Macmillan was revealed as severely limited by patrician thinking, but that thinking was also revealed as closely linked to his integrity and profound sense of duty. What Vaughan was doing was genuine satire because its comedy was deeply involved in seriousness, and therefore contained at least the possibility of being subversive.

Subversion was a much more urgent matter in Cambodia, and he could take his own revenge on the

Sihanouk regime simply by imagining the fate that was awaiting it when the rebels took over. His encounter with the guerrillas near Battambang had impressed him with the knowledge of their determination and their political sophistication: they were certainly what Cambodia needed, and the sooner that Sihanouk's decadent court was swept away the better. He had given up hope in the dark of his cell and then suddenly one day he was hurried away into the shocking glare outside the police station and into the back of a van. He thought they were going to take him from the city and shoot him somewhere in the jungle, but when they took him out of the van they were at the airport. He was being unceremoniously deported, except there was a bizarre version of ceremony in the handing over of his passport in a small plastic bag, and the elaborate displaying of his worldly possessions which they must have commandeered from his flat. They led him to a crate and opened it to reveal his typewriter and sundry other asymmetrical objects such as hats, and then they showed him his two suitcases and opened them to reveal everything else that he owned in Phnom Penh, all arranged with fanatical neatness, clothes sharply ironed and folded, and books placed formally on top of them. All packed to a much higher standard that he could ever possibly have attained. The senior police officer had suddenly acquired quite adequate French and explained that they had done their best to track down all his possessions (as though he had led a major inquiry when Hector's Y-fronts had gone missing). 'Nonetheless,' he said, 'should you find that anything you treasure is not present you need only fill out this form and send it to us and we will do our utmost to track it down.' As he said this he handed Hector a sheet of paper and insisted on explaining the sections where it asked, in Khmer and French, about the nature of the object and its distinguishing characteristics. Hector thanked him very much.

'But you will not want, I think, to return?'

Some questions, Hector thought, are rhetorical, but this one was generically way beyond that. 'No,' he agreed. 'Certainly not.'

Porters were called and, with an expansive gesture of his arms, the senior police officer displayed to Hector the ceremonial placement of the crate and his suitcases on a trolley, followed by the ceremonial wheeling away of the trolley. 'I wish you a pleasant flight,' the policeman said, with a look of deeply humane regret.

'Thank you very much,' Hector said. The policeman accompanied Hector through Departures, up the stairs to the aircraft, and right to his seat and told him to buckle his seat belt. Hector felt exhausted and nauseous during the flight but astonished to find himself flying and alive and made the mistake of celebrating with wine. He slept but was awoken by angry turbulence and thought there must be a clue in the ferociously neat packing of his suitcases: something had changed, someone had intervened, and he had been transformed from a sewer rat into an intimidating grandee. But then he suspected that idea. Now, in Oxford, he understood that, after his desperation in his cell, and then his edgy exhilaration on the aeroplane, he had newly acquired an analytic interest in his mental states, and his mental processes, and it was this unfamiliar interest that made him doubt himself as he gazed towards the Balliol window, which his nineteen-year-old self had gazed through. He fretted about the nostalgia that welled through him like one of those passages of wounded pastoral in Delius, fretted about a new infatuation with the rhythms of the English year, the seasons, the rugger internationals against Wales and Scotland, the Oxford terms – Michaelmas, Hilary and Trinity. His ordeal in that cell had damaged his brain and was making him stuffy and home counties conventional.

He felt guilty, also, about Edith. He was surprised by how much, how badly, he longed to see her, but he felt convinced that he had somehow already been unfaithful to her, that he had been cruel in not telling her immediately what had happened to him. The terrible anxiety he had suffered in that cell made him want to retreat into a tight corner, and hunker down, and see no-one – he didn't want to speak to anyone, anyone at all. He needed to spend time just to re-adjust himself. And Edith, – too much time had passed and it was now too late.

32

David Frost has drowned. The star of the satirical TV programme TW3 was a poor swimmer and he must somehow have got caught out of his depth in a swimming pool in Connecticut where he had been staying with some friends, including Jonathan Miller, Alan Bennett, Dudley Moore, and Waldo Vaughan, who had been reprising *Beyond the Fringe* for an American audience. Much regret was being expressed by these friends that none of them was around to help him: Dudley Moore was especially upset because it was him who discovered the body.

Peter Cook was explaining this to Keith Entwistle as they wandered through the Grand Market: Peter had wanted to be alone and had been dismayed when he encountered Keith, but had lacked the energy to reject his company, so he had passively allowed Keith to wander with him. He had only just heard the news and needed to absorb what it meant, and he understood that he had started to rely heavily on the idea that Frostie was going to help him back into his life in comedy, and that he had more and more come to believe that he couldn't continue in a diplomatic career. The farce with Bopha Devi confirmed his discomfort in the job, because everything he had tried that day in the school had complicated matters further. Irony was his biggest problem because he had defined himself, not just as a comedian and a satirical writer, but as a person, through irony, and he needed that sharp and subtle indirectness, not just to entertain other people but to entertain himself. It frightened him to imagine the need to acquire a mind that bored him, that was compelled to speak discreetly and unironically. He had been officially aware of that need from the start, but he had only recently felt its full force and understood the full implications of the personal adjustments he would have to make if he were to continue.

He didn't want Keith's company because he could only think of boring things to say about David Frost drowning and he didn't want to explain why it was amazing that Frostie's well-being had come to be so important to him. But Keith had noticed that Peter was depressed and had persisted in his questioning to such an extent that Peter had irritably explained that Frost had been so interested in Peter's recent work – with some reservations about its new, Indo-Chinese dimension – that he had suggested that he might regularly use it on television.

'Did you show him *Bedazzled*?' Keith asked.

Peter was absent-mindedly gazing in a shop window that was ablaze with gold jewellery reflected in the streetlights of that early Saturday evening. '*Bedazzled*?'

'Yes, you know, the script you showed me once.'

'No, no. That's not finished.'

'I had no idea that you wanted to go back.'

'I didn't want to talk about it. Don't want to talk about it.'

'No, you never do want to talk...properly about things. That causes problems.'

'It's boring. That sort of talk.'

'I'm very glad to hear it. That your work, I mean, won't go to waste. That would've been a shame.'

Peter was very glad then to see, approaching from the direction of the railway station, his friend Mr. Chang, in singlet and baggy shorts, because he wanted the diversion, and he greeted him warmly in Mandarin, which was a language he knew that Keith didn't understand, and nodded towards the bag that the bookmaker was carrying and asked him if he'd been on a journey. Mr. Chang said yes but only a short one, and Peter, anxious to extend the diversion, declared how much he missed, during the present dry season, the weather betting presided over by Mr. Chang, and how much he longed for its return. Mr. Chang smiled his agreement and said that he had seen Peter the previous week driving a new cream Citroën saloon. That baffled Peter so much that he half-heartedly meandered into a limp Buddhist joke about owning only a lesser vehicle, a scooter, so that Mr. Chang must have been mistaken. Mr. Chang looked irritated by this and wandered away and Peter found himself bewildered by the sense that this Chinese man, with whom he had thought he had such rapport, had been regularly confusing him with someone else. Combined with the news about Frost, he felt this moment represented the lowest point of his obscurity: famous people were recognised everywhere, but he wasn't properly recognised even by a man he had regularly conversed with. He was truly a nobody.

Peter was so disoriented that he actually tried to explain his disorientation to Keith, as Prince Sihanouk screeched from a restaurant, which they were just passing. It was government radio, which broadcast the Prince's speeches, about the glorious Cambodian people and their nefarious enemies, every other day. Keith said that Chinese people probably thought that Caucasians all looked alike, just as Caucasians thought about the Chinese. Peter found it hard to concentrate then on what Keith was saying because he had resolved to get drunk and he was imagining a bottle of Scotch and thinking about the nearest place that he could buy one, but he heard Keith saying that Mr. Chang himself bore a striking resemblance to another unusually tall Chinese man, a man called Zan Jingrun.

'Zan?' Peter said.

'Yes. He's quite prominent in the Chinese embassy.'

'I think I've heard the name somewhere.'

'Zan Jingrun. No-one is quite sure what he does, but whenever the Chinese ambassador is around, Zan is usually there too. And he looks almost exactly like your Mr. Chang. Except he usually wears a Mao suit, and doesn't smile as much as your friend.' At that moment all the streetlights went out, and the coloured lights that decorated the restaurants were also extinguished, but, ignoring the routine disruption, Keith continued: 'He's generally regarded as a sinister figure, there's all sorts of speculation about him, in terms of his connections with the rebels. He's even been seen with Jean Barré. You know I've got a very good memory for faces, but I could easily have mixed up Chang and Zan.' In the darkness, the Prince's voice continued from the restaurant's battery-powered radio, and they heard motors coughing into life as the restaurants started their private generators, and they could see lanterns and candles being lit in all the nearby buildings.

Three weeks later, when Peter had disappeared, and rumours about him had grown, and people were saying, amongst other things, that Peter had connections in the Chinese embassy, Keith would remember this moment, and realise that the rumours about his Chinese connections were based on this mistaken identity.

Peter claimed then that he felt unwell, which was partly true, and needed to go alone back to his flat, which was wholly true, because the idea of his current emotion nakedly in the open, like a thumb not just sore but raw and red, was abhorrent. So he escaped Keith and bought a bottle of scotch and sat on his verandah through the brief sunset and drank. After his second glass he remembered Keith mentioning *Bedazzled* and remembered, also, having taken a brief look at it about a week earlier and casually thinking that there was something odd about its typeface, but dismissing the idea as silly. He wandered inside from the verandah to take another look and flicked through its pages and felt convinced then that it was not the version he had typed. He felt dumbfounded: could someone have somehow entered his flat and rewritten it? He flicked through it again, reading it at random and recognising it all as his own. Was he going mad? No-one could have a motive for rewriting a comedy script. He giggled at the idea that anything he wrote might be regarded as having an urgent political significance. Here, actually, was a comedy idea: a spy breaks into the residence of a comedy writer and edits his material.

He returned to his verandah and drank some more, watching the street life below, and he had no idea what time it was when he stumbled into his bedroom, removed his clothes and collapsed across his bed.

Tap tap tap was the sound that woke him. He didn't believe the sound was possible as he aimed his aching and sweating head towards it and the powerful desire to sleep tugged him in the opposite direction. *Tap tap tap* sounded again and frightened him now because of the image from earlier of an interloper in his flat: had that interloper returned in the middle of the night wanting to confront him face to face? *Tap tap tap* persisted and was coming from the outside of his bedroom window, but he was properly awake now and still thought that was impossible. He walked fearfully across the room and pulled on his dressing gown and pushed the curtains to one side and saw a female figure outlined in the darkness and leaning against the balustrade on his verandah. He unlatched the window and pushed the upper sash downwards and the figure stepped towards him and he saw that it was Ariadna. 'Good evening,' she said. 'May I enter?'

'Er, yes,' Peter said. He pushed the upper sash upwards, then did the same with the lower one. 'Can you duck through here?' Ariadna ducked through into his bedroom. 'Did you use a ladder?' Peter said.

'No, no. I am a trained alpinist. There was a drainpipe and many handholds.'

'Unusual mode of entry, though,' Peter said, as Ariadna dipped her head below the belt of his dressing gown. 'Ah yes, another handhold,' he said, gasping at the strong pressure down there of Ariadna's fingers and mouth. Then he felt himself overbalancing and reached out his arm to steady himself against the nearest wall. 'The physics are decidedly exceptional in this instance, are they not? For what you are doing down there has added greater mass which, on this occasion, is overcoming gravity.'

Ariadna glanced up at him and, her mouth being occupied, used her eyes to silence him for the required fifteen minutes.

Catching his breath, Peter said, 'Are you trained at that as well?'

Ariadna was wiping her mouth with a tissue. 'What are you suggesting?'

'Sorry, nothing. Would you like some beer?'

'Beer, yes. Beer would help, I think. You are very savoury.'

'Savoury. Not sweet?'

With her tongue she tested the taste on her lips. 'Not sweet, no.'

'Not *un*savoury?'

'Salty. You are somewhat salty. Therefore beer would help.'

'I've got some in my refrigerator.'

Peter gathered his dressing gown around himself and headed towards his kitchen. Ariadna followed him as far as his lounge, where Peter had turned on the light.

'What is the purpose of those little pieces – what are they called in English, the little pieces with the dots?'

'The dominoes?' Peter nodded towards a long row of dominoes on his table.

'Yes. They are arranged in a significant fashion.'

'Significant? Yes, very. You've heard of *Rebel Without a Cause*?'

'American cinema. Self-indulgent adolescent drama. James Dean.' She named the film star contemptuously.

'Correct. Well watch.' Peter knocked over the domino at the head of the column. It fell slightly short of the next one in the line. 'You see?'

'No.'

Peter followed the same procedure with the next domino in line and looked at Ariadna quizzically.

'Still no.'

'There's *Rebel Without a Cause*. These are Dominoes Without an Effect.'

33

Yuri Shunin had been mortified and shocked when Alain had approached him publicly in *La Lanterne* because he had simply assumed that the Frenchman would know that what had happened between them must be buried as deeply as possible. Yet there, in that small restaurant, when Yuri was dining with Dmitri and two secretaries from the embassy, – the secretaries had been Dmitri's idea because, he had said, Yuri was becoming a recluse – Alain had approached the table and had swayed drunkenly and had actually grasped Yuri's shoulder. Yuri's three companions had watched in astonishment, and other diners had turned to stare, because Alain's voice was loud as he said in rapid French that something terrible had happened, something very terrible, and that he needed urgently to speak with Yuri.

Yuri blamed himself, partly, that Alain had been so out of control, because he had been avoiding the Frenchman since their encounter, which had left Yuri feeling unsettled and vulnerably uncertain. He was sure that he was attracted to Alain, and even liked him, but there were aspects of the bodily performance that he found impossibly alien, and which didn't express what he meant by being attracted. He needed to resolve that uncertainty, and he knew that Alain's view of it would inevitably be too self-interested to help, but even so it would have been more humane, and certainly safer, to have given Alain a partial explanation. Instead he had been running away, he had been evasive on the telephone, and he hadn't opened his door when he had thought it at all likely that it was Alain ringing his bell.

Glancing around, Alain had evidently understood that his outburst was unwise and had returned swiftly to his own table, and Yuri had managed to behave calmly for the rest of the evening and to endure it for an appropriate length of time before heading over to Alain's flat. As he hurried on foot along the moonlit boulevard he allowed himself to feel the full fury he had been forced to control during dinner and its polite aftermath, and he started to express that fury when Alain opened his door and let him enter. Alain cowered, and Yuri enjoyed the knowledge that Alain was anxious that he might hurt him, but he sensed, also, his depth of desperation, and that made his anger subside.

'I told you about my friend Wilfred?' Alain said.

'Yes.'

'The London police are questioning him.'

'Why?'

'There was an incident in a public lavatory.'

Yuri slumped onto Alain's sofa and scratched the back of his head. Ever since he had started out as a diplomat in Australia he had pondered how fundamentally cultures differed from each other, and therefore how different you would be if you had grown up in Canberra rather than Leningrad: but homosexuality was also like a foreign place with its own customs and laws, and Alain was talking now as a citizen of that country, talking out of assumptions which bewildered Yuri, who felt as though he had crash-landed in this bizarre climate and landscape. Alain had now approached the sofa, and he stood in front of Yuri and reached out his arms. Resignedly, Yuri clambered to his feet and put his arms around Alain, reacquainting himself with Alain's shortness and slightness – shorter and slighter than any woman Yuri had hugged, which admittedly wasn't many.

'I was wrong to involve you,' Alain said.

'You didn't. I'm not.'

'It's just that I am isolated. Even my friends are enemies.'

'I really can't help. I'm sorry.'

'You're right. You owe me nothing.'

'You're right. I don't.'

Alain pulled himself away and collapsed on the sofa and buried his face in his hands. He said, through his hands, 'But you don't understand.'

'You forget: I don't need to.'

Alain removed his hands from his face. 'You are alienated because the world I have introduced you to...'

As Alain paused, Yuri said, 'I have entered no such world.'

'You are denying it again. You are pretending...'

'You always made too many assumptions. That was why I punched you.'

'Certain things about you are undeniable. And a man like me, in the nature of things, comes to specialise in recognising those things.'

Yuri thought that Alain was smug now and he felt a surge of rage. 'You must allow me, however, to judge my own responses.'

'Women, you mean?' Alain glanced at Yuri's fists, which Yuri realised he was clenching and unclenching. 'I don't deny that you might well have those responses...in addition.' He looked exhausted now and said 'Fuck it,' in English, 'I need a drink. You want one?'

Yuri nodded. 'Whisky.' He sat down on the sofa while Alain went into his kitchen for some glasses and poured copious whisky into them.

Alain shook his head. 'Poor old Wilfred. Before they arrested him he was having a marvellous time.' He seated himself on the sofa next to Yuri who shuffled himself away as many inches as he could manage. 'It's funny in a way. Wilfred was convinced that things were changing in London.' He shook his head again. 'Ironic, really.' He gulped his whisky. 'He thought he'd found a brave new world. He got to know a man called John Stephen who owned some shops in a place called Carnaby Street, *very* flamboyant clothes, a real shift in what men are allowed to wear.' He described the clothes in detail and how John

Stephen had once, all in a last-minute rush, created a pullover from a mohair blanket so a pop star could wear it the next day on live television.

'This is all simply trivial.'

'No no, you don't see because you've been indoctrinated.' Alain was almost shouting now.

'You'll wake up your neighbours.'

'You must try to understand,' Alain said more calmly. 'The difference between a tweed suit and a pair of tight-fitting hipsters – that's really not trivial. It's a kind of revolution.'

Yuri understood that Alain was using that word confrontationally. Because Alain was so passionate about this subject, Yuri attempted to share his feeling, to understand what it would mean to regard tight trousers as symbolic. 'I have grown up in a society which has enforced certain rigidities.'

'Yes but so have we all. The West has had its own rigidities, some of them not that different.'

'The rigidities in my country could not be overcome with hipsters.'

'They might help. They might start something. Imagine Khrushchev in pink trousers.'

'I would rather not.'

'Nureyev might easily be wearing tight-fitting hipsters as we speak. There is a whole counter-culture of pink trousers.'

'And you would love, above all, to be there. To be where Rudolph Nureyev might saunter by in pink trousers.'

'I would adore that. Here, in Phnom Penh, in this provincial... I am buried alive. I am growing older all the time, and elsewhere, in London and New York, astonishing changes are starting to happen, and I will never be a part of them.'

'So if it's so important to you why not leave?'

'I can't leave. I'm buried here, stuck here.'

'You are young enough to make a change. You could live a different life.'

'No. That is closed to me.'

'Why?'

'I can't say.'

'Why?'

'I am in bad trouble.'

'What?'

'My life is not my own. I am owned by others.'

'What others?'

'I can't say.'

'Tell me.'

'Even you might be in danger from them.'

'Tell me.'

'You know Jean Barré?'

'Advisor to Sihanouk.'

'Amongst other things. Lots of pies. Lots of fingers.'

'So?'

'He owns me.'

'How?'

'I live the life he tells me to.'

'Yes, but...'

'Blackmail. He lured me in and compromised me. He has some letters, and some photographs. If I tried to go to Europe, he could...'

'Can he be bought off?'

'Money doesn't interest him much, compared with power.'

With deliberate suddenness, in order to pre-empt any response from Alain, Yuri put his glass on the arm of the sofa, and hurried to the door and out of it. He felt sorry for Alain but he resented being implicated in these complexities, which had nothing to do with his own life in Phnom Penh, and Alain's earlier outburst in the restaurant indicated that Yuri needed to distance himself or risk being dragged deeply into incomprehensible intrigue. He slept badly that night, arguing with himself about his own world in Cambodia, which fitted him only slightly better than Alain's. *Slightly* – that was the exaggerated thinking of exhausted insomnia, but even so he knew he could speak less frankly to Dmitri and Ariadna than he could to Alain, where nothing was censored, even if Alain's understanding was limited. An outsider like Alain still thought, as all Westerners did, that it all started with individuals, and life depended on whether you wore tweed or unshrunk denim. Yuri drew upon the knowledge that they lacked and performed his own Marxist analysis of pink trousers, and knew that they must represent the impact on the cultural superstructure of deep-seated economic changes, the start of a boom after the postwar slump. He could say that to Alain and he would listen with mild interest, and the censorship would only take the form of that mildness: he would regard it as a valid point of view, but not see why it explained the most important aspect of flamboyant trousers, not understand that his analysis demonstrated why those trousers needed to be assigned their correct, that is to say minor, significance.

But it was when Yuri imagined sharing his analysis with Ariadna and Dmitri that he started to think he should defect. They would understand his point completely, they would nod earnestly and sagely, and that infuriated him, that ready consensus, and he was contradicting himself now but he wanted to shout at them, 'Yes that's true but it's not the whole truth' and he wanted them to understand a man like Alain could think oppositely to that, but would still be expressing a truth. He wanted to shout 'Flamboyant hipsters!' at Dmitri and Ariadna, 'Tight-fitting pink trousers!' As he set off without breakfast to the Catholic cathedral, set off defiantly to that site of religious worship, he imagined himself in pink trousers and he smiled, enjoying the sense of his own body, conscious of a pleasurable ache in the muscles in his legs and arms and chest, knowing how strong those muscles were and how athletic he was, bounding along Boulevard Monivong, charged with energy, even though he had hardly slept, quickened with happiness and surprised by his vigour. He had no idea how he would make his living if he defected, there was no obvious career for him as there was for Nureyev, but at that moment he didn't care because he was enjoying the knowledge that defection was possible, that he could translate himself thoroughly and be a new Yuri in clothes that flaunted his powerful body.

The service had just started when he arrived and he swiftly chose a pew two-thirds of the way back in the large cathedral with its lofty interior and was still excited so that he felt agitated to be seated. He started to feel hungry during the first hymn and that turned his excitement into anxiety because all the practicalities of defection crowded in on him, and it started to seem impossible, but then he felt anxious, also, about a cowardly backing away, anxious about regrets he might later feel. He was deep in this quandary all through the sermon, which was about the growing dominance of superficial values, of crude materialism, and the sermon was in French and he found it difficult to follow anyway. By the time that the Catholic initiated went up to receive their bread and wine he had sunk into a daze watching them move forward and form a queue. But he was startled out of his daze when he noticed Keith's slim blond girlfriend returning to her seat, and startled more because she suddenly raised her face as she approached her row and not only recognised him but stared a moment and almost halted in surprise and reddened and looked away, very quickly and flustered.

34

'No you're right. There's too little understanding, not even enough *attempt* at understanding,' Edith said.

Bill Noon felt that Edith had interrupted him to say that, and she was looking away from him. It must be his fault, that she was reacting like this, because he knew, and everybody knew, how endlessly patient she was, how endlessly willing to listen. He tried again: 'There are things in battle... When you haven't been in battle...' Edith seemed unwilling to make eye contact with him and he wondered if it was because he was slurring his words and it was too obvious that he'd been drinking. But the drinking had been necessary – otherwise he wouldn't have been able to come and see Edith at the Ambassadorial Residence and try to talk about what was haunting him. It was utterly unlike him, but his state had become extreme: he rubbed his forearm where he had deliberately cut himself and the cut was deeper and more serious than any of the earlier ones.

'Christopher fought in the war, of course,' Edith said. 'He was very reluctant to talk about it. But he did say some things about its horrors, eventually.'

Reluctant, yes. Bill had always been reluctant, had refused in fact, and he knew that silence on that subject was right, and felt ashamed now. He ought to leave, except it had taken such a huge effort for him to come in the first place. 'It's true it's been a common experience for men recently, to fight in a war,' he said with another great heave of effort. Knowing Edith as he did, he was certain it was possible to get her to understand. 'It's very odd, how you can be in one battle after another and come through it and be fine, or nearly so...' Bill faltered because he could see that Edith's attention was wandering, her eyes wandered to the sideboard which was away to Bill's right, so that he also turned to look there, but there was nothing, of course, happening there. He turned back to Edith and gauged fully, for the first time, how pale she looked, ghastly pale, and how exhausted, with deep dark pouches under her dull eyes. He remembered that she was friends with Wilfred and realised that she must be upset about his arrest in London and wondered if she blamed him for Wilfred being sent away. He contemplated an attempt at something mollifying about that, when Edith finally looked him in the eye and spoke.

'I was reading today about hysteria. The Greeks had a theory about women having a kind of mental illness all of their own caused by the womb. They believed that hysteria resulted when the womb wandered about the body searching for a baby. As though the womb believed there must be a foetus there somewhere and so it set off in an endlessly frustrated attempt to find it.'

Bill was distracted by the thought of his own search, because for a couple of weeks he had been setting off near midnight searching the roads with a handgun next to him on the passenger seat. A sort of Russian roulette. It was an attempt to call a halt to that which had driven him to speak to Edith. Three nights ago he had caught sight of the roadblock he had been searching for, but, at the last minute, had turned around and driven home. 'That's a dreadfully sad idea, isn't it?'

Edith smiled wanly. 'The odd thing, Bill, is that men have always wanted to believe that it's women who are mad, but the clear evidence that it's men...that their madness is everywhere...'

Edith was staring directly into Bill's eyes, so that he wondered if she was accusing *him* of being mad. He felt a surge of anger, but it dissipated when he remembered how understanding Edith had been in the past. 'Madness is always closer than you think...'

'Some rulers kill their subjects. Sihanouk writes songs and plays the saxophone and men talk as though that's somehow worse than mass murder, less appropriate. Sometimes it feels as though I have landed in a country where everyone wears their clothes inside out and their shoes on the wrong feet and says their words backwards, and I try to conform but inadvertently I occasionally walk forwards instead of backwards...Or I am at a cocktail party and I forget to stand on my head...'

Edith's asperity shocked Bill, and he felt bewildered as she made a long speech in this vein, about a world all upside-down and topsy-turvy, so that, seated there on that Ambassadorial sofa, he thought he was altogether losing his bearings. He felt like jumping up and running away but then he was unable to move, as though tied to his seat and forced to listen. Did Edith hate him for what had happened to Wilfred? Really detest him? Finally desperate to halt her torrent of speech he said, 'Are you still having bad dreams?' and then regretted it because it was so wrong as a route back to the normality which he now longed for, and because of the baleful look that Edith gave him in response. They stared at each other and Bill measured the distance they had travelled from the point when Edith spoke about lack of understanding and it had seemed possible to raise with her the taboo subject he had come to explain.

'They cling to me,' Edith finally mumbled, 'the dreams cling to me for a long time after I wake. It's a long time before they will admit they're not true.'

Bill couldn't stop himself from jumping to his feet then and charging backwards and forwards across the carpet and exclaiming too loudly, as he stared at the carpet's elaborate Arabic pattern, 'At least you see things there in your dream, you know each time what it was you saw. But often I wake and I'm terrified but there's nothing... There was nothing there to see. All I'm left with is an emotion. And I stare out into the darkness clutched by that emotion...' He halted in the middle of the carpet and turned to Edith and saw that she was shocked and frightened. 'Oh I'm sorry Edith...this is not a conversation anyone is supposed to have... it is not a conversation it is possible to have...' Still looking frightened, Edith gazed at him and turned her hands over in her lap so the palms faced upwards, and he understood that she meant that she couldn't help, and even that she resented being asked, and he took the point, knowing that it was true that this shouldn't happen, not least because he was feeling violent, inappropriately violent in a domestic interior, which was in fact one of the recurrent sins he had been committing for over a year.

After reproaching himself for that, Bill was determined, that evening, to remain calm however much his wife Hilda annoyed him with her incomprehension. So he listened patiently as she lengthily described the marriage ceremony she had attended that afternoon at the Embassy. 'Oh Bill, it was so *glamorous*,' she said. 'Did you know that an Ambassador is like the captain when a ship is at sea, and he can conduct a wedding service? And this nice boy at the Embassy, he's an archivist, Harry Kershaw – perhaps you've met him? – was marrying a local girl, *very* beautiful, I must say. There were real tears in my eyes, it was so lovely, and H.E. was marvellous, he's so *funny* and interesting, I mean Christopher is such a man of the world, so travelled and wise, and he conducts these public events just perfectly. A different class to the musical event afterwards at the reception, with Peter Cook *again* in charge and that Keith Entwistle playing his piano...'

Bill was increasingly uneasy, as Hilda described the ceremony, because he remembered that he had promised to attend it, and he had completely forgotten, and that itself was a sign of how lost he was, that he had gone absent without leave for several hours from the life that everybody else was living. He had wandered away mentally, now, as well, and when he tuned in again, Hilda was saying: '...all so silly and disrespectful and in such poor taste, so immature. All the young people had on little shirts covered in dots, different numbers of dots, and they kept lining up, and the end one kept toppling into the next one in the line, and so on down the line, toppling into the next one, so they all ended up sprawling on the floor and laughing uncontrollably. So silly and immature…'

'Do you think perhaps they were meant to be dominoes, Hilda?' Bill said quietly.

Hilda shrugged irritably. 'The only strange thing, Bill, was that Edith Hartnell wasn't there at the ceremony, the one person you would *most* expect to attend it. The *main* person who is expected at events like these, who we depend upon in the social world of the Embassy. The person who is the beating heart of the Embassy. But the Ambassador, as I said, was just marvellous, and set the perfect tone, which was a little upset by his wife's absence, which everybody commented on, everybody wondered what it could possibly be that would keep her away, and one or two mentioned that she has seemed a little out of sorts lately, a little distant and not herself.' Hilda looked at Bill quizzically, 'And of course *you* weren't there, either, even though you had said *twice* that you would be.'

Bill took a deep breath in the face of the significant stare that Hilda then gave him, the stare that clearly referred to the accusation that she had previously made, that he and Edith were having an affair, which was absurd, except…there was a sense in which Bill did love Edith because he admired so much her sense of duty, her dedication to the Embassy, which was so like what the best sort of soldier must do, and thoroughly selfless too because all the credit went to Christopher and his bosses. And he could feel tears itching at him behind his eyes as he cringed with embarrassment remembering the scene that afternoon, and mourned the rejection that Edith had inflicted on him, worse than sexual because rejecting that incomprehensible, bizarre part of himself that he had wanted so badly to explain.

Bill managed to stay patient through dinner, and then insisted that he wanted to read to Andrea, their daughter, because he had promised her that he would read again to her the story by Peter Cook, 'The Crocodile Princess', which she was so fond of, and which Peter had kindly supplied to him in a typewritten form. After that, when Andrea was happily lying on her side with her hand tucked under her face, he absent-mindedly wandered out to the car with the typewritten page still in his hand, because he had convinced himself that his handgun was sitting openly there on view. He found that it was, in fact, safely concealed in the glove compartment, but, in the process of confirming that, he left 'The Crocodile Princess' on the passenger seat.

Bill worked desperately hard, then, to spend a conventional married evening with Hilda, wishing that such an evening could be routine for him, with Hilda knitting and gossiping about Embassy wives, and him reading a novel by Ian Fleming that Keith Entwistle had lent him, working hard to suppress his distaste for the hero's playboy habits, and to suspend his disbelief in the hero's preposterous exploits. In bed, too, he performed his marital duty and then held Hilda's arm affectionately until she fell asleep, and eventually also fell asleep and was sure that many hours had passed when he woke knowing he had called out because he could hear the echo of his cry, and he could feel Hilda's agitating shuffle in response. He stared into the darkness hearing Hilda settle again and start to snore softly, stared trying to see what it was that had made him shout, that hidden and nameless and shapeless fear, and hearing yet again the word *bivouac* and knowing that he must go out again to his car and drive.

Driving then, Bill was heading through the drab suburbs of Phnom Penh, with their shacks lopsided on their stilts and surrounded by trees, two miles of shacks and occasional pagodas, heading for the long straight stretch where he could push harder and harder on the accelerator. Then he would be able to shed that picture like the needle trapped in its groove, repeating and repeating the broken phrase. The corporal, the top of his head, the steam, the picture all the more pressing because it knew he was heading for that straight stretch, and it was consorting with its subordinates, the memory of lentils boiling, and the word *bivouac*, applied to the picture like an appalling joke. He reached the stretch and heard the roar as he jammed his right foot down hard, hard, and he was flying through the dark with his eyes fixed on his headlights, and *bivouac* was only a murmur, a murmur but still there even when he shook his head, to banish it: 'gallows humour', perhaps, components of a joke but where a joke should never go, about the top part missing. In the case of boiling lentils, the lid of the pan, in the case of the corporal... *Bivouac* – the opposite of funny. The murmur louder now because he had to slow approaching a bend, so he turned around and accelerated again the other way down the long straight stretch.

But half-way along the return stretch it struck Bill as futile and he slowed, and *bivouac* clamoured at him and he knew he needed to search again for the road block and those creatures who had fired at him. He drove absent-mindedly for hours, not conscious of the time, and was surprised to find that it was growing light, and then that surprise coincided with another when he saw, just beyond the scope of his headlights, where their light mingled with the growing daylight, a tree spread across the road and then three men with rifles standing behind it. They were facing in the other direction, so he stopped his car, grabbed his gun from the glove compartment, slipped out of the car and ran with his head ducked down across a paddy field towards a row of sugar palms. From there he could observe the road block and saw that, as well as the three men, there was a Jeep station-wagon with two more men inside. He smiled at the thought that these sort of odds would be easy for 007 and ran out of the palms towards the three men and managed to shoot two of them before they had understood that a madman was running straight towards them. The third one, though, understood quickly enough to fire several shots at Bill and one of them grazed his left leg. He turned around then and headed away from the sugar palms to where the jungle started, feeling surprisingly alive because of the pain in his leg and wanting suddenly to live as he ran through the undergrowth which was partially hidden in mist which was dispersing as the sun rose and he had almost reached the trees as the bullets struck him in the back.

35

The climate of Edith Hartnell, for most of her life, had resembled somewhere temperate like Cornwall. Edith's climate had been stable and easily habitable; then, about five years earlier, she had started gradually to become a different place. Her landscape remained recognisable because she had not, like others, (including her husband) expanded and softened: well, she had expanded a little, but not so she looked transformed. But her climate altered so that she became subject to persistent drought and sudden, overwhelming waves of heat. She was now 'a certain age' but that age was prone, above all, to uncertainty, to disorienting shifts in her weather. Buddhism, however, emphasises fleetingness and change, and Edith was sure that her alterations must be welcomed, that she had left behind one set of possibilities but another had become available. She was not a desert.

Edith was in the bedroom in the Ambassadorial Residence, and had reached, in her sequence of yoga exercises, the fifth, which was 'the tree'. She resisted the temptation, which had been mounting in her, towards Mekong drift, towards floating away, and demanded, of herself, the fixity to stay in that place, in that time. Steadying herself by grasping the top of a chair with her right hand, she placed the heel of her right foot against her left ankle, then against her knee, and finally she used both her hands to insert that heel high inside her left thigh, just under the groin. Then she clasped her hands together in front of her and inhaled deeply through her nose and pushed downwards into the carpet with her left leg, feeling the fibres of the carpet in her naked left heel. She was thrilled because her balance today was so firm, she was breathing deeply, and her body was relaxed yet not wobbling at all but held thoroughly still by her powerful left leg as it thrust downwards.

Closing her eyes, Edith released her right foot and repeated the exercise with her left foot where her right had been. Once again her balance was marvellously firm and, breathing deeply through her nose with her mouth closed, she remembered how she had walked, that morning, to her favourite place in Phnom Penh, the spacious square beside the railway station, where there was a beautiful stupa, light blue and tall, which enshrined a relic of The Blessed One. There each year in front of dignitaries and eighty monks in saffron robes, Prince Sihanouk performed the ceremony of Visak-Bauchea, which celebrated the Buddha's three-fold anniversary – his birth, his enlightenment, and his entry into the final tranquility of Nirvana. Because it was charged with these associations, Edith had chosen it for a small ceremony of her own: she had bought a duckling at the market and then carried it to that square. There she had held the bird, feeling its feathery, agitated warmth and its heart beating with alarming speed, and watching it strain its neck forward and blink its orange eyes, while she prayed and transferred to it her misdeeds and her misfortunes. Seated deep inside the intense heat in the square was a powerful odour of fish sauce. She brushed the bird briefly against her forehead, lifted it up, and released it, and watched it fly. At first it flew fast and straight, but then it weakened and banked and collapsed out of its flight onto the stretch of lawn in front of the railway station, and three boys aged about nine charged towards it.

Edith called out 'Hey, no!' but they were sixty feet away from her. She jogged towards them, remonstrating, but she was still forty feet away when one of them snatched up the duckling and then, noting her noisy approach, he and the other two sprinted out of the square. She increased her speed, conscious that it had been years since she had sprinted, and followed them down a series of backstreets, aware that her knowledge of those streets was much inferior to theirs. She kept catching glimpses of them just as they vanished around corners, but after fifteen minutes of this she was tiring and feeling an affinity with the feeble duckling, weighed down by the farcical inappropriateness of a fifty-year-old ambassadress chasing Cambodians boys with a duckling. Thoroughly out of breath she halted, unsure anyway what she would do now with the bird even if she succeeded in reclaiming it: for what, symbolically, did a duckling represent, which had participated in this chase? She wandered through the backstreets in what she guessed must be the general direction of her favourite square but found herself instead on the boulevard which led to the airport and which looked across the railway line towards Boeng Kak, the enormous lake on the city's northern outskirts. Gazing across that water, she felt a profound sense of futility as she pondered the duckling's altered symbolic status: her soul was truly more like that symbolism, her soul did not resemble a bird that might soar and participate in vast migrations, but a duck that would be shredded and cooked with noodles and grated coconut. And she decided, then, that a westerner such as herself could never really be a Buddhist, that she did not want Nirvana, did not want to be liberated from desire, that she wanted to participate, to be thoroughly involved in the variegated midst of the human muddle.

It was as though in reaction to that realisation that Edith received, two days later, a lengthy, (but intermittently censored), telegram from Hector Perch, apologising for being so long out of touch. Her first response was anger, and the conviction that it was now too late – even making allowances for what had been lost to the Cambodian censor, the telegram's explanation for the delay was insufficient, and that delay was clear evidence that Hector was insufficiently interested in her to give her high enough priority. Later, though, she changed her mind, partly because of the telegram's enigmatic reference to a period of confinement, which she started to understand was deliberately unspecific, indicating an anxiety that the telegram might be intercepted. There was also the phrase 'difficulty telephoning', which suggested an anxiety about the Phnom Penh telephone exchange. Hector had nonetheless supplied his own number, and Edith made several attempts to telephone him, but found herself baulked each time: three times the switchboard connection was severed, each at a different point in the proceedings, twice the telephone distantly rang, but no-one answered, twice a voice answered but not the right one (and one was speaking German), and once a voice answered but crackled and fizzed with static and vanished. She next attempted to send a telegram, even though she found the wording awkward, because she wanted not to commit herself too much in her first response, and finally decided only to ask for more information. But then she encountered the censor, who made her telegram impossible to send though without declaring that to be his actual mission – he argued, remorselessly, over apparently small aspects of content and wording, and inserted a long delay by saying that he needed to consult with his superiors. Edith contemplated bribing him because she had heard Hector say that this would work, if the bribe were large enough, but she shied away, finally, from that. Speaking in very general terms, she consulted Reginald Armstrong for his expertise in communications and he told her that there were growing problems, that communications were being increasingly monitored and obstructed. That intensified her own apprehension that Cambodia was undergoing a sinister change, that there was a deepening atmosphere of anxiety and suspicion.

Reginald surprised Edith, though, by saying (with his eyes unable to meet her eyes) that, if there was someone

250

she needed to contact, she could use his own equipment, and he would set it up for her so that she might speak to someone (for example) in England. Edith was so taken aback that she couldn't reply, and then Reginald managed to look her in the eye long enough to say, 'The Head of Chancery, I know, was a close friend of yours, and this has been a nasty business for him, so I can understand that you might want to make inquiries about him – from members of his family, for instance...' That surprised Edith further, because she wasn't sure that Reginald approved of Wilfred, but it was also said abruptly, like a sudden inspiration, to conceal his underlying pattern of thought. 'But also, of course,' Reginald continued, 'such a conversation would be private, Mrs. Hartnell, and I would leave you to it, once I was sure that I had put you through to the correct number.'

Edith found this all very awkward, especially when, on the first such occasion, no-one picked up the telephone, so that, on the second occasion, she was acutely anxious. This time, however, Hector answered, and they engaged in hesitant, half-bewildered greetings, and then, despite Edith's insistence that they were speaking on a secure line, Hector persisted in speaking in frustrating code, so that it was only subsequent, calmer interpretation that allowed Edith to understand that he had been imprisoned in Phnom Penh. He did make it clear, though, that he was forbidden to return, and that it was dangerous for her to speak at length, and that he wanted them to meet in a fortnight's time in Singapore.

'I can't be sure that I can go,' Edith said. 'I'm really not sure I *want* to go. A long time has passed since I saw you. Since I've heard from you. It can't be the same now. It can't be the same after an interlude that's so long. I adjusted to you being gone. I don't know that I want to adjust back again.'

'I can understand that...' Whatever Hector said then was lost on the crackling line.

'I need to think about it. You know for one thing how much I love Phnom Penh: this would be a terrible wrench for me.'

'This is the first time in my life...' Again the crackling overwhelmed what he said, and Edith couldn't ask him to repeat it.

'There are also practical problems,' she said.

'I will be in Singapore on that day, December 17th, whatever else happens...'

When Edith awoke the following morning, after a night's sleep interrupted by fraught excitement and anguished doubt and wild fluctuations in her internal weather, she had nonetheless gathered enough refreshment to make a clear and determined decision. She was not only going to meet Hector in Singapore but she was going to make it the first leg of a definitive exit from Christopher and Phnom Penh. The ghastly problem, though, was to confront Christopher and tell him: she chided herself for not having warned him previously of anything as major as this, so that her declaration must appear to him to come out of the blue. It would shake him terribly, and he would find it impossible to believe, and Edith shuddered at the thought of hurting him so profoundly.

During dinner that evening Edith was convinced that their Cambodian maid had intuited that something was amiss between Edith and her husband, convinced that Somaly kept glancing at her speculatively each time she brought food to the table. She had to wait until all the staff had left and Christopher had retreated to his study before she could raise the subject of her future. She knocked on the door of the study and found he was gazing at a book of ornithology, a study of the birds of Indo-China. 'That looks interesting,' Edith said.

'It's fascinating in fact. I feel I should've paid more attention to the local wildlife. Should have got to understand it better.'

There was only one chair in Christopher's small study, the one where he was seated, and Edith had to stand just inside the door, so she was self-conscious about standing and reaching out her right hand as though she was reaching for the very awkward point she had to make, like a compromised politician who was desperate to explain. 'I've been meaning, Chris, to explain a dissatisfaction that I've felt...over a long period.'

Christopher smiled wryly. 'You have, occasionally, succeeded.'

The irony annoyed Edith. 'Not remotely well enough. An enormous distance has grown between us down the years.'

Christopher lifted his book from the desk and propped it between his upper thighs. 'No more than other middle-aged couples surely.' He gazed down at the book.

'I'm not at all interested in whatever the norm is.' Edith then described, at length, the history of the growing distance between them, going back as far as Christopher's horribly inadequate response to the baby she lost in Nigeria, and including his treatment of her in Phnom Penh as little more than a high-ranking member of his Embassy staff.

Christopher listened with a long-suffering face, steepling his fingers and swaying his head to the right, his diplomatic tics. 'This is a very biased account.'

Edith was enraged by Christopher's attempt to deal with this as yet another tedious problem in diplomacy. 'However biased it appears to you, Chris, the major point is that my account is how it appears to me.' His dismissive attitude made her determined to shock his complacency. She summoned up a great effort of will, and inhaled deeply. 'And that is why I have decided to leave.'

Christopher started. 'To leave?'

'Yes. To leave.'

The silence lasted so long that it began to whittle away Edith's determination, and she desperately searched for a means of emotional support, ransacking her brain for any form of authority but happening only upon Katharine Hepburn in inappropriate roles, in screwball comedy, in *Bringing Up Baby*, and she shook her head and gritted her teeth (Christopher was looking away in startled dismay) upbraiding herself for not preparing properly. This was one of the most important moments in her life, and she hadn't prepared for it because she had wanted not to focus on it, because of the painfulness it would involve. So instead of being bolstered by Hepburn, she was only suffering interference from her – Cary Grant and a leopard, and worse: *The Philadephia Story*, where the heroine, Hepburn, remarries her husband.

'There is someone else?'

Edith nodded. Brief glimpses of *Woman of the Year* came to her rescue, Hepburn there, apart from that stupid scene at the end where she doesn't know how to make breakfast – Hepburn mostly in that film, calm, successful, self-possessed... 'There is someone else, yes...'

Christopher swayed his head to the right and steepled his fingers. 'All the nice girls love a soldier.'

'Sorry?'

Christopher pulled himself up, with a jerk, out of his slump, so that his book fell onto the floor, and saluted, and, clapping his hands, croakily sang:

"With his pockets full of money and a parrot in a cage.

He smiles at all the pretty girls upon the landing stage..."

Then he shouted: 'Or whatever the soldier equivalent would be!'

Edith felt assaulted by the violent strangeness of his performance. 'I can't...'

'It's Bill isn't it? Is that why he's vanished?'

'Bill?'

'Bill Noon. His wife told me you were having an affair.'

'With Bill? No that's nonsense. He's...'

'Not Bill? Then who?'

'Who it is, is beside the point.'

'I...' Christopher swayed his head to the right, then steepled his fingers. Then he steepled his fingers and swayed his head to the right. He was repeating his Ambassadorial tics, but now at great speed. 'I...' He raised his hands but didn't complete the steepling of his fingers. He jerked his head to the right but didn't manage the slow thoughtful headsway. It was as though the ageing Jack sprang out of his box but the clockwork was terminally damaged and he sprang out again and again at great speed but with always-diminishing spring, and finally his head collapsed and hung limply outside the box.

Edith spent the next two days arranging to send her possessions back to England, and making travel arrangements. But then the Embassy was attacked, and the damage, of all kinds, was so disastrous that Edith felt that she couldn't possibly leave.

36

Cambodians aren't interested in facts. Christopher Hartnell had wanted to say that to Joe Keane: like most other Asians, Cambodians love myth and legend and heroic impossibilities, and they are happy because, unlike Westerners, they don't have that rational and scientific state of mind which is convinced that a notion of objective 'truth' is possible, but which in practice leads to pessimism and gloom. Cambodians were much wiser, Christopher was sure, than Westerners, because there was a legitimate variation on falsehood which was linked to loyalty and love and which spurs people on to brave and generous deeds. But Joe needed to bear this in mind in order to understand that rumour about him, about the Phnom Penh boy dressed up as a woman, – that whether or not it was factually correct was irrelevant to the locals who told the story. Christopher wandered over to his office window and gazed into the Embassy gardens and briefly saw, not the Cambodian dry season, but the English home counties in late autumn, the trees with their remaining dry leaves agitating on their stalks, and a robin on a branch saying *tut tut tut*, and he lamented his inability to make friends with Joe. Something always intervened when they seemed to be getting closer, but Joe anyway wanted younger company, he was at that age when he was desperate not to feel middle-aged, and that was presumably why he was besotted with Peter Cook.

Because Cambodians didn't believe in facts they were prone to believing, for example, in fortune-telling, and to accepting the widespread opinion that the increasing unpredictability of the rainy season was caused by the testing of atomic bombs. And they were gullible when Sihanouk and his Ministry of Information told them that the enemies that surrounded Cambodia on every side were infiltrating the country with agents who instigated revolt amongst the young and the alienated, and with spies who delved for military information, and that they must report to the police any foreigners who struck them as suspicious. It was the atmosphere created in that way which also encouraged the paranoiac fantasies of men like Reginald Armstrong whose warnings continually tested Christopher's patience. First he had warned that Bill Noon was widely regarded as a spy, then he had warned that Bill was being linked with Peter Cook, that they were somehow in cahoots, and then he had warned that it was being said that Peter had a strange association with Zan Jingrun, that sinister denizen of the Chinese embassy. The disquieting thing was that Christopher had a ghostly half-memory of having seen Peter with Zan, a memory that lingered in frustrating shadow, tasting strongly of dried beef and pickled papaya.

Christopher felt profoundly jaded, and hit terribly hard by Edith's declaration of her intention to leave him. By the time that he had arranged with Armstrong for a meeting, the Ambassador had worked himself up into a weary fury about his communications officer, reflecting that the greatest hostility was the one you felt for members of your own side – he had met many Russians he far preferred to the self-important Reginald.

'I promise not to waste your very valuable time, Ambassador,' Armstrong announced, after he had seated himself very stiffly in the armchair Christopher had indicated. 'The fact is, Ambassador, that I have very clear information that the Embassy itself is under a great threat.'

Christopher had a distinct vision of Armstrong's metal prosthesis, aluminium probably, and felt a jaggedly ghastly thrill at the back of his knees, as the vision travelled upwards to the stump. 'You do?'

'Yes, Ambassador. A dire threat. Probably imminent.'

'Can I ask where your information originates?'

'I'm afraid, for reasons you will understand, I cannot divulge that.' Christopher wondered if Armstrong was mentally ill; his disability would certainly isolate him in a place like Phnom Penh, and so encourage aberration. 'What sort of threat?'

'An attack by a mob, probably. The people are being worked up by the Prince and his associates. And I must say, Ambassador, as I have said before, that there is a dangerous sentimentalising of Sihanouk, indulging him because people find it funny that he is a playboy, writing songs and wooing the ladies. But he is a terrible tyrant, Ambassador, terribly selfish and cruel, determined at all costs to strengthen his own position. He would kill masses of people, Ambassador, to do that, kill them indirectly while he goes on playing his saxophone.'

Mentally ill or not, Armstrong spoke very confidently, as though he had some sort of official role. Christopher again contemplated the absurd claim that Alec Crawford had made at the Magdalen gaudy, about Armstrong's covert power, and felt actual tears stinging the back of his eyes. Could the world really be turning upside down? Surely, aside from vicious leg-pulling, if his communications officer had such an additional role, the Ambassador would have been informed by London? It simply wasn't possible that they would undermine him in that way, nor that he would have forgotten information of that sort. Could a letter have gone missing?

'We need to prepare ourselves, Ambassador. I suggest we start by moving away important documents, especially of the more secret sort.'

The man's impertinence was astonishing: it was like being ordered about by a minor clerk in a terrible bureaucracy, or by a car park attendant, and in that ridiculous Cockney accent. But all his certainties were shaken, and he said, 'I see what you mean.'

'Your Residence may not be safe either, so best not to move anything there.'

Christopher had never felt at such a loss. So much of his sure ground had been undermined recently, the business with Wilfred was ghastly, and he felt guilty about that, though he had honestly wanted to help his Head of Chancery, and now he felt it meant the loss of one of his closest friends. Christopher regarded himself as tolerant about homosexuality, but, when he thought about that subject, he felt undermined because he couldn't stop himself from thinking – always, always! – about coarse black hair bristling out of muscular buttocks.

Edith had screamed at him about Wilfred's arrest, screamed and screamed, and it was true the situation was awful, but her screaming was out of all proportion, and she hadn't spoken to him properly for several days. And now he was being told how to do his job by a minor... by a mere... and told by this person with baffling confidence, as though this person really had the authority to speak in that manner. He realised, then, that he felt that Reginald nagged him as a woman would, as Edith, in fact, used to nag him. He stopped engaging with Armstrong altogether as he pondered this: when Edith had nagged him it was accompanied by an assumption that her role in the smooth running of his Embassy was much greater than it actually was, it was a form of presumption, like Armstrong's, a delusion of grandeur. What was also similar, and worse, was that they both, on the basis of that delusion, thought it was their duty constantly to complain and warn, and insist that the situation was much more dangerous than it really was. Still ignoring Armstrong, Christopher realised that Edith had stopped nagging him about a year earlier.

'There are not just practical issues here, Ambassador. We need to show readiness when we are attacked, so that we demonstrate that we are on top of things, that we understand what's afoot in Cambodia. It's also a psychological point.'

Christopher glanced furtively at the asymmetrical thinness of Armstrong's right leg, and worried about the word 'afoot'. 'Thank you, Reginald, I will take on board what you have said, and discuss it with my senior colleagues.'

As Armstrong was limping away, Christopher had thought he would discuss this with Wilfred, not least to decide what was to be done about their communications officer, but then he remembered what had happened to his Head of Chancery.

And it was driven out of his mind, soon afterwards, by yet another visit from Hilda Noon, distraught because her husband was still missing. That was anyway very perturbing in itself, because it was close to a week now, and Christopher had sent out queries along all the channels known to him, in the French, and American, and Australian embassies, and even in the secret services connected to them, especially the ASIS, the Australians who he had often found especially useful. He had even contacted a couple of members of the royal family, and of the Cambodian military, and he had received in reply a lot of specious speculation, but nothing at all concrete. He had wished, during this latest lachrymose visit by Hilda, that he could hand her over to Edith, but remembered that, even if Edith weren't sulking, it would be impossible because Hilda suspected something clandestine between his wife and her husband.

Three days later, at 9.30 in the morning, Christopher was in Joe Keane's office at the U.S. embassy talking to the American ambassador when a brick flew through the window narrowly missing Joe's head. Thinking quickly, Christopher left through the back entrance of the embassy grounds, before the mob had found its way around that side, and dashed past Wat Phnom then down Norodom

Boulevard, to his own Embassy. Other than the ones whose help he most needed, he ordered most of his staff, including Reginald Armstrong, to go home and make themselves inconspicuous, and then he arranged with Keith Entwistle for the Chancery premises to be locked up, with their shutters closed and everything secured behind heavy locks. They also made sure that the servants' quarters were vacated and locked, and they watched the servants chalking, on their doors, pleas in Khmer that their houses be unharmed, and then whole families left the quarters carrying as many of their possessions as they could manage. He disliked having to rely on Entwistle, who was obviously inadequate in a crisis, and missed Wilfred, who would have provided calm counsel, and Bill who would have provided tactical nous.

It was only twenty minutes after the Chancery had been secured that a Volksvagen van pulled up outside the Embassy, and a Cambodian, of venerable age and fastidious tailoring, climbed out and daubed in red *US Go Home* (the same message that was emblazoned in placards on his van) on the pavement and the Embassy gates. Christopher, accompanied by Peter Cook, went out to protest about this: Christopher spoke to the policeman who was on duty about the special status of embassies, while Peter pointed out that Britain was not America and offered to direct him to the correct embassy. Half an hour later, accompanied by their shame-faced teachers, a gaggle of small children wandered past, waving placards saying *US Go Home* and *Perfide Albion*. They were in the vanguard of a large crowd carrying much larger placards with similar messages, but with more variants: *L'Asie aux Asiatiques*, *Vive le Cambodge Pacifique*, and *Perfide Albino*.

Christopher had wanted the two Embassy gates kept open, to preserve a confident sense of business as usual, but the police now closed them, just as he was stepping onto a balcony in front of the Embassy to take a look at the crowd that was amassing in the road outside, and guessed, with horror, that it had grown to about two thousand. It was then that the first object was hurled, a bottle of black ink which shattered against the wall a couple of feet below his balcony, and Christopher hurried inside, as a brass band arrived playing military marches, followed by a Ministry of Information loudspeaker van. A young woman, who struck Christopher as beautiful after the fashion of Bopha Devi, climbed onto the roof of the van and shouted the same slogans as the placards, and she was succeeded by a young man who turned the slogans into chants, which the crowd feverishly repeated. It was the excitement aroused by the chants which seemed to translate itself into the mass stoning of the Embassy from the front of the mob, who were thirty yards away and whose bricks hammered against the walls and windows, and Christopher ordered that the doors be bolted shut, but then the stoning stopped and the crowd climbed over the wall into the garden, about two hundred of them, growing in number all the time. Some attacked the doors and windows, while others were beating and beating at the official cars in the transport yard: they pushed three of them together near the flagpole and were about to set fire to them when the police prevented them, their only intervention of the day.

The Ambassador and his colleagues retreated behind the grilles of the security zone, but then the mob burst into the Consular section where they destroyed and looted everything they could find, and battered the smaller grille with table legs and iron bars, so the Embassy staff retreated even further, into a tiny corridor between the Registry and the Chancery Typists' Office. Christopher realised that it was imperative now to burn the cipher books, and other secret papers, in the Registry, that they must not fall into Cambodian hands, and he said as much to Keith and Peter Cook, but the Registry was unsafe because they hadn't been able to close its shutters in time and long jagged shards of glass and rock kept firing through the window. Christopher and Keith and Peter managed to open the strong room of the Registry and began burning the ciphers, but that was a horribly slow process and they were suffocating inside that small space, and then they heard the mob approaching up the stairs.

Christopher was astonished as he saw Keith run towards the stairs, picking up bricks on the way and hurling them towards the approaching infiltrators. There were fifteen or twenty of them at the bottom of the stairs and Keith stood, on his own, confronting them with a brick in each hand. It must have been the bizarre sight of this single opponent, bespectacled and slightly chubby and with Brylcreem on his hair, which froze the vanguard of the mob for several minutes, while Peter Cook succeeded in burning more ciphers.

37

How could Joe Keane haul himself up out of this clutch? He had fought immensely hard to stay away from the opium, and had managed for a couple of weeks, and then it was like a mosquito was zinging just above the soft tissue of his brain, just above its beige and creased lobes, and sometimes it would land and he could see its tiny hairy legs striding there, and then it would go zinging in the tight gap between that surface and the underside of his skull. That shrill mosquito was trapped in this tiny space, and it was furious.

The attack on his embassy had worked out well for him in the end, though of course he wouldn't have admitted that to anyone, especially to Chris Hartnell, who had been devastated by his own experience, including serious injuries to his gallant staff – Chris was at the end of his rope, and it was much harder for a man his age to adapt in the teeth of such shocking upheavals. The British ambassador was a zombie the colour of stained snow. For Joe, however, it had come as a welcome change to the mundane frustrations of daily life in Phnom Penh, and given him a chance to display his insufficiently acknowledged calibre: everyone agreed that he had distinguished himself in the crisis with his cool professionalism and his shrewd expertise. Soon after the brick flew past his head, he had evacuated most of his staff out of the back exit before the crowd had swelled to the thousands it finally reached, and he had made three judiciously selected telephone calls which had ensured, for one thing, that the police played a more active role in crowd control than they played (certainly according to Chris) in the attack on the British embassy. He, and the three others who remained, managed to keep locking themselves into progressively smaller spaces, and throwing bricks back at the oncoming mob, so that they delayed them long enough for it to be very widely known, and understood, that a siege was underway. That meant that they had to spend only just over an hour in the final space, the strong room, sitting on top of secret documents, (with the door and walls being hammered with chair legs) before the Cambodian authorities felt they had to intervene, in order to pretend they hadn't instigated the riot in the first place. It was exhilarating, actually, to be in the thick of action for once, and even Washington had to take notice when one of its embassies had been invaded, even in a no-account city like Phnom Penh – so his own acumen and courage had been acknowledged in Washington as well.

Action had also meant that, during all those exciting hours, Joe had been spared the shrilling of the skull mosquito. Being rescued was a relief, of course, but it was also strangely disappointing to be forced to resume the quotidian, and to feel again the tiny legs scurry across his brain skin. In the thick of it, Joe had welcomed the siege because he felt it must force a change to happen, even if that involved serious injury to himself, he welcomed even the idea of being badly hurt if it meant that attention would be finally paid to him, and the needed transformation was brought about. So he felt let down when the old routine was back, especially his old self, fretting about a Russian who was as wide-eyed and open-mouthed as a chorus girl but who would want to talk about the inside of atoms, his old addicted mind where he was constantly pacing down endless corridors that ascended into other corridors that ascended finally into a high secret chamber. Washington had noticed him but there was no sign that anything would change, and he was left to deal with the aftermath of the riot like the worst hangover ever anywhere, because the mob had smashed but also burnt – they had broken windows and furniture and pictures, but they had also bundled up carpets and broken bits of wood and set fire to them, so everywhere across the embassy there was broken glass and shattered wood and charred upholstery.

This wounded anti-climax left him in a state of agitated exhaustion, with a merely vestigial energy that was desperate for unchallenging outlets, for self-consciously unwise and self-destructive release. During the siege he had felt in control, he was mastering a very dangerous moment, he was a *mensch* (as a member of his staff, Saul Miller, had said) but now he was once again powerless and ignored. And he felt all the more powerless when, a couple of days into the aftermath, Saul told him a rumour about Ariadna, that Peter Cook, who had pursued her for months, despite his involvement with several other women, had finally succeeded in seducing her – but then, afterwards, he had immediately dropped her. He felt terribly sorry for Ariadna, and resolved, once again, that his own ambitions towards her were to be protective and Platonic, it would be a sustainable friendship, supportive of a vulnerable young woman.

The drab quotidian and the skull mosquito drove him back to Madame Chhum's, but he had always struggled with the forbidden. All his life he had been tormented by freakish, subversive wishes: to punch his father, to muddy his boots and walk across the pristine carpet of his ferociously house-proud aunt, to squeeze the backside of the local priest, to drive into oncoming traffic, to talk dirty to Jackie Kennedy, to throw himself off buildings – always, always, throw himself off buildings whenever he was at the top of one. He had checked with others and they had agreed that, yes, they had these freakish impulses which they would never in fact carry out, but he was certain that they didn't *feel* them as vividly, as uncontrollably as he. Because he dwelt on these impossible desires and let them echo and recur.

Also, it was easy to tell yourself that a visit to Madame Chhum's need not involve the forbidden at all, because it was an important part of the social life of Phnom Penh and everybody went, even staid old Chris Hartnell, though he steered clear of the drug. You could go there but retreat at the point when danger arose, so Joe drove down Norodom Boulevard, past the Independence Monument, to the limits of the boulevard at the poorly-lit southern extremities of the city where the Madame, the Queen Mother of Cambodia, owned most of the houses. He parked discreetly in a lane four hundred yards from Madame Chhum's, then walked down the un-tarmaced street, nodding to the Cambodian gendarme, the Queen Mother's official body guard, who was smoking under a lamp post and casually watching the stilted wooden building, which was lit by candles and spirit lamps, almost hidden by jack-fruit trees, and attended by four impressive limousines whose drivers were laughing together by the entrance. He climbed the steps, smirking with the sense that he had not yet trespassed against his resolutions, and with relief at the familiarity of it all – that route southwards, the boulevard, the familiar lane that kept his car out of sight and away from the Chhum district, and now these wooden steps. It felt like a paradoxical homecoming, because this particular home was so exotic, but he settled into its welcome, kissing the fingertips of Madame Chhum and smiling broadly back at her plump smile, grateful for the refuge which she had provided in the past, that relaxed but robust acceptance by strangers which he had felt was lacking in his embassy staff, and even in his wife.

Sighing with relief to be back in the routine, and tingling with anticipation because he was already catching the heavy-sweet scent of simmering finest-quality opium, Joe removed his suit and enveloped himself in the sarong he was offered, and ordered a Trente-Trois, the French lager, which was his favourite drink in Phnom Penh. A pretty girl (from Laos, she told him) led him along rice straw down a wooden corridor to one of the highest-class rooms, whose floor was completely covered by a mattress, and which was hung with Cambodian mats, whose straw was embroidered in gold and dark brown. The chamber was without a ceiling: through the capacious mosquito net the roof beams were visible, and big fans that ponderously circled, stirring the smoke. The lighting was very dim but Joe could make out four other men in the room, two sitting upright and two lying prone, and there was a very wrinkled woman, also prone, who was preparing a pipe, which she then passed to him.

Joe forgot to resist. Inhaling, he watched the smoke rising through the mesh of the mosquito net towards the fans and he heard the voices around him, important denizens of the city, businessmen and government ministers, French and Khmer mingling, nearby in the dark of his own chamber, but also from the chambers on either side, and all the voices thoroughly contented and slow and deeply considered, innocent of aggression, as his head sank downwards to the mattress.

Their words were hanging like smoke above their heads as though the letters were written there, across the mesh. He felt a mosquito on his face and was sure that it had emerged from his skull, perhaps through his nose, and he remembered mosquitoes crawling on the brightly-lit face of Prince Sihanouk, mosquitoes which were eaten by lizards, and then he saw an owl, astonishingly white, swooping briefly into that glare, and snatching up a lizard and flying off, with the lizard's tail dangling from its mouth. Then he saw himself climbing stone steps that rose between moss hanging among icicles where elongated figures ascended to a landing-place under a portico, the tiny chinoiserie landscape from the frame of Marianne's looking-glass, and then, for what felt like hours, he was ascending steps that wound higher and higher inside a hugely spacious and labyrinthine pagoda.

After those hours he turned his head and looked again at the woman preparing the pipe and found that, this time, she was not the very wrinkled Cambodian – but Ariadna. The jolt that gave him was charged with panic and an acute apprehension of danger.

Ariadna smiled. 'Good evening, ambassador. Is everything to your liking so far?'

'Do you work here now?' Joe asked, then felt absurd.

'Ah no, of course not. But my father told me: try everything you can – within reason. Because trying would broaden me.'

'And I bet your mother said the opposite.'

Ariadna smiled appreciatively. 'You are most astute, ambassador. But, also, I like it here because Madame Chhum and me are great friends, bosom friends, and we laugh together a lot. Madame Chhum has a marvellous sense of humour.'

'Really?' Joe tried to imagine the form that a joke between the Cambodian lady and the Russian girl would take, but reeled, feeling undermined because such alienness brought home the vast scope of what was incomprehensible to him.

'People in Phnom Penh are saying, ambassador, that you were a great hero during that dreadful attack on your embassy.' Ariadna passed him the pipe she had prepared.

Joe was amazed to feel himself blush because it was the first time in over a decade. Blushing had been one of the major humiliations of his youth, exaggerated by his pale skin, and further inflamed, in his shamed imagination, by his red hair. It was a great relief to him that his current blush could not be obvious in the deep twilight of this chamber. 'I only did what was necessary under the circumstances.'

'And yet the accounts speak very highly of your presence of mind and your bravery.'

'Everything gets exaggerated in Phnom Penh – the good *and* the bad.'

'I am sure you have nothing to fear, ambassador, on that account.'

'Oh in *this* city, no-one is immune.' Joe looked Ariadna frankly in the face, and then fretted that she might take him to mean something about her own reputation, and was shocked to find himself blushing again.

'Nonetheless, the whispers on this occasion are very praising. People are saying, in fact, ambassador, that it is surprising that a man of your magnitude is confined to a minor embassy such as Cambodia.'

Trying to conceal his surge of excitement, Joe passed the pipe to Ariadna and watched with interest as she smoked it – he was sure he had never seen a woman smoke opium before. 'Phnom Penh is only a temporary posting for me.'

Ariadna exhaled smoke through her nose. 'It is said that you are very well connected?'

Joe was aware that Ariadna seemed to possess a surprising amount of information about him, and he saw the obvious dangers in that. On the other hand, what damage could she actually inflict given that his masters had treated him so dismissively? 'I grew up with Bobby Kennedy. As boys we went fishing together and were always around each other's houses. In our adolescence we swapped girlfriends quite often...' Joe giggled.

Ariadna laughed heartily. 'And you are still close?'

'Oh yes. Like you and Madame Chhum, we have the same sense of humour. And I played an important role in Jack's campaign for the Senate, and then Bobby's, and then in the presidential campaign. I did a lot of organising and they confided in me all the time. Still do, in fact.'

'They do?'

'Yes, just after the attack on the embassy, Bobby telephoned to say how impressed they had been by how I'd handled it.'

'And so they should be.'

'Yes. Phnom Penh is only temporary. Bobby said to me: "Joe, we want you to get some experience in foreign parts. We need an advisor, someone we can trust, who has had first-hand experience in places like Indo-China." It's a great comfort to me to understand Phnom Penh in that sort of context. And to be kept informed during events like that business over Cuba: Bobby telephoned a couple of times to talk about that.'

'And would you say that you have learned big lessons here?'

'Oh certainly. I learn something new here every day.'

'Yes. Yes. Phnom Penh is so intriguing. That is, I mean: it is *rampant* with intrigues.'

Joe smiled. 'Yes, as you say: *rampant*.'

'And as ambassador, you are thoroughly aware.'

'I am.'

'For example, about the British military attaché.'

'Bill? Of course, yes.'

'Major Noon: he is famous in Phnom Penh. A famous spy.'

'Well I couldn't comment.'

'I am only saying he is famous for that. You know that.'

'But what is said in Phnom Penh, as we said, isn't...'

'But you will know that he attacked the rebels on the road west, the rice road?'

'Of course.'

'And died there?' Ariadna was timing her replies at opium pace, very slow and unaggressive.

'Yes yes of course.'

'And you are aware of his connection with Peter Cook?'

At the mention of that name, Joe felt a wave of dismay.

'Again, I couldn't comment.'

271

'Peter is a friend of yours?' This question had been timed even more slowly.

'That's putting it more strongly than I would put it.'

'He *was* a friend.'

'Yes.'

'Did you fall over?'

'Pardon?'

'Sorry. Did you fall *out*?'

'No no, we drifted...'

Ariadna inhaled deeply. 'He is a fascinating man, Peter Cook. Terribly attractive to women. I would say, in fact – *irresistible*.'

Joe tried to be calm. 'So I've been told.'

'Ambassador, I will tell you a secret.' Ariadna said that, then allowed four or possibly five minutes to pass.

Joe's body was rigid in the near darkness. Finally he had to say: 'Yes?'

'After his death, a document was found in Major Noon's car. A document which was written by Peter Cook. It is written in a code which we have cracked.'

'In code?'

'Yes. In code.'

'I see.'

'You know that Peter Cook is a spy?'

'I couldn't comment.'

'But you know?'

'Of course, yes, I know...'

38

For the first time in his life Dudley Moore felt himself to be thoroughly inside the here and now. He had slept soundly and continuously for nearly nine hours and awoke feeling a great contentment and, as he threw back his curtains, he had glimpsed the mid-December sun above the roofs opposite his flat, and noted how it lit up the frost that covered the roofs and the gardens, and he felt that sunlight enter him, and glow inside his head and his chest so that he was suffused with light. The night before he had done something extraordinary: a beautiful blonde, nine and a half inches taller than him, had approached him after his session playing downstairs at Waldo Vaughan's club *The Red Stoat* – and he had turned her down. He had rejected a woman whose score out of ten would have been close to a perfect ten. That almost made him anxious because it was so unlike him, but he knew that its origins were in this same contentment he was now feeling, which was, admittedly, the product of the huge quantity of sex in which he had recently participated, involving three different women he had juggled simultaneously while also diverting himself with a couple of brief encounters. The huge quantity had actually led to satiation of a kind he had never known, and satiation had led to the here and now.

He switched on the gas fire and enjoyed its small explosion into heat, then he wandered to the bathroom and watched, with enormous pleasure, the water gush from his penis and catch the prismatic light from the window whose frosted glass today had an extra surface of actual frost. When the gush had stopped, he gazed with surprise at his penis, at how it was unprecedentedly happy to sit in its designated place without further ambitions, to accept its place there between his thighs as the placid and modest equal of other body parts. He was surprised because that organ, in its endless pointing outwards towards possibilities and its continual regret at what-might-have-but-didn't-quite-occur, had been the crucial antagonist of the here and now, had urged him always towards the elsewhere, the past and the future. In the kitchen he noticed a packet of green tea which had been recommended to him as a concept and then insistently given to him as an object by an American friend who was a beatnik and a Buddhist, and he made himself a mug of the murky infusion and returned to bed to drink it and sit and contemplate the world further from the new vantage of his hereness and nowness. He saw, like a revelation, that his room was shockingly untidy, so, when the tea was finished, he set about picking up books from the floor and arranging them on his bookshelves and sliding long-playing records inside sleeves and then next to each other in an orderly series under the bookshelves and picking up trousers and underpants and dumping them in a pile in the kitchen to be washed. It was when he moved a pair of trousers that he found the script called *Bedazzled*, by someone called Keith Entwistle, which he remembered having received from his agent a couple of weeks earlier.

It was lucky for that man Entwistle that Dudley's unusually contented mood led him to make another cup of green tea and light a cigarette and seat himself back in bed and flick through the script first of all and then find himself sufficiently intrigued to read it with more careful consideration. It was based on the Faust legend, which Dudley knew from the opera by Gounod, where a tenor is visited by the devil and has all his wishes granted. As a comedy idea it reminded him of something, which he couldn't quite place, from the days of *Beyond the Fringe* – it was the sort of intellectual premise that Jonathan Miller might have invented, perhaps. But here it was all elaborated with deft skill, and the Faust part, the character called Stanley Moon, could almost, uncannily, have been written with him in mind, it was so well suited to his strengths as a performer.

That evening was the first anniversary of the opening of *Red Stoat*, Waldo Vaughan's club in Soho, and Waldo had invited him to a special event there, which he had called *Gangster Night*, which sounded like a fancy-dress party, but there were no indications, on the invitation card, that anything specific need be worn. Dudley arrived early and saw Waldo surrounded by a big group of men, and in conversation with the vast, burly writer, Roger Law, the 'Tiger from the Fens'; there were a dozen or so other men, mostly young but one or two slightly older, who all shared with Waldo his swarthy looks of someone Spanish or Greek, with dark hair and skin and bristling eyebrows. As the evening got underway these men distributed themselves around the tables – Dudley was watching developments closely and was surprised to see that all the guests were men. He overheard the Waldo lookalikes, a couple of times, talking to each other and noticed that they spoke the same east European language, Bulgarian or something, which he had heard Waldo speaking on the telephone. Waldo had been accused, by newspapers, of being funded by the Russians: perhaps that was true, after all, and they had provided him with bodyguards?

Usually the comedy started early, but it was some time before Waldo climbed the steps to the stage and smiled broadly into his microphone and said, 'Hello and welcome to *Gangster Night*, the special invitation event to mark our first anniversary. This evening we are concerned to celebrate, above all, our good friends the Proctors, those captains of local industry, who have given us such a warm welcome in Soho, and who themselves chose this evening, some time ago, as one when they would demonstrate their strong feelings towards us at *Red Stoat*. My associates and I decided that we should reciprocate, that we should respond in the terms which the Proctors have made distinctively their own.'

At this point Roger Law and the Waldo dozen headed towards the tables situated at the furthest point from the bar, and Dudley understood that this was where the Proctor contingent were seated. He decided it would be a good point at which to move behind the bar and chat there to his friend Anthony, the barman.

'I personally,' Waldo continued, 'like to regard the Proctors as satirists. Violence, in their hands, is a very effective device, which works, in a Brechtian way, you might say, to uncover the implicit workings of the State and of international capital, where violence is ever-present but hidden. In their own business dealings, the Proctors, with marvellous, confrontational directness, deploy violence as a strategy that satirically mirrors the more complex, indirect violence that surrounds us on a daily basis. They are impressively hard-hitting, and their alienation techniques are radically telling. So this evening we are mounting a tribute to them and inventing a performance whose style will acknowledge their influence to everyone who is aware of their work.'

Waldo then nodded at Roger Law, who featured conspicuously in the intense but brief encounter which followed and which led to several of the Proctor gang being carried out and three others consenting to be led, on foot, from the club. The celebrations afterwards took place in the basement of *Red Stoat* where Dudley played piano, and lasted until four o clock in the morning. During that time, Dudley pondered the *Bedazzled* script and thought that he would ask for one of the scenes to be removed: the one where his character became an Oriental potentate whose saxophone-playing caused a big river to reverse the direction of its flow – that scene struck him as out of place with the others. He befriended one of the Waldo lookalikes, who was a jazz enthusiast Dudley allowed to take over at the piano on a couple of occasions: his name was Geraint, and, as they spoke together, Dudley realised that he didn't have a foreign accent, but a strange British one, and he told Dudley that the language spoken by him and Waldo and his friends was Welsh.

39

'You have a close relationship with Zan Jingrun, of the Chinese embassy?'

'No.'

'You meet in secret locations across Phnom Penh. What do you discuss?'

'We have never met.'

This was the third day of Peter Cook's interrogation, and since the second day he had been attempting to make his answers resemble, word for word, his previous answers to the same questions. His predicament was obviously alarming, and yet it felt so often that he had committed a misdemeanour in school, and had been summoned to the headmaster's office, that it was difficult to take it seriously. His interrogator repeatedly gave the impression that he was expecting someone else to arrive, expecting something different to happen: Peter saw him, on the first day, and then on the third, pacing around the compound and checking his watch, and his interrogator became, as the days passed, more irritable, and appeared more frustrated, and Peter heard him once arguing loudly with one of the guards. Was there truly something missing in the interrogation, or did the interrogator only want to make Peter more nervous?

'You are sufficiently proficient in Mandarin to speak to Zan in his native tongue?'

'On a good day...'

'With a following wind...

Peter smiled at his interrogator: 'With a following wind and after a solid breakfast of kippers and eggs boiled for precisely two and a half minutes, my Mandarin is "sufficiently proficient".' As he had done fifty times before, Peter made a quotations sign with his index fingers six inches in front of his face. He noted, in response, that tired, rueful smile of his sharp-faced interrogator, which he had spotted, for the first time, the day before.

'You have inveigled yourself into the good books of Prince Sihanouk. For what purpose? What were your instructions?'

'Ooh I love...'

'A spot of inveigling in its own right and just for its own sake. I'm an amateur inveigler, I am. I do it just for the sheer love of inveigling.'

Peter laughed. His interrogator's English was impeccable, but even the hint of a Russian accent, combined with his patronisingly mechanistic parody, added another dimension to the comedy of inveigling. Peter looked at him more closely and noticed with surprise that he was unshaven today – on the first day his interrogator had been immaculate in a light-blue lightweight suit, and his hard bony face had accentuated the sense of sharpness about him, everywhere, from his close-cropped blond hair to his shiny black shoes. He had moved with staccato but vigorous precision and asked his questions in the same style. But today there was some blond stubble on his chin, and his tie was a little loose.

'You are close...'

'To the American ambassador...'

'Joseph Keane. Unusual for someone...'

'So junior. Yes, that's true.' Peter shrugged. Boredom made him change his mode. 'Alright, I'll come clean. There's a secret link between myself and Zan, and Sihanouk, and Keane.'

His interrogator straightened in his seat and nodded encouragingly.

In a confidential whisper Peter said, 'We are all supporters of the English football club Tottenham Hotspur.'

The interrogator raised his hand and shook his head, 'No, please. No.'

'The other day, Jingie said to me, "Pete why don't you and me and Joey and Snookie drive up to that away game in Newcastle? Snookie's been working much too hard recently. I mean," he said, "Snookie's a genius and all that, slaving away all day in the Royal Palace, playing off the superpowers against each other, encouraging Russia in the morning and America in the afternoon, and all that. But there's only so much a man can take. I mean all work and no play etc, etc, he needs a break, and that game up there, you know, the Spurs could really..."'

'Yes thank you, Mr.Cook, that will do.'

They had snatched Peter just after midnight, after an evening of drinking, not far from his flat. A couple of minutes earlier, he had stopped to gaze at two tall bamboo poles and two white flags shaped like a crocodile – white, the colour of mourning, and a wreath with a photograph in the middle of it, stiff and formal, of an earnest young woman. Death varies from one country to another, Peter was drunkenly musing, when a powerful hand, from behind, clamped a sodden, pungent handkerchief over his mouth, and he was pushed into the back of a jeep. The building they brought him to, after a long, bumpy journey, was in a clearing deep in the jungle, but it resembled a hunting-lodge in central Europe, with an air of half-hearted bureaucracy – a notice with instructions about how to respond if there were a fire, doors painted in dark, official green and with dense spring-cartridge locks, all displayed under light bulbs with very low wattage.

When he first arrived, two guards forced Peter successively into five different rooms, each time (until the fifth) ordering him to strip off all his clothes, and each time asking him his name, his occupation, and his date and place of birth. The first room was in complete darkness but it appeared quite spacious, and Peter, naked, seated himself at first in a wooden chair trying to calm himself. But then he wandered through the room searching for somewhere to lie down comfortably, because he was exhausted, but he kept colliding with tables and chairs, so he thought the room might be a canteen. Eventually he found a bench and he stretched out on that and fell asleep but the two guards burst in soon afterwards and woke him up, and ordered him to get dressed. The second room was extremely cramped but with a high ceiling and an intensely bright light, and the fat guard shouted at Peter to undress, as though it was shocking that he was now clothed. The room was too narrow for Peter to stretch out so he seated himself and hugged his knees and tried to sleep, but the light shocked the inside of his eyes. But then the light flickered and faded away and Peter could hear the two guards arguing with each other, in incomprehensible Russian, before they re-entered the room and took him to another, which was a little less cramped and where the light was not quite so intense. Peter could hear the two guards arguing again after they left: the fat one seemed to be lower in rank than the small, slight one, but the small one was slovenly looking, unbuttoned and tarnished, and the fat one's moustache bristled constantly with indignation. Peter was in this third room only briefly before the fat guard marched him to a fourth, which seemed medical in nature because there was a table with a neat row of scalpels. This time, after Peter had undressed, the fat guard ordered Peter to peel back his foreskin, then he contemplated the scalpels matter-of-factly, but was interrupted by the small guard bursting in and shouting at him. Peter wondered if the altercation between the guards was part of a process of disorientation, which was a prelude to brainwashing, but both guards appeared then to lose heart. They showed Peter finally to a bedroom, which contained a single bunk bed, a sink with a toothbrush and toothpaste, a wooden chair, and a desk, which was covered in long scratches. Sleepless, Peter wondered if they had brought him there to force him to write comedy sketches.

'You have communicated, employing coded messages, with insurgent elements. How well do you know Hok Suhana?'

The same questions in a different order: this one started day four. 'I know Hok Suhana slightly. He is a schoolteacher.'

'You know that he is also a notable insurgent. You have worked alongside your colleague Major Noon to establish close ties with these elements. Your military attaché has also passed to them these coded messages.'

'My work and Bill's are very different. His rank is much higher than mine. I am an assistant assistant to an assistant...'

'I notice, Mr. Cook, that you speak of Major Noon in the present tense?'

Peter had not, on any of the nights, slept well in his hard bunk with jungle noises alarming the thick darkness, shrieks and bellows and murmurs impossible to identify – some in the distance, others jarringly close, as though just outside the wooden walls of his bedroom. He recoiled exhaustedly from whatever this latest insinuation meant, coming after so many other bewildering, world-upside-down interpretations. For the past four days he had reeled between disbelieving altogether in what was happening to him and receiving it with a sense of *déjà vu*, the notion, charged with both conviction and disbelief, that he had lived that moment before when he was someone else. 'You have no right to detain me here, it's a breach of every possible diplomatic rule, and Britain and Russia...'

'Who said that we are Russians?'

Peter shrugged dismissively.

'It strikes me, Mr. Cook, that you are not as frightened as you should be. I take that to be another benefit of your privileged background, your expensive school, and your tip-top Cambridge college, and your dilettante dabbling in popular entertainment before your arrival here, where the man in charge is an old chum of your father's. So you are not frightened because your background leads you to believe you are immune, that you are protected wherever you go, even deep in a jungle in Indo-China.'

'When Princess Margaret paid a visit, recently, to Vietnam, listening devices were inserted in the light bulbs in her hotel room... If you had been efficient enough to perform the appropriate surveillance on me, if you had placed such devices in my flat, for example, you would be aware that I am not a spy.'

'We did do that. And it is true that we found nothing incriminating, but we found, nothing, either, that proved your innocence. We took a journal from your flat, and that makes very interesting reading.' The interrogator reached into the briefcase that was next to his feet and produced Peter's journal, and opened it. 'What, for example, did you mean when you wrote: "It feels, sometimes, as though I'm living in the wrong genre?"'

'Well...the main thing I've learned in my diplomatic life is that all the politicians are merely players strutting and fretting and staging big publicity events like the Cuban Missile Crisis (knock 'em dead, knock 'em dead) because Russia and America both need to be the biggest star on the planet...and then there are others with a subtler agenda, publicity-wise, the subversive types, 'Les Autres', who *vawnt to be alowwwnn...*'

The two had been raising their voices, but now they gazed at one another. The interrogator's sad smile seemed to indicate genuine puzzlement, and Peter noticed that he was still unshaven, and his tie was even looser, and he looked older – nearer forty now than the thirty he had looked at first.

'That was excellent pho soup you brought me last night. Did you cook it yourself?' Peter asked. On previous nights his food had been brought to him by one of the guards, but, on this latest occasion, it had been his interrogator who brought him his meal, and the food had been superior to the Russian dumplings and cabbage and pork, which had preceded it.

'What makes you say that? The cook is still here. The guards are still here. And I am trained, anyway, in martial arts.'

It hadn't occurred to Peter before, but the building felt less occupied on this fourth day than it had before, and his suspicions were further aroused when his interrogator refused to allow him the evening walk, into the jungle margins, which he had previously been allowed. The change alarmed Peter: he understood that, for a man of action, it might offer an opportunity, but for him it suggested an instability that was threatening. But then, also, lack of sleep, combined with the constant under-presence of suppressed fear, was creating a hallucinatory atmosphere that made it impossible to judge anything confidently.

It was after a long ramifying fugue, on the fifth day, about the World Inveigling Championships, just after a section about the small margins between world-class inveigling, inveigling at the absolutely top level, and inveigling just below that level, that Peter's interrogator emitted a loud scream and punched the table shouting, 'Stop! Stop!'

'It takes its toll, doesn't it?' Peter said, 'this living in the jungle. All those lizards in the bathroom. They take their toll. Did you know that there's a single tree in the Cambodian jungle that has more ants than the whole of the British Isles?'

The interrogator put his hands over his face. A couple of minutes passed before he said: 'you mean *species* of ants?'

'You might say that, Mr. Interrogator, but you are mistaken. Because formicographers have identified this tree and it's one single heaving pullulating conglomeration of ants from its formicating roots to its formicating canopy, and these ants are marching up and down its trunk all day and night bumping into one another carrying bits of leaves...'

'What is your relationship with Sihanouk's daughter? It is said in many places in Phnom Penh that you and she were caught *in flagrante* in a cupboard.'

'No, no. Because I am not her type. You know her nickname?'

The interrogator wearily shook his head.

'See you later, interrogator. Not for a while, crocodile. Young Bopha is universally known as The Crocodile Princess. Can you guess why?'

'I have heard that name, but not...'

'She is aroused by crocodiles, and only crocodiles. The odd cayman, and occasionally an alligator, at a stretch. It's those rows of ferocious teeth, they excite her, unbearably. And their bumpy pachydermy torsos and tails. And risk excites her in general. So she made me dress up as a crocodile and meet her in that headmaster's office. I was the innocent party entirely.'

'Maybe it is true, in fact, that you are a world-class inveigler. That in fact that has been your function in Cambodia, to inveigle at the top level with Sihanouk and the others. You are Prince Charming fighting the Cold War with suave *savoir faire* and puerile jokes and silly voices...'

'So cruel...'

'And yet, it seems to me, Mr. Cook, that your style is actually that of a woman. Like a beautiful woman who uses her charms to distract and seduce powerful men. It is not at all manly, what you do.'

Peter slumped in his seat. For the first time there was an air of genuine threat in his interrogator's manner.

'What was it you said on the second day about repetition?' The interrogator was mournful now.

Peter shrugged, and said, almost apologetically, 'That your job is mired in repetition. Like a worker on a production line, or a comedian on tour who has to tell the same jokes again and again, so by the time he gets to Scunthorpe he has told them fifty times and the boredom makes him want to kill himself.'

That night Peter had dozed off and was awoken by the sound of an engine starting up. He checked his door and found it was unlocked, and he wandered through the building and out of the exit and found that the jeep had gone, and wandered back into the building and found that it was empty. Still glancing frantically around himself he chose the narrow road in front of the building and sprinted into the jungle.

40

Edith Hartnell was increasingly annoyed with herself because she had lapsed so much into a drifting lassitude. So much had happened, yet her position, her duties and her daily habits, remained the same except that they lacked what had previously lifted them out of banality – the humour and diversion, and perhaps even love, that had been supplied by her closest friends, Hector and Wilfred. For days she had been drifting around Phnom Penh, aimlessly wandering the streets, and finding herself constantly drawn down Avenue Daun Penh towards *Hôtel le Royal* where Hector had first lived when he came to Cambodia. It was there, in 'the Raffles of Phnom Penh', that she and he had spent their first improper times together, in a room where she imagined that the air and the light shuddered as they do above a bonfire, because below it the bougainvillea spread around the building and climbed upwards inflaming the light and the air.

She often, now, seated herself, surrounded by noisy old French rubber planters, at the bar of *Hôtel le Royal* drinking a glass of pernod, the drink which Hector introduced her to, and which they regularly drank together in the same seats, and she sometimes even climbed the carved wooden staircase and walked along its endless, half-lit corridors.

She had become a hungry ghost. Buddhists believe in realms that precede rebirth, the lowest that of animals and the one just above it of frustrated spirits who are at the mercy of desires that can never be satiated and which therefore trap them on the earth. These hungry ghosts can sometimes be briefly glimpsed and are depicted in popular art as shadowy forms with small pinched mouths and distended bellies. Edith sipped her pernod, and noticed its effect, because she had always been easily affected by alcohol, and stroked her stomach, thinking *hungry ghost.*

Humans might glimpse her out of the corners of their eyes. Except it wasn't desire that confined her, quite the opposite: desire would take her to Singapore and her meeting with Hector. (And she hadn't yet informed Hector that she wasn't going to meet him there, and that was wrong, he ought to know quickly, but that was another thing she was allowing to drift). What was confining her was lingering, undesirable loyalty, to the Embassy and to Christopher, especially now that he was so shattered by the attack on that building which was so much more to him than a place of work. Of course, he wouldn't talk about it at great length, but it was entirely clear that his world had been overturned, that he felt betrayed by people he had trusted, and that he felt foolish because he could never have believed that Cambodians would behave like that because he regarded them as somehow both fatalistic and fun-loving, as incapable of action because lazy and slightly decadent, and deeply unserious.

It was early on a Friday afternoon, with a week to go before Christmas, and Edith allowed herself, which was very unusual, a second pernod, before she set off again for her aimless wandering. With that tang of serious aniseed, Edith experienced a recurrence of the nightmare that had awoken her that morning: the National Bank of Cambodia, that reddish-brown edifice, had imploded, and burst open, and thousands upon thousands of 500-riel notes had overflowed into Norodom Boulevard and were strewn on sandbags and spiked on the barbed wire that was for some reason sprouting everywhere on those central boulevards.

She was struck hard by the fierce glare as she stepped outside, and was conscious of how woozy she was from the alcohol, and how fragile the heat made her feel. As she walked she told herself that there had also been positive effects of the recent events, especially between Keith and Sandie. Keith's act of bravery, in the face of the mob inside the Embassy, had surprised everybody, but it had crucially delayed the mob so that others there could run to safety. He had been struck on the head by a stone but had fortunately not been felled and had managed also, eventually, to get to safety. He had spent a couple of days in the hospital but had insisted on leaving earlier than the doctors had advised, and this too raised his status amongst his colleagues, who now treated him with unfamiliar, and slightly disoriented, respect. Keith's manner had also changed – his diffidence was gone and he carried himself with a new authority. Edith had known that it was this which had altered Sandie's attitude to Keith, and that Sandie only wanted to have this new attitude sanctioned by Edith when Sandie had asked to talk to her, and so Edith had adopted, during their meeting, quite a passive approach, smiling and approving the respect which Sandie was showing to Keith. Edith had been conscious throughout, however, that there was some other question which was bothering Sandie, and which she was never quite able to bring to the surface: Edith assumed this to relate to Sandie's continuing attraction to Peter Cook, but there was obviously no future in that, and Edith had been very happy to hear that Keith and Sandie had become engaged to be married.

She entered the park and was grateful for the opportunities for tree-shade that it offered, feeling dozy because of her midday alcohol and the exhaustion which had been mounting in her from interrupted sleep. It was partly her doziness that made her blink a double-take when she saw Reginald Armstrong behaving very oddly towards a tree. Stupefied, she halted and watched him: she had noticed him first because of his characteristically lop-sided stance inside a group of trees about forty yards from the path where she was strolling. But then she saw him reach into a hole in one of the trees and extract from it something that resembled a letter. He glanced around himself anxiously, then took a knapsack from his back and placed the letter inside it, then he took another letter (this time with a brown envelope unlike the white of the one he had extracted from the tree) and thrust it deep into the same hole from whence he had extracted the first letter.

It was when he stiffly turned from the tree that Reginald caught sight of Edith. His first motion was to turn away, but he immediately reversed that, turned and acknowledged Edith with a brief raising of his hand, and limped towards her. Edith at first felt embarrassed for him, as though she had caught him in a perverted act with that tree, but, as he approached, she understood that he must be a spy. All embassies were said to have at least one, and she had often entertained herself by speculating who it might be, and she and Wilfred had often joked together about it – but Wilfred had always insisted that Bill Noon was obviously a spy, far too obviously in fact. But Wilfred had also once, after one of their visits to the cinema, fantasised about Reginald as a spy, and had concocted a cruel, but hilarious, story on that subject that compared him to Long John Silver, and involved doubloons and a parrot.

Edith had indicated a bench where they might sit together, but they had said nothing beyond comments about the heat after several minutes there, and during that time Edith had reviewed incidents in the past which now appeared to confirm the spy hypothesis, odd moments of insight, of surprising knowledge about the context of new events. She kept trying to resist this line of thought and to invent a conversational starter, but, each time she thought of one, its triviality became too flagrant in the face of the image that sat between the pair of them on that bench, the image of Reg reaching into a tree and producing a letter.

Finally, Reginald said, 'I was never meant to be this person, this man that I am now.'

Edith wondered if Reg was not, in fact, a spy, but mentally ill, because his tone was so desperate, and he had pulled his face so extremely. 'No, I'm sure…'

'There were many ways, that day needn't have happened that way.'

'That day?'

'I had left that place, and I was called back to it. Called back to it on a bureaucratic whim, a nothing.'

'Please, Reg, calm yourself. That day? That place?'

'I was called back there, so some papers, quite trivial papers, could be gone through, for a second time. For a *second* time. Trivial, trivial papers. And it was while those papers were being gone through that the grenade, that grenade…'

'Reginald, please, look: people are turning to stare at us. Calm yourself, please, and stop shouting.'

'I'm sorry.'

'A grenade?' Edith understood now that Reg wasn't talking about a recent event. 'When was this?'

'I was nineteen, Ambassadress. It was 1944.' He was calm now.

'I see.' So Reg was trying to explain a bigger context.

'Nineteen. I was meant to be a different person, but then that day… That place.'

'Yes, I understand.'

'And the grenade rolled towards us. And I could have chosen, like the others there, to run away. Often, often, Ambassadress, I have imagined running away like them. Often, often. Imagined the scene and done the obvious thing. The sensible thing. Run away, run away.'

Was this just a diversionary tactic? Was Reg such a brilliant spy that, when he was so flagrantly uncovered, he could divert attention towards such an emotive subject?

'But you didn't run away?'

'No, no. And that wasn't brave, as young Entwistle was during the siege. It was stupid.'

'What did you do?'

'I kicked the grenade.'

Edith glanced at Reg's right trouser-leg, the emptier one. 'I see, Reg.'

'And the grenade exploded just at that moment.'

'Yes.'

'So I became a different man to the man I was meant to be.'

'Yes.'

'But I have never shirked my duties.'

'You are invaluable, Reg.' Edith shuddered at how patronising that sounded.

'As *you* are, Ambassadress. Some of the most invaluable work is done by the inconspicuous people, like you and me.'

Was he referring directly to spying now? For spying was certainly meant to be inconspicuous and Reg would have an advantage like that, he was inconspicuous because people actively turned away from him, afraid to stare, not wanting to think about the inside of his trouser leg. Actively not seeing him. But she baulked at the idea that she resembled, in any respect, a disabled man – baulked because she recognised the truth of it, because it was true she endlessly performed unacknowledged service, and true she had been physically impaired in the process. 'That can make you terribly weary,' she said, half to herself.

'But it must continue, Ambassadress. It is *vital* that it continue. Without it, Britain would go under altogether. And then the world would suffer, because the world needs Britain to continue its good work.'

Edith recoiled inwardly from Reg's fervency. She had long ceased to feel that about Britain. 'No doubt you are right, Reg.'

'I know there are many who are backsliders. Many who want to eschew their responsibilities.' Reg turned to Edith then and stared at her significantly, and Edith wondered if Reg somehow knew that she had been contemplating a move away – perhaps he had overheard, on his wireless equipment, her conversation with Hector?

'No, no, Reg. We must continue, you and I. The inconspicuous ones. Who *also* serve.'

Reg then launched into a very long, tedious speech about all the many duties she performed as Ambassadress, and how apparently tiny they were and yet how utterly crucial. And it was the telling tedium of that, combined with her knowledge that Reg was exactly reproducing the official view, about the unavoidableness of her unheralded role, that clinched her decision. She realised then that her apparently aimless wandering about Phnom Penh had actually been part of the decision-making process, but it was Reg's eloquent description of her lifelong role that finally propelled her towards Singapore and Hector.

41

After a short sprint into the jungle, Peter Cook realised, or remembered from his reading, that this was no way to survive: he was moving far too quickly and his head was uncovered. He stopped and stared at the ground, assailed by a stench like rotting mushrooms. He was very reluctant to return to the building where he had been imprisoned, but he knew that he ought to return there in order to steal from it anything that he might be able to use in what might become a lengthy trek through a rainforest. He ambled reluctantly back, half-heartedly concealing himself by ducking down and keeping to the edge of the jungle road – he felt indecisive because he understood even less, now, about his current situation than he had when he was being interrogated.

He had been certain that the building was deserted but when he approached it again he felt less certain. Perhaps they had set him some sort of trap? Hidden their vehicles, and were waiting to ambush him, as part of a psychological game? Because, all along, his interrogator had seemed ineffectually to be attempting psychological tricks. Feeling absurd, as though he was being compelled to participate in a children's game, he ducked down and galloped towards the building, self-conscious that his long legs under his bowed torso, like an accelerated Groucho, introduced an unwelcome comedy if anyone was actually watching him. He knew that his own room contained nothing of jungle use. The first, previously prohibited, room that he entered contained five beds with metal frames and there, in a cupboard, he found a knapsack, slightly torn, but serviceable, and three military caps hanging on hooks. He tried on all three and put the one that was slightly too large in the knapsack and the one that was slightly too small on his head, ignoring the threads that were hanging down from its peak – *you must never wear a pith helmet because branches will knock it off your head. But a hat is crucial because insects fall on your head all the time in the jungle.* He hurried from one room to another, constantly darting his head around: in the kitchen, in a drawer next to the sink, he found a sharp knife and a pair of scissors, and he cupped his hands under the tap and drank as much water as he could stand.

Jungle Survival, by Captain Hilary Pecksniff-Protheroe, was a commanding voice as he entered another room, one he fancied had belonged to his interrogator, where he found the other vital object – a flannel sheet (not cotton, and a blanket is too heavy) that he could wrap around himself at night, when the temperature would fall dangerously low. As he was pushing that sheet into the knapsack, he noticed that this room was at the back of the building and that, through its window, he could see another road into the jungle. Was that the road on which he had arrived? It had been dark then, and Peter had been too overwhelmed by his ordeal to notice where the road had ended in relation to the building.

Which road should he take? The one at the front or the one at the back? He felt himself slipping into a reverie about the symbolism of taking one road rather than another, certain now that he had taken the wrong road years back which had led to this moment, when he was stranded in the jungle. But his interrogator's bedroom was no place to slip into absent-mindedness.

Throwing the knapsack over his shoulder, he dashed outside the building, and then behind it, and along the other jungle road far enough to conceal himself while he pondered. There appeared to be thinner vegetation by the side of this road, which must surely indicate that it was used more frequently? This thought propelled him down this behind-the-building-road, combined with the half-formed idea that he would try out this road for a little way, and turn back if it began to look untrustworthy. *Your stride must be steady and sustained*: running had been very wrong, but he had read the survival manual only for comic material so it was uncomfortable to use it in a serious jungle, to translate it into actual steady and sustained strides. His memory of Pecksmith-Protheroe was selective and he tried, as he strode steadily along the uneven road, to re-read it retrospectively, selecting for practical information rather than comedy. Native people, he remembered, walked along a jungle path at the fastest end of walking, just slower than running, and they could walk like that all day – but then native people were no doubt much fitter than him.

Most intimidating was the knowledge all around him of pullulating life, the thrusting, competitive trees, the teeming and scheming creatures so unlike the pond life of his Devon childhood, the friendly frogs and neighbourly newts, and in the woods there teddy bears would have their picnics, whereas here – and he remembered then to tuck his trousers into his socks, to stop his ankles from being bitten. He ought to have boots, and, since he didn't, he might have to make holes in his shoes, halfway along them, to release the water that would collect inside them. He had thought that shoe-holes might be funny, if he adapted the idea somehow, but he couldn't remember why. He was now seriously in the wrong genre, but he had to adapt, and he proved to himself that he was adapting by seating himself by the side of the road, removing his shoes, and using the kitchen knife he had skilfully scavenged to poke holes into their leather in precisely judged places. After he had walked at top pace for an hour he felt reassured because his chosen road was still stretching ahead like a determined, purposeful road, a road that could be trusted to head in the right direction, and a road that had been shrewdly selected by a jungle survivor.

Confidently, then, he contemplated the concern that eating and drinking might be the next challenge, and congratulated himself on his capacity for forethought, because he wasn't even hungry yet. He had found no food or drink in the building, and nothing that would contain tap water: but then a doubt arose about whether he had taken this need seriously enough to look exhaustively for a container that he might have improvised. He shook his head to drive away that doubt – this was a rainforest, after all, and there would be no shortage of liquid. *Lianas contain drinkable water* he remembered and glanced around for the vines that figured so prominently in *Tarzan*, and noticed them proliferating above his head, but then remembered, also, that some vines contained, not water, but a *milky, viscous sap*, which is poisonous. Bamboo might be a safer option, because, in some varieties, water was trapped inside its sections, and you could identify that by shaking them. Sixty yards or so down the road he spotted a stand of bamboo and, when he reached it, he shook each of the tall plants in turn, but found that none of them made the noise of interior splashing he was hoping for. That alarmed him, and he contemplated the possibility of dying of thirst in a place where floods of water constantly poured down and soaked the trees and the earth. Struck by this, he stood for a couple of minutes vacantly shaking an ominously silent bamboo.

Shaking that bamboo might easily, under other circumstances, have been funny, and, a couple of miles further down the road, Peter thought that it would raise his spirits if he could transform his predicament into comedy. He set his mind to work on that, but a sharp anxiety kept interposing itself whenever he pictured a man alone in a vast rainforest, and, whatever angle he approached the picture from, it kept on feeling monotonously frightening. After another hour of walking, it occurred to him that the comedy that his predicament most resembled was the cartoons of a man stranded on a desert island, which always sprouted a single palm tree and was about six feet in diameter. The ocean surrounding the man was, by implication, even vaster than this jungle, and the man was shown as progressively more dishevelled, with long hair and an even longer beard, and with ragged clothes, and sometimes he was standing in a big rotund pot where cannibals were cooking him.

That didn't help, and started to unnerve him even more with an anxiety that his mind was thoroughly unsuitable for the jungle, that it would be catastrophic in the same way if you were wobbling on the edge of the high diving-board and were assailed by obsessions with your hairstyle or the bulge in your trunks. He started to feel hungry, and remembered, but only in fragments, the edibility tests for jungle plants, that you must avoid plants with milky saps, with the exception of coconut, dandelion and goat's beard. What is goat's beard? It figured in his memory only for its sound, which might work in a punch line, and he hadn't bothered to look it up. Best to avoid eating for as long as possible, or to wait until he was tired when he could stop and spend some time in one place testing different plants. The desert-island beardy man was food for cannibals, but he was never shown foraging for his own food, but then his island was half the size of a tennis court. He noticed several varieties of toadstool feeding on a decaying log by the side of the road, and one of the varieties resembled giant red ears: *the edibility test, I am afraid, is ineffective for fungi.*

The book had said that attacks by wild animals were much less likely in jungles than people imagined, and that *it is advisable to make as much racket as you can manage*, because animals will then simply avoid you. So Peter thought that singing would work best and shouted a medley of songs by Elvis Presley for some distance, but then found that the song he could manage with least effort was a hymn he remembered from his childhood: *Onward Christian soldiers/ Marching as to war/With the cross of Jesus/ Going on before.* At first he didn't listen to the words as he bellowed them at the road and the trees, but then he did, and wondered why they came so easily to him, and whether, after weeks in the jungle, he might emerge as a bearded and shaggy-haired and ragged and devout Christian, like a manic prophet.

He tried to suppress his knowledge of growing thirst, but the singing made him slightly hoarse and that compounded the problem, so he forced himself to shake the next stand of bamboo he passed, and was relieved to hear water splashing inside it. He cut it open with his knife and drank from the stalk, and then felt encouraged enough to test some nearby plants for edibility. He found a plant whose leaves looked plausible and tested it for *contact poisons* by crushing the leaf and rubbing a little of its sap (which wasn't milky) onto the skin of his inner wrist. He waited for fifteen minutes, staring repeatedly at his watch, and noted that his skin didn't itch or burn, and then he placed a small piece of leaf in his mouth, and left it for five minutes, and found no bad reactions, so he chewed it, and found it very bland but that it didn't burn and wasn't bitter or soapy. He swallowed the liquid but spat out the pith, knowing he needed to wait many hours before he could be sure, but he plucked off several leaves and stowed them in his knapsack. He found himself unrecognisable in performing these actions, and confirmed that when he pondered what he needed to do about sleeping, that *spending the night on the jungle floor must at all costs be avoided* because it was rife with dangerous insects. Just as he was thinking that he noticed, on the right side of the road, the scattered wreckage of an aeroplane, and then, shrugging off the pointless feeling that he had strayed into the margins of someone else's story, he noticed that the largest part of the wreckage was the half-intact fuselage – intact enough to provide a night shelter just at the moment when his thoughts had turned to that need. *Check the surroundings of your jungle bed for insects and snakes.* He gazed around the fuselage suspiciously, and remembered to check above it for rotten branches, and then he urinated behind a tree, wrapped the flannel sheet around himself and climbed into the belly of the broken plane.

He felt exhausted lying there, and yet he couldn't sleep except briefly, because of the hardness of his bed and the lack of a pillow and, above all, the exotic horror of his predicament, and he wondered if the attempts, by his interrogator, to play psychological games, botched though they were, had nonetheless had some delayed impact, because, half-asleep, he found himself skidding away from himself: fuselage...broken belly of...goat's beard...desert-island ocean impinging...one-legged Tarzan...rotund pot...onward Christian...broken belly...edibility won't work...shaking a silent bamboo...

42

It is snowing in the village in the Cotswolds where Christopher Hartnell will retire. It is the 20th of December and early in winter for such a heavy snowfall, it has been snowing relentlessly for almost two days, and six inches of snow cover the church steeple and the pub roof and all the gardens and the village green and the cricket ground. The villagers have worked constantly to clear the roads and pavements and paths, but the snow is so constant that they are endlessly covered once again by fresh flakes. The children of the village are enraptured and are using anything they can find as a sledge, and the Thames is frozen and the younger people are skating on its surface of darkly-glinting glass. Drifts are piled high in corners, and the sides of exposed objects such as roofs and gravestones are crusted with deep swaths, which are freshened constantly with pristine snow. For miles around road and rail have frozen to a standstill, and the telephone connections are severed, so the village is entirely isolated. Christopher, in a heavy overcoat, wanders briefly into his back garden to scrape some left-over scrambled egg, and fragments of toast, onto the snow to feed the brave, beleaguered robins and blackbirds. He turns his face upwards and watches the snow swirling downwards, follows its sudden spirals and hesitations and sideways drifts, and allows it to tumble across his cheeks and into his eyes. Then he returns and pokes the vivid fire in his hearth, and lifts his copy of *Our Mutual Friend* and wanders briefly to the window to watch the snow, and returns to his armchair, thoroughly safe and snug, and with no need to speak to anyone, no need to think on his feet about the most diplomatic gambit to drop into the conversation.

The chill and brilliant whiteness of that vision accompanied Christopher as he wandered in his luncheon hour through broiling Phnom Penh, brooding about Edith's departure. Which was a relief, actually. But very surprising, because Edith had never before shown any aptitude for subterfuge, and never betrayed any romantic inclinations, having always been admirably practical and no-nonsense. Shocking, actually, this sudden change, but a relief because he had found her recent dissatisfactions terribly irksome, and he welcomed the restful quiet she had left behind. Nonetheless, he was angry, so angry that he couldn't focus at all on his work, because his anger kept surging back and fighting off the preoccupations he ought to have. That Edith should choose that ranting left-winger, Perch, infuriated him, but it was entirely typical of that type that he should creep around secretly indulging himself with another's man's wife.

Over on Sisowath Quay, at the edge of the Tonle Sap, Christopher heard the river hissing as the tide changed, and watched a flying fox spread its huge wings as it lifted itself out of a mango tree, and felt another surge of fury as he entered a café where he had only been a couple of times before, remembering that he'd once enjoyed the fish soup there. He had only taken a couple of steps inside, however, when he noticed Sandie Hamilton sitting at a table with a young man who was only slightly familiar to Christopher: only familiar, that is, as many people are whose faces you repeatedly see in a small town. Christopher set off towards them, but then realised that Sandie was upset, and he backed away to observe them – they were far too engrossed with each other to notice him. The man, who was bald except for a small stranded tuft at the top of his forehead, reached across to Sandie and tried to take her hand, but she pulled her hand away forcefully and shook her head with great determination. The man slumped back in his seat, desperate, and with tears in his own eyes, but then he reached forward again and this time Sandie allowed him to take her hand. Christopher unsettled himself because he felt a start as he recognised a charged sexuality in the taut chest and powerful shoulders and determined arm of the man as he reached across the table, and he thought about Wilfred, and hurried out of the café. Wilfred, who was fined £50 by a magistrate and advised to see a doctor about his aberrant inclinations, and who was still feeling too humiliated to return.

Christopher had no idea what this scene with Sandie meant, except it looked very inappropriate for a girl who had just become engaged. He remembered that Sandie had once denounced Keith to him, implied he was a spy, and that had annoyed Christopher because he knew it was just petulant, that it had something to do with things going wrong with the pair of them as a couple. She had claimed that Keith was close friends with a Russian diplomat, thick as thieves, she said, and that Keith had once been approached by a Russian in Oxford, trying to recruit him. So preposterous! You had to give the Russians more credit than that: they understood how the English class system worked, and that was why Burgess and MacLean had been so valuable, because they were sons of the establishment, and knew how to open the most important doors. But look at Keith in comparison! The Russians wouldn't touch him with a punting pole because all the important doors would be slammed in his face. But now, also, there was this disturbing business with the vanishing of Peter Cook. So soon after the disappearance of Bill Noon, it must confirm what a number of people had always said, and which Christopher had never wanted to believe (partly because it meant the Foreign Office – as Alec Crawford had told him – had indeed kept him in the dark about goings-on inside his own Embassy). Cook and Noon were both spies, and had been in cahoots together. Odd combination, but they had always got on surprisingly well.

That evening, Christopher wondered if he should have a chat with Keith about the scene he had witnessed with

Sandie, but shied away from the idea because he might be thought to be interfering. He was dining alone, which he found very restful, though there was an odd moment when a shuddering ache crossed his chest and into his left arm in a peculiar wave, but he dismissed it as another of those twinges that age brings. He exchanged a few words with the cook, who commented on how well the Embassy seemed to be restoring itself; Christopher found that shared perception very gratifying. He felt a pang, however, when he realised that his not being able speak to Keith on such a personal matter indicated a distance between them, which was partly to do with age, and that insinuated in him suddenly a feeling of being marginal. Perverse of him to care, because for some time he had longed to shift into a margin to rest and think in peace, but this feeling of distance was surprisingly chilling – the world was shifting towards the young in ways he knew he didn't fully grasp.

He turned in to bed early, sure that a good night's sleep would shake off his melancholy, but he needed to pee a couple of times in the first couple of hours before he finally fell into a deep sleep. He woke suddenly, after a long sleep, with the knowledge that something was badly wrong. A great pressure was sitting on the left side of his chest and extending into the upper part of his left arm. He sat up in bed and found that the usual tinnitus in his left ear had amplified into a roar, as though a hundred thousand angry cicada were shrilling between his ears. He tried to stand but the roar in his head dizzied him, and a wave of severe pain crossed his chest and forced him back down. He needed to formulate the best course of action, but first he needed the lavatory so he raised himself strenuously and crossed the landing and seated himself and felt the excrement rush out of him and wiped himself but worried that he would need some sort of operation and must be very clean so he took a flannel and soaked it and rubbed soap into it and washed himself carefully there trying to ignore the soaking of his pyjama trousers that were still around his ankles. Then he dressed himself and found his address book and tried to work out who it would be best to telephone, noting, ponderously, that it was just after 6 a.m. and that Edith and Wilfred were unavailable, and that none of the Cambodian staff had telephones. He rang a couple of the Embassy staff who were in his address book, but received no answer, they must be deep sleepers, then he thought of Joe Keane, who might have staff in his residence who would be up and about at that time – but no, that was inappropriate. He wasn't sure what the etiquette was for heart attacks, but telephoning the US ambassador felt uncomfortably in breach of it.

The pain was muddling his thinking. He would drive to the hospital. He searched for his car keys, and found them, finally, on the desk in his study, then he strode to his car and started it and put it into gear, but then felt an especially acute pain that made him gasp and search for air with the back of his throat. The pain was crossing him in waves, and some of the waves pushed down deeper and harder than others, and it was too risky to drive when a very powerful wave might knock him out altogether. He slumped back in the seat and stared at the steering wheel. He would walk over to Hilda Noon's place, which wasn't all that far, maybe a quarter of a mile.

Ten minutes later he was walking on the broad boulevard, and it was still dark and cool, and people were just beginning to stir on the pavements, and the Phnom Penh sparrows were starting their insistent cheeping, and he noted a large lit-up hoarding with a portrait of Sihanouk in a uniform with a sword and a knowing smile. He stopped several times to gather his strength because the distance to Hilda's place had multiplied by fifty times. Finally he reached the street, which was poorly lit, but he recognised the white columns on its ground and first storeys and he passed through the porch and knocked as hard as he could on the front door and called out feebly, 'Hilda! Hilda! Are you there?'

There was no answer, and he sank to the ground, and rested his back against the door, and stared at the little yellow balustrade that formed part of a portico behind the columns. When he had gathered more strength he knocked again on the door, and then, soon afterwards, he heard a voice just above him saying, 'Hello. Who are you?' It was the voice of a little girl, and he realised it was the daughter, the Noon daughter, and he raised himself a little and saw that she was peering out at him, just her eyes and nose, through a small hole that had opened up where the louvres in the door had rotted and broken.

'I'm the Ambassador. I met you a few times. Do you remember?'

'No.'

'I work with your daddy.'

'My daddy had to go away for a while.'

'Yes, I know. Your daddy knows me very well. And your mummy. Would you help me please and go and get your mummy?'

'My daddy is a soldier. He's very brave.'

'Yes I know. But I'm not very well. Would you please go and get your mummy?'

'My mummy says I must never wake her until it gets light.'

'This is different, though. This is special you see, because I'm really not very well at all. I'm really *very* poorly.'

Christopher had turned away because it was uncomfortable turning towards the door from his seated position. Alarmed then by the silence he twisted back to look and saw that the girl had gone. He gasped with pain and called out, 'Hilda! Hilda!'

'Look!' The girl was back again.

Christopher twisted back and saw that she was pushing something through the hole in the louvres, and he took it in his hand. 'Oh thank you,' he said.

'I've been crayoning. I've been a good girl, not waking mummy.'

'It's very good.'

'That's my daddy. He's in a war.'

'Yes. I can see that.'

'You need to get your mummy now you see, though, because this is very special so you can wake her, because your daddy is here with me and he wants to see you both. It's very good now to wake your mummy because your daddy's here, and he wants to see you both very quickly.'

Christopher strained then to hear sounds inside the house and heard nothing except the cicadas shrilling inside his ears for a long time until finally there were footsteps and Hilda Noon opened the door looking sleepy and bewildered. Christopher explained and watched her close her eyes and sigh deeply and shake her head.

'I'll get the car keys,' she said.

43

After a couple of hours of walking on his second day in the jungle, Peter Cook reached a place on the road where another road branched away from it, so that he had to choose which to take. The dilemma struck him so much like a blow that his knees buckled and he sank to the floor and remained seated there, cross-legged, staring at the two roads for half an hour. Lotus Buddha, terribly slow old vehicle. The roads were equally wide, the jungle on each side of them was equally thick, the light was equally dusky, subdued by the density of the same canopy above them. But one road would save his life, and the other would envelop him in thick leaves and snuff him out.

The night before, he had finally fallen asleep for a couple of hours, and, when he awoke in the broken fuselage, he was still half-dreaming about the dried-up tadpoles from his childhood, the tadpoles dead on his pillow, and a dreadful sadness seated itself on top of him, so heavily that he felt he couldn't move. Only the thought that snakes and poisonous insects were slithering, or hopping, around nearby at the level of his nose, drove him to a sitting position. Staring now at the two roads, the image of those tadpoles recurred, and overwhelmed him with inertia. Then he noticed approaching him, down the road that branched away, a group of about ten leeches sliding along: he watched them with inert fascination and allowed them, in that passive state, to get within six feet of him, and then they raised themselves up, sitting up on their lower suckers, and he knew that their angled stiff bodies were attracted to him, that they could smell his blood. They were fingers raised to warn him.

You must at all times keep checking that leeches have not latched onto your person. This was one of many injunctions he hadn't followed properly – he hadn't, during the night, protected himself enough from mosquitoes and was now itching in various tender parts of his body. The sight of the erect leeches shocked him from his stupor and propelled him down the primary road, away from them, because they were an ill omen for the branch road and surely, anyway, the primary road was the best bet? Another instruction he had forgotten was to dry his clothes overnight because clothes in the jungle are relentlessly wet, and now, as he hurried along, he could feel a sliminess inside his shirt and trousers as they slid against him in the rhythm of his stride. After a couple of hours of walking he stopped and munched on the leaves he had been carrying in his knapsack and which appeared not to have had especially bad effects after the edibility test. He gazed, as he chewed, at a peacock in a nearby tree, and knew that his physical discomforts were badly lowering his morale and told himself that the road he was following was a jungle thoroughfare and must therefore have regular traffic which would, sooner or later, rescue him.

As he started on his third leaf, however, he was undermined by a feeling of uncertainty about such a rescue. Vehicles on this road might easily belong to Russians heading to the jungle fastness where they had imprisoned him. Or they might belong to subversive elements who hid themselves in the jungle, and who might have their own designs on a British diplomat. If a vehicle approached on this road, should he run towards or away from it? He was convinced that there was an obvious answer to this question, and it was a sign that his mind had turned that he could no longer understand what it was. As he was thinking that, he noticed, high up on a tree that was nearer to him than the peacock's tree, a lizard, and then, as he was gazing at it absent-mindedly, it suddenly sprouted wings and flew across the road and deep into the dense trees on the other side. Its flight was beautiful and eerie – but surely impossible, and, from that moment onwards, Peter thoroughly mistrusted his mind.

After another couple of hours of walking, just after another stop for bamboo water, he reached an open stretch of ground and, noticing that, in the middle of it, there were two long rough lines marked out with stones, realised it was an airstrip. That was puzzling, and he wondered if his best hope of rescue might be to wait for the next plane: it must be in regular use because it would otherwise be overgrown very quickly. But, again, the anxiety about what faction controlled it drove him across the swath of tussocky grass towards the jungle on the other side. But there he was dismayed to find that there was no longer a road but only a narrow path. Perhaps he should turn back? But the turn in the road was now a whole morning's walk away, and the prospect of admitting that he had chosen the wrong road, and only being, by the end of the day, close to where he had started it, was too depressing to contemplate. So he plunged along the narrow path, hoping it might soon become a road again.

Instead he found that the path narrowed almost into nothing, but his head was swimming and he found it impossible to stop plunging further into the dense trees, the high jungle grasses and strangled thickets of bamboo. He noticed, often now, signs that elephants had passed through, sometimes recently, with their dung still steaming and the vegetation flattened. He heard, once, a ferocious grunting, and turned and saw a herd of wild pigs rushing through the undergrowth. Then he reached a stream, with gravel tumbling through it, and he followed that for a mile, climbing over boulders stacked up high and drifts of sand, and then the stream widened into a deep, stagnant pool that was too wide to skirt around, so he had to wade through it. He was now thoroughly lost and the stream opened three more times to these pools which he had to wade through, so that his clothes were soaked and he was drooping with exhaustion, and there was thick undergrowth to force himself through and fallen trees to climb over. Then he heard the sound of water roaring, and he waded through the undergrowth towards it, realising it was a waterfall, and was amazed when he reached it to see that the stream there plunged about fifty feet. Behind its cascade of water there were thick ferns and moss, and rainbows thrown up by the ferocious spray surrounded it.

That sight shook him profoundly. He edged away from the steep drop, and found, eventually, a more gradual descent, and then he rested on a flat boulder at the bottom of the waterfall, and dozed. When he awoke he was terribly thirsty and hungry and he drank from the waterfall, and found some fruit in a tree that had been eaten by monkeys and so couldn't, surely, be poisonous, and he devoured it, though it was hard and slightly bitter. It was growing dark and beetles started to shrill, and there were bats and a large owl hunting. He lay down again on the boulder and watched the moon rise through the opening in the jungle made by the waterfall, and watched the moonlight suffuse the spray and the mist, and felt that, in his feverish state, as a curious blessing. And that moment would recur to him often later: just as the dried-up tadpoles aroused melancholy, the waterfall opalescence of moonlit mist and spray would arouse a knowledge of the possibility of resilience, of continuing to fight back, that meant his responses would be different to what they would've been. Meanwhile, on that flat boulder, he fell asleep again.

Mosquito bites awoke him sometime later – he couldn't tell how long he had slept, but he knew that he had once again behaved foolishly. He wrapped the flannel sheet around him, knowing that he should find, or construct, a more elevated place to sleep, but he felt overwhelmed by self-pity, and by fear aroused by all the bizarre shrieks and bellows that surrounded him. So he lay in a frozen stillness, unable to move and unable to sleep. As soon as it started to get light he rose to his feet and set off again into the jungle, forcing his way again, for hours and hours, through high grasses and bamboo thickets, until he found another stream, and then he was surprised when a path suddenly appeared, and even more surprised when he found, after an hour of walking, that it led to a village.

The villagers were amazed to see Peter, and they welcomed him with smiles. The only sentence of Khmer they could understand was 'Do you speak Cambodian?' but they led him into a wooden building which resembled other Cambodian buildings in standing on stilts six feet high, and whose roof was thatched with palm-leaves, and whose floor was rods of bamboo. Peter was alarmed that they all seemed to have skin diseases, and he noticed a man about his own age with a huge weeping sore on his leg, but he felt desperately grateful to them for their friendly welcome and for the rice and eggs which they gave him to eat, and for their safely elevated floor where he could lie down to rest. Even there, though, he struggled to sleep because his circumstances were so alien that he felt he was losing any firm sense of who he was, and he spent an hour, deep in that tropical jungle, recalling the childhood sights and sounds and tastes of Torquay.

Exhaustion finally ensured that Peter slept, and the next morning he felt refreshed, and after a breakfast of more eggs and rice he felt strong and confident. Four of the villagers, three men and one old woman, pointed fervently in the direction he needed to go down the jungle path, pointed smilingly as though this direction was the simple answer to all his problems. So he set off, marching at a fast pace, and covered an enormous distance on that day, and ate and drank from a small picnic, which the villagers had assembled for him. He also remembered that *throughout Indo-China, attap basha can be used as a building material,* and he experienced a moment of profound competence when he recognised, from a photograph in the jungle survival book, four of the broad-leaved plants growing close together, which he could easily use as the basis of a shelter, combined with the ground sheet which the villagers had given him. So he slept easily that night, with a powerful sense of self-satisfaction, as a man of many competences.

His confidence diminished rapidly the next day, however, when the path diverged three ways, and he was once again compelled to make an impossible choice. He spent most of the day walking the path which he had chosen, because it headed closest to the direction of the parent path, but he sank further and further into despair: and then he discovered the Tree of Ants. There it was! The tree, which he had often described, the tree which contained more ants than the whole of the British Isles. Horrified, he stared at this tree, ten yards to the side of the path, and recognised it, and it truly was, as he had often predicted, one single heaving pullulating conglomeration of ants from its formicating roots to its formicating canopy, with huge ants marching up and down its trunk bumping into one another carrying bits of leaves. He stood and stared, and drank some water from a pitcher plant, even though it was thick with insects, and tasted like urine, or tasted like urine smelled. And he closed his eyes, then, and saw a vision of limping men, because he was sure at that moment that there was a secret pattern, which he hadn't discerned before, a connection between Reginald Armstrong, Bill Noon and Joe Keane. Reg with his prosthesis, Bill with his war wound, and Joe with his crushed and stabbed leg – in Phnom Penh, Peter had been surrounded by limping men!

Soon after the Tree of Ants, and as though conjured by it, Peter started to encounter a sight which he knew was impossible, and which confirmed that he was sinking into madness, and which made him remember the equally impossible flying lizard. For he entered a place which looked as though the jungle had fiercely desired a section of

Angkor Wat and had seized it in a grotesquely fertile embrace, so that the trees and the flowers and the fungi had interbred with Buddhist temples, and given birth to chimeras of plant and stone, and masonry and vegetation were wrapped around, and interpenetrated, each other. The faces of apsara, handmaids of the gods, stared at him out of tree trunks. Bamboo was growing out of a gateway under a face tower, one of those conical towers with the face of a god staring out of it, and the bamboo had wrapped itself around the face, over the closed meditating eyes of the god. An enormous *linga* was being strangled by lianas.

Terrified, Peter charged along the narrow path beyond this place of abomination, and continued to sprint and then jog and then walk for hours and hours as fast as he could, finally exhausting himself so much that he sank to the ground and slept deeply and stupidly on the jungle floor. When he awoke he was amazed to hear a familiar sound, which was so unexpected in that place that he couldn't believe at first what it was. It was the barking of dogs. He rose to his feet and hurried along the path and heard another astonishing noise – steam shovels! After another quarter of a mile the jungle started to thin and then he caught sight of the sea and then he emerged from the jungle close to where a railway station was being constructed, and he recognised Sihanoukville, the new port on the Gulf of Siam.

44

'Derivative, Keith. All style, no substance, mate.'

'But it's witty don't you think? Not art, but witty and fun?'

Keith Entwistle had invited Yuri over to listen to the long-playing record of the Dudley Moore Trio that Dudley Moore's agent had sent him. Keith had loved receiving it, because it made him feel connected with London, where so much was starting to happen. 'But listen to those filigrees in the right hand…'

'Filigrees! Pah! It's Errol Garner with a silly simper. On his white face.'

Keith was hurt by Yuri's irritableness, because he was feeling so happy, and he wanted his friend to share it. He had spent a marvellous Christmas with Sandie, they had been so perfect together. She had cooked a wonderfully traditional Christmas dinner, and they had eaten turkey wearing party hats and they had got drunk together and enjoyed such passionate, yet cosy embraces and long kisses on her sofa, and he had walked back to his flat in the warm darkness feeling excited yet calm in a way he had never felt before. He knew that their marriage was going to be perfectly contented because they were so thoroughly compatible.

He felt so strongly about this that he had to describe it in detail to Yuri, who listened to him throughout with a wistful smile, but he winced when Keith finally said, 'You can't imagine, at all, what it's like being with Sandie, unless you've been close to her the way that I have.' And Keith reprimanded himself for his insensitivity. It was horribly wrong to have said this to Yuri, who had for so long spent a lonely and uneventful time, and was obviously pained by Keith's apparent one-upmanship. Trying to make amends, Keith said, 'But after Sandie and me are married you must come over and dine with us and we can spend long evenings together. I've been teaching Sandie about jazz.'

'I would've loved to do that, Keith, but they're moving me. They're sending me to Washington D.C.'

'No! Really?' Keith felt upset, 'Well, that's...It's a shame. But it's a promotion for you?'

'Yes. Yes. A promotion.'

Keith was still twitchy with embarrassment at his gaffe next day in the cyclo on his way over to the hospital – but at least he had managed mostly to rescue the situation with his parody of Joe Keane. Keith had elaborated a fantasy about meetings in Washington between Yuri and Keane, who was also on his way to the US capital after distinguishing himself in the assault on his embassy, and Yuri and Keith had laughed together about this picture of a Phnom Penh reunion between a Russian and a member of the US government.

When Keith arrived at the hospital he found Peter Cook already seated at the bedside of the Ambassador. A nurse was also there, taking the Ambassador's blood pressure; young, rural-dark and plump, and with gold in her teeth, she scolded the Ambassador for resting his right ankle on his left. Wagging her finger and smiling, she warned him that such a posture would restrict his circulation.

While Keith was seating himself, he heard Peter and the Ambassador resuming a discussion about lizards and whether there was a lizard that could fly, and then he listened while Peter described a series of species he had seen in the jungle – birds, reptiles and small mammals – and the Ambassador explained what they were. During this exchange, Keith pondered Yuri's denial that the Russians had been responsible for Peter's ordeal. Whoever had done that, he told Keith, it hadn't been Russians, who would never behave in such an outlandish fashion. It was good of Peter to venture as far as the hospital because he was, himself, still recovering – he had suffered badly from exhaustion after his ordeal, and had told Keith that the experience had shaken him so badly that he would never be the same again. (As always, however, Peter's manner had been so coloured with irony that Keith had found it difficult to judge the level of seriousness in Peter's declaration.)

The Ambassador was recovering well from what had been only a moderate heart attack. But he was going to take an early retirement, and he described at great length, and surprising detail, the life he planned to live in a village in the Cotswolds. Peter genially declared that they must stay in touch because, thanks to Keith's help, he was also on his way back to Britain where he was going to resume his career in comedy.

As Keith and Peter were finding their way out of the hospital, however, Peter adopted a more sceptical attitude towards Keith's help. 'But you put your own name on that script when you sent it to the agent?'

'Yes. But I thought you wouldn't allow me to send it using your name because you kept saying you had put all that behind you.'

'So it was purely altruistic on your part?'

'You were never suited to the diplomatic life. And you needed a strong decisive push to go back to the life that did really suit you. That's why I did that.'

And that was partly true.